THE LAST ELIGIBLE
BILLIONAIRE

PIPPA GRANT

1

Hayes Alexander Rutherford, aka a billionaire who would give his fortune to never see another single woman again in his life

THERE'S EXACTLY ONE THING A MAN WANTS AFTER TWO weddings, a funeral, a clandestine overnight drive, and an unfortunate incident with roadkill, and it is not more drama.

It is *never* more drama.

Or more people.

Or a complete and total disaster in what's supposed to be a haven.

Yet instead of falling into bed at my private retreat on a small island off the coast of Maine, with the French doors of my bedroom balcony open to let in the sound of the ocean waves rolling to shore while I escape into a mindless oblivion to recover from the past few weeks, I've arrived to a problem.

Someone has broken into my estate just as surely as the sun is breaking over the clouds off the horizon as it rises over the water.

The back door to the main house is unlocked, the lights

are on, dirty dishes and clothing are scattered all over the covered porch, someone's piled paint-stained rags outside the laundry room, and the refrigerator is gaping open.

Worse?

There's cheesecake in my refrigerator.

Cheesecake, pink wine—no, I don't care what kind it is, not if it's *pink*—three bags of peanut butter cups, two Styrofoam containers of god only knows what, a massive raw steak, a bottle of Tabasco sauce, and a stick of butter. All inside the refrigerator that *should* have its doors closed but doesn't.

I stick my hand into the fridge.

Room temperature.

The wine bottle isn't even sweating anymore, which means the doors have been open so long the damn refrigerator has ceased to function at all.

Worse?

This means whoever broke into my house ruined cheesecake.

How is it that the cheesecake is the most egregious of my intruder's sins?

My head aches. My body is stiff and sore. I might have a touch of whiplash, I definitely smell faintly of skunk, I'm exhausted, and someone—an unauthorized *someone* who should not be in my sanctuary after all the lengths I went to in order to reach this place anonymously and undetected—is letting *cheesecake* go bad in my open refrigerator.

This should not be the most appalling error of the morning, yet here we are.

I'm rapidly becoming irrationally angry over spoiled cheesecake.

One hand on my phone, the other wrapped firmly around my regrets in ditching my security detail, I make my way through the living room to the staircase. There's a subtle hint of music drifting from somewhere above, mud prints on my wood floor—both human and animal—and a maroon jacket embroidered with a smiling hot dog hanging on the banister.

This keeps getting worse.

For god's sake, Hayes, call the police, my mother would say. *You're already not the catch your brother was. Don't ruin what little good looks you have left by confronting the ruffians.*

Reason enough to do this myself.

If I were a tad uglier, perhaps the fortune-hunting bachelorettes that I can't seem to avoid would be less inclined to bat their lashes my way.

Not that their attention has *anything* to do with my looks.

Who needs looks when your bank account has as many zeroes as mine, and when your mother is as encouraging as mine? Provided you have the right pedigree and pass her background check, that is.

The scent of something sweet and unexpected tickles my nose, and not the way cheesecake would.

This is a nose-tickle of perfume. Given the increasing volume of the echoing music—is that "I Will Survive"?—and the yowling to go along with it, I don't believe I'm about to find my property manager here taking advantage of my absence to live it up.

While I'm hardly an expert on the man, I'm positive he's not the girl power song type.

Which means I'm about to find my squatter in the bathroom.

I make my way down the hallway to my suite and gently press the latch. The door swings easily and soundlessly as I push it open, revealing another disaster of clothing strewn about my bedroom and increasing the volume of the singing drastically. Two bras dangle off the mirror over my armoire. A box of tampons sits open on the floor outside the bathroom door. Four pairs of muddy shoes are scattered about the floor, perilously close to the Turkish rug beneath my bed.

But the mess is nothing compared to the singing.

Dear *god*, the singing.

There's not a human in my bathroom. There's a hyena stuck in the awkward stage of puberty, sucking down a helium balloon, and then letting it all go in an off-key rendition of the world's worst karaoke song.

Not helping the headache.

Not helping the bone-deep exhaustion from the travel to get here stealthily.

Not helping my desire to be completely alone, away from the world, away from scheming socialites and my mother and wedding cakes and funeral flowers and the weight of generations' worth of expectations that have landed squarely on my shoulders now that I'm not only the new chief financial officer of my family's company, but also, rather quickly and unexpectedly, the final unmarried male billionaire under the age of eighty-three on this entire planet.

You'd think being nearly forty would give me all the freedom I need to tell *anyone* meddling in my personal life to fuck off, but my family's fortune started with children's cartoons in the 1950s and has continued with family-friendly movies, television shows, streaming networks, amusement parks, and branded merchandise, with most of us still front and center as the modern family of dreams.

We're the very pillar of perfection.

The Rutherfords do *not* engage in scandalous behavior publicly, even mild infractions involving a slip of the tongue, no matter how much I'd like to climb the Brooklyn Bridge and let out a massive *fuck* some days.

And if I think my relatives' attempts to introduce me to dozens of women who will be the next *woman of my dreams* is irritating, it's nothing compared to the brow-beating I'd get for not living up to the family name.

The song changes, and my squatter launches into an off-key accompaniment to "thank u, next."

It is too damn early for Ariana Grande and her lovely voice *on-key*.

Forget a pubescent over-heliumed hyena *off-key*.

I take two steps farther into my bedroom and spot my intruder through the crack in the bathroom door. Three more steps, and I can clearly see her.

In a manner of speaking.

Her hair is wrapped in a deep blue towel, my black silk robe dangles from her shoulders, her face is coated in green *something*, and she has one leg propped on the edge of my elegant tub, where she's—

Dear god, tell me she is *not* doing what I think she's doing.

She wails along with the lyrics that I frankly can't understand, and also which don't seem to be lyrics that should be wailed, while she gives a hard yank that momentarily interrupts the singing as she yelps in pain.

She is.

She's waxing her bikini line with one foot perched at the edge of my marble soaking tub.

While wearing my robe.

The very audacity of this woman.

Invading my home.

Leaving litter and dirty dishes and soiled clothing on every available surface.

Disregarding all respect for cheesecake.

And standing in my bathroom, grooming herself while ruining already questionable songs.

This ends.

Now.

I step through the open doorway, ready to toss her over my shoulder and then off the balcony. "What in the *devil* do you think you're doing?"

She spins, screams, and then, with ninja-fast reflexes, grabs an industrial-size bottle of shampoo, *also* from the edge of my tub, and hurtles it at my head.

"Stop!" I order.

"Intruder!" she yells over the infernal music. "Marshmallow! Attack!" She grabs a towel and flings it at me too.

I dodge it easily, though my weary body would prefer this was unnecessary. "*Stop*."

For the love of every Razzle Dazzle film ever made, why did I finally choose today to ditch my security team?

Her robe—*my* robe—is gaping open, revealing creamy skin, lush breasts, and half-waxed *not going there*, but her state of undress doesn't stop her from diving across the bathroom to my vanity, where she grabs a tube of toothpaste and throws that at me too. "Thief! Murderer!"

I take three steps toward her, and an electric toothbrush comes flying my way. "Who the hell do you think you are?"

"*Help!*" she yells. "Marshmallow!"

I swat aside a flung box. What the fuck is *marshmallow*?

Is she kinky? Is it her safe word?

Does she think I'm a stripper? Or a paid companion?

And I thought this couldn't get worse.

She grabs the towel stand that sits in the middle of the vanity, but I reach her and wrestle it out of her grip before she can send that flying also, snagging her hands to keep them from causing more damage.

"What," I breathe in her green-goop-covered face, "are you doing in my house?"

She flips her wrist, ducks, and escapes my grasp, diving for the closet. "This isn't your house!"

Is she playing technicality games? Christ on a crumpet, I hate talking to people almost as much as I hate that I'm still having to shout over this infernal music. "It's sure as fuck not *your* house." Whoops. There I go with the *fucks*. Apologies, Mother. "What are you doing here?"

"*Marshmallow!*" she bellows. She's spinning in a circle, muttering about *too many damn doors*, the towel on her head

6

tilting, robe flapping open and giving me more of a view than I want of any woman today, and I finally catch on.

Fear.

She's afraid.

Slow on the uptake, Hayes?

I grunt to myself, fist my hands in my pockets, and lean in the closet doorway, forcing myself to calm down and look at her like a math problem instead of as a fleshy ball of emotions who's latched on to a hair dryer and is aiming it at me like she can blow me out of the doorway.

"Who are you?" For the record, it's damn hard to keep my voice steady. I used up every last drop of my peopling skills five minutes into my brother's wedding reception last night and had to fake it for another six hours. I have nothing left to employ for patience with this woman today, but she's between me and overdue alone time.

She shifts back and forth on the balls of her feet, towel drooping, robe swaying, hair dryer still aimed at me. The green goop coating her face is getting spots, like she's sweating through her face mask.

"I rented this house fair and square, and you need to leave."

"I *own* this house, and I didn't rent it to *anyone.*"

"Prove it."

Prove it? "You have no idea who I am, do you?"

"Are you kidding me?" she mutters. "*Another* one? *Marshmallow!*"

"Stop yelling *marshmallow.* What the hell—"

It's the last syllable I utter before I realize what a *marshmallow* is.

It's a dog.

A large, black-and-brown, long-snouted, pointy-eared, teeth-baring, snarling attack dog.

I have a feeling I'm about to be its breakfast.

This day truly can't get any worse.

Begonia Fairchild, aka a woman who would like to stop regretting every last decision in her life. Any day now. Really…

Go on a post-divorce retreat and spoil yourself in a place *without internet or cell signal so your mother can't reach you for a couple weeks*, I told myself. *Look, there's a lovely beach mansion rental miraculously in your budget that just came available. It must be fate*, I told myself.

And it was.

For two glorious days.

Now?

Now, I'm interrogating an intruder while my dog holds him against a closet wall, with no cell service to call the police, and the full knowledge that my dog will most likely stop growling any second now because he is truly the world's worst guard dog, and the last bit of leverage I have against this mansion-invading murderer will be gone.

"Who are you? And don't pull any of that arrogant *you should know who I am because I'm so important* baloney," I order the man currently held hostage by my dog between clothing racks in a corner of the massive closet.

What kind of a bathroom has *four* different doors?

This one.

That's what kind of bathroom.

And it was cool yesterday, when I was renting a beach mansion with a bathroom so large it has two closets and a private hidden sitting room, but today, when I needed to make a spur of the moment decision about which of the four doors to lunge toward, I went the wrong way, and now I'm trapped in a closet with an intruder who's glaring at me like *I'm* in the wrong.

I have two weapons at my disposal.

One's the hair dryer, which is only scary if you've ever had one short-circuit and almost catch your hair on fire while using it, and the other is my phone, which gets no signal in this house—thank you, obscure wireless plan—and which I'm finally able to silence inside the pocket of this robe, killing Ariana Grande's voice probably as surely as this man is about to murder me.

"My name is Hayes Rutherford, and this is my house." His voice is quiet and controlled, and he has a commanding air about him that might be the tux—side note, *who breaks into an island mansion in a tux?*—or it might be that anyone named *Hayes Rutherford* innately carries around an air of importance.

Why does that name sound familiar?

And why does the fact that he claims that's his name immediately assure me that he's not going to kill me?

Probably because if he were planning on killing me, he'd tell me his name was Freddy Krueger or Mr. Death or Chad, because god knows I've had enough Chads in my life. The universe would definitely send a Chad to murder me.

But this man—Hayes Rutherford—is staring at me expectantly as though he's just answered every last one of my questions, and while the tic in his jaw suggests he'd like to strangle me with the cord on this hair dryer, the rest of his expression says *I am entirely over this bullshit*.

He's not *old*. Maybe upper thirties, early forties at most, based on the lines at the edges of his eyes and the strands of silver dotting his dark hair rather than overtaking it. He's clearly in good shape. No fluff hanging over his belt, his rolled-up shirtsleeves showing off what I'd call forearm porn in any other circumstances, posture straight, tendons straining in his neck.

And there's a single lock of hair falling across his broad forehead like it's tired of behaving, or possibly it just doesn't have any fucks left to give about doing what it's supposed to do.

Are those one and the same?

I don't know.

But I do know I should've been enjoying cheesecake for breakfast right now, and if I don't get this hair dye out of my hair soon, there'll be no chance of *I didn't see you standing there, Begonia* ever again, because my hair will glow so bright, astronauts could see it from Mars.

As if that's my biggest worry when *there's an intruder trapping me in a closet*.

If I try to dash out of here, Marshmallow will think it's playtime, and I give myself a fifty-fifty shot of getting through the door before this Hayes Rutherford person attacks.

And then it clicks. "Oh my god, *Hayes Rutherford*. Like the president, but backwards. Did your parents do that on purpose?"

He blinks one slow blink at me, and I get the impression no one has ever asked him that in his entire life.

Note to self: Do not make jokes about presidents' names with a burglar who might have murder on his mind.

Other note to self: If I'm living out a horror flick, I am definitely the first victim. It's always the vain one who gets it first, which is *so stupid*, because I'm not vain. I'm having a single morning of pampering myself in a luxury bathroom. This has happened approximately five other times before in my life. The pampering part, I mean. Not the luxury bathroom part. I'm usually pampering myself in a bathroom a third of the size of this closet. It is definitely a first for a luxury bathroom.

And one final note to self: I'm growing more and more confident by the second that he's not planning to murder me. But I still don't like this situation.

Marshmallow, my Shiloh shepherd, is slowly calming down. I have maybe twenty seconds before this *Hayes Rutherford* person realizes the dog's more likely to flip the lights off and shut the door in here than he is to actually bite.

Poor Marshmallow.

His best wasn't quite what they were looking for in service dog school.

"Yes," Hayes Rutherford finally says. "That's exactly it. My parents have a presidential sense of humor."

"You're lying."

He makes a face like there's a fly attacking his nose. "How did you get in here?"

"With the code. I rented this house for two weeks. How did *you* get in here?"

"Where did you rent this house?"

Have I mentioned that I'm over men? Because I am *so* over men. "You didn't answer my question."

"I've answered your question six times. I own this house. Where did you rent it?"

"Vacation rental site. And you answered that question *twice*, which doesn't make me believe it any more than I did the first time. How do you have a vacation rental house *that you don't know is a vacation rental house*?"

Something else flickers in his eyes—annoyance, I think—and for the first time since he nearly gave me a heart attack in

11

the bathroom, I realize he might actually own this house, and there's a reasonable chance I'm not supposed to be here.

Marshmallow seems to realize it too. He tilts his head, goes back on his haunches, and gives a final *harumph*.

It's a *harumph* of *of course you should've known renting this house for fifty bucks a night was too good to be true, Begonia*. He lies down and curls one paw under his chest.

I cut a glance at the row of suits, shirts, and jeans lined up neatly on hangers in the closet. The dresser in the bedroom is full of men's underwear and socks and the funniest assortment of pajama pants. There's a study on the main floor, stocked with books and family photos that I haven't looked at closely, because I assumed it was merely ornamental fluff to go along with the posh feel of the rest of the house.

But is this man in those photos?

Is this really his house?

It *did* seem odd that there were clothes and personal effects scattered about, but then, the last time I did a vacation rental, it was me and four of my college girlfriends renting a place in Panama City Beach, and not a swanky mansion like this. It made sense that popular spring break destinations would be as sparsely furnished as possible, given that it would usually be college kids pooling pennies to rent them, and that upscale luxury homes on quaint islands off the coast of Maine would have more amenities.

But again—*fifty bucks a night*.

When the listing said *unexpected vacancy, special deal*, I should've known.

I *really* should've known.

Am I—am I here *illegally*?

Welp.

I wanted an adventure.

Looks like I'm getting one. Might come with a mugshot.

My mother will love that.

But *I have a vacation rental agreement*. I can't get arrested for trespassing when I have a rental agreement.

Can I?

Am I responsible if I didn't know I signed a fraudulent agreement?

"Will you please put that damned hair dryer down?" he mutters. "And for god's sake, tie the robe."

I look down, squeak, then jerk my head back up while I aim the hair dryer at him and try to pull the two sides of the robe together with my other hand. I'm standing here with my cooch hanging out and at least one nipple pointing at him.

"*Turn around.*"

He aims his eyeballs at the ceiling. I yank the robe shut, tie it, then aim the blow dryer at him once again. "How do I know you're the owner? What if you just *know* the owner? Or what if you're casing the joint to figure out when the house will be empty next?"

"You've found me out. I'm a burglar. I'm the tuxedo burglar, and I only burgle while wearing last night's formal wear. Whatever shall I take first?"

"Sarcasm is *not* attractive on you."

"I don't believe you're in any condition to make observations about anyone else's attractiveness."

I gasp. Did he just—he *did*.

He called me ugly. "Marshmallow, bite him in the balls."

My dog lifts his head, bites the edge of a pair of jeans, pulls them off the hanger, and delivers them to my feet.

My intruder—*Hayes*—makes that face again like he's considering all the bad decisions he's made in life that led him to this moment.

Or possibly I'm projecting.

But is this a bad moment? Does it have to be a bad moment? "Marshmallow, you know those don't fit my hips. If you want to help me dress, get something out of my suitcase."

My dog grins at me. This is his favorite game. *Look what I know how to do, Mommy.*

Hayes squeezes his eyes shut and pinches the bridge of his nose. "I need to see a copy of this rental agreement."

There's nothing like being an obvious inconvenience to a man to make a woman believe his original intention wasn't murder. Not saying I won't annoy him enough that he'll want to hurt me for other reasons—my ex-husband says I have a gift—but at the moment, I feel weirdly safe.

"It's in my email on my phone. And if you're not in the family pictures downstairs, I'm calling the police. I'm happy to work this out with you, but I need a show of good faith. You have to let me get dressed and cleaned up, and then I'll show you the agreement."

His nose twitches.

Because he's afraid of the police? Does he come here to get in trouble? Are those not family photos downstairs? I didn't look very closely in the study, because it felt wrong to work on watercolors in a room where I could've caused real damage if Marshmallow decided to help, and while I adore looking at family photos, I assumed they were staged and not the *actual* family that lives here.

"You have five minutes to get dressed and meet me downstairs with this rental agreement, or *I'll* be the one calling the police. Are we clear?"

"Twenty minutes."

"Five."

"Fifteen."

"Five."

"Thirty."

"Three." He pulls a phone from his pocket, like he's about to dial the police *now*.

And that's when my dog decides it's playtime.

I see it coming in slow motion. Marshmallow's eyes landing on that phone. His brain clicking. *Chew toy! Chew toy!*

14

His eyes light up, his jaw opens, his back legs engage, and in one quick snap, he's stolen the phone.

And here we go. "Marshmallow!"

My hundred-pound dog pivots, launches forward, dashes from the carpeted closet to the tile-floored bathroom, skitters, gets his balance back, and sprints away.

And Hayes Rutherford, Mr. Fancy Pants with bloodshot eyes and a tic in his jaw and flaring nostrils and a stick up his butt—though maybe that's not entirely his fault—turns the kind of glare on me that would've incinerated me on the spot a year ago before he takes off after my dog.

3

Hayes

OF ALL OF THE ANGLES IN THE WORLD, CORNERS ARE BY FAR MY least favorite.

Specifically, being backed into a corner, which is exactly what I am now, because my squatter has realized something very, very dangerous.

"*Oh my god,*" she gasps through a pant. "You're *Hayes Rutherford.*"

After chasing the dog all over the damn estate, she and I are now in the study, which is where the infernal animal finally decided my phone needed to go.

The furry beast trotted in here and deposited it right beside the wireless charger on the desk as though it knows how to charge a damn cell phone.

I'm breathing heavily. My eyelids hint at swelling and my throat tickles and my sinuses clog as I snag my phone and shove it back in my pocket. The woman is bent over gasping for breath like the last place she ran was to an ice cream stand.

Her towel is gone from her head, her hair a sloppy mess pasted to her skull with some kind of goo in it. Her skull itself is an odd red color, which is leaking onto her green goop and turning it an unnatural shade between sewer brown and *repulsive*, and her robe is gaping open almost as much as her mouth as she stares at the row of family photos on the built-in bookshelves currently at her eye level.

"Your name," I order.

The dog barks as though it thinks it can answer that question.

I point at it. "And get that nuisance out of my house. *Now*."

"You're from *those* Rutherfords. The Razzle Dazzle Rutherfords."

There goes any chance I might have of privacy while I'm here. My mother will know my whereabouts in approximately forty-two minutes, because a woman whispered my name—it's like rubbing the genie's magic lamp—and she'll arrive with at least one eligible bachelorette in tow within four hours.

They're all together for Jonas's post-wedding brunch. Won't take but a limo ride, a helicopter ride, and then a private plane ride for her to reach the small airport on the mainland, and she'll charter a ferry herself to get here to me on the island.

"Your. Name." I repeat.

"Begonia. I'm Begonia. Oh my god. I had your brother's posters all over my wall when I was a teenager."

My eyelid twitches. *Begonia?* If that's her real name, I'll eat my left shoe. "Begonia who?"

"Oh, are we doing knock-knock jokes?"

I try to breathe deeply through my nose, but my nostrils have swollen shut. "What's your last name?"

She doesn't answer right away.

"Or I can go through your purse," I mutter.

She straightens, touches the gunk on her hair, then the gunk half-smeared off her face, and blinks shiny green eyes in my direction. "You're the first person to ask me that. Sorry. I need a minute." She sucks in an audible breath and fans her face. "Wow. Didn't expect it to hit me like that. Sorry."

There's a madwoman loose in my house. What kind of person cries over being asked her last name?

A jilted bride, my new sister-in-law's voice offers in my head.

A new widow, my uncle Antonio's voice chimes in.

A woman who had amnesia and just regained her memory only to discover her friends and family thought she was dead and moved on without her, my cousin's voice squeals.

Some days I dislike that my favorite family member has an addiction to Korean dramas.

Or she just discovered she was adopted and understands now why she's always felt like she didn't belong in her family, Keisha's voice adds, and this time, I can picture her sly grin, because while she might be my favorite family member, she's not above trying to play matchmaker like the rest of them. She's also adopted herself—by my mother's brother, though her romantic spirit suggests she's more Rutherford than I am— and she's an exquisite case study in nurture versus nature. *She's just like you, Hayes. She doesn't fit. But she's actually adopted, and you're just weird.*

I'm not *weird*, though it's taken me years to shake off the label in my own head. I just don't fit what people expect of a Rutherford. I like math instead of people. I'd rather read historical biographies than talk about the character arc of a romantic lead in a Razzle Dazzle movie.

I puked once getting off of a Razzle Dazzle Village roller coaster ride, which was photographed and filmed for all of the world to see, and the media liked painting me as the oddball for ratings.

God knows they didn't get anything else clickbait-worthy from my family. Everyone else is too perfect.

They all fit the mold.

Even Keisha, who's something of a disaster, though thanks to not having the Rutherford name, she's not frequently linked to us.

But even she had a better media debut. Mine was accidentally being interviewed by a swarm of bloodthirsty paparazzi when I was separated from my family during a movie premiere when I was about six years old, and I got so flustered that I clucked like a chicken instead of answering questions until my father saved me.

I shudder at the memory and once again wish I were somewhere else. I should've gone to the house in Nantucket instead if I wanted to get any work done in peace, but the Nantucket house belongs to my mother, and I couldn't have hit the first button on the alarm panel without alerting her to my whereabouts.

I stood half a chance here.

"Fairchild," Begonia says. "My name is Begonia Fairchild."

Don't do it. Don't do it. Don't do it. "And that's difficult to say, because…?"

Dammit.

I did it.

"I picked it after my divorce." She flashes her bare left hand and a goofy smile while she blinks quickly. Is she flirting with me, or does she have something in her eyeball? "There was no way I could continue being a Dixon, and I never really felt like Bidelspach fit me the way I wanted it to, so I decided to be Begonia Fairchild. My dad would've liked it. He was way more the *peace, love, and prosper* type than my mom ever was. Give me fifteen minutes to shower and put some clothes on, and I'll pull up that rental agreement for you and we'll figure out what's going on here. Did you want some cheesecake? I got enough for a party and I figured it would last me all week, but I can go get more if we eat it all this morning. Oh my god. You're Jonas Rutherford's strange older brother. I can't believe I'm standing here in your house. And I didn't mean strange in a bad way. That's just—"

"Stop talking."

"—what the teen magazines always called you. I'm sorry. That's a bad habit. I won't say that again."

"You'll shower, pack, sign a non-disclosure agreement stating that you weren't here and you've never seen me, and that you acknowledge I'll sue for ten million dollars in the event you break your word, and then you can leave."

I'm being an ass. I generally dislike being an ass, but I'm beyond controlling my frustration and anger today.

I want to fucking *sleep*, because after I sleep, I have to dig deeper into some inconsistencies that I found in the Razzle Dazzle books right before Jonas's rehearsal dinner the other night, when I was trying to distract myself from thinking about my cousin Thomas's funeral and my new role in the company.

The dog whimpers and lies down, covering its nose with a paw like it knows it's in trouble.

"It's okay, Marshmallow," Begonia says softly. She blinks up at me. "I truly am sorry. That's rude of the tabloids to call you names, and I should know better than to repeat it. I'm a little flustered. It's not every day that I—well, that I meet someone related to my teenage crush. But you probably hear that enough that it's annoying."

I don't, actually. I'm excellent at avoiding people, especially people who would have crushes on my brother.

So yes, right now, it's highly annoying.

I let my body language answer for me.

She straightens, touches her cheek, pulls her hand back to look at her green fingers, and grimaces. "Right! Shower, dressed, and I'll make you some coffee and cheesecake while I sign that non-disclosure agreement for you and we figure out who's staying and who's going where. My lips are zipped. I won't breathe a word. I won't even ask for a picture. Cross my heart. And I'm sorry Marshmallow took your phone. He —well, he sometimes thinks he's someone's annoying little human brother instead of a dog." She frowns. "Do you eat cheesecake? I know there are cheesecake pop stands on every corner at the Razzle Dazzle parks, but I guess that doesn't mean you eat it, does it?"

I point to the doorway.

"Right. Upstairs. Right." She takes two steps, then tilts her head. "Why *are* you here dressed like you came from a party? I've been here for two nights already, and the host on the vacation rental site must know you well enough to have not expected you, so—"

"While you're showering, I'll note all damages to the house and prepare a bill for you."

She squeaks.

I point harder.

"You should know that the handheld spout in the owners' suite shower was already broken when I got here. I made a note to report it to the host when I have cell service again, and I hardly minded, because the rain shower spout is the coolest thing ever. Who needs the handheld spout when you can pretend you're showering in a rainstorm instead? Also, Marshmallow isn't the first dog to stay here. I know most owners are picky about dogs staying in vacation rental homes, so it was amazing that this one said pets were welcome. We were a little surprised by the dog hair caked in all the runners on the stairs, but it wasn't a big deal to us since we knew Marshmallow would be leaving some of his own. And—"

"Stop. Talking."

Her chin wobbles.

Dammit.

I stalk around the desk toward her.

She backs toward the door, the dog copying her movements.

"March," I order.

"I *knew* it was too good to be true," she mutters while she angles toward the door. She's not talking to me. She's talking to the dog. You can tell by the way she's started in with the baby talk. "Who rents a house like this for fifty bucks a night? It's like that time we signed up to go sailing with that Groupon and got there and the captain was drunk and forgot he booked three hundred people on a boat built for seven."

I stifle an annoyed sigh as she turns the corner and heads up the stairs to the main level.

"But that turned out okay, didn't it, Marshmallow? I really wasn't supposed to be on that boat that day. This will turn out okay too."

Perhaps for her.

For me?

If I don't find my emergency supply of Benadryl soon, this house won't be where my mother and her eligible bachelorettes find me.

No, that'll be the hospital.

4

Begonia

OH. MY. GOD.

I've crashed a Rutherford family property, and I'm currently naked, in Jonas Rutherford's older brother's bathroom, with the door shut while I hold my breath and squeeze my eyes closed under the rain shower spout and pray that I didn't leave the hair dye in too long.

Although, my bigger problem might be that I need to make an appointment to get my eyes checked.

How did I not connect the dots the minute Hayes identified himself? *Oh, funny, your name is a backwards president*, I said.

Your name is a backwards president.

Maybe it *would've* been better if I left my hair dye on long enough for it to soak through my scalp and burn off some of my slower brain cells.

In my defense, normal people don't expect family members of celebrities to walk into the bathrooms where they're waxing their pubic hair, so it's not like my brain should've immediately picked up on that. And Hayes isn't a clone of Jonas Rutherford, whose posters really were all over my wall when I was younger, but they're similar enough in the eyes and mouth that I should've picked up on it.

Or maybe not.

There's something so blunt and rough about Hayes's features, whereas Jonas is the right amount of rugged to walk that line between boyish heartthrob and all-man lady-killer.

Not that blunt and rough are wrong on Hayes.

Under other circumstances, I'd call him attractive.

Okay, fine.

Under *these* circumstances, I would honestly call him hot. I know exactly what's wrong with me that a broody, cranky man in a tousled tux is doing it for me—he's commanding in a way that Chad could never master, and he just has this *air* about him. It's mystery and danger and intrigue and *adventure*.

And goodness knows I'm here for the adventure, though I wouldn't have minded if that adventure was the other Rutherford brother.

The one who feels significantly safer at the moment.

I used to tell my mom I was going to marry Jonas. Specifically, the version of him that starred in *That Last Summer*.

That was the only Razzle Dazzle Studios movie where he came out of the ocean in a wet T-shirt that clung to his pecs and abs. The movie where he raced across an entire island with his heroine in his arms because she stepped on a jellyfish and had an allergic reaction, and then he cried when he almost lost her. Of course he didn't lose her—no one ever dies in a Razzle Dazzle film, unlike those awful Nicholas Sparks movies—but *he cried*.

It was the most romantic thing my fourteen-year-old heart had ever seen.

On top of the wet T-shirt being the raciest.

People picketed the studios over that film because it was too close to bare skin, which Razzle Dazzle *never* shows.

Hyacinth, my twin sister, preferred him in *Inn the Know*, a slightly older film with a younger Jonas starring as the teenage son of a single dad running a small inn. He had a romance with his teacher's bookworm daughter while his dad fell in love with his principal.

The smolder, Hyacinth would always sigh. *They should've picketed this one for that smolder.*

But my point is—I'm very, *very* convinced at this point that I'm not supposed to be renting this house.

If Hayes himself doesn't own it, his family does, and there's no way in h-e-double hockey sticks, to quote the one and only time Jonas Rutherford ever came close to cussing on screen, that the Rutherford family would rent their coastal island mansion to random people for fifty dollars a night.

And here I am, not just staying here, but making an utter pigsty of the place.

For the record, yes, I would've picked up after myself before I checked out in two weeks. But I *like* the mess.

It's the mess I need to make before I can put myself back together again, when I have to be organized for the school year.

This summer is supposed to be about me making all the messes and digging through them to find myself again. Trying new hobbies and getting reacquainted with old hobbies—like the watercolor kit I did yesterday and accidentally spilled all over the place in the kitchen—and reading for hours on the swing in the wildflower garden and riding the bike from the shed into town to buy flowers for myself and walking along the rocky shoreline and playing with Marshmallow.

Remembering who I am when I'm not Mrs. Chad Dixon. Analyzing how I ever got to be the woman who put up with being unhappy for so long because *this is what marriage is,* and *you made a commitment, Begonia.*

Getting a solid foundation back under myself so I never, ever, *ever* fall into those patterns again.

I wanted an adventure.

It appears I'm getting a different version, but it'll still be an adventure.

As if it'll matter, since Hayes apparently wants me to sign something agreeing to never talk about this. I'm assuming I won't even be able to tell Hyacinth if I sign his non-disclosure agreement.

Is that weird?

Or is it a standard thing when the rich and famous find accidental guests in their homes?

How often do the rich and famous find accidental guests in their homes?

How did this even happen?

Three sharp knocks on the door pull me out of my head. "Yes?" I call.

"It's been seventeen minutes," Mr. Crankypants says.

"Can't rush beauty," I call back as I get a strange little rush in my heart at that bossy voice again. Then I wince as I process what I just said. "Or presentability, in some cases."

"You have two minutes before I shut off the water and toss you off the balcony."

I'd like to say I'm confident that he's joking, but I don't actually know if someone of his status would joke about that.

Money can buy anything, right? He could probably buy his way out of being guilty of murder.

"Almost done," I call. "Are you ready to see the new and improved Begonia Fairchild? Gotta warn you, it'll be surprising after what I looked like when we met."

He doesn't answer.

Apparently he doesn't do small talk.

Or possibly that cold he seems to have is making him cranky.

I should definitely offer him a cup of my dad's miracle tea, except I don't have the ingredients with me, and I have a sneaking suspicion I wouldn't be let back through the gate if I ran into town to pick things up.

I crank the water off, pop open the glass shower door, and reach for the towel.

My hand connects with the towel hook, but no towel.

It's not on the ground.

It's not on the heated towel rack across the bathroom.

In fact, *all* of the towels are gone.

So are my clothes.

"Marshmallow!"

My dog pokes his head through the doorway, tongue lolling happily like he's not the reason the door's gaping open.

"Where are the towels?" I ask him.

He plops his rear haunches down and keeps smiling that bright doggie grin at me.

"This is no time for hide and seek," I tell him.

He leaps to his feet, barks once, and takes off out of the bathroom again.

"Dammit, dog, I put you outside," Hayes snarls.

I shoot a glance at the mirrors. I can't reach the closet to look for more towels without crossing in front of the door, and without my entire naked body reflecting into the bedroom, where my unexpected host is apparently waiting for me, and the idea of *knowingly* being naked in front of him makes me squirm. "He can open doors," I call. "Do you mind waiting downstairs? And possibly tossing in a couple towels on your way out?"

No answer.

"Hayes?" I call.

Still no answer.

"Um, Mr. Rutherford?"

When he doesn't answer once more, I decide he's already gone.

If he's not, it's his own fault if he gets a show.

"I'm naked and walking to the closet for a towel," I call just in case. He's already gotten an eyeful of me. Not like this could get much worse.

Still, when I step out of the shower, the cool air around me making my skin pucker, I dart as quickly as I can toward the closet and the rack of extra towels.

"Good *god*," that male voice yelps in the other room, startling me just enough that I turn, and that's when I realize my mistake.

Porcelain tile floors and wet feet do not mix.

My right foot goes sliding one way. My left foot the opposite. I windmill my arms, bang one on a doorframe while the other catches the vanity countertop, and I manage to stop myself, legs spreadeagle, beaver still only half-waxed, hair dripping behind me, before I slowly slide the rest of the way to the ground.

Huh.

Look at that.

I can still get forty percent of the way into doing a split. And they said my body would betray me with age.

What did they know?

Definitely not that there's an uncomfortable pull in my left hip joint and that my right knee doesn't like this.

"Could you *please*, for the love of all that has ever been holy, *put on some goddamn clothes*?"

I twist so I'm covering as many bits as I can, and I catch a glimpse of him trying to turn in the bedroom so that he can't see me.

It's harder than you'd think, what with the mirror over the dresser facing the mirror for the bathroom, and the way he's standing and I'm squatting, and while this maybe isn't the most embarrassing situation I've ever found myself in, it's high up there.

I wasn't planning on being naked and vulnerable in front of a man this morning, yet here we are, and my body is betraying me over it.

It takes me a second to make my voice normal. "Relax, Mr. Rutherford. One, you've basically already seen it all. Two, I tried to warn you. And three, it's not like your mother's catching us in a compromising position. I'm *positive* this isn't the worst thing to ever happen to you. It's pretty high up there for me though, so if you don't mind waiting downstairs for just a couple more minutes—"

"Will you be wearing your own damn clothes?" He's shoving his fists into his eye sockets.

That can't feel good.

And it's bruising the part of my soul that knows that most people like me.

Most.

Awesome. He's in the same category as my former mother-in-law.

Granted, these are unusual circumstances, but I'm trying to be nice here, and he's all *grump grump crank snarl grump.*

"So long as Marshmallow didn't distribute them all over the house, yes, I'll be drying off and putting on my own clothes."

"Your dog needs to go back outside."

"He gets lonely if he's outside alone for too long. Also, since he can open doors, if you didn't lock them all, he'll find a way back in."

He mutters something while I regain my balance enough to carefully duckwalk the rest of the way to the closet, covering as much of myself as I can, but undoubtedly giving him a solid view of my ass the whole time, if he's even look-ing, which I suspect he's doing his best to *not.*

When I pop back out two minutes later completely

PIPPA GRANT

wrapped in towels, he's not in the bedroom anymore. And I understand why when I finally make it downstairs after getting dressed and tossing as much of my stuff as I can into my suitcase without *taking too long*.

He's showered too, and he's wearing a pair of the pajama pants that were in the dresser in the bedroom. The gray pair with the dancing hamster pattern all over them, to be specific.

That's why he was in the bedroom.

He was getting clean clothes.

His dark hair is damp and unkempt, like he got bored in the middle of towel-drying it, and it's dripping water onto his white T-shirt while he leans against the kitchen island and scowls at his phone.

If it weren't for the scowl sharpening all the features in his angular face, I'd think he was a completely different man. He looks approachable in pajama pants and a white T-shirt.

Like a normal man, instead of a fancy rich man totally inconvenienced by my dog and me.

Like a man just out of the shower, getting ready for break-fast with the woman he ravaged the night before, unhappy that someone in his office is calling him in early when he'd rather eat his guest out on the kitchen counter.

Stop it, Begonia.

I force myself to focus on the pile of dishes on the island, which is a stark reminder that my dog and I are definitely an inconvenience.

Must you leave your dirty cereal bowl on the counter, Begonia? I have better things to do than pick up after you.

Chad was a financial advisor with one of the big firms in Richmond, always up before the sun checking the markets, falling asleep listening to financial podcasts every night, while I'm just a high school art teacher who doesn't get to do art for fun nearly as often as you'd think I would, and who sometimes gets her head stuck in the clouds. *I make the money, you do the dishes. I make the money, you do the laundry. I make the money...*

You get the idea.

So, yes, I left my dirty dishes all over the kitchen yesterday.

And yes, Hayes is sliding me a death glare that suggests he, too, prefers life neat and orderly. And that's *before* Marshmallow trots into the kitchen, flips the lights off with his snout, and opens the dishwasher.

Hayes slides a look at me, then at the fridge, which is also gaping wide open.

Dammit.

How long has that been open?

Oh, no.

Is my cheesecake ruined?

Here I go, wincing again. "He was raised from birth to be a service dog, but he flunked out of the program when he started doing all the things he'd learned because he wanted to, instead of only on command. I have things Marshmallow-proofed at home. We have a good system. He's out of his element here."

"Your dog called my mother."

I don't know what precisely that means to Hayes Rutherford, but I have a terrible feeling it's not good, and that it's making every bit of me being here even worse.

5

Hayes

THIS WOMAN CANNOT STAND STILL, AND NEITHER CAN HER FACE. She's had approximately a dozen shifts in expression as she's absorbed the news that she can't possibly understand about her dog calling my mother. It's actually strange to see her skin moving, white and smooth, rather than green and flaky and crumbling every time her lips twitch one way or her forehead wrinkles another way.

She's fully clothed now, in tattered jeans that hug her hips and a pink crop top hoodie, but her feet are still bare, showing off toenails painted all random colors, no rhyme or reason. And her hair—I'm not entirely certain what color she was going for, but it's somewhere between burgundy and purple, and it's giving off a fluorescent shine, as though it could double as a beacon were we to get stranded here and need to signal for help.

It's quite bright. Impossible to miss.

"Well, I hope Marshmallow was polite and didn't bark

your mother's ear off," she finally says. She flits to the fridge, glances inside, grimaces, closes the doors, and then heads to the island, where she piles plates and bowls and utensils. She carries them to the sink, smiling indulgently at her dog, who's now gazing at me like I'm some kind of dog god. "Good boy, helping Mommy with the dishes."

"The contract, Ms. Fairchild." I don't tell her my mother's left me six voice messages and is now not answering my return call, which means there's zero doubt in my mind that she's taxiing down a runway right now.

Did they track my phone?

Did they know last night that I was leaving?

Was I followed?

I was certain I wasn't followed.

Begonia pulls her phone out of her back pocket. "Of course. Sorry. Nervous habit. Not that I like cleaning, but I—never mind. The contract. It's right here in my email..." She swipes her finger over the screen, and after a moment, she bites her lip.

I cross my arms.

She hits the screen harder.

"Is there a problem?"

"No, no. It's just thinking. I like your pajama pants. One of my students found that old video of the dancing hamsters late last year, so we did a unit on the art of the early internet memes."

I frown at her.

She gestures to my crotch. "The dancing hamsters on your pants. I assume you're a fan? Or were those a gift?"

"Hamsters have nothing to do with your contract."

"I have the contract. I do. But my email program seems to have had a little glitch and emptied all the emails that were in my inbox, and I don't get service here, and there's no wifi, and...and that was supposed to be exactly what I wanted, but it's a little inconvenient right now that I need to download my inbox again and I...can't."

"Inconvenient," I repeat.

She tosses the phone on the counter. "I paid for this house! And Mr. Ferguson sent me instructions on how to get to the island and which golf cart company to use to get to the gate with my luggage, and to play a game where I said I was Marilyn Monroe, which makes so much more sense now, for the record, and he sent the code, and I wouldn't know any of that if I wasn't authorized *somehow* to be here, even by someone who shouldn't have authorized me. I'm not a thief. I'm not a trespasser. Do you believe in fate, Hayes? Because I saw this house come up on the vacation rental site—one minute it wasn't there, and I got lost in my search and started it over, and then *poof*, here was this house, and it was fate's way of saying *I'm sorry you married the wrong person and took too many years to realize it, here, go enjoy coastal Maine for a couple weeks*, and *gah*, that sounds like I'm trying to sob-story you into letting me stay, but I'm not. I'm just telling you what happened, and you don't need to feel sorry for me. I just want you to know I honestly thought I was supposed to be here."

My headache is back, and the longer that dog sits there switching between watching her load the dishwasher while she babbles, and gazing at me like it's a teenage girl and I'm my brother at a movie premiere, the more my sinuses clog up again.

"Give me your phone."

She pauses in the midst of wetting a rag. "Are you going to make my dog eat it like he did yours?"

For the record, twitching while your head is pounding isn't enjoyable. "Yes. That will solve everything."

Her face screws up in irritation. "I'm trying *very hard* here."

"And I have a headache, I haven't slept in two days, and I wanted peace and quiet and to be alone, and *this is my house.*

Give me your damn phone so I can find this damn contract you claim to have so that I know who I have to murder."

"I don't have signal, and I—"

"Give. Me. Your. Damn. Phone."

She closes her eyes, sucks in a very large breath that has her chest rising under her pink shirt, and blows it out like she's counting to three thousand.

When she opens her eyes again, I swear she's muttering to herself about wishing it was my brother here instead of me. But she hands me the phone with very controlled movements, like she wants me to know I'm trying her patience, and like she thinks I'll truly care about where her patience sits when she's trespassing in my house.

"Does your family know you say *damn*? That's not allowed in any of your movies."

"Unlock it," I order softly.

She flips it around to her face, swipes up, and then hands it back to me. "If I find out you're Hayes Rutherford's doppelgänger and that *you* are really the one who's not supposed to be here, I'll do something we'll both regret."

"Believe me, Ms. Fairchild, if I could be anyone else right now, I would be."

Her nose wrinkles, and she goes back to attacking the countertops. "Why would you want to be anyone else? You're financially set, you have a good reputation, your family is lovely, and there's literally nothing in the world you can't have." She lifts a hand. "Yes, yes, except this house to yourself at this exact moment. And no family is ever as perfect as they look on TV. I'm aware. You're inconvenienced and imperfect. So am I, Hayes. So am I. But I'm rolling with it, and I think you'd be happier if you tried to do the same."

I connect her phone to the hotspot on mine, which gets weak signal, but signal nonetheless, then order her email to download while she yammers as she flits about the kitchen, continuing to gather dirty dishes and dumping them in the dishwasher, then wiping the counters down.

"How many people did you have over?" I ask.

Her nose wrinkles. "Just me and Marshmallow."

I eyeball the dishwasher, which is close to full.

"Oh, that." She flaps a hand at her mess. "It's been such a long time since I decided where we should eat that I don't actually know my favorite foods anymore. I'm sampling them all. Do you know I'd never had curry before yesterday? There's a soup and sandwich shop over in town with a curried chicken salad and it was *so good*. I'm thinking of offering to do some bussing in exchange for tips and tricks on how to make my chicken salad that good when I go home. I'd never ask for their actual recipe, but if they wanted to share the brand of curry powder they use, or any *you should know to never combine these ingredients* suggestions, that's all I need."

She never stops talking.

And her email is downloading, and *dear god*, she has three thousand unread messages.

No, four thousand.

No, still going.

She's not a squatter. She's an assassin, sent to murder me by making me twitch to death at the sight of her *Jesus Christ on a curry sandwich, thirty-four thousand unread messages*.

"You need psychological help," I tell her.

"My therapist said I probably only need to check in every three to six months. She was *massively* helpful during the divorce. And I still have daily work to do on myself, but I'm up for the hard work, and that's the important part. Well, that and all the hard work I've already done. Scoot over, please, and I'll get these bread crumbs behind you."

I shift, glance around, and the disaster that was my kitchen is now a workable space, aside from the dishwasher still hanging open.

The refrigerator's open again too.

I'm twitching all over again, watching her put my kitchen back to rights. "Could you please make that dog go live outside until I've removed you from this house as well?"

She visibly stifles a sigh, then squats and smiles at the dog. "Marshmallow! Go catch a butterfly! Go catch a butterfly, you good boy!"

The dog barks, wags its tail once, and trots to the back door, where it noses the lever, uses a paw to swing the door open, and slips outside.

Begonia makes one last pass through the kitchen, shutting the dishwasher and the refrigerator door. She dusts her hands together, then beams at me. "Coffee while we wait?"

"No."

"*No, thank you, Begonia, but it's a very kind offer to share your special coffee of the month club coffee with me,*" she says, affecting a baritone.

I slowly lift one eyebrow in response.

And Begonia, in what I'm rapidly deciding is true Begonia form, squints at me. "Does your family drink the same coffee that's served at your theme parks, or do you have, like, a private coffee plantation where you grow and harvest your own? With—what is it? Civets, right? Civets eat the raw coffee beans, then digest them, and when they're harvested on the other end, they're super fancy and delicious in a way you wouldn't think considering what the beans have, erm, been through."

"I don't drink coffee. I drink the blood of people who piss me off."

She laughs. "Oh, wow, do you have any idea how many of my students quoted that line to me last fall? I didn't see *Trick or Date*—my ex really didn't like Razzle Dazzle films—but my kids *adored* it. They even said Jonas was hot for an old guy. Teenagers, right? Thirty-something is *not* old, but maybe he should start playing roles more mature than college kids? I mean, it was great that your family finally moved him up from playing the high-schooler, but—"

This woman is getting on my last nerve, and she thinks I'm making jokes. "I'm printing the non-disclosure agreement, and then you can leave. Immediately."

My phone buzzes as some emotion I'd prefer to ignore flashes across her face. Truthfully, I'd prefer to ignore all emotions.

They make life entirely too complicated.

As does my brother's text message.

Mom's on a plane with Amelia Shawcross. If you're hiding at your place in Maine, I recommend drowning a sack of puppies. Got a great prop guy who can make it look real and a semi-reliable paparazzo who owes me a favor. Alternatively, dash off to Vegas and have a shotgun wedding with the first person you meet who'd have you. Let me know if you go with the second option, and I'll have Caspian draft a good prenup before you land.

All I wanted was six hours of sleep before digging into the inconsistencies that everyone else in Razzle Dazzle's corporate real estate division overlooked to figure out why we seem to have a small leak in our bank accounts.

Instead, I have a modern flower child with the world's most obnoxious dog making a mess of my house while my mother's on her way here to convince me to marry a Wall Street heiress who needs a husband who won't mind when she flies off to visit her secret lover in Cambodia.

Suppose it could be worse.

She could be bringing Paisley Windsor too. Mom's convinced Paisley's a misunderstood socialite who needs a little consistency in her life, and that with the right paperwork, she, too, would make me a good wife.

Anything to avoid a repeat of my early twenties when I believed in love.

"Does your eye always twitch like that?" Begonia asks. She's flitted into the living room, where she's gathering scattered clothing and paint rags, slowly but steadily erasing the evidence that she was ever here. "You seem like you're under an unhealthy level of stress. *Way* more than I'd expect for you finding an unexpected guest in your house. Is everything okay?"

I open my mouth to ask what a *healthy* level of stress would be when finding a squatter in my house, but before the words can form on my tongue, the back door swings open again, and her dog trots in, carrying a wooden statue in its jaw.

"*Marshmallow!*"

He drops the statue, sits back on his haunches, and regards her with a faux innocence that's utterly diabolical while I process the rest of what I'm seeing. "What the *fuck*?"

Begonia falls to her knees and grabs the small wooden statue. It's roughly eighteen inches high, and rubbing its head as she's doing will *not* fix what that dog has done. "Just needs a little polish and freshening," she says brightly.

"*Maurice Bellitano carved that.*"

She goes pale. "*The* Maurice Bellitano?"

"That's *my grandfather*. Your dog *chewed off the head of Maurice Bellitano's carving of my grandfather*."

"Oh, god," she whispers.

We both stare at the statue in her hands.

While my grandfather was more rotund than the slender statue, the high-waisted suit pants, the suspenders, and the loafers are undeniably him.

The head used to be as well, but now there are gnaw marks in my grandfather's eyeballs, his nose is gone, and the scally cap he always wore is missing half its brim.

I shift my attention to Begonia.

Her expression leaves *zero* doubt that she knows exactly who Maurice Bellitano was, and exactly how priceless that piece of wood in her hands is. "Oh, no no no..."

And now my head is going to explode.

When my mother sees this—

Wait.

Wait.

I look at my phone again.

Then at Begonia, a squatting divorcée with her poorly-disciplined dog and her glowing hair and her disaster all over my entire house.

An idea takes hold at the root of my brain.

It's a terrible idea.

Worse than terrible.

The consequences, the repercussions—if this backfires, it could do far more harm than good, and cause more problems than the situation I'd like to extract myself from.

But if it works, it could give me exactly what I've wanted and needed for months.

Years, even.

"Do. Not. Move," I order. "Do not think. Do not breathe. Do not *move*. Do you understand?"

She's kneeling on the floor, one hand on her dog's collar, the other gripping my grandfather's chewed head, staring at me with wide-eyed fear again. "My brain and my instincts are very much at odds over understanding right now, if I'm being perfectly honest."

"And for the love of god, *do not talk*."

I need to think.

And I need to do it quickly.

6

Begonia

I'M DUCK-WALKING AROUND THE ROOM, GATHERING MORE OF MY belongings and writing the inscription for my tombstone in my head—*here lies Begonia Fairchild, who had only just begun to find herself when her dog inadvertently destroyed her childhood idol's brother's prized and priceless wooden carving of his grandfather*—when Hayes Rutherford, whom to this point I had assumed to be a completely sane, if not slightly out-of-touch-with-the-common-people kind of guy, returns to the living room after a short phone call that he was speaking too softly for me to overhear, and announces, "Congratulations, Begonia. You're now my girlfriend."

I blink at him, rub my ears—are they full of wax?—and then blink at him again as his words filter from my ears to every other part of my body, some of which should *not* be listening to this. "I'm sorry, *what*?"

He points to the carving, which makes me cringe.

I studied Maurice Bellitano in college. I spent three semesters re-taking a class on carving because I wanted to *be* Maurice Bellitano, but my talents lie elsewhere.

My soul aches with the knowledge that my dog has just chewed up a priceless piece of art. I lift the surprisingly light carving. "Was that from Maurice's early years? It has some inconsistencies from—"

"It's a Bellitano original, and yes, I can prove it. Even if I couldn't, who would the courts believe?"

"Do you know that you have a choice every day to *not* be the kind of guy who thinks everything is a personal insult? It's okay to let things go. Research says it actually makes us happier to assume everyone around us has good intentions and sometimes screw-ups happen."

Hayes Rutherford is unswayed. At this point, I'm pretty certain a twenty-foot ocean wave couldn't budge him. He's laser-focused on me, and whatever he's about to say next, it can't be good.

"I can bill you for the damages to that statue, among the rest of the damages you've caused to this house and the grounds, or we can come to an alternate arrangement whereby you present yourself to my mother and the world as my girlfriend, and I don't financially ruin you for life."

That is *not* what I expected him to say, and it takes me a minute to find an appropriate response. "You live in a very strange world."

"Two weeks, you said you paid for? That's plenty of time for us to get engaged as well."

"*Excuse you?*"

"We won't get married. The very idea of it is beyond comprehension, and the legalities would be a larger headache than it would be worth. But I have no desire to be inundated with family trying to save me from my bachelorhood now that the entire world is watching me, and you have very few options for enjoying the rest of your vacation, much less your entire life, if you don't sign here."

He presents me with a small stack of papers as I lean back on my heels. I'm still on the floor, which is good, because my legs probably wouldn't support me right now. Absorbing weird news is best done as close to the ground as possible. Marshmallow tilts his head, clearly thinking that Hayes has lost use of his better sense too.

"What is this?" My skin flushes hot and cold as I skim the first page of the document, but it's so full of legalese that the only thing that truly leaps out at me is that it has my full name and address on it. "Oh my god, is this a set-up? Did Hyacinth win some kind of *win a date with your favorite celebrity* game, and give the prize to me instead, and then Jonas couldn't make it? *You knew I was here.* Is Jonas coming? Oh my god. I haven't watched his movies in at least eight years. They all got to be the same after a while, you know? Don't tell him I said that. And then Chad didn't like anything with actors who were more handsome than he was, because Chad was a douchewaffle, and I can call him that because my therapist says I shouldn't feel bad for not liking people on occasion, and people I'm willing to divorce fall under the umbrella of people I'm allowed to not like. I haven't even watched the reruns of *Hollybrook and Mistletoe* that used to run each December. Do you still play that every year? Has it aged okay? I can't remember all the specifics now, but I—"

"This is not a set-up, and you will *not* be meeting my brother. You'll be staying here, playing the part of my girl-friend, and distracting my mother and the rest of my family when they try to introduce me to women, and I'll be either working in the study or disappearing to New York for meet-ings." His face wrinkles again, his nose doing that *is there a fly on me?* twitch again. "If I absolutely *must*."

Stay here. With this man who's making me extremely uncomfortable for a variety of reasons I shouldn't even be thinking about, considering I barely know him and he clearly

43

dislikes me. *You have a type, don't you, Begonia?* "You have lost your ever-loving mind."

"Quite the contrary. It's the most efficient plan. I have no desire to have my family parade me around like the last eligible duke in some nineteenth-century historical novel, and the only thing that will stop them is a belief that I'm already involved with someone, and the further belief that if they don't back off, I will finally snap and marry someone so completely wrong for the role of my wife. You're here. I don't have to go search in town for anyone else, and you're clearly unsuitable. You've passed an initial background check, you have nowhere to be until school begins again in late August, and I demand compensation for both damages and the inconvenience of *not being fucking asleep right now*."

"You ran a background check on me?"

"Begonia Florence Fairchild, nee Bidelspach, formerly Dixon, employed by Tobin High School as an art teacher, three speeding tickets in the past year, your Netflix account is suspended because your credit card payment failed, daughter of Helen Nolan and Daniel Bidelspach, who divorced when you were seven. Father passed when you were seventeen. And if you spill the details of anything inside the agreement to your twin sister, Hyacinth, all will be null and void, and you'll owe me ten million dollars."

I squeak.

It's the only noise I'm capable of making.

"A more thorough background check is still ongoing, so if there's anything I need to know before I tell my mother I'm madly in love with you, you'd best speak up right now."

"*In love?* This *is* a set-up."

He frowns. "If this were a set-up, I would not have certain images in my head that make me finally understand the term *brain bleach.*"

Oh. My. God.

He's picturing me naked, waxing my bikini line, and

telling me he finds me unattractive. "Now I see why Jonas is known as the charming Rutherford brother."

"It's a fake relationship, Ms. Fairchild. I have no reason to charm you, whereas you have every reason to convince my mother that we're madly in love. You may take this very generous offer, or you may see me in court. I'll give you fifteen minutes to decide."

"How do I know you're not a serial killer with enough money and family connections to cover up all your crimes and this isn't just the way you play with your victims first?"

"I suppose you don't. Fourteen minutes and fifty-two seconds, Ms. Fairchild. I'm tired, and I expect my mother soon. You'd best get reading."

I eyeball the stack of papers and promptly toss them aside. "Why don't you just tell your mother you don't want to date anyone?"

He stares at me like I'm suggesting he go dance naked in the middle of town while blowing a kazoo to the tune of "YMCA." Not that that specific scenario popped into my head because I did it purely to annoy Chad in that brief window of time between consulting a divorce attorney and the paperwork being ready. And now I'm wondering if *that* will show up in his background report.

"It's almost adorable how little you know about the upper class, darling," Hayes says.

I recoil. "*Darling?* We need to work on terms of endearment. *You.* You need to work on terms of endearment. Also, you need to think this through a little more. Assuming I accept your argument that you, as a grown man, are incapable of just telling your mother you don't want to date anyone, what in the *world* makes you think she'll just accept that you're dating me?"

"If she doesn't, I'll promise to go to the press with all the details about how we started dating before your divorce was finalized. And lest you think I'm incapable myself of convincing my mother that I'm in love, bear in mind that I've been forced to watch Razzle Dazzle films from the cradle. I may not enjoy acting, and I may not understand the appeal of the god-awful films coming out of my family's company, but that doesn't mean I don't know how it's done, and if there's one thing I do *very* well, Ms. Fairchild, it's whatever I set my mind to. And I'm determined to convince the world that I'm very much in love with you. It's the most efficient way to restore my peace."

I gasp.

He's fiendish on an *evil cartoon overlord intent on destroying the world* level. If the Rutherford family is still as dedicated to being the perfect, charming, non-controversial family that they were all through my childhood, then threatening a public scandal is probably akin to vegetarian socialites getting caught eating cheeseburgers, which shouldn't be a *thing*, because who doesn't cheat on their diet every now and then? Could we *please* stop judging people for being human?

Also?

It's oddly erotic—and empowering—to think of a man wanting to claim to have fallen madly in love with me while we were having a clandestine affair when I was legally married to another man.

I think I'm turned on.

By a man.

Who's being a complete and total asshole, and I don't call people assholes lightly.

It's not really in my nature.

It's taken me a year of therapy to call Chad a douchewagon.

You wanted an adventure, Begonia.

And it's not like I'm not going into this with my eyes wide open.

Marshmallow swings a look at me, and I can't tell if he's

thinking I'm an idiot to consider this, or if I'd be an idiot to walk away.

I study Hayes, looking for any sign he's having the time of his life yanking my chain here. "There *aren't* any details about us dating before I was divorced, because we just met."

"Once again, *darling*, you are so naïve in the ways of the world."

It's probably wrong to get a little thrill every time he implies I'm ignorant in how the rich operate. It's like I can't wait for him to educate me. "Just how terrifying is your mother, *boo-berry*? She always seems so nice on talk shows and during red carpet interviews."

I'm rewarded with a nose twitch. "My mother is a menace. She wants me married. I'm uninterested. So you'll run interference, I'll have peace and quiet, and I won't tell *her* what happened to the statue of my grandfather."

"Why does she want you married?"

Well. Would you look at that? The *have you been living under a rock?* look is apparently universal across all socioeconomic statuses. "Do you read the news, Begonia?"

"Been a little busy getting divorced here, Hayes. Also, I gave up celebrity gossip around the time Violet Quinn checked into rehab and every channel had a live newsfeed of the clinic she was supposedly staying at. It felt like such a violation of her privacy when she was in such a low place, not to mention everyone else who could've been exposed on national TV for being near the place, and it made my stomach hurt."

He studies me briefly like he's trying to decide if I'm for real before sighing and scrubbing a hand over his face. "Eleven minutes, Ms. Fairchild. If you intend to reject my settlement offer, I suggest using your eleven minutes to gather what you can of your belongings before I forcibly throw you out."

"I can't really be the best partner in crime if I don't know why we're committing the heist. Why does your mother want you married? Is it like, normal mother stuff, with her insisting you've waited long enough to give her grandbabies? Does she still do your laundry and she's tired of it and wants another woman to take over raising you instead? *Oh my god*. If you tell me you're gay and your family won't accept that, I'm sorry, I won't be your fake girlfriend, but I will one thousand percent be the person who gets arrested for telling every last one of them off. Is that it? Are you in love with a man? *Oh my god*. Razzle Dazzle has never done a film with main characters who aren't straight, have they? *Oh my god*."

Marshmallow growls.

He knows what's up.

And Hayes—Hayes looks *amused*.

God help me.

He's rakishly handsome when he smiles, and that is *not* helping things. "My mother knows better than to insist I raise a child merely to satisfy her urges to hold a baby. I'm well aware of how to send my laundry out for cleaning without needing any assistance, along with conducting every other chore and task necessary to be a fully-functioning adult. And I am not in love with a man, but you're still welcome to give my mother an earful about the homogeny of Razzle Dazzle's films. Congratulations, Ms. Fairchild. You've just convinced me more than ever that you're the right woman for the job."

My heart squeezes. So does my vagina, which is like, *hello, what?* That hasn't happened in months. "Did you just call me *attractive*?"

"Dear god, no. Rather annoying, actually. Which is perfect. My mother will have her hands so full trying to get rid of you that she'll leave me alone completely. Add in her fear that I'll find someone even worse after you if she doesn't back off, and this is perfect. The document, Ms. Fairchild. Last chance. Are we doing this the easy way, or shall I get my attorney and the sheriff on the phone?"

7

Hayes

BEGONIA FAIRCHILD MIGHT HAVE PASSED AN INITIAL background check and signed the contract to play my fake girlfriend while never giving anyone the details under threat of financial ruination, but she's also a tenacious pain in the ass.

Perfect for when my mother gets here.

Right now?

When I'd prefer to find a bed that her dog hasn't shed all over so that I can sleep without waking up covered in hives and unable to breathe?

Right now, I'm considering the idea that a prison sentence for murder would *also* get me out of being attractive to the majority of the segment of the world's single women who would like to snag the world's last eligible heterosexual male billionaire.

Yes, only *the majority*.

I'm aware it wouldn't solve my problem completely.

Conjugal visits are apparently a turn-on in some circles, which was much funnier when I suggested that as the theme of a Razzle Dazzle movie to make my brother shut up after he won his Oscar.

"So if we've been talking on the internet for the past six months, that means we'll know a lot about each other," Begonia says as she dusts the bookshelves lining the fireplace. "*Moby Dick*? Really? Do you read it, or is it a conversation piece? There's nothing wrong with reading commercial fiction instead of literary classics."

She makes air quotes around *classics*, and I feel my face twitching. "The only story we need is that you find cranky assholes irresistibly charming."

"That's the plot of half the Razzle Dazzle films. No one's going to believe it."

"Quite frankly, Ms. Fairchild, I don't need my mother to *believe* us. I merely need her to know I'll make the family look bad in the press if she insists on presenting me with a parade of eligible women she'd like me to marry."

She frowns again. "I don't—*oh. Oh.* It's not about telling your mom no, is it? It's about the time and energy it takes every time she throws another woman at you. Or is it about disappointing your mother? Do you have mommy issues? I never thought I did until I announced I was divorcing Chad, and now I'm the disappointment."

"Congratulations, Ms. Fairchild, you have confirmed that you do, in fact, listen three percent of the time."

"My listening skills are fine. It's your communication skills that need work. You had two options there, and you just said I listened. That's not answering the question." She waves the feather duster at me, sending particles floating into the shafts of light pouring in through the east-facing windows and making me flinch.

Billions of dollars in the bank, the majority of which I made on my own with wise investments as I took control of my trust fund, and then a bit of fun with bitcoin mining, and not a solution to be bought for basic environmental allergies. "One more thing you'll be certain to tell my mother you find charming about me. Where the devil did you hide—"

The gate phone rings in the foyer before I can finish asking where she's hidden fresh sheets. Begonia brightens, and her dog barks out on the screened-in porch, where he's been locked away to cause minimal mischief.

"Oh, visitors!" Begonia tosses the duster onto the fireplace hearth and darts for the foyer. "Don't worry, I'll send them away. Unless they brought food. I definitely need to get over to town to get some food, since Marshmallow ruined everything in the fridge."

"Don't tell them—" I start, but she's already answering the video intercom, which I haven't upgraded to Bluetooth, because I *like* living in an old-fashioned world.

At least when I'm here.

"Hello?"

"Hello, this is Mayor Kristine Turner. We heard the owner's back in residence. Just wanted to check and see if he needs anything?"

My shoulders creep up to my ears. "Tell her no," I order softly, staying out of sight of the camera myself.

"Oh, no, we're good," Begonia chirps. "I'll be coming into town in a little bit for supplies, but for now—"

"I can bring supplies," the mayor interrupts. "Does Hayes need food? What about his favorite wine? My mom's happy to make him her famous sponge cake. We know how much he loves that. Is he still allergic to strawberries and dogs?"

For god's sake. I march into the foyer, stand to the side, and hit the button to hang up the connection. "I said, tell her no."

"*Hayes.* That's rude. Don't hang up on people. How do I call her back?"

"You don't. No one in town needs to know I'm here."

"They already know you're here. Also, you're allergic to dogs? How does she know you're...*oh my god*. Did she pretend to be your girlfriend another time when you were hiding from your mother here?"

The intercom buzzes again.

Begonia reaches for the button to answer, but I snag her hand—and then her other hand—before she can answer it. "Do. Not. Pick. Up. The. Intercom."

She blinks up at me with bright green eyes under that glowing magenta hair. Her lips part, and her tongue darts out to sweep over her plump bottom lip. "Why?"

I'm suddenly very aware of the fact that I'm holding onto her wrists, that her skin is smooth as silk, and she has three freckles—and only three—beneath the outer corner of her left eye. "Because I said so."

"Someone who knows you love her mother's sponge cake is *clearly* a friend, so what's the big—" She cuts herself off, glancing at the small monitor showing Kristine standing at the gate, shifting back and forth on her feet, smiling hopefully. "You dated her, didn't you? You seriously dated her."

"Do not confirm for anyone that I'm here. Have I made myself clear?"

She nods, but there's entirely too much going on in her expression. I've known a woman or two in my lifetime who've thought loudly.

Begonia doesn't merely think loudly.

She uses a bullhorn.

And right now she's broadcasting that she'd very much like a jumbo carton of popcorn to go with the tea I'm denying her.

I glower at her.

She visibly gulps and pulls her hands away. "There are fresh sheets in the laundry room. I'll go fix up the bed. Do you know when your mother's getting here? I'm great with parents, so if you wanted to go to sleep, you're welcome to, and you can trust me to charm the pants off your mother. Which guest room does she like? I'll get that fixed up too, and take the one in the basement for me and Marshmallow."

"Your dog can sleep in the basement. You'll be in my room."

"I—"

"For the farce to work, Ms. Fairchild, you'll be in my room."

She looks at the video monitor once more, where Kristine keeps reaching out like she wants to hit the buzzer again, but keeps having second thoughts. "Can I at least tell the mayor I'll let her know if I need anything?"

"No."

"You're incredibly unreasonable."

I'm incredibly tired of people who have no right to make demands of me thinking they're entitled to my time. "It's a perk of being me."

She doesn't answer.

Even her face gets quiet.

And that's possibly more disconcerting than anything else about this entire situation.

8

Begonia

NOTE TO SELF: FAKE DATING A BILLIONAIRE MAY NOT BE BUCKET list-worthy.

So long as I don't end up in prison, accidentally do something that would get me fired from my teaching job, or get murdered, I'm sure I'll still find something positive out of the experience, but right now, I'm sincerely doubting I'll have anything good to say about Hayes Rutherford when this is over.

Case in point?

Fifteen seconds ago, when a perfunctory knock sounded on the door, he sighed heavily, put away the phone he's been staring at non-stop while I've been needling him for information so we could pull this off, looked at me, and said, "I hope you're half as good with parents as you are at annoying me," then walked to the foyer, swung the door open, and said, "Mother. What a surprise," in that way that says it wasn't at all a surprise to see her.

And now, I'm staring wide-eyed at three of the most gorgeous women I've ever seen in person in my entire life.

Giovanna Rutherford leads the pack. Hayes's mother is one of those women who reminds me of a bird. If I wanted to stay as skinny as she is, I'd have to live on a daily diet of three chickpeas, a shot of vodka, and four hours of being yelled at by a personal trainer named Guy, then two hours of therapy to get over the four hours of being yelled at. She has fewer crow's-feet in her seventies than I do in my early thirties—and don't ask about how flawless her white skin is, without even a hint of a single sun spot—her pantsuit looks like it was woven by angels and fitted by Tim Gunn or the *Queer Eye* guys, and her chin-length hair is such a lovely shade of silver that it could be braided into a chain and used as a necklace.

Or possibly I'm having an irrational girl-crush reaction to being within inches of Jonas Rutherford's mother.

I wonder if Hyacinth is picking up on my freak-out over our twin radar.

Not that I have time to worry about that. The two women behind Giovanna are giving off major diva vibes.

The first is a stunning dark-haired, brown-skinned woman with more curves than a mountain road and more poshness in her pinky nail than I have in my entire body. The second is a striking alabaster-skinned redhead—and I mean a natural shade of red, unlike mine—who has lust written all over her expression when her brown eyes shift to Hayes.

Giovanna gives me a once-over, then hands me her gloves as she plucks them off her hands.

My fake boyfriend's mother has *traveling gloves*, while I'm standing here dripping in sweat from running around picking up and changing sheets, my hair glowing fuchsia, and with a streak of what I hope is dirt and not paint from an undetermined source swiped across my left boob.

It's probably a good thing I opted to *not* wear my *Artists Do It In Full Color* T-shirt.

"See to it that my luggage is taken to the guest quarters upstairs and make Amelia comfortable in the room down the hall," Giovanna orders me. "Charlotte will take the en suite in the basement."

"Carry your own luggage, Mother," Hayes says. "Begonia isn't here to serve you."

"Ah, my sweet boy. So cranky when you're tired." She pats his cheek, turning her back on me like I'm the hired help, which would make a lot more sense than what I signed paperwork agreeing to. "Have you had anything to eat today? That never helps either."

"Neither do uninvited guests."

"Hayes."

"Mother."

"I realize you're old enough to take care of yourself, but it's been a difficult two weeks, and you shouldn't be by yourself right now."

I fling myself between them and grip Giovanna's hand, pumping it enthusiastically, because *oh my god, I'm touching Jonas Rutherford's mother*. "Mrs. Rutherford. Hi. I'm Begonia. It is *so good* to meet you. Hayes hasn't told me much about you, but then, you could probably say the same about what he's told you about me, couldn't you?"

She smiles at me, but it's one of those patient smiles that I give my students when they try to convince me that a blank canvas is *art* just because they didn't want to do the assignment.

Or possibly like that smile my mother gave me when I told her I was divorcing Chad.

"I'm sorry, I have no idea who you are," Giovanna says, smile still in place, patiently letting me continue pumping her hand without pulling away.

I wonder if this happens when she visits the Razzle Dazzle Village amusement parks. Strangers accosting her and shaking her hands and telling her thank you for being part of the family that runs their favorite vacation spot.

"Relax, darling, I'm quite all right with it if she doesn't like you." Hayes slips an arm around my waist, his fingers resting above my hip. It's an intimate gesture suggesting we're much more acquainted than we actually are, and it should make me uncomfortable—I don't need another overbearing man in my life, even if I'm mostly game for fake-dating a billionaire—but instead of my common sense reminding me that this is pretend, my vagina reminds me that it's been somewhere between twelve and eighteen months since a man's touched me for anything other than a handshake or a hug among colleagues or family. I don't remember the last time Chad and I had sex, but I do remember it wasn't any more memorable than a handshake, which is the only thing that made it memorable.

"Begonia, meet my mother, Giovanna. Mother, this is Begonia Fairchild. My girlfriend."

My mom looks *nothing* like Giovanna Rutherford.

But I know that disappointed mother face.

I know it *very* well.

It disappears nearly as quickly as it appears though, which makes me wonder if Jonas got his acting skills from this side of the family.

"Ah, again?" she murmurs, fake smile still plastered on.

A-*ha!* I was right.

He's used fake girlfriends before.

Possibly including the mayor here.

And now I want to know how that one went down. It couldn't have been terrible if she was willing to come ring the gate bell.

Or does he just have very, very poor taste in women?

Of all the time to have my internet speed dependent on a hotspot on someone else's bad wireless connection, the moment when I need to google my new fake boyfriend's relationship history is *not* ideal.

"Yes, Mother, I have a girlfriend *again*," Hayes says. "Begonia and I met on a Snarflings World forum while I was incognito, moved private chats to phone calls, and I asked her to meet me here. She had no idea until this morning who I actually am, nor to whom I'm related, and I'd prefer if you don't make her uncomfortable."

Wow.

He's good.

Except I wouldn't be caught dead within seventeen miles of a Snarflings World forum, since it was Chad's favorite television show and I never really got it.

Aliens trying to correct things wrong with Earth and always getting it wrong?

They could've tackled world hunger or environmental disasters, and instead, they were like, *we must save humans from Cheerios.*

It was so absurd it wasn't even funny.

And now I wonder just how odd Hayes really is, and also if he knows that little detail about Chad from his background check on me.

Just how thorough can a background check be if it's done in ten minutes?

Once again, I'm back to wondering if he knew I was here, but the circle of questions is more likely to make my head hurt than it is to convince me to run, so I stay, smiling brightly.

"You can take your own luggage to your rooms," Hayes continues, "or, more preferably, to one of the other accommodations in town across the island."

"Did you run a background check on her?" the dark-haired diva asks. She's familiar, but I can't quite place her, and this isn't a *Did I meet you at Cracker Barrel?* or *Was your brother one of my art students?* kind of familiar.

Is she an actress?

"Begonia, this is Amelia Shawcross," Hayes says. "We went to grade school together. And this is Charlotte, my mother's personal assistant who deserved a Sunday off but apparently didn't get it. I assume there's a security detail making the rounds outside. You'll meet them soon enough as well."

Amelia takes my hand for a handshake that feels very practiced. "Hayes and I got married in second grade."

"Oh, that must've been adorable." I beam at her. "I married my dog when I was nine. My sister and I were arguing over who got to be the bride and who had to be the bridesmaid, so we decided to take turns, but when Mom heard me talking about a honeymoon with Oreo, she freaked out over what the neighbors would think, so Hyacinth never got to be Oreo's second wife."

Hayes chuckles, and the sound wraps around me like a blanket made of chocolate lava cake. "Isn't she adorable?"

"Quite...normal." If Giovanna's appalled, she's hiding it well.

Amelia shakes her long, thick hair and smiles a vulture's smile at me. "You probably shouldn't tell that story in mixed company if you don't want stories about yourself having sex with a dog spread across the tabloids. Have you ever dated someone famous, Begonia?"

"Just Oreo. He ate the mayor's wife's roses and made the local papers for it. Mostly because he wasn't smart enough to stop after the first thorn made his tongue bleed." I turn my beaming smile up at Hayes, and yes, I'm well aware that my dog being famous has nothing on the level of fame these people deal with every day. "But I'm attracted to smarter creatures now. And Oreo's tongue was okay. It wasn't as bad as the news made it sound. Plus, he was recovering from the ol' snip-snip and still had a lot of painkillers in his body when it happened."

The looks on their faces are priceless.

I can't wait to tell Hyacinth that Jonas Rutherford's mother will never forget me.

Obviously, I'd prefer it was for a better reason, but a girl has to work with what she's got. And honestly? The idea of the whole Rutherford family sitting around a Christmas tree, fire roaring, laughing about *that time Hayes pretended to be dating a girl who married her dog who went small-town viral when he was drugged-up and snip-snipped* brings me a little joy.

Do people on Fifth Avenue talk about the things their pets do that aren't normal or polite?

They always seem so stiff, like they need the little things to laugh at.

"Are any of you hungry?" I ask. "I think we have crackers. There was, erm, a refrigerator malfunction, so we're out of butter. I can use the house phone to order a Tuber to have some lobster rolls delivered. Have you had the lobster rolls from Clickety Clack? They're *delicious*. And I think it's adorable that there's a local named Mr. Tuberman who runs the *Tuber*. It's like *Uber*, but not."

"They know where Clickety Clack is if they're hungry, darling," Hayes says.

Giovanna's lips go flat and tight.

"Don't be a bear," I whisper to Hayes. "They'll think I'm a bad influence."

"It's not you, Bernardia," Amelia says.

"*Begonia*," Hayes corrects. "Though I prefer to think of her as my bluebell."

"Of course you do. I was always your azalea."

Amelia Shawcross.

It clicks.

Holy sweet da Vinci on toast. "You were on *Dancing with the Stars*."

"Amelia's multi-talented." The smile Giovanna aims at Amelia leaves no doubt just how much the older woman likes her. It's a Sesame Street smile, except Giovanna doesn't want Amelia to be her neighbor. She wants her to be her daughter-in-law. "She's quite brilliant in her day job on Wall Street, runs a popular finance blog, *and* would've won that season if they hadn't let a former cheerleader with seven years of dance training into the competition."

"You kicked ass," I tell her sincerely. "I don't know how you kept up with everything while you were doing dance lessons for the show too. Seriously amazing. My sister and I couldn't stop talking about how we would've been so exhausted after the first thirty minutes of rehearsals, but you killed it like a major lady boss. Such a great role model for young girls everywhere. High five, rock star."

I lift a hand.

All three women stare at me like I'm an alien.

I glance at Hayes and find that he, too, seems completely befuddled.

"You don't celebrate each other's successes?" I ask.

"And you wonder why I like her," Hayes says to his mother.

That's all the warning I get before he grabs me by the hips, spins me so our bodies align, and lowers his mouth to mine.

My first instinct is to protest, but I ignore it.

Not because I'm contractually obligated to, or some other legal nonsense reason.

But because if these people truly don't celebrate each other, then who am I to interfere with Hayes's plans to *not* get set up with one of them?

Also, I haven't been kissed in months.

Months.

Well over a year, for sure.

And I like kissing. I like being close to someone. Skin to skin. Breath to breath.

Intimacy.

I don't miss Chad.

I miss *intimacy*.

Hayes wraps one arm tighter around my waist while he settles his other hand at my nape, his fingers spreading over my scalp and making my nerve endings stand up and rejoice. He licks the seam of my lips, and I melt.

I'm no longer Begonia Fairchild, lost child in search of herself.

I'm a puddle of paint in every color of the rainbow, swirled and glittered and beautiful and wanted, or at least, I can pretend I'm wanted.

For just a minute.

I miss being *wanted*.

I part my lips, touch my tongue to his, and while a hazy part of my brain tries to remind me that *this is just for show*, when he teases my tongue right back, my vagina leaps to her feet and throws her bra at the stage where Hayes is performing the encore of all rock show encores.

"*Hayes,*" a distant voice says.

I ignore it.

He ignores it.

This is a spectacular kiss.

I would believe this kiss if I were watching it.

He could make you come in thirty seconds if he kissed your pussy like this, a little voice whispers.

There's a shriek in response, and I realize that's not me shrieking.

Nor is it my vagina recoiling in fear that we're not ready for pussy-kissing.

It's an actual shriek.

"*Dog!*"

Dog.

Dog.

Marshmallow.

I wrench myself out of Hayes's arms and spin away. "Marsh—"

"*Sit*," Hayes orders.

He's right behind me, and I can feel his chest heaving against my back.

I can also feel—*oh*.

Oh, that's not good.

I mean, it *is*, but—did he enjoy the kiss *that* much? Or does he have a hair-trigger erection?

Focus on the dog, Begonia.

For once, Marshmallow has followed an order.

And he's now sitting in the middle of the living room with a lacy pink bra draped over his head.

A lacy pink bra that is *not* mine.

My gaze flies to the luggage that the three women dragged in behind them.

And then back to my dog.

"*Marshmallow.*"

"Put. It. Back," Hayes says.

Marshmallow whimpers, rises to his feet, and skitters across the floor to drop the bra at Amelia's feet before army-crawling to Hayes's feet, where he plops all the way down, then lifts his eyes at my fake boyfriend like he's begging to still be loved.

"Good boy," I squeak out.

Giovanna's gaping at me.

Amelia lowers herself to the floor, lifts the bra with a single finger, and rises again, draping it over her shoulder with a meaningful look at Hayes.

Georgia O'Keefe have mercy, I am in an entirely new social class, with entirely new rules, still reeling from that kiss, and I'm pretty sure my fake boyfriend is being propositioned with a bra that my dog dug out of another woman's luggage.

Adventure?

Oh, yes, Begonia.

You are getting an adventure.

9

Hayes

THE PROBLEM WITH INFINITY IS THAT YOU CAN'T COUNT TO IT.

I'm trying.

I'm *desperately* trying.

I'm at six million, four hundred twenty-three thousand, two hundred sixty-one, with my eyes closed, a sheep pictured for every increase in count, allergy medicine consumed, headache medicine consumed, and my brain will *not* shut off.

"Are you mad at me?" Begonia whispers in the dark.

I stifle an irritated sigh. "Whyever would I be angry with you, my darling bluebell?"

"Sarcasm still isn't attractive on you, but I'd probably be cranky if I hadn't slept in seven days too."

Three. Not quite three.

"You should've told me about the weddings and funeral," she adds. "Your mother and Bachelorettes One and Two are *not* buying this fake relationship, because I don't know enough about you."

She's on a pile of blankets on the floor—the side away from the door—because I refused to let her sleep in the closet, and she refused to sleep in my bed with me. This entire day has been one disaster after another, after two intense days of wedding-everything, and now I can't fucking fall asleep.

I sigh again and roll to my left. The dog has been successfully locked away for the night, the French doors are cracked open to the balcony, letting in a hint of the cool salty breeze off the ocean and the sound of the surf rolling to shore. The sheets are clean and dog hair-free, and Begonia insisted on vacuuming in here herself after dinner to make sure the room was as clean as possible.

I should be dead asleep by now.

"Were you close to your cousin?" she whispers.

"Begonia. Be quiet."

"I didn't sleep for almost a week after I moved into my apartment when I left Chad. I was bottling up everything inside, lying in bed at night second-guessing myself and wondering where I'd gone wrong. I thought I could've done something differently, and that I'd been a bad wife when I'd tried so hard to be a good wife. Then there was my mother, insisting I was a fool for leaving a decent man and that I'd be alone forever. It took Hyacinth coming to see me and telling me she couldn't sleep because I couldn't sleep, and that we needed to talk it out so we could both sleep again. So we did. We talked it out, and then we both slept."

Don't ask. Don't ask. Don't— "Why the hell couldn't *Hyacinth* sleep?"

"Cosmic twin connection. Just like I had horrible cramps when she was in labor both times."

I sigh.

She rustles on the floor, and a moment later, the light flips on in the bathroom.

I growl softly.

She did a decent enough job distracting two of the three

women at any given time today so that I could get the study set up for the work I need to start on tomorrow, but she's inept at managing three high-maintenance women at once, so I was never alone.

Amelia wanted my opinion on business topics and her website and to ask how long I intended to play boyfriend to a common high school art teacher.

Charlotte wanted to know what she could fetch me to make my life easier, and I'm fairly certain she would've fetched me herself in lingerie if I'd moved my face the wrong way.

My mother wanted to know how long I plan to be here, if I realize the dangers of dating a *civilian* unfamiliar with life as a Rutherford, and why I would ever choose to date a woman with not just a dog, but a dog who was clearly talented at uncovering things best kept in drawers and closets.

And Begonia was loud even when she was quiet.

She has a special talent.

Tomorrow, I'm kicking my mother and her guests out of my house so I can relegate Begonia to a guest room with orders to keep everyone out and invent creative stories about how madly we're in love so that when we break up, I'll get at least a six-month window before anyone starts hounding me again.

If I could take off in a private jet and parachute myself to the ground somewhere over an uninhabited tropical island that was miraculously stocked with food, alcohol, and an internet connection so that I could tackle all of my new duties for Razzle Dazzle remotely, I would in a heartbeat.

"Sit up," Begonia says, suddenly near me.

Something earthy and feminine tickles my nose. Flowery, but not unpleasant. I open one eye and peer into the darkness at the woman nudging my shoulder. "What are you doing?"

"Helping you get to sleep. Your mom said dogs and

strawberries are your only allergies. You're not allergic to lavender too, are you?"

"No."

"Good. I lit some lavender incense. Breathe deep. It'll help you relax. And sit up and scoot down."

"No."

"*Sit up and scoot down*. Don't make me get your mother."

"My mother would welcome any excuse to throw you out."

"You really don't understand who you've asked to be your fake girlfriend yet, do you?"

I know that I'm completely uncomfortable with how lovely that scent is, along with once again feeling blood surge to my cock the same way it did when I kissed her earlier.

I needed to convince my mother that I was falling for an ignorant disaster of a woman, not trick my body into thinking there was hope for a companion the next time I wanted physical release.

Instead, I have—well.

I have *Begonia*.

In my bedroom.

Lighting *incense*.

And bending over me with her breasts swaying beneath a low-cut nightgown that's somehow simple cotton, yet the most erotic thing I've been up close and personal with in weeks, and oddly preferable to that pink lace bra her dog so helpfully pulled out of Amelia's luggage.

"Yes, yes, you're a terrifying woman," I say. "It was your master plan all along to lie in wait here so you could surprise the *weird* Rutherford brother and score yourself the last eligible billionaire on the planet, and now you have me right where you want me."

She twists my ear, and I barely stifle a startled shriek of outrage that my mother would hear.

She growls softly. "Sit. Up. And. Scoot. Down."

I'm not sleeping.

Might as well be entertained.

I do as she orders, and the infernal woman takes a seat, cross-legged, on my pillow, then pats her bare thighs. "Lie down. Face up."

"I'm certainly not planning to return to that pillow face-*down*."

"Don't be an ass. *Lie down*. I'd very much like to not fake being madly in love with a grumpy-pants for the next two weeks, and that means you need to get some sleep?"

I refuse to consider if it's curiosity or the threat that has me reclining back onto the bed, settling my head into Begonia's lap, but soon, that's exactly where I am.

"Close your eyes and take a deep breath," she says softly.

I should not trust this woman, but my body is exhausted, my mind is beyond rational thought, and the lavender scent is rather nice. So I do as she orders, letting my eyelids drift closed while I inhale.

My body stiffens when she threads her fingers through my hair, but then she applies pressure to my scalp, and goose-bumps race across my flesh.

"Tell me if I hurt you," she says softly.

I grunt a response.

"Listen to the waves," she whispers as she rubs my head. "Just breathe and listen to the waves."

I've taken fake girlfriends before. Once at my mother's request when her best friend's daughter had been caught in a compromising position and needed her reputation salvaged. My mother wouldn't have been disappointed if something had come of that relationship, but there was no chemistry, and even if there had been, I wouldn't have trusted it.

The other times are hazy now.

It's like Begonia is cleansing my brain of those memories. "Strong fingers," I murmur.

"Is it too much?"

I try to shake my head, but it won't move. It's becoming cement in her hands. Cement on the shore, with the surf rolling in and out over it, but a dry surf.

No water.

Just lavender.

Her fingers move down my scalp to my neck, stroking the tension away with firm hands. Jonas has massages regularly. Weekly, possibly.

I don't.

I don't like strangers touching my body.

I shouldn't let Begonia touch me, but if we're going to fake intimacy, then I need to be comfortable touching her.

Letting her touch me.

Letting her rock me to sleep on the boat.

I want a lobster pillow.

I want her to use those hands on my cock.

Does her pussy smell like a spa?

Could I crawl inside and hide in there?

Am I—am I falling asleep?

There's a muted knock somewhere in the distant sludges of my sleepy brain, and then my mother's voice, both loud and quiet at the same time. I can't understand what she's saying, and I don't want to.

I want to lie here, in my boat, with a woman's hands stroking my neck and scratching my scalp, helping all the lights inside my brain flip off, until I finally float away, on my back in a rowboat with a fuchsia-haired mermaid in a cotton nightie smiling at me from the prow.

Begonia

WHEN I SKETCHED OUT A PLAN FOR MY TWO WEEKS ON Oysterberry Bay Island, I figured I'd start my first Monday tackling something that's always scared me. There's nothing like making Monday your bitch to start the week on a high note, and if you fail at making Monday your bitch, you blame it on Monday being Monday, and start over on Tuesday.

It's not like having a major failure on a Friday and then having to suffer through the weekend with regrets.

But instead of heading to the dock in Sprightly, the little town on the other end of the island, for the sailing excursion I booked with a gnarled old sailor guy who *promised* he wouldn't let me drown, Marshmallow and I have snuck into town early for a lot more grocery shopping than my credit card would prefer, and probably more than I should carry back on the bike I used to get across the island.

I have a fake boyfriend's family to charm.

THE LAST ELIGIBLE BILLIONAIRE

And there is absolutely no better way to do that than with down-home cooking.

Unfortunately for all of us, I'm not much of a chef, but considering it doesn't take a genius to figure out Hayes wants to be alone, this will probably work to his advantage, and then I'll be rewarded with more free time to explore the island and get in that sailing adventure later.

I'm pushing the bike down the dirt path along the rocky shoreline while Marshmallow dances in and out of the waves when a golf cart approaches. I start to move to the side of the path, then realize who's in the cart, and my heart does a slow somersault.

The past twenty-four hours have been so unexpected and strange that if I hadn't snuck out of the bedroom where Hayes was sleeping early this morning, I wouldn't believe it's all real.

Yet here he is, driving a golf cart with Amelia Shawcross seated in the passenger seat, her thick black hair billowing in the breeze and her eyes hidden behind sunglasses, a second golf cart with three of Giovanna's bodyguards following them closely.

Hayes is scowling as he pulls the cart to a stop in front of me. "Darling, I told you not to leave the estate without security."

The last thing Hayes said to me last night before passing out cold was *Bubbles melt in the mermaid boat*, and he didn't mention security once before that.

But I smile at him, and it's not actually hard to find that smile.

Even scowling, he looks less grumpy than he did yesterday. Or maybe I'm projecting a belief that he needed more sleep, or maybe it's that he came to get me himself instead of just sending security, or maybe it's that the dark scruff growing out on his chin and cheeks, coupled with the black jeans and Henley, make him look more rugged than fancy, and a scowl on a rugged man is from a way different place than a scowl on a billionaire finding an unexpected nearly-naked guest in his bathroom.

And now I'm thinking about how he wasn't wearing a shirt when I made him let me into his bed last night, and wondering how naked he was, and once again debating with myself if I can use this change in my own plans to ask a favor of him as well.

"We were out of food." I gesture to the bike handles, laden with canvas bags of groceries, hoping I don't look like I'm mentally stripping him, because I'm not.

My favor has nothing to do with finding him attractive. It's just a *thing*. That's it. "No strawberries. But I did get more cheesecake."

"This is what Charlotte is for," Amelia tells me.

"Oh, but I love the market. It's so quaint and charming, and they have a nut butter maker, and I got a sample of the most delicious fresh almond butter that I've ever had in my life. Don't worry—I got a jar to share, because you *have* to taste this. It's so good. And the market also let Marshmallow in with me, and no one minded when he carried my mangos around the store for me."

Hayes makes a noise that might be a simple hiccup or might be regrets laced with *dear god, don't ever speak of your mangos again* as he slides out of the golf cart. "Come, Begonia. Sit. I'll load up the bike—"

"No, no, I'll ride it back, if you'll take the groceries. And I'll start brunch when I get home."

Amelia doesn't say anything else out loud, but I'm pretty sure she's once again thinking *that's what Charlotte is for*.

Poor Charlotte.

She's *clearly* in love with Hayes, and he has no idea.

Or maybe he does, and he's very, very good at playing obtuse.

And maybe she's not actually in love with him, because

maybe she has better taste than that, but has great admiration for him because he's…good…at something she admires.

Whatever that is.

Feel sorry for the man for clearly having a rough few days? Yes.

Admit he's attractive in a rugged, grumpy way, and possibly not the horrifying bear I thought he was yesterday? Maybe.

Want to fall in love with him?

Absolutely not. Love and I are on a break, and when we decide to give it a try again, it won't be with a man who makes me sign a contract agreeing to be his fake girlfriend.

I want to be wooed, and I want to be someone's equal.

Not gonna lie though—I also want someone to pop my post-divorce cherry, and I am nothing if not in tune with signs from the universe.

In all the time since I left Chad and started this journey toward being single, this is the first time I've *wanted* to consider having sex again.

Sleep in the same bed with someone? Of course. I don't like being lonely. Especially at night.

But sex? Nope.

"Get in the golf cart, Begonia."

After he fell asleep last night, I extracted myself from beneath his head, climbed onto the other side of the king-size mattress, and slept so-so for about six hours, our bodies continuously drawing closer together until I'd jerk awake and scoot to the other side of the bed again, his deep breathing as constant as the rolling tide outside and the soft breeze fluttering the curtains surrounding the balcony doors.

And I thought.

And this morning, slipping quietly through the aisles of the grocery store, listening to the whispered gossip around me, I thought some more.

This is fake.

It can be a lot of fun.

And maybe, just maybe, whenever this farce is over, both of us will have gotten something out of our arrangement.

Goodness knows I've already gotten more than I bargained for.

I met *Jonas Rutherford's mother*. And she thinks I'm dating her other son. And *Amelia Shawcross* is staring at me.

This is way more adventure—in a peopling kind of way—than I thought I'd ever get in my whole life.

So I'm all in with this fake relationship thing.

Still, knowing what I'm supposed to do and why, coupled with what I want to ask *him* to do, makes it more difficult to slip my arms around this man's shoulders. So does the way my heart kicks up when I go up on my tiptoes to press a kiss to his scruffy cheek. "No. Walk me home instead."

His muscles bunch, but he mimics my movements and settles his hands on my hips. "It's not safe to wander off the estate by yourself when you're dating me."

I smile brighter and slip my fingers through his hair. "Are kidnappers going to dash out from behind that rock and carry me off to torture me behind the lobster shack?"

"You're being ridiculous."

"There *is* a possibility some nosy busybody with a camera will take our picture and perpetuate this crazy story where the world's last single billionaire is madly in love with a divorced art teacher from Virginia. That would probably be a serious hit to your reputation." Thank you, market tabloids, for filling in more details to his story while I waited to pay for my groceries.

The world's last unmarried, male, heterosexual billionaire.

With Jonas getting married to his actress girlfriend, his single cousin, Thomas, dying in a horrific car accident, and Mathias Randolf, the software billionaire, eloping in the Caymans—with friends and family present, including Hayes —all within the last two weeks, that means I truly am fake dating the world's last single man with a ten-figure bank account.

I'm the only thing standing between Hayes and the dozen women I overheard wondering if he was single and wanted to meet them or their niece or granddaughter.

And Amelia Shawcross.

And who knows how many others?

"My patience is in short supply, Ms. Fairchild."

"Then you definitely have to walk me back to your place. Just breathe that air. Isn't it amazing?" I suck in a huge breath, demonstrating how to breathe for him, not because he needs it, but because I never would've said this to Chad, and I *need* to practice saying the things I want to say when they don't cause anyone harm.

Chad would've said, *Get in the cart, Begonia,* and I would've said, *Yes, Chad* while thinking *He's such a stick in the mud, but at least this way we don't argue over it.*

Peace over happiness.

What good was the peace when it robbed me of the little joys in life, like a few extra minutes of breathing in the fresh salty air while my dog chases sea birds and tries to catch the waves in his mouth?

Hayes's nostrils quiver, like he's trying to test the air without letting on that he's following instructions, and just like last night, when he laid his head in my lap and let me help him relax, a tight band around my chest eases.

My pulse is still running high, and there are goosebumps racing across my skin, but the nerves aren't about if I'm doing this fake girlfriend thing right, or if I've agreed to a deal with someone who actually wants to hurt me.

I think he's doing the best he can with whatever demons are haunting him, and for one small moment, I'm giving him peace.

I like giving people peace.

But I'm done doing it at the expense of my own happiness.

"Hayes, your mother wants to know if she should send Charlotte into town for coffee, or if we're bringing some back," Amelia calls.

I lean around Hayes and smile at her. "Everything's set in the pot in the kitchen. It's my special coffee-of-the-month-club coffee. From Ecuador this month. And it's delicious. All she has to do is hit the power button."

She doesn't smile back.

I lift my eyes to Hayes. "People in your social circles *do* know how to hit the power button on a coffee maker, right?"

"If not, there's always Charlotte."

I blink. "Did you—did you just make a joke?"

"No."

His delivery is so straight-faced, I crack up. "Well, you should've. Jokes lower blood pressure too."

"So does getting home and getting to work. Get in the cart."

I stroke my fingers into his hair, pretending I don't notice when his entire body goes stiff against me, and *definitely* pretending I don't notice a new pressure on my belly right below where his belt sits. Is he easily turned on, or has it just been that long for him too? "Walk me home. It'll take an hour, and it'll clear your head before you disappear to do all of your work and leave me to entertain your mother and your ex-wife."

A strangled noise rumbles from his throat. "She is *not*—"

"Grade school wives who are super successful all on their own don't often come back when you're still single at your age, and when they do, they definitely don't get on a plane with your mother at the drop of a hat to go check on you at a secret hidey spot just because they had nothing better to do," I whisper. "She's here because she wants you."

"Congratulations on your powers of observation."

"Walk with me. It's what a boyfriend would do."

He doesn't sigh out loud, but his expression looks like my mother's when she wants to, and she's had *so* many reasons to sigh silently at me in the past few months. *He doesn't beat you, cheat on you, or degrade you, Begonia. I don't understand why you'd throw away a man like that when there are so few good ones left.*

"Amelia." Hayes releases his hold on my hip and turns, one hand still gripping the bike. "We'll be walking home. Please take the groceries."

Her lips purse. "Are you sure that's safe?"

"I have the mayor on speed-dial if anything happens."

I can't see Amelia's eyes, but I'm positive they're twitching.

As they should be.

You'd think a woman with glowing magenta hair couldn't be incognito in a small town, but apparently no one recognized me as the tourist staying at the big island estate today, since I had brown hair the last time they saw me, and I got to eavesdrop on all the shoppers talking about everything from Hayes's affair with the mayor here two years ago to how long Giovanna might be planning on staying, given the amount of luggage she brought with her to, yes, who would also like to date him.

And I'm betting Amelia knows the part about Hayes dating the mayor here.

"There's no room for the bike on the cart," Amelia says. "And there's no room in the security cart either."

"We'll walk it back," I tell her. "Along with —*Marshmallow!*"

There he is.

That's my dog.

Soaking wet and leaping up into the driver's seat of the golf cart and trying to kiss Hayes's second-grade wife.

"Down," Hayes orders before I can take a full step toward

the cart, and miracle of miracles, Marshmallow hops off the seat.

He also shakes his whole body right in the space between us all, coating every last one of us in sea water and sand.

Amelia's nostrils flare.

That muscle in Hayes's square jaw twitches.

And Marshmallow flops to the ground at my fake boyfriend's feet, gazing up at him with blatant adoration coming out on every tongue-lolling pant.

Poor Marshmallow.

We are *so* out-classed here, and he has no idea.

Probably best that way.

I should get back to working on not caring too.

Hayes

Amelia has barely driven the cart out of hearing range, the security cart accompanying her but lighter two men who are keeping a respectful distance, when I hear my name, and it's not coming from Begonia.

"Hayes! Hayes, hi. Everything okay out at the estate?"

I eyeball the woman responsible for me being here, on a dirt road, instead of safely on a golf cart headed back quickly to the pile of figures and new responsibilities I need to sort through today, *away* from the prying eyeballs of the single women of Sprightly.

Begonia smiles brightly, then grabs my hand and squeezes. "She can't hurt you. She'd get fired as mayor, and trust me, after what I heard at the market this morning, that's the last thing she'd jeopardize."

"For the record, this is the last place I want to be." And I mean both standing here, in the open, and also walking beside Begonia, who is so very damn bright and sunny and seemingly trustworthy, which I find completely untrustworthy.

"But it's such a beautiful morning. That has to make it a little better," Begonia replies with a *Begonia* smile.

The world will either *eat her up*, as they say, or chew her out for that smile. And the fact that I've never been able to judge which is exactly why I'm now the CFO of Razzle Dazzle while my brother and father are the creative geniuses picking our film and television line-ups every year.

"I'm so glad I ran into you this morning," Kristine continues. She's in her late thirties, white with mousy brown hair and a nose slightly too large for her face. Once upon a time, she was the perfect bland choice for a date when I wanted to feel like a normal person whose every move isn't scrutinized by the press or well-meaning family members. "Seems like you might be having connection problems with your gate intercom system. Hamish is still around if you need an electrician."

I stifle a wince as I turn and nod to Kristine as she descends the dune from the main road just outside of town. "Ms. Turner. Lovely weather."

"Good job," Begonia whispers with a hand squeeze.

Kristine is smiling brightly at me, but it's not a *Begonia* smile. It's far more awkward and inquisitive. "I called the sheriff's office up at the point and let them know you were back, so they're watching out for any unusual activity, though I see you're not as alone as we thought you were. And we activated the Oysterberry Bay gossip chain. Nobody's gonna bug you, and if you need anything at all, just give me a holler." She looks down at where Begonia's fingers are linked in mine, and a rare flash of guilt pokes me in the gut.

Dating Kristine was another act of rebellion the last time multiple family members decided they had *the perfect woman* for me. Thank heavens, Thomas ended up divorced not long after that, and Mathias Randolf landed on the list of the world's dwindling single billionaires when stock in his healthcare software skyrocketed, so I was given a brief reprieve from scheming family members and their devious friends.

A reprieve that is now over and carries with it more grief than I can admit to in public.

"Glad to see you back," she continues. "I tried to get in touch when Blaine left and his girlfriend stayed, because it felt unusual, but nobody at your office returned my calls. The sheriff checked in every now and again, and it didn't seem like she was robbing you, so we had no choice but to let it go."

That's in line with what my head of security told me late yesterday afternoon.

I haven't been back to this house since my ill-advised romp with Kristine two years ago. In that time, my long-standing property manager out here took a few liberties, including moving himself into the main house, and then got kicked out by his girlfriend, who decided to shove it to all of us by listing the house on a vacation rental site.

Hence Begonia's presence.

With clear expectations of the house being empty for the foreseeable future, when in actuality, she would've been getting another visitor today, and three more tomorrow, because Blaine's girlfriend double-, triple-, and quadruple-booked the house for the next three years.

The only reason Begonia was alone yesterday was that her intended co-occupants came down with food poisoning and couldn't travel.

My security team is handling the details of taking care of every part of the issue.

"I love your island here, Kristine," Begonia says into the settling silence. "Everyone's so friendly, and the shops are adorable. You must love living here."

Kristine eyeballs our hands once again, then gives Begonia

a flat smile. "Couldn't imagine living anywhere else. Great place for keeping in touch with what's important."

"You can really feel the love all over. This is the best hidden gem I've ever visited. But don't worry—I won't tell anyone. Too many tourists would ruin it."

"We aim for just right."

"You're doing a spectacular job."

Begonia beams.

Kristine smiles back hesitantly, like she doesn't want to but can't help herself.

I saw my mother do the same yesterday when Begonia spilled the take-out lobster rolls she'd insisted on ordering for dinner for all of us. *And there's one for the floor, and one for Marshmallow, and one for a reminder to me to be less clumsy next time. We all have our moments, don't we? Here. Take mine. I ate too much cheesecake yesterday anyway and I'm still not hungry.*

"We should get going," Begonia says brightly. "Lots to do today. Thank you so much for all of your kindness. Marshmallow! Drop the crab and c'mon, boy. You don't want that thing biting your nose or tongue or your ears. Who's a good dog? Marshmallow's such a good dog."

She waves at Kristine with a non-threatening smile. "He's smart, but not always bright, you know? And we love him exactly as he is."

With Kristine fully smiling back now, Begonia tugs my hand, and then we're back on the path, me holding the bicycle with my other hand, her dog racing ahead of us with a live crab in its mouth.

We look like we're in a damn Razzle Dazzle film.

But while Jonas always plays a character who's charmingly baffled by his feelings for his on-screen love interest, I merely feel awkward and uncomfortable at suddenly being alone and the very picture of romantic perfection with the woman who put me to sleep last night.

How did she manage that?

She's a virtual stranger, and when my brain starts spinning, there's nothing that will calm it.

Except, apparently, lying in Begonia's lap, with the scent of lavender mingling with the fresh sea air, getting a head massage that I never should've agreed to in the first place.

Maybe it was the incense. Is it possible to be overly sensitive to incense? I've never used the damn stuff before.

"Why did you get divorced?" I ask Begonia in the silence. It's better than getting lost in my own head.

Also, I should know these things for the inquisition that'll be coming from my mother. She clearly suspects this is fake, which means I need to improve my game if I don't want to have to threaten to make a scene with the media.

And the truth is, I don't want to have to threaten to make a scene.

I've made my peace with the media, but that doesn't mean I go looking for opportunities for my social life to be featured.

Walking back with Begonia was, in fact, the better option for keeping up appearances.

"He didn't like my dog."

"You didn't adopt the dog until after you filed paperwork."

"Just how thorough was that background check, and did you memorize it?"

"Why did you get divorced? As your boyfriend, I should know."

She lifts a thoughtful gaze to me. "You should, shouldn't you? Okay. I'll tell you. But first, you have to tell me if you've ever had a pet."

Any other woman I've ever dated would've asked about my history with Kristine, and while Begonia might come off as flaky, I suspect she's wiser about the world than the casual observer might notice when she hides it behind the compliments and bubbles of her personality, though time will tell if those bubbles are real or put-on. Either way, they're suspicious.

"You don't want to ask how many other women will be arriving on my doorstep vying for my attention?"

"Oh, you think there'll be more? Will there be any actresses? Oh! What about famous artists? Wait. They probably don't want you for your money, and your personality isn't exactly the type that usually jives with artists. We like to be the temperamental ones in a relationship, and we love being broke, because it gives us something to complain about. Oh, barf. Tell me you're not expecting a bunch of lady CEOs. Don't get me wrong, I admire the crap out of them for the things they accomplish, and Amelia is lovely in her own way —I mean, she can't be *barf* when she was on *Dancing with the Stars*—but give me someone who wants to talk about how difficult clay can be in humidity, and I'll have a new BFF."

Her eyes are sparkling like she doesn't expect me to know what a *BFF* is.

Who am I to disappoint? "Clay is related to bank failure Fridays?"

She squeals with laughter and pokes me in the bicep. "You did it again. You made a joke. Sleeping was really good for you, wasn't it?"

"Please tell me you don't drink coffee. Or that you've already had six cups today. One or the other. Nothing in between."

"Nope. I'm riding the high from horrifying your mother when she came into our bedroom last night."

I jerk to a stop. "My mother came into the bedroom last night?" That wasn't a dream. "What did you say to her?"

"I shushed her and told her you'd had a few long days and that you needed your sleep." She tilts her head. "She was really horrified. Is it a Rutherford family thing that you're not supposed to be shirtless with a woman in bed in real life in your own home?"

"Yes."

She studies me, and when I tug her hand to move again, she doesn't move. "Is it the hair dye? I was worried yesterday about leaving it on too long, but I actually like how bright it turned out. It's like, *hello, world, Begonia is ready to experience all of you again*. But hair dye isn't against your family's principles and image, is it?"

"Yes. It's the hair dye."

"Are you always a bad liar, or are you just trying to make me stop talking?"

"Yes."

The confounding woman laughs. "So sleep doesn't make you more charming. Noted. Were you up early enough to see the sun rise? It was glorious this morning. Like Monet painted it. I know it's totally cliché for an art teacher to say Monet's her favorite, when I could pick Berthe Morisot or Alfred Sisley, or a non-impressionist, but Monet's colors are like—looking at his water lilies collection is like seeing the full potential of my soul on display. They make me happy and peaceful and hopeful all at the same time."

I frown. "Have you been to Musée Marmottan Monet?"

"No, but it's totally on the bucket list. I started a Paris fund the day I left Chad, and if I budget right, I can get there in two years."

Her face is shining, eyes lit up, her smile wide, as though the idea of pinching pennies to afford a trip to Paris to see a gallery featuring hundreds of pieces by her favorite artist makes her happy.

And not a small amount of happiness, but more excitement than I've ever felt over anything in my life since—

Dammit.

Since I got my first pet. "When I was six, my parents got us a puppy for the holidays. I came down with a horrible cold the same day and lived in utter misery for a week while hugging that damn dog at every opportunity until my nanny suggested I was allergic to it."

She squeezes my hand. "I'm sorry. That's heartbreaking."

"We had fish tanks instead for the rest of my childhood."

"My dad ran a summer camp. Mom hated it, which is why they got divorced, but I loved it. Hyacinth and I spent every summer there, running wild and playing on the ropes course and shooting archery and swimming in the pool and riding horses and fishing in the lake. We had minnows for bait, but neither of us could bear to actually hook them, so we'd sneak them back to our cabin and try to raise them as pets."

"We had jellyfish and stingrays in our tanks."

Her eyes go wide, and after a moment of her eyebrows arching wildly, she bursts out laughing. "Of course you did."

A reluctant smile tugs my lips. "There was a very large grouper that I named O-face."

She snorts. "You *didn't*."

"I was informed quickly that the grouper preferred to not be mocked for its expression, and it was renamed Theodore. And the octopus that I named *Octopussy* was rapidly renamed Harrison."

Her laughter mingles with the sound of the surf, and for the first time since my phone rang with the news two weeks ago that my cousin Thomas had passed, I feel as though I can take a full breath.

It's one small moment of peace without the weight of grief and familial expectations and my sudden status as the world's last eligible billionaire bachelor.

This is the respite I sought when I left New York for Maine.

She was right to insist we walk, for more reasons than appearances.

"Hyacinth named an entire batch of minnows after all the roles Jonas played one summer," Begonia says.

My sigh is so automatic, I can't stop it.

"Do you not get along with Jonas?" she asks. "Or does it just annoy you that everyone thinks he's so perfect?"

"You accused me of setting you up yesterday, but I'm beginning to wonder if the opposite is true, Ms. Fairchild."

"Don't *Ms. Fairchild* me, *Mr. Rutherford*. I saw you in dancing hamster pajama pants. Fancy doesn't work between us anymore. Also, I work with teenagers, and I have yet to see *any* set of siblings who adore each other all the time, even the ones who like each other most of the time. It's not natural to not have conflict with your family. If Hyacinth was as famous as Jonas is, I'd probably sigh like that too. And we might be twins and adore each other, but we fight plenty too. Hello? Signed non-disclosure agreement? You have a very rare opportunity to bare your soul to someone who won't repeat a word, won't judge you and who's had enough therapy in the past year to probably say some very insightful things about your life that just might make you smile more often. Hit me with it. What's the story with you and Jonas?"

"He got married."

"You wanted his wife for yourself?"

"Dear god, no. I didn't want to be the richest single man in the world. It makes me a target for more attention than—"

"*Hayes!*" someone calls from the road above. "Oh my gosh, *Hayes!* That *is* you. Hi! Hi, I'm Martina."

"In short, it makes *that* happen," I finish on a sigh.

"Back off, lady," Begonia calls. "This one's mine."

The elderly woman's brown face scrunches in irritation. "Well, aren't you an impertinent little twit. I was just being friendly to a neighbor I've never met."

Begonia grins. "Sorry. I'm terribly jealous. I thought you wanted him for his butt in these jeans."

Martina fans her face. "If I did want him, and I'm not saying I do, but if I *did*, could you blame me? I might be old, but I'm not blind."

"Keep being fabulous and putting yourself out there."

Begonia flashes her a thumbs-up, then smacks my ass, which has the unfortunate effect of making me picture her naked breasts, and that is not *nearly* as unappealing as it was yesterday when they were surprise naked breasts. "We need to get going. Hayes is late for work, and if he doesn't work, he can't afford to treat me to a lobster dinner on a sunset cruise."

Begonia winks.

The old lady titters. "Oh, you're a cheeky one. A billion-aire not affording a lobster dinner. Ha! Come say hi at the flower shop, Hayes. Your girlfriend deserves it. I like her."

"How the devil do you do that?" I mutter to Begonia as she waves at the woman and tugs my hand to get us moving again.

"Do what?"

"Make friends with anything that moves."

"All people just want to be accepted for who they are. It's not that hard to tell someone they have a nice haircut or a great smile or excellent taste in butts."

"That sounds exhausting."

"It brings me so much joy to see people happy. Way worth the effort."

"All people?"

"I don't like to think about people who don't deserve to be happy, which means I basically refuse to acknowledge they exist, unless I have to, like when I think they're a tuxedo-clad murderer bursting into my bathroom, so in my little world, yes. All people."

I cannot fathom looking at every person I come into contact with as someone who *deserves to be happy*. Not when so many of them give me headaches.

But Begonia—Begonia took my headache away.

I could argue she gave me a scalp massage and lit her lavender incense because it makes her life easier if I'm more agreeable, or because if I was unconscious, she could've found more Maurice Bellitano originals for her dog to chew on, or that she was planning to copy my driver's license to try to steal my identity and bank accounts, but between her saucy grin, her background check, and her utter horror at what her dog did to the carving of my grandfather, I can't find it inside of me to believe anything she's done since I found her in my house yesterday has been a purely selfish act.

Sorcery with that head rub, possibly. Selfishness, no.

She's had ample opportunity to rob me blind if that was her intent, and if she's looking for a hair sample for god only knows what reason, she could've waited until I got out of the shower and not had to touch me in the meantime.

And for as much as I don't trust her, I don't believe she'd be snapping pictures of me in my sleep to sell to the tabloids or anyone else.

"Your mom said you just took over as the Chief Financial Officer for Razzle Dazzle—does that mean long hours and endless meetings? And can you really do it from here with limited cell service?"

"We'll go to Paris this weekend," I announce.

She stops. "*What?*"

"You've never seen Musée Marmottan Monet. A weekend trip to Paris for you to see Monet's waterlilies is pocket change to me, and an impromptu date in Europe will solidify the rumors that I am not, in fact, *eligible*."

She's staring at me like I've kicked her dog. "But—but I haven't earned it yet."

"You—pardon?"

"It's an incredibly generous offer. I don't mean to imply I don't appreciate it. I do. That's so thoughtful and kind, but while it's pocket change to you, to me, it's the entire experience of saving and anticipating and savoring the idea. Like Christmas morning. Do you live for those five minutes when you're tearing through the wrapping paper, or do you live for the months from the minute you start making your wish list and talking to your friends about what you're hoping to get? And like, dreaming about the pony you'll find in the back-yard, even knowing that your dad declared bankruptcy this year and can't afford a pony. Plus knowing that your mom and stepdad would never get you anything that would make poop that has to be cleaned. But you spend all those months dreaming and waiting anyway until that moment when you see the tree and the presents under it, and it's like, the joy of the possible?"

She's speaking English, and I think I follow what she's saying, but I can't at all comprehend why she'd say no. "You would rather *anticipate* seeing your favorite paintings than actually *see* your favorite paintings?"

Her glowing smile slowly drops off her face. "Never mind. You're right. We should go to Paris. It'll keep up appearances. *Marshmallow*! Sweetie, don't eat the rock. Where did—oh. Yes. Okay, good boy. Good boy helping push the bike back to the house."

The dog's latched onto the bike's other handlebar and is attempting to walk on its back legs on the bicycle's other side, helping push it along.

"He could've made such a great service dog, but he doesn't take orders well." She's talking faster, like she's grateful for the subject change. "He knows how to do all the things, but it's like he's missing that part of his brain where he understands that he's supposed to do it when people tell him to, instead of when he wants to. And he went through three owners who thought it was cute at first and then couldn't live with him, and so I adopted him because he deserves to be loved for who he is, flaws and all, and so do I, so we make a good pair. Especially now that I've figured out how to Marshmallow-proof my apartment."

Ah. Of course. She's worried about leaving her dog. "The animal will survive without you for a weekend. I have competent staff who can arrive within a day to learn his eccentricities before we depart. And we need to keep up appearances."

She bites her lip and looks down at the dirt road. "I don't actually have a passport. That's the other issue."

"I'll make a phone call."

"That's cheating."

"I live in a world where my every public move is under scrutiny, where I'm judged based on the fantasy world of the films my family puts out into the world rather than on the world we actually live in, where people befriend me for every reason except enjoying my company, and where my acquaintances are just as likely to double-cross me as they are to follow through on their promises. So if the other side of that coin is that I can make a phone call to have a passport application expedited, then I'll make the damn phone call."

She gives me another of those looks that I'm coming to dread. "You're very suspicious of the world and its intentions."

"Welcome to my life, Ms. Fairchild."

"So why do you trust me?"

"I don't so much trust you as I trust that I can destroy you if I need to."

The damn woman doesn't so much as flinch. Instead, she studies me as if she's trying to peer into my soul and decide if I have it in me to crush a high school art teacher who was in the wrong place at the wrong time.

Having been labeled *the weird one* from a young age simply because I wasn't what anyone thought I should be, having spent my entire life feeling like I don't conform to my family's expectations, taking years to grow into my too-serious, too-angular, awkward face and body while everyone else in my family just seemed to *fit*, and knowing how very vulnerable it can make a person to be on the wrong end of a rejection at exactly the wrong time—the truth is, I couldn't intentionally hurt her.

I don't enjoy hurting people any more than I enjoy being a dick. And I enjoy it even less when being an asshole is necessary.

Like now.

I refuse to feel guilty about it—this is *my* estate, and I didn't wish for this situation any more than she did—but I'm realizing I'm not angry with Begonia.

I'm angry with the world, and I'm taking it out her.

To be fair, I take it out on everyone, but in this instance, I can acknowledge it's not her fault.

She'll realize I'm right about Paris once we get there. And I'll make sure she has a nice time.

I have to.

The world will be watching.

"I'll find a sitter for Marshmallow and go to Paris with you," she finally says, "but only on one condition."

"You're mistaken if you think you have room for negotiation, Ms. Fairchild."

"I'll find a sitter for Marshmallow and go to Paris with you," she repeats, "and in return, I want you to have sex with me."

I draw to an abrupt halt while the dog tries to keep going, leading to him yanking on the damn bike handle while I gape at Begonia.

She peers back expectantly like she hasn't asked for a larger favor than my bank account.

"There it is," I mutter. "We'll be ending this relationship the minute we get back to—"

"Quit being a pompous ass who thinks this is about me taking advantage of you and *listen*." It's the schoolteacher voice, which, unfortunately, despite all the reasons it *shouldn't*, causes blood to flow south to my cock again.

"You don't have to kiss me, you don't have to look at me, we don't have to have the lights on, and we can keep touching to a minimum," she says. "There will *definitely* be multiple forms of birth control in place, and I'll sign whatever you need me to sign, agreeing to whatever you need me to agree to in the event of something unexpected happening."

I make a noise, but she keeps talking.

"I just—I haven't slept with anyone since Chad, and I want to move on. Physically. I need to take that leap, and I'm not quite afraid of it, but I haven't been putting myself out there either, and you're here, and we're pretending to be dating, and you've already seen me naked, and your mother caught us in bed together, and I wouldn't even care if you wanted to call me by someone else's name to make it palatable enough for you, so—"

This time, when I make another unintelligible noise, she pauses.

But only for a moment.

"Never mind. Never mind. Forget I said anything. This is a terrible idea. I'm done talking. Fine. We'll go to Paris. I'll ask Kristine for someone here on the island who's good with strong-willed and over-trained dogs, and I'll go pop my post-divorce cherry with some lovely fisherman in the village once our two weeks of fake-dating is over."

I stare at her without blinking, completely still. I've been asked to sleep with a woman so that she can add a billionaire to her body count. I've been asked to sleep with a woman because she claims she finds me sexy and desirable. I've been asked to sleep with a woman when we've both been drunk. I've been asked to sleep with a woman because *I'm into the weird ones* and she believed all the rumors that started about me when I was in college.

But I've never been asked to be a woman's first post-divorce romp, where we're pretending we're not actually fucking *each other*, just because I'm *convenient*.

And while my brain is horrified, my body—well.

My body still remembers what her hands felt like on my scalp last night, and what it felt like to kiss her when my mother arrived, and how easy it was to grip her hips not ten minutes ago while putting on the show for Amelia and my security detail, and it's eager to see this through.

Even in the dark.

Calling each other by different names.

She shakes her hand out of mine and keeps walking. The dog attempts to push the bike to keep up. I make a noise at it, and it shrinks back on its haunches and gives me the same wounded look Begonia's worn more than once in the past twenty-four hours.

"Begonia."

"I know, I know. We have to get back to the house together and look like everything's fine. Just—I need a minute, okay?"

"*Begonia.*"

"*What?*" She spins and glares at me. Her cheeks are flaming red, nearly as bright as her hair, and her bright eyes are clouded over.

I swallow hard. I don't know which one of us is right and which is wrong here, which is unfortunately standard in my world.

It happens when you trust exactly no one. "I'll be finished with work by four, so we can take the sunset cruise for dinner. If you don't have a dress you'd like to wear, I'll have Charlotte take you into town to go shopping. My treat."

"I don't want your money, Hayes."

"You can't fake-date a billionaire without taking advantage of it, bluebell. It's just money."

She's sad.

I'm offering her Paris and shopping and romantic dinners, and ignoring her off-the-table offer to let her save face, and she's *sad*.

Confounding woman.

"Thank you for your generosity," she finally says stiffly. "I'm sure I have a dress in my luggage that will work, but if I have to be in something new to be seen in public with you, I'll clear my calendar for this afternoon and go shopping with your mother's personal assistant. I'm sure it'll be a wonderful time to get to know her better."

At least I'm getting one thing right about this fake relationship.

We've mastered the art of irritating the shit out of each other.

12

Begonia

GIOVANNA RUTHERFORD IS GOOD.

When Hayes and I get back to the house, me feeling like an open book with one cover flap caught in a shredder, him quiet and grumpy and probably about to throw me out of the house, his mother is in the kitchen, wearing an apron that makes her look like Donna Reed, chopping vegetables with a gorgeous hand-thrown pottery mug sitting beside the thick wood cutting board.

Whether it's my coffee or something stronger inside that mug is anyone's guess.

"Good morning, dear." She sets the knife aside to go up on her tiptoes and peck Hayes on the cheek, then greets me with a cheek peck too, like we're not swimming in this aura of *oh my god, I asked him to have sex with me and call me another woman's name* horror.

Which she doesn't know, of course, but she probably has ten billion reasons of her own to not like me, which makes her warm greeting suspicious in a way I wish it didn't have to be.

"Begonia," she says pleasantly, just like Donna Reed all over again. "You're looking fresh and lovely this morning."

I dig deep, deep, deep into my joy well and find a smile that almost feels genuine. "Thank you, Mrs. Rutherford. You look like you belong in a movie."

And then I cringe to myself. Is that like calling my pretend boyfriend's mother a total faker?

"She's had a lot of practice," Hayes says, earning himself an eye roll.

It's a patient, amused eye roll, and once again, I don't know if it's real, or if I should look around for cameras. I hope Hayes and I were pictured together out in town, because I want to talk to Hyacinth, and I don't know if I should or shouldn't until it's public knowledge that we're dating.

The point is for this to be public knowledge though, right?

Unless we're done dating, because I'm *that* level of awkward and embarrassing and disappointing as a fake girlfriend.

But if we were photographed together and we make the news, then the only thing I can't tell Hyacinth is that it's fake. If her twinstinct is working at all, she's probably trying to call or email me right now. And since downloading my email again yesterday to show Hayes my contract for the house meant seeing three new emails from my mother with *You should get back together with Chad* as the effective subject line of each, I'm avoiding email.

Again.

Even though one simple message—*Mom, I'm dating a billionaire now*—would solve almost all of my issues with my mom.

Probably.

There's still a large part of me that knows she'll start telling me how to keep him, even though telling my mom that I've moved up in the world of dating was no small part of the appeal of agreeing to this plan.

I really need to talk to Hyacinth.

At the same time, I hope she's too busy with the kids and hasn't picked up on my disastrous morning.

I like that twinstinct means I know when she needs me, but I hate that twinstinct also means she knows when I need her.

I need her to *not* know that I need her. For her sake.

Marshmallow shoves into the middle of the circle of the three of us, licks Giovanna's hand, then continues on into the kitchen, where he noses open the silverware drawer and a random cabinet.

"Close it," Hayes orders him.

If Marshmallow were a child instead of a dog, that soft whine would mean *but I don't want to.*

"I'll get it." I move toward the kitchen, but Hayes grabs my hand and repeats his order to my dog.

Marshmallow goes all the way down to the floor, settles his chin between his paws, and gives Hayes the *but I'm such a cute puppy and I did my best trick for you* puppy dog eyes.

"What a sweet dog." Giovanna pats Hayes on the arm. "Go take your Benadryl and stop tormenting the poor thing."

This is not the same woman who gasped and recoiled in horror at the sight of me rubbing her son's temples last night. And I'm pretty sure I didn't have any nipple showing, and I *was* wearing underwear, which she also couldn't see, because Hayes's head was in the way.

Maybe she really thought we were faking and that was proof positive that we aren't.

Or maybe all of us are better on a good night's sleep.

Except me and my glorious awkwardness.

But then, I wouldn't call what I did last night *getting a good night's sleep.*

If I had, I never would've made that outrageous suggestion.

Have sex with me, fake billionaire boyfriend. I'm sure no one has ever suggested using you for sex before, so surely you'll be fine with me doing it.

Idiot, idiot, idiot.

He's trying to get *away* from women who only want him for what he can give them.

And I'm trying to get away from men who see me as nothing more than a live-in maid with benefits.

"I'll finish chopping the vegetables," I offer to Giovanna. Maybe I'll have an onion malfunction and need to disappear to douse my head in the ocean a few times to rinse the onion juice out too. That'll put my brains back in straight. Especially since the water's not more than fifty-five degrees. "You can go put your feet up and enjoy your coffee."

"Nonsense. We'll chop vegetables together."

"Where's Charlotte?" Hayes asks.

"Sleeping in. She's earned a day or two off after all the wedding excitement. Shoo. Go on. We know you can't wait to get back to work. Begonia will come find you when brunch is ready. But let me get you a cup of coffee. It's delicious."

He's giving her the same look he gave me in the closet yesterday when I was trying to explain that I had every right to be in this house, and the same look he gave me ten minutes ago when I proposed he be the first to lubricate my lady-bits post-divorce.

"You're going home today," he says.

And that means shopping for a dress with his mother's assistant is out—thank god—so this farce is hopefully about over. I overheard someone in the market mention that one of the local B&Bs had a sudden opening. If I act quickly, Marshmallow and I might be able to talk our way in, just long enough for me to figure out what else my budget can afford for vacation for the rest of my two weeks.

I could try something on the Gulf of Mexico. Or further south along the Atlantic. No need to stay in Maine.

"No, I think we'll stay another few days," Giovanna replies. "Amelia hasn't been out here since you were teenagers, and I promised her we'd explore town together. There's a lovely new art gallery I haven't seen yet. And then I get to know Begonia better, and we all make sure you're not working too hard. Goodness knows *that* takes a village."

The undercurrents in the kitchen are strong enough to drown even the bravest social swimmers, so I duck it all and slip over to the coffee pot, grab a fresh mug—have I mentioned I adore the homemade pottery here? It's gorgeous, and I have so much respect for the talent it takes to make it— and I pour a cup, then realize I have no idea if Hayes takes his coffee black, or if he prefers it doctored.

"You're going home today," Hayes repeats while I decide when in doubt, fix it like I'd fix mine. That's what I did with Chad when we were dating, and it was enough to prompt him to propose.

I suspect Hayes takes his black, like his soul, and doctored fancy might be enough to make him throw me out too.

That would be a little bit of a relief right now.

Giovanna clucks her tongue. "Hayes, the house is plenty big enough for all of us—"

"Which doesn't change the fact that you weren't invited."

"I don't care if you're ten or sixty, I'm your mother, and I know when you're in a mood and need to be checked on. This lone wolf routine—"

"Yes, I'm clearly alone and suffering for being here for a private getaway with my girlfriend."

Silence settles behind me.

All except Marshmallow making a whimper that suggests he's caught in the crossfire of a glaring contest.

Don't turn around, Begonia. Do not turn around and do not drop the sugar and do not move if you want to live.

Hayes breaks the silence while I stand frozen, a table-spoon of sugar hovering over his coffee. "Begonia and I will join you in New York early next week."

Paris *and* New York? I'm so startled, I drop the full heaping tablespoon into his coffee. The metal clatters against the ceramic, making me cringe.

No way to hide when you're clanging spoons in coffee mugs.

"*Next week*?" Giovanna says.

"I'm fully equipped to telework from here while I learn my new role this week," he says over my muffled squeak of surprise. "And then I get to spend the weekend with Begonia *without* you."

"Hayes—"

"I want time alone with my girlfriend. Go away."

I'm tipping the creamer into his coffee when he slips behind me, puts an arm around my waist, and kisses my neck.

My nipples leap fully erect and my vagina asks if it's play-time and I spill cream on the counter.

I could pretend *this* is popping my post-divorce cherry if I hadn't actually *asked him that out loud*.

Hayes covers my hand with his, guiding the creamer container back to safety. "Thank you, bluebell. Just the way I like it."

"Wait," I gasp, way more panty and needy than I would prefer to sound in front of his mother. "Cinnamon first."

I knock over the paprika and the oregano in the small spice rack on the counter in my lunge for the cinnamon, but I pull myself together, unscrew the lid, and sprinkle the *right* amount of cinnamon into the top of his coffee.

"Hayes doesn't take cinnamon in his coffee, dear," Giovanna says.

"He's trying my favorite since I couldn't shut up about it,"

I say at the exact same time Hayes replies, "Begonia insisted it's delicious, and she's right."

Oh my god.

We're on a fake-relationship-wavelength.

And he's still pressing his body to my back, one arm still looped around my waist, making me want to suck my stomach in.

I asked him to have sex with me and now he's touching me.

I have to talk to Hyacinth.

Like, *now*.

"Remember, darling, you promised no tomatoes in those eggs," Hayes murmurs into my hair, loud enough for his mother to think he's whispering sweet nothings but soft enough for only me to hear exactly what he's saying.

I think.

"Making you happy is my favorite thing in the world," I reply, louder for our audience.

It's a Razzle Dazzle line. It's a total Razzle Dazzle line. Not long after we turned twenty-one, Hyacinth and I had a weekend of bingeing as many of our favorite Razzle Dazzle films as we could fit into two and a half days, and drinking every time a main character said the line.

We weren't falling-down drunk at the end of the first ten-hour marathon, but we'd gone through more vodka shots than we thought we would. And I have no idea if they still use it, but as of about ten years ago, they'd used it plenty.

"If only I didn't have to work today," Hayes replies, and I almost choke on air.

That might be the second-most common line ever recited in a Razzle Dazzle film. At least six scenes have flashed through my head with various actors on various sets.

And is that—is that a *twinkle* in Hayes's eyes?

No.

I'm imagining it.

He reaches for the coffee mug and takes a sip.

And if it weren't for the way half his face twitches before he turns and lifts the mug in his mother's direction, I'd swear he was being completely honest when he says, "Delicious. I'll never drink coffee another way again. Mother. Pack your bags. You can stay for brunch, and then you're leaving by two. I'll book your ferry myself."

He stalks out of the room like that's that, no room for argument, and I catch myself rolling my eyes.

But not before Giovanna catches me too. "So he's not your first boyfriend who likes to issue orders?" she murmurs.

"He's a man." I sigh heavily. "We have to put up with the ego to get the rest of them."

She blinks at me once, and then Giovanna Rutherford laughs.

And not just any laugh.

This laugh comes with a *snort*.

And a fart.

I am not kidding.

Giovanna Rutherford, Jonas Rutherford's mom, matriarch of the world's most perfect family, billionaire in her own right, just laughed so hard that *she farted*.

Hayes pauses, jerking his head in her direction as she covers her mouth and pretends she didn't fart. "Oh, goodness. *Snort*-laughing doesn't happen often, does it?" she says.

I don't know if I'm nodding or shaking my head. Somewhere in between, definitely. We're just gonna pretend that little fart didn't happen.

"Giovanna? Are you okay?" Amelia floats into the kitchen on a pillow of gilded perfection—okay, she's walking, but it's like she's trained in the art of walking like you're floating on a cloud-pillow—and her brows are perfectly arched like she's both amused and concerned.

Giovanna slips an arm around my waist. "Begonia has quite the sense of humor."

The man being mocked continues his petulant stalk away.

And he's still carrying the coffee I made him, which I'd bet he'll be feeding to a plant before too long.

"A sense of humor is a nice change," Amelia says. "Didn't you say his last girlfriend was an engineering grad student?"

"Oh, what kind?" I ask. "My stepfather's a civil engineer. You wouldn't think he had a sense of humor, but Hyacinth and I used to distract him all the time with knock-knock jokes. It'd take him out of a bad mood like *that*. Mostly because he had about seven thousand of them memorized, and we only had to laugh at the first dozen or so before he'd yell for my mom to come listen too, and then we'd disappear."

Amelia blinks at me.

Giovanna clears her throat, a smile still playing on the edges of her lips. "You're quite laid-back, aren't you?"

Today? No. No, not at all. "The sun's shining, the scenery is gorgeous, and I have a cantankerous boyfriend with a heart of gold under all his gruff. What's to be upset about? Unless you're the kind who gets hangry, I suppose. *Marshmallow*! Put the knife down. You know you can't cook."

I slip away from Giovanna, rescue the chef's knife from my dog, and tell him to go chase butterflies.

It's literally the only command he regularly takes from me.

"It's interesting that Hayes doesn't mind your dog." Amelia slides onto a stool across the high counter that separates the kitchen from the dining nook. "He made me give up my dog when we got married in second grade, and I'd swear he's only gotten more uptight since then."

"Oh, he doesn't like Marshmallow." I smile at her as I scrub the knife. "I gave him an ultimatum. Me with the dog, or no me at all. Honestly, I thought he'd tell me to pack my bags, but I guess I'm worth taking daily allergy medicine for."

I'm being catty with Amelia Shawcross.

Definitely time to go dunk my head in the ocean.

"Do you have plans this afternoon, Begonia?" Giovanna asks. "We'd love to have you join us in town."

"Such a treat," Amelia agrees.

I'm fairly certain she means *we'll find the most remote corner of the island and tie you to a rock where, if you're lucky, someone will hear your screams and come rescue you before the tide rolls in and the seagulls peck out your eyeballs.*

For the record, I *rarely* pick up on the subtle dangers of love triangles.

Love triangles?

Is it a triangle when Hayes has made it abundantly clear he wants to be a hermit for the rest of his life and is only using me to hide from the woman his mother wants him to date? Is a love wall a thing?

And why is his mother being so nice to me?

Is she killing me with kindness?

I need Hyacinth. She has just the right amount of cynicism in her bones to be able to guide me through this.

Plus, she reads gossip rags, whereas I just got to study the headlines in my brief time in the checkout line at the market this morning.

She'll know if there are rumors that Amelia wants Hayes for real, and not just because she wants to make Giovanna happy.

"You're...staying?" I ask as delicately as possible.

"Cantankerous with a heart of gold, I believe you said?" she replies. "After two weddings and that devastating funeral, you'll excuse me if I want to make sure he's fine for myself. Do you have children, Begonia?"

"Just Marshmallow."

"I couldn't sleep if I wasn't here to see for myself that he's fine. It doesn't matter how old or self-sufficient your children get, there's no replacing a mother's worry. So forgive me for staying an extra day to take my son's new girlfriend shopping while still hovering closely enough to be here if he needs me.

My security team is excellent, so we won't have to worry about being interrupted if we don't want to be."

"Oh, but everyone in town is so nice."

I get matching bland smiles from the two rich ladies in the room.

It's a clear *stay in your lane, Begonia*.

And I know my lane.

My lane is entertaining Hayes's mother and her guest so that he can get his work done, and so that he doesn't throw me out of his house.

This is what I wanted.

Adventure.

New experiences.

A chance to live in a world I'd never be able to experience otherwise in my tiny little existence working in a high school in a suburb just outside of Richmond.

And if we *are* photographed together, and they make it into the gossip rags, and Hyacinth sees them and shows my mother, that wouldn't be a bad thing.

I'm actually counting on it.

So today, I'll make brunch with Giovanna, then I'll spend the afternoon shopping, go on a dinner cruise with Hayes tonight—Georgia O'Keefe help me if he was serious—and find myself a few new goals for my nest egg, since I'm apparently seeing Monet's waterlilies this weekend.

This is all good.

Even if Hayes makes me sleep in the closet so I'm not tempted to try to talk him into having sex with me again.

And hey, now I get to say I mortified myself in front of the world's last eligible billionaire bachelor.

Not *exactly* the experience I was hoping for, but I'll roll with it.

That's what this trip is about.

Time to get back to my purpose. I'll live this up and find myself again if it kills me.

13

Hayes

My mother has not left. Amelia has not left. Charlotte has not left.

All three of them, *plus* the dog, are accompanying Begonia and me to the pier, where I've chartered a private boat for a lobster dinner at sunset.

It takes three golf carts to get here, thanks to the extra security detail, and the only reason Begonia isn't on a bike is that skin-tight mermaid dress she's wearing.

She may as well also have a mermaid's tail for as fast as her feet are carrying her from the cart down the wooden plankway to the small yacht.

Her dog's stuck to her as if it's afraid I'll throw her overboard.

And the worst of all?

I made exactly zero progress on digging into Razzle Dazzle's financials while sequestered away in my office, because Begonia's voice was on repeat inside my head the entire day.

And that discrepancy that's bothering me?

It's less than a thousandth of a percent of the company's operating budget. The FTC wouldn't blink. The board won't blink. Yet I'm incapable of thinking about anything else while I'm supposed to be acquainting myself with my new role, which is big-picture strategy rather than staying buried in the minutiae that I've enjoyed so much since joining the Razzle Dazzle payroll.

Or possibly it's a difficult enough problem that it's keeping me from the *other* thing I can't stop thinking about.

I want you to have sex with me, Hayes. Be my new first. It's not personal. Any dick would do, and yours is convenient.

"Evenin', Mr. Rutherford," a white-bearded sailor calls as we make our way toward the boat at the end of the pier. "Sea's a little choppy tonight, but don't you worry. You're in good hands."

Begonia slips her arm through mine and squeezes hard.

Death-grip hard.

Her new dress this evening was courtesy of my mother's insistence—which is not to say my mother approves, for the record, but rather that my mother is willing to play dating chicken with me, and see which one of us blinks first.

It will not be me.

She should know this by now.

Regardless, the end result is that Begonia is wrapped in a sparkly green crepe fabric, showing off an obscene amount of cleavage that she's attempted to cover with a silk shawl, but that I can still picture in my mind and will probably still be picturing the day I die as an old, crotchety, lonely man. I'm reasonably certain the strappy heels are new too, and that she's never had the pleasure of having her hair done by anyone like Charlotte before either.

The Begonia of earlier today would've been like one of the

many Razzle Dazzle film leading ladies being swept away with excitement over undergoing a magical transition from frumpy to fairy princess for the symbolic ball, with sparkling eyes and a pounding heart and romantic sighs and twirling dance moves. But the Begonia of right now, who's swaying into me and slowing her steps, either has a severe issue with one of her undergarments and can't breathe, or she's terrified of the boat. Or, possibly, something worse.

"Are you ill?" I murmur.

"I'm great," she squeaks.

"Is that dress cutting off circulation?"

"Breathing great. Veins and arteries running in tip-top shape."

The dog growls low in its throat. It's not a threatening sound. More like it's calling her a liar.

"*Begonia.*"

My mother and Amelia both turn and peer at me.

"Problems in paradise?" Amelia asks lightly.

I'd be irritated with her, except I know what she wants, and it's not to cause another woman harm.

It's a marriage of convenience that would make her family happy.

We'd be well-suited for marriage if I weren't so opposed to the institution in general.

And also if I weren't allergic to a third thing I failed to mention to Begonia: being manipulated.

I am very much allergic to being manipulated.

"Can I talk to you for a second?" Begonia whispers.

"Of course, darling."

"I won't make us late, I swear."

"The captain won't leave without us, even if we take two hours."

She makes a noise that I'd call a whimper on any other woman.

On Begonia, it could mean anything from *oh, look, there's a pretty flower that would be so much prettier in the daylight!* to *we can't get on the boat because the sea monsters will eat us.*

Thirty-six hours of knowing the woman, and I'm already well aware of her extremes.

"Spit it out, bluebell," I murmur.

"The last time I got on a sailboat on the ocean, it tipped over, and I almost drowned. I mean, I didn't actually, but I felt like I might for a minute, and I haven't been able to get on a boat since. My intentions aren't bigger than my fears in this case."

"If you don't want to go—"

"I do! I do. I was supposed to go sailing this mor—while I'm here—because I want to get over it, but—"

"This morning," I interrupt. *I was supposed to go sailing this morning* is what she was about to say, I'm positive.

Her face flushes again. "It's not important."

Of course she had plans. She's Begonia. She probably has a massive itinerary of various adventures she was intending to try out all along the coast while vacationing here. "How many excursions and side trips had you booked that you've now changed?"

"It doesn't matter."

"*Begonia.*"

"Shh. Your name-saying privileges have been revoked. Actually, your talking privileges have been revoked, period. I'm trying to tell you that I'm going to get on that boat, but I'm a little nervous because the last time, Hyacinth saved me, and she's not here, so if I fall off the boat and once again come face-to-face with a killer manatee who decides I need to be his lover, I won't have her twinstinct to save me."

"There are no manatees in Maine, and even if there were—"

"But there are other sea creatures, and they're like Marshmallow. They're not normal when I'm around. Manatees aren't killer, I know, but I swear to you, that manatee had a look in his eyes that either meant, *you're the girl I've been waiting for, Begonia*, which is totally creepy, by the way, or *you are the prey I've been waiting for, Begonia*. I'm a very good swimmer, but if I fall off this boat, there's no telling what might happen."

I'm doing my utmost best to not stare at her like she's three bananas short of a fruit basket, but I'm apparently not succeeding, because her face twists up and she glares at me.

"Fine. *Fine*. I'll get on the boat. It's an adventure, and I wanted an adventure, and I know that you're so *big* and *powerful* that you'll order the seas to quit chopping and they'll calm down and rainbows will appear and three whales will serenade us with a blowhole symphony, from a safe distance, of course, and everyone in town will talk about how talented you are for decades to come."

She's talking with her hands again. I lean back a little to stay out of the way while she keeps rambling.

"And it wasn't a horny manatee. I lied. I made up the lie, and Hyacinth told it so many times I started to believe it, but the truth is, I actually get seasick, and I *hate* that I get seasick, because I want to go cruise around the world but the one time Chad and I took a cruise, I puked on the first day and got put in quarantine in the ship's hospital because they were afraid I had norovirus, and being in an enclosed space on a cruise ship meant that I was ill the *entire trip*, so I didn't enjoy it at all, and I really, *really* want to learn to enjoy it, but I don't want to puke in front of your mom and your second-grade ex-wife and your mom's Hayes-hungry assistant, and if I'm puking, and I *do* fall overboard, I don't know if I'll actually be able to swim, because *you can't swim while you're puking*. I can kayak. I can canoe. But *I can't freaking sail*."

"Is everything okay?" my mother calls.

"I'm failing to have the proper appreciation for the horror of the run in Begonia's hose," I call back.

"Apologies, Begonia," she replies. "God knows I've tried,

but his understanding of pantyhose falls into the same bucket with his ego. They're both completely hopeless."

"The boat won't tip," I tell Begonia quietly, "nor will you fall off, nor will you throw up, but if any or all of the above happen, I swear on my firm belief in the magic of the world, Marshmallow will save you."

She squeezes her eyes shut. "I spent the past year getting divorced after four years of being married to a complete stick in the mud, and two years before that dating him, and I'm trying *so hard* to remember who I was before him, but there are still a few things that scare me or make me super uncomfortable."

Once again, I'm ordering myself to keep my mouth shut, and once again, I'm failing. "And those other things would be...?"

"Paragliding, being squeezed to death by an anaconda, and lightning bugs."

"*Lightning bugs?*"

"One flew up my nose and got caught in my sinus cavity when I was at a party I wasn't supposed to be at in high school, and you do *not* want to know what it took to get it out, which is really sad, because I have such great memories of chasing lightning bugs with Hyacinth at Dad's summer camp, but now..." She blows out a breath, then looks beyond me, lifting a hand. "Excuse me, Captain. Have you ever lost anyone on a dinner cruise?"

"Only Boone Decker."

My heart nearly stops in my chest as I turn and look at him. My mother's gaping. Amelia too. And Charlotte looks like she's about to pass out.

The old captain cackles. "Just yankin' your chain, Mr. Rutherford. Ain't ever lost anybody. Come on aboard. We're aiming for some fun with your dinner tonight."

"Who's Boone Decker?" Begonia whispers. "Why does that sound familiar?"

"Founder of Rhythm Airlines," I murmur to her. "Disappeared off the coast of France ten years ago with the authorities on his tail for insider trading."

"Oh! He was making a joke."

"Yes, Begonia, he was attempting to make a joke."

"You naughty man," my mother says to him as she accepts his help onto the gangplank to the yacht. "I sincerely hope the rest of your entertainment is less morbid."

"I'm a sailor, ma'am, but I'll do my best. Evening, Ms. Shawcross. Lovely dress. Color of lobsters. Gonna have to watch out for mermen jumping up into the boat tonight, won't we? Charlotte, my dear. Glad to see you get to eat tonight too, for once."

"We always make sure Charlotte gets what she needs, Captain Hollingsworth," my mother says stiffly.

"Except you," Begonia says softly to me. "Have you ever looked at Charlotte like that? Because I'm pretty sure she's in love with you."

"No."

"No, you haven't thought of her as a potential girlfriend, or no, you don't think she's in love with you?"

"Is this conversation helping you to get on the boat?"

She eyes the captain and the vessel.

Then she glances up at me with what I'd call a devious smile on any other woman.

On Begonia, it's so out of place, it could be indigestion or a heart attack.

"I have a twenty stuffed into my cleavage," she whispers. "Do you think if I slipped it to him, he'd close up the boat and leave with your mom and Amelia and Charlotte before we can get on it? We could have a picnic on the beach."

"With what food? All the shops are closed for the evening."

She clucks her tongue. "Such little imagination."

When she reaches into her cleavage, I cover her hand with

my own, refusing to think about my fingers brushing the swell of her breast.

She freezes.

I freeze.

Except for my cock.

My cock is most definitely *not* frozen.

And the way her lips have parted—not helping.

Not helping *at all*.

I clear my throat and snatch my hand away from her firm flesh. "It will require something larger than a twenty-dollar bill."

"Nonsense. Captain Hollingsworth seems like a reasonable man."

I sigh heavily. "Stay here." I point to the dog. "You too."

And then I stroll the rest of the way up the gangplank to the boat, about to do something I'm positive I'll regret.

14

Begonia

HAYES TOUCHED MY BREAST.

I know, I know, *grow up, Begonia.*

But this isn't a junior high *oooh, he touched your buuuuu-uttttt* moment.

This is a grown-up, Mr. Stiff and Proper and Cranky accidentally brushed my breast with his hand and it made goosebumps race over my skin and my nipples tight and my panties wet and none of it matters, because he rejected my proposal this morning, and now, he's openly staring at me as we eat the Cranfords' leftover crab cakes and the Perwinkles' homemade bread and the Browns' hand-picked sugar snap peas from their garden, while sitting next to a campfire on the beach.

I swipe at my mouth. "Do I have crumbs?"

"This is oddly delicious."

He's so adorable.

No. Stop it, Begonia. He's aloof and cold and you cannot save him, so don't even try.

I swipe at my mouth again, but this time, I'm trying to rub the smile off so I can match his seriousness. "Even commoners on coastal islands have to eat, and sometimes they like their food to taste good."

"Yoohoo! Mr. Rutherford? We won't look if you want to kiss on Ms. Begonia here, but we heard you were having an impromptu romantic date, and we thought you might like some music."

I glance up the small hill to where three locals are descending with violins, and I can't help clapping my hands. "Oh my gosh, *yes*! That is so sweet of you!"

"You haven't heard them play yet," Hayes mutters.

"Don't be so negative. How often do you get serenaded by people who rarely have an audience?"

"You'd be surprised."

"Hush and eat your peas, or there's no pie for you. And if that pie tastes half as good as it smelled while it was baking this afternoon, you definitely want pie."

His gaze lands on me, lit only by the crackling fire, and I suddenly wonder if he *wants* "pie" to be a euphemism.

That searing look says yes.

Or it might say *I'm going to murder you in your sleep.*

"We'll take a minute to get warmed up, and then it'll be nothing but the best music you've ever heard outside of a symphony hall until our fingers fall off or you decide it's time for you or us to go home," the ringleader of the violinists calls. They're setting up a little way down, like they know just the right amount of space to give us so we can enjoy the music but still hear each other talk.

"Thank you so much for giving us music," I call back with a smile. "I'm sure you have better things to do tonight."

"Just the dishes." All three of them laugh.

I smile at Hayes. "What's the strangest place you've ever been serenaded?"

He holds my gaze while he sips discount wine out of the silicone cup that the local post office manager donated to our picnic tonight. "I was with Jonas in Los Angeles, with limited security. He was coated in stage make-up that made him look approximately sixty-five for a *fifty years later* scene, and he wanted a cheeseburger from a local joint just outside the studio's gates. Seemed safe enough, but a small gang of teenage girls spotted him and recognized him."

I laugh. "Hyacinth totally would've been in that group. So you were serenaded in a burger joint?"

"No. We took off at a run, and we ended up thinking we'd lost them when we dove into a single port-a-john at the edge of an alleyway, but teenage girls are terrifyingly smart, and they surrounded us, belting out the tunes from that god-awful film where he played a rock star until security arrived and rescued him."

I try to stifle a giggle, and I fail miserably. It takes me a minute to stop long enough to whisper, "At least you know this performance can't possibly stink like that one."

A rare smile tilts his lips behind his wine cup. "I concede your point."

Maybe it's the wine. Maybe it's the campfire under the stars. Maybe it's the first notes of the violins sending music out into the world. Or maybe it's his smile.

Whatever it is, I can't stop myself from leaning over and pressing a kiss to his cheek. "For appearances," I whisper.

He's stiff as my former mother-in-law, but he slides a hand around my waist, tugs me close, and tilts his head to mine, capturing my lips in a long, slow, languid kiss.

My hand wobbles, and he takes the flexible cup from my hand, still kissing me, coaxing my lips apart, his large hands gripping me more firmly, and all I can think about is my horrible proposition earlier.

Does this mean he'll do it?

Does it mean he'll have sex with me?

Or is this for appearances?

Hayes Rutherford should taste like charcoal and day-old dishrags, but instead, he tastes like sin and temptation. He's in a tux, on a homemade quilt loaned to us by a woman he dated once, the firm muscles in his arm brushing against my chest while his fingers dig into my hip and waist and his thumbs rub up and down over my dress. The sea breeze is making the kiss salty, the violins settling into "Serenade in G Major," and I wonder if this is what it would be like to make love to him.

Quiet.

Intense.

Thorough.

A light flashes behind my eyelids, and he breaks off with a muttered curse.

"Hey! *Hey*! Get back here."

The music stops, and one of the ladies playing takes off at a run up the hill. "Paparazzi! *Paparazzi*!"

The cry is echoed above, like the whole town's on alert.

"Go back to playing," someone yells in the distance. "We'll get him!"

Hayes glances at me, but his gaze doesn't meet my eyes. "That will be quite effective in convincing my mother to stop throwing other women at me for a while. Thank you."

A startled gasp slips out of my lips. "*You knew*?"

"Hush, now, darling, the sea has ears." He takes his wine cup again. "And I'm sure my security detail will do what's necessary."

He knew. He knew there was someone waiting to take his picture, and now he can't be seen with another woman without being labeled a playboy, and his family couldn't possibly have *that*.

He set us up.

He's not kissing me because he's thinking about having sex with me.

He's kissing me because we have a deal, and the deal is to keep his family from trying to play matchmaker.

He doesn't want to date *anyone*.

I'm suddenly grateful that we're in the dark, lit only by a fire, because it's not the fire making my cheeks hot.

It's the warring feelings of wanting to kiss him more while knowing he'll only kiss me for convenience.

Self-respect, Begonia. Have some self-respect.

The violins pick back up. Marshmallow rolls onto his back with his legs curled over his belly, dozing peacefully in front of the fire. And Hayes returns his arm around me as if this is precisely where he wants to be.

My movements are stiff and unnatural as I cut off a block of cheese and hold it out for him, silently inviting him to continue the ruse by eating out of my hand.

His jaw tightens, but he leans in, his lips gliding across my fingers and making my stupid body shiver in response as he takes the morsel with his mouth.

"Why do you want to be alone so badly?" I ask quietly.

He stares at the fire while he chews, and even after he swallows, he doesn't answer me right away.

I don't rush to fill the conversation, despite every instinct inside of me screaming for me to say something to make the awkwardness go away.

Smoothing things over, eliminating the tension, making people feel good about themselves—that's what I'm good at.

Asking hard questions and waiting for answers that might not come?

That's for people who are not me.

"I don't wish to be alone," he finally replies. "But my life doesn't lend itself to any other option."

"Why not?"

"Begonia, you tried to offer to write my mother a check for

the dress you're wearing while simultaneously asking her not to cash it for two weeks until your next payday. You bought cheese from the clearance bin at the market this morning, and you promised Kristine we'd use a dryer sheet when we wash this quilt before returning it to her tomorrow. When I say *you wouldn't understand*, you have to trust that you truly could not possibly understand. It has nothing to do with your character or your intellect, and you've done nothing wrong, but *you cannot understand*."

"So people have taken advantage of you and your money your whole life, and you have trust issues?"

He snorts softly. "Drop it, Begonia."

"Will you have sex with me if I drop it?"

His whole body jolts, and I end up on the receiving end of a glare that should be setting someone's hair on fire.

And I laugh.

I shouldn't.

The first man I've made a real pass at since my divorce is glaring at me like I'm the most inconvenient thing in the world, and I'm laughing.

I pat his knee. "Don't worry," I whisper. "I'm working on finding my self-respect so that I actually enjoy it when I finally have sex again."

He squeezes his eyes shut and sucks in an audible breath through his nose, nostrils flaring, jaw ticking, aura screaming *will this night never end?*, and suddenly, it's not funny anymore.

Concentrate on the picnic, Begonia, I remind myself. *Enjoy this lovely picnic.*

The entire little town came together to make sure we enjoyed ourselves on the beach tonight. But for the kindness of strangers, I'd be having a leftover egg bake from this morning all by myself in the garden back at the mansion.

It wouldn't have been a bad way to spend the evening.

The gardens are lovely, and so are the stars, though the egg bake wasn't entirely edible.

But instead, there are violins, a campfire, a homemade quilt, more delicious food than a dozen people could eat in two days, marshmallows for roasting over the fire—Marshmallow roasting himself near the fire—and an apple pie and wine in glow-in-the-dark silicone glasses to finish it off.

All while we're wearing formalwear.

And there will be pictures in the paper, so I'll be able to talk to Hyacinth all about it as soon as I get a cell signal again when I'm in New York next week.

And I'm going to *New York*.

There's so much to be grateful for.

But my companion is not currently one of those things.

And he probably won't ever be.

15

Hayes

BEGONIA TALKS IN HER SLEEP.

While I'm lying in bed, tossing and turning and accidentally brushing her leg with my knee time and again after waiting until she was asleep to even come to bed, she's having an entire conversation with herself about goats in trees being painted wrong on the side of the banana boat.

Have sex with me, Hayes.

It's all I can think about.

It's all I thought about through dinner. All I thought about while kissing her for the cameras. All I thought about while walking back to the estate, her swaying slightly as she told me hilarious stories about getting caught swapping places with her twin sister during their teenage years or the trouble they got up to at summer camp—clearly, her favorite place in the universe—chattering away with her strappy heels dangling from her fingers, all of her together making for the very epitome of a Razzle Dazzle romantic comedy heroine.

And yet, a naked Begonia writhing beneath me and moaning my name is all I can think about.

And it shouldn't be.

Fake dating her was a terrible idea, and now, thanks to myself, I'm stuck with her as my pretend girlfriend for as long as the tabloids milk the story.

This should be a good thing.

And it would be a good thing.

Everyone knows a Rutherford would never cheat on his partner, so I don't even have to be kind in turning down advances, which will still come, because the world is still convinced I'll never get married, so this is clearly temporary.

Dammit.

I *will* have to propose. Or possibly blackmail her into an actual marriage.

And that thought doesn't shrivel my testicles as much as it should.

Begonia Fairchild is a beguiling minx who shouldn't be allowed in public with all of that sunshine and kindness and naïveté that's either an exceptional act or proof positive that my world will destroy her.

My conscience is suddenly betraying me. Possibly because on top of knowing just how poorly this relationship could end for her, I'm genuinely beginning to like her.

I don't like liking her.

Liking her leads to trusting her, and trusting her leads to her betraying me, and her betraying me leads to me being publicly single, and then my mother or my aunt or my grandmother or my father's assistant's mailman's financial advisor will know *the perfect woman* who would fit into my world as though she was born there—which she most likely will have been—and I'll finally cave and marry a woman simply to be done with this ridiculous notion of being the world's most sought-after billionaire bachelor.

Don't mistake me. I appreciate the luxuries my life provides.

But there are two sides to every coin, and money comes with a price.

And this is why I'm prowling around the kitchen at three AM, looking for something to eat that will soothe an unsootheable ache that's only made worse every time Begonia shifts closer to my side of the bed in her sleep.

"Insomnia?" my mother says from behind me, startling me so badly that I drop a jar of local honey that Begonia picked up at a small stand after she left the market this morning, which was another story that also involved nearly being attacked by bees after sampling every flavor.

The woman does nothing *small*. She throws herself all the way into everything.

The jar cracks on the tile floor and splits, much like I feel my brain is about to do. The sticky brown substance creeps out from the splintered jar as I try to mitigate the damage. "Don't come in here," I mutter.

"I'm so sorry, sweetheart. I didn't mean to startle you. Did you not get enough dinner? The lobster was delicious. We missed you."

Here we go. "Don't start."

"Hayes. We both know what you're doing here."

"Removing myself from the public eye to mourn my cousin in private while I acclimate to my new position at Razzle Dazzle and take solace in the company of someone willing to let me be my own cranky self in the meantime?"

"Is that what this is?" She slides onto the stool across the high counter, one eyebrow raised in that mom look that always came with inquisitions when Jonas and I were younger. *And did you try your best at school today, or were you taking the easy way out because learning about conjunctions didn't sound fun? What did we tell you about playing with the spa in the solarium while adults aren't around, and now look at this mess.*

Someone better grab a towel. Did you think about the fact that your grandmother's vase was on the fireplace mantle before you started tossing that basketball at each other? Accidents happen, but I trust you'll make better decisions next time.

It's been a long time since I've been a kid.

Still have to squash the feelings of guilt though. "Do I get a say in my life?"

"Hayes. Of course you do. But…"

"I'm nearly forty years old. You don't get a *but* here."

"You're dragging that girl—"

I send her a sharp glare as I continue attempting to mop up the honey. "Woman."

"You're dragging that *woman* into your life just to annoy everyone around you, when you know you could have your pick of so many more appropriate women."

"You're treading on dangerous ground, Mother."

"She stopped and danced to the street performer music this afternoon, Hayes, and *someone tipped her*. Her dog attempted to steal a man's walker. She stopped at a tourist stand to ask for brochures about skydiving. *Skydiving.* She's flighty and unpredictable and completely ignorant of the ways of our world. Turn her loose with a reporter and god knows what she'd say, and that egg *thing* this morning was horrific. Don't pretend it wasn't. The longer you string her along like this—"

I cut her off with a growl.

Of course Begonia danced in the street to random music, asked about skydiving, and of course she can't cook but will give it her all anyway. As for her dog— "Did the dog return the walker?"

"Yes, but *Hayes*. You know that's not the point."

"Isn't it?"

"The point is that she's just as terrible of a choice as your last rebellion girlfriend, and we all know how this ends."

My last *rebellion girlfriend* was nothing like Begonia.

Nor did we have a contract.

I learned my lesson.

But Begonia—she's an even more excellent choice than I could've imagined, and it's causing me heartburn.

She knocked on four doors in an evening gown, asking if anyone had any leftover food they could share with her and her billionaire boyfriend, since we didn't get to the shops before they closed and we wanted to have an impromptu picnic on the beach. And she would've knocked on more, but those four were all it took to activate the phone tree for the whole damn town to show up with a feast for three dozen.

I've been on this earth nearly forty years, and I've never had a private meal on a beach catered by strangers and their leftovers, with music provided by random townspeople unexpectedly and exquisitely talented with violins, while my date and I watched the half-moon rise over the ocean and talked about nothing consequential at all, but still had a more pleasant conversation than I've ever gotten from small talk at charity galas and movie premieres.

I've been around the damn world, and tonight was the first date I've had in my entire life that didn't center around how much opulence my money could buy, but on how very real and charming the world could be all on its own.

And *that*—that is my biggest problem with Begonia Fairchild.

She takes more pleasure in there being oxygen available on this earth for us to breathe than I take in a garage full of Rolls Royces, vacation homes on nearly every continent, more money than I could spend in twenty lifetimes, and all of the other little luxuries that that money affords me.

She's the best-worst fake girlfriend.

And I'm growling at my mother, because that's what you do for the woman you're pretending is your world. "You have two options, Mother. You can accept that I love Begonia and welcome her as one of the family, treat her with the same dignity and respect you'd honor any other woman with, and stop attempting to sabotage our relationship behind her back, or you can leave. *Now*. I choose her. I realize you think you have my best intentions at heart, and I have no doubt you mean no harm, but I get to decide what I want. Not you. Not society. Not some arcane system of *rules*. And if you can't respect that, then perhaps *you* aren't what's best for me either."

There's a flash in the living room just behind my mother.

A glowing, neon fuchsia flash.

Begonia.

Fuck.

My mother spins, and her eyes go wide. "Oh, dear," she whispers.

She's not the completely perfect housewife she lets the media paint her to be, but she's never intentionally cruel either.

I'm still glaring at her as I leave the honey mess on the floor and stalk out of the kitchen, playing the part of the doting boyfriend because I have to, ignoring the whisper in the back of my mind that if I couldn't sleep *before* Begonia overheard this, there'll be no sleeping for an eternity if I don't make sure she's okay.

Despite my best intentions, I think I might like the woman and her spirit.

"Gone," I tell my mother. "All of you. Before Begonia's out of bed in the morning. Understood?"

"Hayes—"

"Understood?"

The house alarms blare to life, honking and shrieking and leaving no doubt that Begonia's attempting to remove herself from the situation instead of standing up for herself.

"And handle that first," I yell over the noise. Security will undoubtedly be rolling into the house in moments.

The door off the study is open, and I pause long enough to

enter my code and kill the alarm before stepping out into the night. "Begonia?"

She doesn't answer in the darkness, but her dog bounds toward me, skitters to a stop inches from my bare feet, and plops into a sit, tongue lolling, eyes reflecting the interior lights. I hear Amelia or Charlotte inside—the entire household is apparently awake now—but I leave the questions to my mother and pull the door shut behind me.

"Where's Begonia?" I ask the dog.

He leaps to his feet and jerks his head, like he's saying *follow me*, which he probably is.

I caught the damn animal trying to pull toothpaste out of a vanity drawer in the bathroom earlier this evening, and I surreptitiously listened in from the study while everyone was making breakfast, and the dog *very* clearly growled when Begonia said she was adding a little mint for spice to the egg catastrophe that everyone pretended was delicious.

I could like the dog if he didn't make my eyes water and my nose plug.

He disappears into the gardens, and I switch on my phone's flashlight app to follow his progress, until he leads me to Begonia sitting on the porch swing overlooking the sea, her knees tucked up under her nightgown as the swing sways slightly in the breeze.

"You sh-sh-should g-g-go b-b-back in-inside." Her teeth are chattering.

Naturally.

Summer evenings on the coast here tend toward the chilly side. It's usually a comfortable chilly, but not for a woman in a thin, spaghetti-strapped nightie.

I pull my own T-shirt over my head and plunk it over her, trapping her arms and all, then settle onto the bench swing beside her. "Apologies. My mother—"

She sniffles.

I freeze.

"Thank you for the sh-shirt." Her voice is small, as though it's shrinking with her personality, and thick too, like her throat is full of unshed tears. "But you're c-cold too. You should—"

"I prefer the chilly weather. It matches my cold, dead heart."

I'm reasonably certain she'll tell me my heart isn't cold or dead, but that's not what comes out of her mouth.

What she says instead may be infinitely worse.

"I divorced Chad because he didn't defend me to his mother when she called me stupid and a waste of his intellect."

I study her profile while her words fully sink in. "Seems her accusations were misplaced."

"We were trying to have a baby, and she blamed me for us not getting pregnant too. The doctors said I was perfectly fine and healthy, but his sperm had motility issues, and she managed to twist that so that it was *also* my fault for not feeding him enough fruits and vegetables, and for nagging him until his swimmers went into hiding. He didn't argue with her when she said that either."

I know the line I'm supposed to say.

I've heard it come out of my brother's mouth at least a dozen times in various different Razzle Dazzle films.

But telling Begonia her ex-husband and former mother-in-law don't deserve her isn't my place.

I'm not her hero. I'm the man trapping her into pretending to be my girlfriend so that *my* mother can insult and degrade her.

"I apologize for my mother." My hands are lying in my lap. I don't have the right to hug this woman, to offer her physical comfort. It's my fault she's here, if only because I didn't make sure this property was being cared for as well as

I assumed it was. It's my fault she's reliving the reasons she got divorced. It's my fault this odd little ray of sunshine is hiding in the dark. "Regardless of what she suspects we are, she was wrong to speak ill of you."

"For two years, I waited for *my husband* to do what my fake boyfriend did in under two days. The man who's supposed to love me couldn't do for me what the man only pretending to love me would do to keep up the ruse. That's really pathetic, isn't it?"

"Love isn't rational, but it's not pathetic either." *Christ*, I hate how many Razzle Dazzle films have all the cheesy lines. It's hard to be real when you feel like you're reciting a movie script. How the devil does Jonas have relationships in real life without feeling like he's faking all of it?

"Do you know the worst part?" She's whispering so softly now that I have to crane to hear her.

"It bothers me that your story *can* get worse."

"My mom didn't understand. *Doesn't* understand. She thinks I shouldn't have divorced him and that I should ask him to take me back because *Begonia, he didn't hit you, he provided for you, and he let you spend time with your friends*. That's what my mom thinks a good relationship is."

I don't have any idea what an angry rhinoceros sounds like, but if I were to guess, I'd say it sounds remarkably like the rage welling up inside me right now. "And my mother wonders why *I* don't want to fall in love," I mutter.

"You would be good at it."

"I grew up watching my family get richer and richer off of fantastical and over-romanticized depictions of relationships while every woman I was ever attracted to ultimately proved to want nothing more than my money, my connections, or my family name. I would *not* be good at love, because I have no idea what real love, in the real world, looks like."

She tilts her head in my direction, rubbing her nose on my

shirt, then pausing as if she's inhaling the scent of it, and my damn cock goes hard.

Not the time, Woody-boy. Not. The. Time.

"Real love looks a lot like changing your plans at the last minute to humor someone having an irrational panic attack, and then defending said flake to your mother, because you know no one's perfect, but you're willing to accept them just as they are, flaws and all, knowing that they're doing their very best, every day, and wanting to help them along that journey every day for the rest of your life."

Heat prickles over the back of my neck, belying the derisive snort coming out of my mouth.

"I know you won't ever love me," Begonia whispers. "I know this is pretend and temporary and just one more adventure for me, and something convenient for you. But I just want me to know, you know the right things to do to love someone. It's not your fault if all of the women in the world aren't willing to do the same for you. It's actually a damn shame, because you would be quite a catch for any woman willing to see you for the man hiding under all those walls."

Of all the women in the world that I could've found naked in my bathroom and bullied into pretending to be my girlfriend so that the world would *back the fuck off*, it had to be *this* one.

Her dog sets his head in my lap, sniffs my aching cock, and harumphs back at me when I shove his snout away.

"You don't know who I truly am," I say gruffly.

"I don't. You're right. But I know enough. And I don't blame you for not believing me. I probably wouldn't believe me either if I were you."

I'm simultaneously furious and horny and in desperate need of wrapping my arms around this woman, and I don't know how that happened.

But I know I feel better when I give in to the urge to pull her against my body and press a kiss into her hair, inhaling not the scent of my luxury shampoo, picked and stocked by my mother's staff, but of something soft and flowery and innately *Begonia*.

She'll never be the woman I love.

But for the first time in a long time, I believe I've found someone I could call *friend*.

16

Begonia

THE NEXT SEVERAL DAYS ARE WEIRD. GIOVANNA AND HER entourage are gone when I finally get up Tuesday morning after all the drama in the middle of the night. Hayes moves into the guest bedroom and informs his security team that *no one* beyond the two of us and my mutant dog are allowed on the property, and that I'm *to be accompanied* at a *respectful distance* for any trips I'd like to make into town or the surrounding areas.

Though we basically don't see each other while we're at the house, and he ends up having to work through the whole weekend—or so he says—rather than taking that impromptu trip to Paris, he still makes a point of taking me to lunch at the lobster shack in town or the soup and sandwich shop so that I can make him confirm for me that yes, curried chicken salad is the best.

And honestly?

I prefer that to Paris.

And I also don't.

Paris would've been showy and blingy and uncomfortable, overly-romantic for the cameras, whereas this feels almost real when we're together.

And the *real* part is what bothers me.

I don't love Hayes Rutherford, but I could get addicted to our conversations, to his attention when I'm talking, to that soft near-smile that overtakes his lips when he's watching me doing things that Chad would've grimaced over and asked me to never do again.

Like stopping in a small tourist shop on our way to dinner to have ourselves drawn as cartoon heads.

Or shrieking in joy at finding my first clam during a dig after talking him into taking two hours out of his workday for stress relief.

Or shuddering every time we walk past a boat.

I feel *seen*. But it's still not *real*.

We have a romantic dinner in the garden one night, where he points out the boat sitting offshore taking pictures of us and tells me to *act normal and like we're in love*.

Saturday night, I convince Hayes we need to spend the evening in the crowded bar, listening to mostly terrible karaoke, some of it provided by yours truly, of course.

I do love singing.

Singing does not love me back.

When we're on our dates-for-show, he tells me about the job responsibilities of being CFO for Razzle Dazzle, which is way more boring than being a movie star. Or an art teacher. I tell him about my favorite parts of my dad's summer camp, about Hyacinth and me agreeing to only get each other terrible things that make us both laugh until we pee our pants every Christmas, and about things my students have said, done, and *arted*. On our last night on the island, when I drop my favorite student story on him during dinner at the bistro overlooking the sea—it involves a clay giraffe, parent night, and the word *fuckerella*—he snorts clam chowder through his nose.

If we were in a real relationship, I'd offer him a blowjob to apologize for the pain, but we're not, so when we get back to the house, he retreats to his bedroom, and I retreat to shower in the shower to end all showers. I don't know what kind of showerhead there will be in New York tomorrow, and just in case it's not the rain shower kind, I want to enjoy it one last time.

But when I sneak down to the kitchen for a cup of tea, he's at the high counter, freshly showered himself, his dark hair that perfect amount of damp to make me want to picture him naked, his chest covered with a gray T-shirt, those adorable dancing hamster pajama pants hugging his hips again, and he's fiddling with my phone.

"You keep saying you don't have cell signal here," he says.

"That was kind of the point of looking at this part of the country for vacation." I wince, because I don't usually avoid people since it's not kind, but— "My mom can't call."

"But you miss talking to your sister." He hands it back to me. "You're on the wifi now. It'll carry a call."

And this is precisely why Hayes Rutherford would make the best *real* boyfriend. He pays attention to the little things, fixes what he can, and understands what I need before I realize I need it.

And I want to kiss him senseless for being so kind and thoughtful.

But he's not my real boyfriend. He's a man that I've agreed to pretend to date who just happens to occasionally do nice things, especially when he's had enough sleep and enough time away from his office.

"Don't listen to the messages from your mother," he orders. "I would've deleted them myself but your dog wouldn't let me. Her emails too. Why the *fuck* is she still asking if you want to get back together with your ex-husband when she clearly knows you're dating *me*?"

I glance at the list of voicemails. The *dozens* of voicemails. Four from Mom for every one from Hyacinth, who *definitely* knows, because she still reads the tabloids.

Hayes has a legitimate question. Mom *has* to be thrilled I've upgraded to a billionaire.

Maybe he heard her wrong. She couldn't possibly be saying I should get back together with Chad now.

I could listen to *one*. Just to test the theory.

"If you hit that button, I *will* throw that thing into the ocean, your dog's opinion be damned. She doesn't believe you can keep me, and she thinks you need to cut your losses before you piss him off more." Hayes has his head buried in the fridge, rooting around for cheesecake, I'd bet, not looking at me, but still seeing right through me.

And that's the most maddening thing.

He's so *normal*. And attentive. And a strangely good cook, and also very polite about telling me my own cooking skills suck without telling me my cooking skills suck, but the note taped to the fridge yesterday—*Begonia, there's chicken salad in here. I forbid you to spend your vacation time trying to top it when you'd enjoy making sand castles so much more*—very clearly implied he likes edible food and is willing to make it himself to provide for both of us so I don't have to cook something we'll both regret, and he respects that I'm here to have fun at the same time.

Chad never cooked, and he always expected me to find something edible, so we ate out a lot, and then he complained about the credit card bill.

You're shocked.

I know.

"I'm calling my sister and I'm telling her you still have a few things to learn in bed," I tell Hayes as I drift toward the back door.

"I'd expect nothing less."

I smile.

He knows I'm lying. I couldn't insult him if my life depended on it.

Other than the whole *be my fake girlfriend or I'll financially ruin you* thing, and his perpetual case of the grumps, and the two of us pretending neither of us keep thinking about me asking him to have sex with me, he's a decent guy. We're in a weird situation, and he's dealing the best way he knows how, especially considering he's balancing his privacy and desire to *not* be the world's current most famous bachelor with keeping his family's name untarnished.

He can't exactly tell the tabloids and his family and probably more than a small handful of women to go fuck off, not when he's a Rutherford.

Well, he could.

But he cares about his family and their reputation too much to do it, and that says more about his character than his note that I found taped to the inside of my door yesterday morning informing me that if I attempted to cook eggs one more time, he'd personally murder all of the chickens on the island so that there were no more eggs for me to abuse.

He's such a liar.

He'd re-home them before he'd murder them.

Although, that would take interfacing with the locals, and while most of the locals are kind and respectful of his boundaries—yes, even the ones I heard plotting to set him up with themselves or their personal favorite single women before they realized he was involved with someone—you can spot the tourists, and he's *definitely* an object of lust among certain demographics in the tourist crowd.

I don't usually notice until he starts touching my hand or my knee, or leaning in closer and making bedroom eyes at me when we're out in public, but then, I don't understand why people would chase a man just for his money.

So I get why he wants a fake girlfriend, and I get why he has trust issues, even if maybe I don't understand all the nuances.

I probably won't be sharing with him that his threat of bankrupting me wasn't actually as terrifying as he thinks it is either.

Convenient? No.

But survivable? Yes.

My dad did it. I could do it too. And I took so very little in the divorce that the only thing I'd miss is if I had to sell off my great-grandma Eileen's old dildo collection.

She painted them and sold them at traveling art fairs. The leftovers aren't used.

Probably.

Before I can dial Hyacinth, my phone rings in my hand, and her face lights the screen. I head for the back door, check that the house alarm isn't set, and then sneak out into the rapidly fading evening sunset.

"Hey," I start as I answer the video call, but she barrels over me, her face a mirror of mine, but hers is brimming with the thrill of impending gossip.

"*Oh my god, Begonia, you are a fucking ROCK STAR!*" She glances away from the screen. "No, Jerry, I won't watch my language in front of the kids when my sister is dating a *fucking billionaire*. This is *appropriate* usage of the word *fuck*, okay?"

"Hey, Jerry," I say to Hyacinth.

"B says hey," she calls. Then she's back facing me. "Talk. Now. Fast. Before Mom figures out we're talking and tries to beep in. She is *losing* her *mind*."

"So this thing just kinda happened." I have to be careful. She'll know when I'm lying, and my face is very bad at lying, especially to Hyacinth. But there's *so much* else to talk about. "And I met his mom. And we're going to New York tomorrow. And you can't tell the news that if they call, okay? It's actually possibly scandalous that we're dating so soon after my divorce? I don't know that part for sure, but it's like, *the Rutherford family*. Frowning wrong at a camera is scandalous, right? And apparently there are security considerations with travel plans, blah blah blah."

"*Gossip Minute* just posted a picture of you from dinner tonight and it looks like you're giving him the Heimlich. All I can say is, *what?*"

"I told him the clay giraffe story while he was eating clam chowder."

Her face twists like she's both horrified and amused, which is fair. The clay giraffe story is legendary. "*Begonia*. You can't keep the world's last billionaire bachelor interested if you're trying to kill him!"

"Hy. *He survived*. And you can't tell me any of his other options for dinner companions would've been *nearly* as entertaining. He's never dated a commoner before. Wait. No, he has, but none quite like me. He thinks the fact that I use drug store shampoo is adorable. Confounding, but adorable. Also, *oh my god*, he has this hundred-dollar-an-ounce hand cream from this spa called *Silver Crocus*, which is just the best name ever—wait, excuse me, it's Silver Crocus *hand crème*, spelled with that funky symbol over the first e, and I keep calling it *cremm-aye* just to watch him stare at me like I'm one of those poison frogs that supposedly just went extinct, and yet he found me in the wild. Like, shocked and worried but still enthralled and like he can't believe the very last poison frog in the world is his?"

"Only you, Begonia. Only you."

"I don't have any expectations that this is forever—I mean, who marries their first boyfriend post-divorce? Other than Mom, who loves being married?—so I'm going to enjoy the thrill of the ride while I'm on it, you know?"

"Is it…*thrilling*… in *all* the ways?" she asks.

If I tell her we're sleeping together, she'll know I'm lying.

If I tell her we're not, she'll figure out this is a ruse. Hello, pickle.

I need to pick my truth carefully, so I lean into something that's so true it hurts. "The first time he kissed me, it was like, *oh my god, is this what I've been missing*?"

Her eyes light up and she squeals, shaking the phone like she's making excited happy hands and forgot she's holding it.

"Shh! I don't want to talk about it." I'm flapping my hand too, which is making Marshmallow think it's time to play. He leaps, then bows down on his front paws, back end waving in the air. I pull a jerky stick out of my pocket and toss it out into the night. "It's like…sometimes you just want to enjoy something without analyzing it too much, you know?"

"Analyzing is most of the fun."

"Do I need to talk to Jerry about that?"

She laughs.

I try to.

But honestly? Sometimes I worry about Hyacinth. She married a guy who doesn't hit her, who provides for her, and who doesn't cheat. Mom's definition of perfect husband material. He also gets on her nerves sometimes, and they have lovely children together, but I just feel like…

I feel like she settled.

And I don't want to settle anymore, so I don't want her to either.

And I can't tell her that, because I have to let her live her life, even when I don't like it.

"Enough about Jerry," she says. She knows. She knows where my brain goes, even when I feel disloyal and I don't want her to. We're both trying to respect each other's life choices, and I know she was on Team Mom for a while over my divorce, even though she never said as much. "Have you met Jonas yet? Oh my god, I'd probably ask if I could lick him if I ever met him. Yes, Jerry, you knew that when you married me. Hush. He's on my freebie list, not that it matters, because he's a Rutherford, and he's married now, which means he won't let fans lick him anymore. Not that he ever did. But you can rest assured you're the last man I'll ever lick, okay?" She drops her voice and pulls the phone closer to her face so all I can see are her eyes and nose. "Do you think he'd let me lick him if we were in a dark room with no witnesses?"

"You're ridiculous."

"Is Hayes as weird as the news says he is?"

"*No.* They just like to have something salacious to report, and *he doesn't fit the mold* is as juicy as it gets, which makes him an easier target than the rest of the family. He's such a nice guy, Hy. And—cone of silence?"

"I won't say a word, unless it's to Mom, and only under extreme duress if it'll improve the situation."

"His mom doesn't like me, but he told her off for me."

My sister gasps. "What the fuck's wrong with his mom?"

"Oh, don't be like that. I'm a suburban art teacher who's recently divorced, can't cook, and doesn't know which fork to use during a seven-course meal, and he's the world's last eligible male billionaire. Of course she's concerned. I would be if I were her. And did you see my hair?" I lift the phone to highlight the disaster that's my short glowing hair.

It's a disaster that I love, for the record, but I can still acknowledge that it's a disaster.

Hyacinth growls at me. "His mother needs to know you're a fucking *catch. Shut up*, Jerry! If you don't like my language, take the kids outside and play a damn game with them! Sorry, B. He's taking the kids out now. As I was saying. His mother's had an awful lapse in judgment, and I'm sure she'll see the error of her ways soon. So long as you don't cook for her."

I wince.

"*Begonia.* Tell me you didn't."

"I didn't know I was meeting her and I got nervous and stayed nervous for the entire time she was here! But it won't happen again. At least Marshmallow didn't do anything crazy like find a vibrator in her luggage and deliver it to my room. *That* would've been awkward."

There's a beat of silence on the phone, coupled with a strangled noise from the balcony above me, confirming my suspicions that Hayes is listening in to make sure I don't say anything he'll regret, which I have clearly done, since I didn't mean to mention that thing that I'm pretending didn't happen.

Then there's another beat of silence, both on the other end of the phone and also above me on the balcony, while neither Hyacinth nor Hayes asks how I know it was his mother's vibrator, and yes, I know it was hers, and no, I'm not saying anything more about it.

I wince again. "You should see this estate, Hy. It's on the southern tip of the island, so we can see both the sunrise and the sunset from the gardens, and Hayes rowed himself out here in a rowboat to get to me the day after Jonas's wedding, because he didn't want to wait for a ferry, and that's *hot*. Here. Let me remember how to flip my camera, and I'll show you the sky here. The sunset is *so* gorgeous tonight. Pinks and blues and purples…" I trail off while I try to remember the right combination of buttons to press to flip the phone around while not hanging up on my sister.

"Tell me you don't have Giovanna Rutherford's vibrator in your possession."

"*No.* It's back in the nightstand drawer in the guest bedroom, and *you are not welcome here* until it's reunited with its owner, and do you know what else? *Good for her*. Now, can we *please* discuss how my boyfriend has the most delicious chest known to man? You think Jonas is hot. You should see Hayes without his shirt on."

"Hair or no?"

"Yes. And it's like, not just a token amount of hair, but it's also not like a rug. It's just right."

"Are his nipples even?"

"Will you *never* quit mocking my poor high school boyfriend and his crooked nipples? That's how his body was made, Hy. Knock it off."

She wiggles her brows. "And his…?"

"Sorry, I actually had to sign a non-disclosure agreement about that part. It comes with dating a billionaire from the country's most famous family, apparently."

"You *didn't.*"

"I did. And if I had a little more money in my vacation fund, I might've hired my own attorney and asked him to sign one in return, agreeing to never mock my art or my cooking in the event that we break up."

"Oh my god, Begonia. Only you. Fine. Tell me he's at least treating you to the rarest oysters and albino lobster and gold-crusted chocolates that will make your poop glitter."

I laugh. "No, but I think he would if I asked. But I don't want the fancy stuff. I like just having lunch or dinner with him out at the cute little local places with all the funny people who tell stories about the times they've spotted him out here, or what they do in winter, or that time that a carton of lobsters spilled at the grocery store and they kept finding them in random places under the shelves."

She smiles. "And once again, only you. Are you really just hiding out in Maine with him for the next forever?"

"No, he's taking me to Paris next weekend to see Monet's water lilies."

She frowns. "But you were saving up for that."

I wave a hand again. "I'll find another dream to save up for.

"Another dream as big as seeing Monet in Paris? It doesn't *get* bigger than that. And you were so excited about anticipating it for the next four years."

"*Two.*"

"Begonia. You spent every dime in your first rainy day fund for Paris when you heard about Marshmallow and hopped a plane to fly halfway across the country to rescue him. You can lie to yourself about how long it takes you to save up for something, but you can't lie to me. I'm your *sister*."

"Quite obviously so," Hayes says behind me, startling me so badly that I drop the phone. When I recover it, all I can see is Hyacinth's textured ceiling, suggesting that she, too, has dropped her phone.

Her face pops back into view, eyes wide, mouth gaping open. "Oh my god, it's you."

"Your tea, darling." He sets a steaming mug on a small picnic table tucked in amongst the wildflowers, then drapes an arm around my shoulders and kisses my temple. "Hyacinth, I presume. Lovely to meet you. From a safe distance. I'm off to bed, darling. Don't be long, and don't let your tea get cold."

He lifts a hand and waves to my sister, then disappears behind me again.

"You should see your face," Hyacinth whispers.

"You should see yours," I whisper back.

"Make sure to tell him I'll kill him if he hurts you. And then go jump his bones, okay?"

I nod, even though there will be no bone-jumping.

Him moving into the other bedroom made that *very* clear.

I manage to get off the phone without Hyacinth catching on that this is all just for show.

But I'm starting to wish my heart would remember that part.

He made me tea.

Chad never made me tea.

And Hayes Rutherford isn't my soulmate.

But he's doing a damn good job of resetting my standards in the meantime.

17

Hayes

Leaving Maine and returning to New York is inconvenient at best and a disaster-in-the-making at worst. We've barely touched down in Albany before I'm itchy for coastal air and lunch in a colorful lobster shack with townspeople who proved themselves nearly as adept at helping me maintain my privacy as my very well-trained security staff.

"Where's the Empire State Building?" Begonia has her nose pressed to the window of my private jet, peering out onto the small private airfield. "Are we facing the wrong way?"

It takes my head of security murmuring to her that we're not in the city, but rather upstate, for me to realize I was unclear. "Razzle Dazzle's corporate offices moved out of Manhattan several years back in an effort to give our employees more space for their families to live and play," I tell her.

She frowns. Marshmallow, who's in a bright purple vest

and has been almost well-behaved the whole flight, also frowns. "Because they didn't want to live in the city, or because it's all about appearances?"

"Yes." I rise and gather my coat. "And it also significantly reduced the burden of real estate upkeep costs. I have to get straight to the offices. Nikolay will escort you to Sagewood House."

"Can we detour somewhere fun in Albany, or do I have to go straight there to drop off my luggage?"

"Correction. Nikolay will see to it that your bags are delivered to Sagewood House, where I will meet you this evening, and he'll accompany you anywhere you'd like to go between now and then."

Her smile shines brighter than her hair. "Can I see your offices?"

"You'd be bored to tears amidst the gray walls and suits, my dear bluebell. Go explore the art exhibits and museums by the river." I nod to Nikolay. "Make sure the staff is aware that Marshmallow needs extra supervision."

The man's lips twitch. "Naturally, sir."

I make a show of kissing her goodbye, which I enjoy more than I'll admit even to myself, before tucking her into the first of two limousines waiting at the edge of the taxiway. She's breathless, with pink staining her cheeks and her pupils fully dilated when I close the door myself.

If my dick wasn't hard as a goddamn rock, I'd be preening like a fucking peacock right now.

I turn and open the door once again, lean in for a final kiss, and whisper, "My uncle is also in residence at Sagewood House, so we'll be sharing a bedroom again. Until tonight, my dear bluebell."

She squeaks.

I shut the limo door again, and I stride to the vehicle waiting behind it. When I slide into the rear seat, Razzle Dazzle's vice president of operations' executive assistant,

Therese, crosses her legs beneath her pencil skirt and gives me a smile that sets my teeth on edge.

"Good morning, Mr. Rutherford. How do you like your coffee? I'll text ahead and have it waiting. Your nine-thirty has been rescheduled to six, your mother made a reservation at The Brunch Café for you at one, we've combed through the applicants for your own executive assistant as requested and scheduled interviews for you starting at two, and Mr. Okimoto requires a word as soon as we arrive."

"Cancel the six o'clock, cancel lunch with my mother, forward me the candidates' resumes, and call my uncle Antonio and inform him he's moving into Sagewood House for the next two weeks. Also, tell anyone you're talking to Antonio, and I'll have you fired."

She bites the end of her stylus and studies me for a long moment before dropping it back to her tablet and casually brushing her long hair back, pushing her breasts up as she does so. She's technically not my executive assistant, but that won't stop me from issuing orders. "Of course, Mr. Rutherford. And your coffee?"

"I don't know. Call my girlfriend and ask her."

"Her phone number, Mr. Rutherford?"

I blink.

I don't have Begonia's phone number.

How the *fuck* do I not have Begonia's phone number?

I didn't need it on the island, but I should've thought— and I didn't—and *fuck*.

Robert, the second-in-command on my personal detail, visibly fights a smile as the car pulls away. "Got it right here for you, Ms. Therese."

"Thank you, Robert."

I don't speak to either of them the rest of the ride, instead burying myself in email on my work cell phone, nor do I acknowledge when my personal cell phone vibrates with an incoming contact card from Robert.

Good man.

He'll be finding a new bottle of his favorite brandy sitting on his doorstep this evening.

Since my parents persuaded me to come work for Razzle Dazzle on the financial side of the business a few years after I finished my master's degree, I've split my time between the New York and California offices, so walking into headquarters today should be nothing new.

But it's the first time I've walked in since my cousin Thomas passed unexpectedly, leaving the chief financial officer position vacant and me as the supposed best man for the job. Last week was spent communicating with the technical team, getting all the correct files unlocked and access granted, digging into active and upcoming issues, and having virtual meetings with various officers inside the company to get up to speed. Being back in the office now is the first time I've had to bother with things like personal assistants, a schedule full of meetings with officers and executives, and sitting in a chair once occupied by a relative I wish I'd spent more time with.

We rarely saw each other outside the office, and with my former role as associate vice president of financial affairs for parks, real estate, and development keeping me nearly as busy as the CFO position kept him, we rarely saw each other *inside* the office either.

It was a rare relationship that required little talking and less drama. While Keisha will forever be my favorite relative, I've realized I didn't know what I had with Thomas until he was gone.

Also not helping?

Thomas's executive assistant is out on maternity leave and won't be returning. The one modicum of peace I've clung to after his death is knowing that he was able to see his daughter before the accident that claimed his life.

While my family won't publicly claim Mirabella or her

mother as Rutherfords, they'll both be well cared for. And lest you think we're heartless bastards who put our reputations above all else, the decision is as much Thomas's secret girl-friend's as it is ours.

She doesn't want to raise her daughter in the limelight that comes with being part of my family.

God knows I understand that to my core.

But it means that I need a new executive assistant, and when I leave my office at quarter to two, there's a wall of women crammed into my foyer who immediately leap to their feet.

There's a damn *wave* going on in my office as if we're at a baseball game.

I look at Therese. "Did you schedule the interviews simul-taneously?"

She lowers her cat's-eye glasses and smiles at me. "Of course not, Mr. Rutherford. But we did stress to all of the applicants that timeliness is important."

I look at the wall of women again, and I turn and retreat into my office.

I don't want to pick an assistant.

I want—

Fuck. I want to not be here.

I'm dialing Begonia's number before I can think twice.

"Hello?"

"Begonia. I need—"

"Hayes! Hi, sweetie. Did you know downtown Albany has a performing arts center called The Egg? It's *amazing*. And Nikolay said the right thing to the right person and we got this unbelievable behind-the-scenes tour that—"

"You know people," I interrupt.

"Quite a few of them, yes."

"Good. Come here. Now. I need someone to interview executive assistants for me."

I can *hear* her blinking. "Can I—can I speak freely in front of Nikolay?" she whispers.

"No."

She growls.

Begonia.

Begonia *growls* at me.

"What the hell kind of noise was that?" I ask.

"That's me breathing very deeply before I *don't* remind you that people like *you* don't call people like *me* to do the things that you have other *way more qualified people* to do for you."

"I don't trust them."

Fuck me.

That truly is the root of all of my problems.

I spin in my chair and peer out my top-floor window at downtown Albany. I can't see The Egg, which is apparently exactly where Begonia is right at this minute, but I know roughly where it is and I can't stop staring in that direction, hoping the buildings between us will disappear so that I can see her waving at me and telling me I'm being ridiculous.

And she's right.

Powerful men from rich families *don't* call the woman they found naked in their bathroom barely over a week ago and ask said woman to *pick their new executive assistant.*

"I don't understand people," I say slowly. "I don't know if my temporary executive assistant is hitting on me or trying to annoy me, and I don't know why everyone thinks getting married is some pinnacle event to be celebrated when it looks like shackles and chains to me. I know numbers. I was born and raised to be if not in this exact position for Razzle Dazzle, then damn close to it, and I know I can't do my job without help, but I don't know how to find the help, but you—you knock on doors and ask people for food not because we can't afford it, but because you somehow *know* it would actually make other people *happy* to help. You know why people tick.

You could probably tell me what Nikolay wants for Christmas, who his last girlfriend was, why they broke up, and if he has a favorite sports team, but I—"

"A ride in a hot air balloon, Sheila with the shoe collection, she didn't like his hours, and the Copper Valley Thrusters, because he likes their mascot, just like me, but he said it first, for the record," she whispers.

My heart squeezes.

When it comes to people, I get very, very little right.

With Begonia—I trust her.

And if she fucks this up, I'll just fire whoever it is I hire on her advice, and I'll start over from scratch.

With *four* applicants vetted by human resources, who will all be fired if they allow my waiting room to fill up like this again with applicants.

"Will you *please* come interview these hundred women who want to be my executive assistant? I'll buy you diamonds and pearls and cancel Paris and take you somewhere else instead, and order you golden chocolates so that you can—I won't finish that sentence, but I *did* listen to every word your sister said about it."

"Hayes, you don't have to buy me gifts for me to do the little things."

"This is *not a little thing*." I'm too old to crawl under my desk and hide, but I want to.

And wanting to is a bad, bad sign.

We should've stayed in Maine.

I could've done everything remotely.

I can still go back.

"Have you had lunch?" she asks softly.

"Yes."

"What was it?"

"I don't know."

"What's your favorite meal?"

"Begonia—"

"Your job applicants aren't going anywhere if they're worthy of working for you, Hayes. Where are you?"

"Locked in my office."

"Good. Stay there. I'll be there in twenty—no, Nikolay says ten minutes, but we have to stop to get you a lunch that'll taste good enough for you to remember it, so definitely twenty minutes, and then I'll handle everything. Also, can I tell Hyacinth about this?"

"*No.*"

"Good gravy, I'll leave out the part where you look human and vulnerable, okay? You're really, really great at a lot of things, but asking you to interview a hundred women on your first day back in the office after a death in your family sounds like something your mother would dream up in a really bad Razzle Dazzle film."

I freeze.

She's fucking right.

And if not my mother, *someone* in my family set this up.

"Do *not* call your mother," Begonia orders. "Let me."

I stare harder in the direction of The Egg, and I picture Begonia straightening her spine and smearing on blood red lipstick—no, not blood red.

Neon magenta.

To match her hair.

And while I don't feel very *chief financial officer*-ish in this exact moment, I find I can breathe again.

"Begonia."

"Yes, Hayes?"

"You're a very good friend. Don't fuck me over."

"Someone hurt you very badly, didn't they?"

Yes.

Yes, they did.

"Tell Nikolay to bring you here and then run out for whatever else it is you're convinced I need. I'll see you in ten minutes."

18

Begonia

I LOOK AT HAYES'S SQUARE-JAWED BODYGUARD AS I DISCONNECT my phone, and my face must be showing *something*, because his eyes start twinkling and he wipes a hand over his mouth like he's trying to hide a smile.

"Mr. Rutherford is not a fan of pizza," he tells me.

"Then where's the best fried chicken in town? He needs something orgasmic. Coconut cream pie. No, too many people don't like coconut and we haven't had that discussion yet. A fudge brownie sundae and fried chicken and biscuits. *Biscuits*. We definitely need biscuits. I've tried everything else. It's time for comfort food."

"This way to the limo, Ms. Begonia."

My phone rings again as I start to follow him, and I'm answering, assuming it's Hayes again, before my brain can process the name on the readout, and suddenly I'm gaping at my phone in horror while my mother's voice rings out. "Hello? Begonia? Begonia, are you there?"

Marshmallow whimpers, cowers to the ground, and covers his face with his paw.

Nikolay mutters something to him in Russian, then jerks his head at me like he's saying, *Come. The billionaire is waiting, and if you think your mother's terrifying, wait until you see Hayes Rutherford displeased.*

And now I'm rolling my eyes.

I've seen Hayes angry, and I'd rather relive that moment he found me in his bathroom seven thousand times over than take this call with my mother.

But I'm a grown-up, so I put the phone to my ear and reply to the woman I've been avoiding. "Hello, Mom."

"You're dating the world's last eligible billionaire!"

"No, Mom, we're having a torrid fling and I'm on my way to have loud, noisy, earth-shattering sex with him in public in a park just to horrify people, and then I'll—"

Nikolay makes another noise, and I realize other people could overhear me and take me seriously.

And then I'd cause a scandal for Hayes, whose family is expected to model ideal, buttoned-up family perfection every waking minute of the day, and now I'm mad.

Why can't they be allowed to be *normal*? And have fuck-ups and *scandals* and regrets?

Why do they have to look like the epitome of perfection when perfection isn't freaking possible and the pursuit of perfection only makes them miserable?

I mean, I assume there's a part of them that's miserable.

Look at poor Hayes.

It sounded like it cost him his entire bank account to tell me he trusts me. That's not normal, and it's not fair, and I hate it.

Marshmallow whimpers and rubs his body against me while we march out of The Egg and to the car waiting on the street. "I'm kidding, Mom," I say loudly. "Of course we won't do that."

Nikolay winces.

I know, I know. I'm not very convincing. I shouldn't have been convincing when telling my mom I'd be doing *wicked, wicked things* in public, but my temper is awful.

At least, I *feel* like it's awful.

Hyacinth laughs at me every time I tell her I had a temper tantrum. I'm apparently not very good at them.

I should put *learn to have better temper tantrums* on my bucket list.

"Are you getting married?" Mom asks. "Is this a rebound thing, or is this a potential forever thing?"

Nikolay opens the door to the limo, and I climb in after Marshmallow. "It's a one-day-at-a-time thing with a guy who stuck up for me when his mother insulted me."

She sucks in a breath. "His mother? Giovanna Rutherford? You met his mother? And she didn't like you either? Dear god, Begonia, what did you do to her?"

"I breathed wrong, Mom."

"Begonia! You can't go around breathing wrong when you're dating a billionaire! Especially around his mother! What's she going to think about the way I raised you?"

"I don't know. Maybe she'll think you raised me to date normal men, since that would make more sense for where we lived and the social circles we move in?"

The car pulls away from the curb, and I start to ask Nikolay if we can get some alcohol for me too, but then my mom's talking again.

"Your father had some *very* exclusive clients at his summer camp a time or two. There was a Norwegian prince one year, and the son of an oil baron another year. We should've made sure you spent more time with them to learn rich people manners."

"Wasn't that before Hyacinth and I were born?"

"Don't bother me with details, Begonia. The point is, you have a very rare opportunity, and you need to not waste it."

"Marshmallow! Oh, no! Silly doggy! How could you spill that strawberry daiquiri all over the inside of this priceless limo! Mom, I have to go. Marshmallow and I are in trouble with the billionaires again."

My dog stares at me in horror, like he can't believe I just threw him under the bus, while I hang up on my mother.

"I'm so sorry, baby." I hug him tight, holding my phone up on the other side of him to change my mother's ringtone so that I won't make the mistake of answering without thinking again. "I promise I'll buy you six new chew toys and a big fluffy bed with my next paycheck. You know she'll forgive you, but I would've never heard the end of it if I told her I was the one who stained the inside of a limo."

Nikolay stares at me.

I sigh. "She wanted me to stay married to a man I didn't love because she doesn't think I can take care of myself. She means well, she just...wants different things for me than I want for myself."

"What do you want?"

Dammit. That's not supposed to make me cry. "For someone to love me just for me."

He nods once. "I hope a penis grows out of your mother's forehead."

"She means well," I insist again.

"If she meant well for you, she'd pay attention to what you want. Not what she wants for you."

I ponder that on the rest of the drive to the Razzle Dazzle corporate offices, but the minute the complex comes into view, everything else fades out of my mind. "It looks like a little village! Like from one of the movies!"

Nikolay nods. "Mr. Rutherford believes people work best when they feel at home."

"Mr. Rutherford—Hayes?"

"No, ma'am—his father. Mr. Gregory Rutherford."

"Why does Hayes hate it? He told me it was dull and boring."

"What one learns to appreciate depends on what one is surrounded with, ma'am."

The limo turns a corner, passing an adorable little bookshop and a tea house that both remind me of the streets of shops at Razzle Dazzle Village. All the buildings are three or four stories tall, so I assume the offices are above.

I hope they're just as quaint on the inside.

We turn another corner, and a stately gray brick building comes into view. "City Hall?" I guess.

Nikolay nods. "And the executive offices."

"Hayes way undersold this."

The limo glides to a stop at the steps to the fake City Hall building, and Hayes himself pushes through the glass doors to greet us.

His hair is disheveled, like he's been running his fingers through it, and his square jaw is tight.

So are his eyes.

When I was little, I used to think Hyacinth and I would take over running the summer camp for Dad one day. But then the divorce happened, he declared bankruptcy, and he died, and the summer camp is no more.

But I've never wondered if I would've realized it wasn't what I was supposed to do if Dad hadn't had to sell it.

I've always assumed I would've *happily* taken over running the summer camp, but that it wasn't in the cards from the universe.

And now I'm wondering if Hayes was born to do great things *not* related to Razzle Dazzle Studios.

Is he trapped? Does he feel obligated? Is he misreading the signs from the universe about other opportunities he has, or is he ignoring them, or is he just having a normal rough day because of upheaval in his family?

What would he do if he'd been born like me, to ordinary

parents in an average family just outside the suburbs, instead of into a world-famous family with ridiculously high standards set by the world around them?

He reaches the limo and pulls my door open before Nikolay makes his way around the car to do it, and then he's offering me a hand. "Begonia."

"Hayes."

Our palms connect, and my stomach drops.

In the good way, for the record.

As soon as I'm all the way out of the limo, he pulls me close, our bodies lining up while he presses his face into my hair. "Everyone will be watching us closely, so be on your best behavior," he murmurs.

"I didn't think you were dating me for my best behavior," I whisper back.

"I meant your best *pretending to be madly in love* behavior. And for god's sake, please weed through the disaster in my lobby. Diamonds and pearls, Begonia. Diamonds and pearls."

"I don't want diamonds and pearls, but I'd take a day pass to Razzle Dazzle Village for Hyacinth and her kids."

He pulls back and stares at me like *I've* grown a penis out of my forehead. "We need to work on your standards and expectations."

I wince. I'm so bad at asking for things. "Is it too much? I'm taking advantage, aren't I?"

"Yes, Begonia. Giving away three single-day passes to Razzle Dazzle Village would completely bankrupt the entire operation."

Marshmallow growls and shoves between us.

"Agreed, Marshmallow." I rub his head. "Sarcasm *still* isn't all that attractive on Hayes. It's a good thing he has other redeeming qualities. And Hyacinth has two kids *and* a husband who should probably go with her if we want Hyacinth to have a good time. So four passes, please."

"Find me an executive assistant, and she'll book the whole

damn family a week-long private adventure with all the frills and fripperies."

"Oh, that's too mu—um, I mean, thank you." I pause. "Also, can you say *fripperies* again?"

"No."

"Please? It was adorable. In a manly, rugged way, I mean."

He visibly stifles an eye roll, takes my hand again and tugs me up the stairs, bypasses the metal detectors in the entryway that looks every bit as much like a government office would, almost like this is used on movie sets when they need city halls, growls at the lone guard in the building who looks at Marshmallow wrong, and then we're all crammed into an elevator together.

It's a lovely elevator, but it's a little small for two large men, me, my dog, and the sudden knowledge that my fake billionaire boyfriend actually expects me to pick out a proper executive assistant for him.

"Did you take your allergy medicine this morning?" I ask.

He answers with a *duh* look.

I wave a hand in his general direction. "Is it the job, or is it me?" I ask.

Nikolay coughs and turns around, which doesn't do much good, considering the elevator walls are lined with mirrors.

Mirrors etched with the Razzle Dazzle logo, but still mirrors.

Hayes is spared from answering when the elevator stops and the doors open, and—

"Whoa," I whisper.

"I'll be in my office. Tell me when you're done."

He kisses my forehead, looks at the throng of women squeezed into the waiting area, all of them rising to their feet or going up on tiptoe and peering at him, and he sighs so heavily I feel it in *my* toes.

It's like he's on display at the meat market.

"Hayes," I whisper.

His dark eyes meet mine, and I don't know if that's sadness or desperation or regret or hope, but I know whatever's going on in his brain and in his heart, it's not pretty. "Please don't tell me you can't do this."

"I need a kiss for good luck. And to stake my claim."

"That's not proper, Begonia. I'm still a Rutherford."

"It's necessary for my process."

He studies me for one more beat, and just when I think he's going to kiss me—*please, please kiss me*—instead, he turns to the room at large. "This is Begonia. She's my girlfriend. We're madly in love, and she'll be doing the pre-interview screenings. Anyone who disrespects her will immediately be dismissed from consideration for the job. Am I clear?"

Murmurs and head-bobs affirm he's made his point.

"That was less helpful," I whisper to him.

"I have faith in you, my bluebell."

He drops my hand and strides through the sea of women, leaving Nikolay, Marshmallow, and me to watch.

And I realize I've already decided at least four of the women won't work out at all, because I don't like how they're looking at his ass.

"Just point, and I'll escort them out," Nikolay says to me.

"I can't really tell someone they can't have a job just because I'm feeling jealous."

"You know people," he replies. "Point. Do not feel bad. It's now, or it's several inappropriate passes at work later. This world is cutthroat, Begonia. Consider what Mr. Rutherford needs, and I'll handle the rest."

My nose wrinkles. "She definitely has to go," I whisper, trying to subtly gesture to a white redhead in a killer mauve business suit who looks at Hayes wrong as he marches past her and into an office, where the door is quickly shut behind him.

"She's not interviewing, Ms. Begonia. Therese is already

an executive assistant here, merely filling in until Mr. Rutherford hires his own."

Well.

If that's not motivation to get started, I don't know what is.

I clap my hands as if I'm standing in a classroom, and the entire sea of women turns to face me. "Alright, ladies, let's do this in an orderly fashion. If anyone has to use the restroom, it's—Nikolay, where is it?"

He points to a hallway to the left.

"It's there," I say, pointing in the same direction. "Don't be shy about taking care of your own needs, because you can't take care of Mr. Rutherford if you don't take care of yourself first. If anyone can't handle taking care of herself first, no one will judge you if you quietly see yourself out, and I wish you all the best. This world really doesn't teach us to take care of ourselves, does it? But can you imagine if we—erm, sorry. Right. Interviews. I want you all to line up shortest to tallest, leave your shoes on, yes, and we'll get started in height order for the first few interviews before I mix things up again, because that's completely random and nothing any of you have any control over. Questions?"

No one so much as peeps—or moves—and I'm starting to get funny looks.

Nikolay clears his throat. "You heard Ms. Fairchild. Please line up."

This will *not* be pretty.

But Hayes is trusting me to help out, and this is just one more adventure I didn't expect.

Time to keep rolling with it.

19

Hayes

I'M HIP-DEEP IN FIRST-QUARTER FINANCIAL DATA, IGNORING MY ringing phones—yes, *phones*—and pulling my hair out over the post-it notes decorating the surface of my desk to remind me about who wants to meet with me when and about what for the next infinity. The lunch Begonia insisted Nikolay bring me tasted like sawdust, though I blame work rather than the food. I'd rather be working on the data with the discrepancy in the real estate books, and I'm about to surrender to the urge when someone knocks on my door. I'm agitated that I'm supposed to send this data to someone three levels below me for error resolution. I'm agitated that my father's agitated with me for rescheduling a meeting with him. I'm agitated that the vice president of corporate development has called six times to reiterate the same thing, as if I didn't hear his request the first time, and that six other vice presidents have called with mundane greetings, congratulations and condolences, and small talk, and I'm agitated that there are so damn many vice presidents and chairpeople in this damn company.

In short, I'm agitated, I feel ill-prepared to execute this job, which means I feel as though I'm letting my family down despite the fact that I've increased all of our fortunes tenfold with my instincts about the stock market and bitcoin and global currencies, and I'm in no mood for one more person to demand my attention.

"Go away," I call to the knocker.

The door swings open, and a very frazzled Begonia gives me the kind of look my mother sometimes gives my father when he's being a total twat. "Your executive assistants, my lord." She bends at the waist, sweeping her arm as if we're on a Broadway stage after performing a historical musical, and a warm glow spreads through my chest.

But two women appear behind her, and there goes that glow.

"*Assistant*," I say. "Singular."

"*Assistants*. Plural. Two. Because it's utterly ridiculous to think that *one woman* can do everything from fixing your coffee to booking your travel to handling your dry cleaning to managing your complete calendar when managing your calendar alone is a full-time job, and do *not* get me started on the last time Therese took a vacation since there's no one to cover for her and she still has to go do work for her other VP when you leave for the day, and yes, I *did* go to the pub around the corner and tell them to charge you for her lunch, dinner, and all snacks for the next week. If you don't start valuing the work of the people who make your life run, *we are done, Hayes Rutherford. Done.*"

She turns her back to me and points at the two people, one tall Black woman and one average-height white woman. "And do *not* put up with any insistence that either of you work more than forty hours a week. If he has to drop off his dry cleaning on his own, or hire a personal assistant outside of your working hours to tend to his coffee and make his dental appointments, then that's what he'll have to do."

"Begonia—"

She swings back to me. "Happy employees are productive employees. Fight me."

She's so very ruffled and tired yet still sparking with an undeniable *Begonia* energy that I find I can't stop an unexpected smile.

And honestly?

I can't find fault with her logic.

Razzle Dazzle's corporate offices *do* have room for improvement.

I saw the surveys myself last week. Most executive assistants are doing far more than calendar and coffee management.

"We can fight later, my love." I rise and study the two women.

Neither of them drops their gazes from my face, neither of them smiles, and neither of them winks or makes pouty lips at me.

Dear god, I hate the pouty lips the worst. "Ladies. Pleasure to meet you both. I'm sure you'll find me cranky and difficult and say horrible things about me behind my back, and I honestly don't care, so long as my office runs smoothly."

Begonia puts her fists on her hips and glares at me.

"I'm being honest, bluebell."

"*Names*, Hayes. You haven't even asked their *names*."

My lips part, and an all-too-familiar sensation settles in my gut.

Unfortunately, this time I know I've earned it.

"Apologies, ladies. This is quite the awkward start, isn't it?" I'll have to fire them both and start this whole process over again. They undoubtedly think I'm easily pushed around, and I can't do my job if I'm having my assistants issuing *me* the orders.

But I asked for Begonia's involvement.

I should've known this is what I'd get.

She sighs. "Stop making that face. No one's questioning your authority, and you don't have to fire anyone. Technically, you haven't even hired them yet, but I might break up with you if you don't." She nods to the white woman in a crisp blue suit. "Merriweather has six older brothers and can handle your attitude and won't blink at strange requests, because she's already seen them all." And now she gestures to the Black woman who's wearing nearly the same ensemble as Merriweather, but in ivory. "Winnie color-coded and reorganized your calendar faster than Therese could on the twenty-fourth time I made her race a candidate, and Therese does *not* like to lose, so she wasn't just playing to get out of helping me. Be yourself, Hayes. That's why I picked them. So you could be yourself."

"That lets us be *ourselves* too, Mr. Rutherford," Merriweather says.

"I quit my last job because my boss couldn't handle me pointing out errors in his spreadsheets," Winnie adds. "Begonia assures me your ego can handle it. If she's wrong, Merriweather will have to handle you solo, and I like her. I don't want to have to leave her and make her deal with you all on her own."

"You're competent with finding errors?" I ask. "Databases, spreadsheets, balance sheets?"

"The day artificial intelligence takes over and I can date a computer, my life will be complete. I *live* for logic."

I tell myself the relief I feel is knowing that at least one of these two is machine-sexual and not at all attracted to me, but it's probably more that Begonia has potentially found competence among the personalities that she interviewed.

Begonia beams. "Therese scheduled you all for a getting-to-know-you breakfast at eight tomorrow morning at that adorable brunch café behind City Hall so you can verify for yourself that I'm right and they're perfect and make everything official. But it's past my dinnertime, and past my dog's dinnertime, and I get ugly when I'm hangry, and Marshmallow—well, you know what Marshmallow does even when he's not overdue for dinner. Also, please ignore anything anyone tells you about an incident with an umbrella and a coffee mug, and yes, it's worse than it sounds."

Once again, I'm smiling at Begonia. "Ever seeing you angry in any manner would be quite the sight. Merriweather, Winnie, I look forward to working with you."

"Good job. Now, take me home. I'm famished." She turns, hugs both of the women as if we're not in an office. I'd correct her, but it's Begonia.

This is how she operates.

I saw her do the same thing nearly every time we left a restaurant in Sprightly and after our impromptu picnic on the beach.

Corporate life doesn't match up with Begonia, and I wouldn't want it to.

"Good luck tomorrow," she calls to both women as they head for the doors, neither of them looking near as frazzled and tired as Begonia.

But for the first time in my life, I find myself wondering if my potential employees are wearing masks, or if they truly have that much more stamina.

It's difficult to out-stamina Begonia.

As soon as they're out of my doorway, she pushes it closed, collapses on the sofa behind the door, and drapes her arm over her face. "That was like doing an entire week of first days of the school year at once. And don't you dare consider not hiring both of them. You will *love* them. I have a feeling."

There's a perfunctory knock, and Therese sticks her head in. "Winnie's former employer says she's difficult and he wouldn't hire her back if she was the only person who could save him from being drowned in a burning barrel of oil."

How many times have I sighed today?

I've lost track.

"He's the dickhead from the Brouchard Corporation that all of my friends have warned me about," Therese continues. "If you don't hire her, *I'll* quit, and if I quit, this entire company will fall apart. I was humoring you when you threatened to fire me this morning because I thought it might be worth the divorce settlement to stay on your good side in the event that you broke up with Begonia, but honestly, I hope she breaks up with you for herself. You're difficult. She deserves better, and I don't want you anymore."

Begonia's lips curve up in a smile. "Be that tiger, Therese. You tell 'im."

"Also, it turns out the real reason there were fifty women in your office is that there was a glitch, and all of the candidates that HR had rejected received emails telling them to show up at the same time. There *are* four more qualified candidates if you'd like to speak with them."

"Not just yet," Begonia answers for me.

My phone rings, undoubtedly my mother calling to demand what in the hell I've done with the company during my first day in the office.

I ignore it and rise. "Thank you for your assistance, both of you. Begonia. Time to go home."

"I have no idea if your helicopter is ready," Therese says. "I told Nikolay that was his job."

"*Rawr*," Begonia says. But she's barely gotten the sound out of her mouth before she bolts upright, miscalculates, and tumbles off the couch. "*Helicopter*? Please tell me that's a billionaire joke."

"Sagewood House is over an hour by car. We're taking the helicopter."

She gapes at me while I pull her to her feet.

Therese pats her shoulder. "Only the best pilots for the Rutherfords, Begonia. You're in good hands."

"It's on my bucket list." Begonia's voice has suddenly turned into the squeak of the mascot of Razzle Dazzle's largest competitor. "But over a glacier in Alaska or into the heart of a dormant volcano in Hawaii. You know, so I can die in paradise and not over upstate New York."

I put a hand to the small of her back, oddly grateful to have her back within arms' length. "You keep saying you want adventure, bluebell, and then you keep being afraid of it."

"It's not that I don't want to take a helicopter ride. I do. But I need mental preparation time to be in a small metal whirlybird of potential death, and *my dog*."

I open my mouth, and no words come out.

Therese eyes me, then Begonia, and then quietly steps out of the office as Nikolay peeks in. "Bird's ready, sir."

"Marshmallow *cannot* get in a helicopter. You—you go on ahead without me. I'll take the limo. Or I'll stay in that adorable little inn around the corner and I'll see you in the morning."

"The inn is for show. It's office space behind the façade. Your dog will be fine."

"He'll open the door and leap to his death!"

Once more, my mouth is open, my lips are moving, and no sound comes out.

Not because I doubt her.

More because as I give it more thought, I'm afraid she might be right.

Opening an airplane door was beyond the dog's strength.

A helicopter door might not be the same.

Right now, the damn dog's trying to bite the trunk of a small tree in the corner as if either the tree is a chew toy, or he's decided his next career move will be *interior decorator* and the tree is in the wrong place.

It could honestly be either option with that dog.

Begonia's eyes go shiny.

And that's how I find myself holding a hundred-pound beast in my lap, getting dog hair all over my suit and up my nose, making me wish Benadryl came in ironman strength as we make the flight from Razzle Dazzle headquarters to my estate farther south in the Hudson Valley. Nikolay guards one door. Robert is shielding my pilot should the dog attempt to climb out of my lap and help fly the damned chopper. Begonia's plastered to the other door.

And Marshmallow keeps staring at me as though I'm the bloody King of England, and he's my loyal court jester.

This dog is going nowhere.

He thinks I'm his god.

"I had fun today," Begonia says, one wary eye still trained on her beast. "I'm exhausted, and I'll probably sleep like the dead for about two days to recover, but it was fun. Not the part where I had to tell like fifty women that they probably weren't right for the job, but the part where I got to meet so many fascinating people."

"Human resources will be a headache when I tell them I want two executive assistants."

"I haven't had enough food or playtime today to offer to do that for you. Besides, you're the boss. You could order *everyone* to have at least two executive assistants, and they'd have to do what you told them. You should too."

My nose itches almost as bad as my throat, and my sinuses are beginning to clog, even with the daily allergy medicine regimen I started in Maine. But it's oddly tolerable.

This might be gratitude. "You'll have to mention that to my father. *He*'s the boss."

"Do you think he'll like me as much as your mom does?"

This eyeball twitch has nothing to do with my allergies. "Most likely."

"Thank you for your honesty."

I nod to her. "You should look out the window."

She's sporting bags under her eyes, her bright hair is mussed in a way that makes me think she just crawled out of bed, and it's a good thing there's a very large dog blocking the view of my lap. And she still finds a smile for me.

I rarely find a smile for anyone when I'm hangry and exhausted.

I rarely find a smile for anyone when I'm *not*.

Yet here she is, supposedly both, smiling as she turns to peer out the window.

And, just as expected, she gasps.

"*Oh*, Hayes, this is *beautiful*," she whispers. "Do you get to see this every day?"

To this point in my life, I've avoided the corporate offices as much as possible, but I've still made this journey often enough that I know what she's asking. "No. I'm generally working during my commute."

"No wonder you're grumpy all the time."

Nikolay's lips twitch.

I try to glare at him, and instead, I sneeze all over the dog.

Begonia turns away from the view, cringing. "Oh my gosh, I'm so sorry. Marshmallow's sorry too. For his fur making you sneeze, I mean."

Marshmallow doesn't look sorry.

He looks like it's an honor to wear my snot. The damned dog's tongue is lolling out as he pants, looking for all the world like he's flirting with me the same as half the women and at least three men in the snack bar today.

If they're not kissing my ass because they want to date me —and honestly, why *anyone* would want to date me is beyond me—then they're kissing my ass because I have power and money and connections.

Not for the first time in the past few days, I wish I'd been born into a family like Begonia's.

My nose twists again, and Nikolay silently hands me a handkerchief.

"Oh, wow, look at that fancy house." Begonia's staring out the window again. "It's *massive*. It's not a house. It's—is that a hotel? And the lawn! It's so green. I know, I know, grass is green, but it's like—it's like it *glows*. It's preening because it knows it's the proverbial red carpet for whatever celebrities and CEOs and royals can afford to stay there. And *the fountain*! When I was little, Hyacinth and I would sometimes check this book out at the library all about the world's greatest fountains, and we used to tell each other we'd live in gorgeous mansions with fountains in our driveways, but naturally, we didn't. I don't think I'd want to. Can you imagine the upkeep on a fountain? And it's not like a fountain like that would've fit at summer camp, and I wanted to live at summer camp more."

She spins, beaming at me, and her smile drops away.

I have no idea what my face looks like, but I do know one thing.

Begonia's just realized that the *hotel* she's gaping at isn't a hotel.

It's Sagewood House.

And where every last one of my former girlfriends would've fussed over its beauty, none would've quite like Begonia.

And none would be having second thoughts.

It doesn't matter that I've known her a little more than a week. I can *see* the second thoughts.

"I'm gonna need a minute," she squeaks.

"It's a house, Begonia."

"Chad's company had a holiday party at the fanciest hotel in Richmond one year, and there were passing servers with cocktail weenies on trays, and he got so mad at me when I called them cocktail weenies, and said he didn't want to take me places when the hired help outclassed me."

My first assignment for my new assistants will be to find Chad's address so that I can personally go beat the shit out of him.

I'm a damn Rutherford. We don't beat the shit out of anyone. We watch a fucking Razzle Dazzle film and hug.

But I will beat the ever-loving shit out of Chad Douchecanoe Dixon for making Begonia feel inferior for merely being who she is.

"Begonia."

She doesn't look at me.

"*Begonia.*"

I get a squinty-eyed cringe. "Yes?"

"It would be the highlight of my life if you were to ask my mother to serve you cocktail weenies while we're at Sagewood House."

She flaps a hand about. "Sorry. I'm being ridiculous. It's because I'm tired. If I wasn't—"

"I would rather be back in Maine too."

Her eyes finally connect with mine, and it's like watching a puzzle click into place. She nods, and she probably has no idea just how regal that simple action is on her. "Okay. One more adventure."

"Sagewood House is a home. Feel free to treat it as such, regardless of how it looks."

I've said many, many things to Begonia that I never would've said to another girlfriend. And I don't think it's the non-disclosure agreement and the fraudulent nature of our relationship insulating me from having to mean it, though I do mean it.

I think it's that she's Begonia.

20

Begonia

My fake boyfriend's house has a helipad and looks like a museum from the outside—and I assume on the inside too—and I'm trying to embrace *someday, I'll tell my great-nieces and nephews about the time I had an adventure pretending to date a billionaire and sleeping in his mansion*, but I might be hitting overwhelm for one day.

So when Nikolay opens the sixteen-foot-tall front door and gestures us into the marble-floored, crystal-chandeliered entryway after our short limo drive from the helipad to the circle drive and portico, and voices well up somewhere deeper in the house, beyond the curved staircase, I whimper.

Hayes looks as exhausted as I feel. There are bags under his eyes that I won't be pointing out, and his shoulders are drooping, which I also won't be pointing out. But he pulls them back, glances in the direction of the voices, and then nods to Nikolay. "Take Begonia to my quarters, please."

"This is *all* your house?" I whisper to Hayes.

"I needed someplace large enough to breathe whenever my mother decided to drop by."

I snicker-snort. It echoes in the massive foyer, and the sound of my own snicker-snort echoing makes me involuntarily do it again, until I'm at risk of laughing until I'm crying.

Have I ever been this tired in my life?

If Hyacinth were here, she'd tell me I'd hit the dangerous side of slap-happy and needed a cheeseburger, a vodka chaser, and bed immediately.

But Hyacinth isn't here, which means I'm leaning on Hayes's arm and trying to telegraph to him that that's exactly what I need when there's a squeal, then a flash of sparkly red, and the next thing I know, a literal rock star is shoving me out of the way and leaping on him.

"*Hayes*! You're *back*!"

Keisha Kourtney is decked out in a red sequin bodysuit and cape, her platform red sequin boots hooked behind Hayes's back as she presses a resounding kiss to his cheek, which he tolerates with a level of affection that quite honestly pisses me off. Her short, jet-black hair is shaved on one side and dangles to her chin on the other, and sparkly diamond earrings lined with ruby chips dangle from her ears.

"Quit being a showboat," he tells her as he pulls her off of him and sets her back on her feet. "What are you wearing? Can you be a little more ridiculous?"

She grins widely and turns to me, instantly smothering me in a massive hug. In her platform boots, she barely comes up to my chin. There's more superstar per square inch in this woman than should be possible, and I want to adore her for it, but I can't quite get there, because *she just jumped my boyfriend*.

An actual damn *rock star*. Molesting my boyfriend in front of me.

My *fake* boyfriend, but she doesn't know that.

And I feel like the sludge leftover in the pan after

everyone else has eaten all of the grits—dried up and leftover and ready to be washed down the drain and put out of my misery—while her olive skin is glowing and her makeup is flawless and her eyes are bright and clear, unlike the rest of us.

"Oh my *god*, you must be *Begonia*! We are going to be *best friends*. Do you like kale smoothies? Say no. Please say no. If Mildred makes me eat one more kale smoothie, I'm divorcing her, and the only thing that ever works to get me off the hook is *I don't want to make other people watch me drink that shit*."

"Begonia, meet my cousin, Keisha," Hayes says. "Keisha, let Begonia go. She's in desperate need of a nap and a shower and dinner away from you."

"Cousin?" I echo faintly.

I'm still getting squeezed to death by the tiny rock star. A rock star who's married, apparently. This is what I get for not reading the gossip pages.

"I'm the black sheep," Keisha whispers dramatically. "Can you *imagine* the Rutherfords being related to a *lesbian*?"

A smile plays at Hayes's lips. "Stop it. We claim you in public. Sometimes in private too."

"It's scandalous," Keisha assures me, like she *likes* the idea of being scandalous.

"Hyacinth would adore you," I blurt.

"Oh my god, is she secretly your wife and you're using Hayes as your beard? Begonia and Hyacinth! That's *adorable*! Mildred? Millie? Honey, you need to change your name to Neesha so we can be as cute as Begonia and Hyacinth, mm-kay?"

"Stop making me out to be a shrew, you drama queen," an affectionate voice calls back. "If anyone's changing their name, it's you, to *Kildred*, *Killie* for short, because that's what you're doing to all of us. You're *killie* us."

"Keisha." Hayes has pulled out the Boss Voice. "Let

Begonia go. You can interrogate her later. Possibly next year. Or next decade."

"He is such an old maid," Keisha whispers to me. "Come join us. Dad's here, and he whipped up some of his famous guacamole, and Millie made her famous sangria, and Aunt G asked the chef to actually make a real meal, so we're having picanha and pão de queijo."

"Brazilian steak and cheese bread," Hayes murmurs to me.

Keisha rolls her eyes at him. "Don't be so boring. Which would you rather eat, Begonia, steak and cheese bread, or picanha and pão de queijo? And wait until you try the fried bananas. Oh. My. God."

"The guacamole?" I say.

She laughs, then beams at Hayes. "Someone I don't claim to be related to at this exact moment invited Liliane Sussex-Williams. She's here too."

"Begonia and I are both eating in my quarters. If you're still here in the morning, I'll see you then. Don't be here in the morning."

Hayes nudges me to the stairs.

Marshmallow sticks to his side.

Nikolay gives me a *hurry up* look, and so I do.

But first, I smile at Keisha. "It was nice to meet you."

"Oh my god, *same*. We're going to be—"

"Hello, Hayes."

Holy. Mother. Forking. Cannonballs.

I have no idea who the woman swinging her hips as she strolls into the foyer is, but she *owns* this place. She's tall and slender, white, with thick chestnut hair, symmetrical features, bright green eyes, and her clothes fit her as though the entire reason pantsuits were invented was so that this woman could one day wear them.

She's what you'd get if Bella Hadid had a love child with Marilyn Monroe, except instead of being carried in a uterus, she was incubated inside the rarest rose and infused with the essence of phoenix wings and golden unicorn horns.

And she's holding a hand out to Hayes as if she expects him to kiss it.

He could have *this*, and I asked him to have sex with me purely for the sake of helping me get back in the saddle.

No wonder he turned me down and has been avoiding talking to me about it ever since, except to kiss me when we have an audience to make it *look* like he wants to tear my clothes off.

And despite knowing he doesn't actually want me, a very large, very angry green beast roars to life inside me.

"Hi!" I leap in front of him, take the goddess's hand—and yes, I have to reach about as high as my nose to grab it—and jerk it down to waist-level to pump it. "I'm Begonia, and *oh my god*, I can't believe I'm meeting Angelina Jolie. *Hayes*. Why didn't you tell me Angie would be here? Can I call you Angie? Oh my god. Can we get a selfie?"

The woman extracts her hand from mine and glares down at me with a look that could melt a diamond.

Actually, I wonder if it has.

Someone should call the scientists.

"Did you just call me *old*?" she demands.

"What? No! Oh my gosh, Angie, you're not old. You're *gorgeous*. You're timeless. Don't let what any of those awful paparazzi say about you bother you. You're above all that." This woman, however, will never be on my good list for implying that Angelina Jolie will get old.

None of us are perfect, but Angie really is timeless to me.

"Begonia," Hayes says gently, his voice slightly strangled, "this is my old friend Liliane Sussex-Williams. Liliane, this is Begonia. I quite adore her, and I marvel every day that she puts up with me."

Keisha has disappeared, but there are strangled noises coming from a nearby room that I'd call muffled laughter if I wanted to take the time to analyze it, which I don't, because Hayes claiming me is making me feel warm and fuzzy and a little horny, despite the fact that I know it's for appearances only.

I have yet to actually see Mildred. Nikolay is showing the first signs of discomfort I've seen on him all day, and based on how his stomach sounded after lunch, I *know* it's not the first time he's *actually* been uncomfortable.

"Hayes and I are engaged," Liliane informs me.

I clap my hands. "Oh my gosh, first I get to meet his second-grade wife, and now his fiancée! Is this like a rich people betrothed-at-birth sort of thing? That is *adorable*. Or are we testing out the next Razzle Dazzle plotline? Do you do that? Play-act plotlines to see which ones the unsuspecting guests don't realize are plotlines?"

Superman has nothing on this woman. I'm pretty sure she's slicing and dicing my spleen with that look.

And in the words of my dear sister after a particularly craptastic day, I have zero fucks left to give.

Hayes isn't a freaking piece of meat, and I'd feel that way even if he hadn't threatened to sue me if I didn't pretend to be his doting girlfriend.

"We are *not* engaged," Hayes murmurs.

She eyeballs me, makes a very obvious decision to not say whatever it is that would prove they're engaged—*ha!* It's totally an *our parents want us to get married* thing, I *knew* it— and instead turns to Hayes. "You should have her examined by the family doctor."

She gives me one last look, her attention lingering on my mid-section, though I have no idea if she's calling me chubby or if she's trying to determine if I'm carrying his love child, before turning to sashay deeper into the house again, with a casual, "We know where this is going in the end, Hayes, and I'm a patient woman, but only *so* patient, and you'd best remember that," tossed over her shoulder.

Marshmallow growls.

"Quiet," Hayes orders. "For now."

Marshmallow harumphs, but he sits back on his haunches. These two.

It is utterly unfair that Hayes is allergic. They're soulmates.

"Do you ever consider changing your name and moving to a cabin in the Alps where no one can find you?" I whisper to him.

"Every. Damn. Day." He puts a hand to the small of my back again and gives a gentle push, but unlike every other time he's steered me somewhere this past week, he keeps his hand on me as we make our way up the grand staircase.

And I do mean *grand*.

The stairs are marble. The banister is sleek polished wood, and the balusters are decorative cast iron, and the whole staircase sweeps a circle around the low-hanging crystal chandelier so that I can see that every bauble on the damn thing is free of dust as we reach the next floor.

I'm pretty sure a dust-free crystal—or diamond?—chandelier beneath an arched foyer ceiling is the ultimate sign of wealth.

If I had one like that, I wouldn't even notice it needed dusting until the light couldn't make it through the dirty crystals anymore, but there's no mistaking that this one is spotless.

"Does everyone in your family follow you from house to house like this all the time?" I'm still whispering. I don't know if the walls have ears, or what the acoustics are like here.

"Not usually. Exceptional times." He pauses. "Except for Uncle Antonio. He adores me. Would've been in Maine except he hates seagulls."

Nikolay coughs in the foyer below.

"You weren't trying to make her like you," Hayes

PIPPA GRANT

murmurs to me before I can ask questions about this seagull aversion.

He's on to me. There are very few people in this world that I dislike on sight, or who I'm not motivated to win over on sight, and this Liliane person just got added to the very short list of two, with the collectiveness of Chad and his circle now being the other one. "Who? Your fiancée?"

"She is *not* my fiancée, despite what her mother would like to believe."

"Figures. You're not good enough for Angie anyway. No offense."

A full smile curves his lips. He barks out a laugh, and someone hand me a parachute.

I'm falling.

I'm falling hard, and fast, and it is a *long* way down.

21

Hayes

BEGONIA IS STARING AGAIN.

It should be annoying, but instead, it's making *me* examine every bit of my life with fresh eyes.

Again.

We're sitting before the wall-mounted fireplace in the den of my private suite, her lounging in a black silk robe and white terrycloth slippers from my closet, her hair once again wrapped in a towel, me in jeans and a Henley after both of us showered—separately, at her insistence, as though she was afraid I would suggest joining her, which I would've done in a heartbeat if she looked any less worn down and unable to resist the charms of anyone with half the personality of a garden troll—and she's staring at the candlelit tray of food on the table between us the way I wish she'd stare at me.

I'm reasonably certain it's not the black cloth napkins, the china, the crystal wine goblets, the candles, or the silver that have her captivated, her hand hovering above the serving tray piled with a dwindling supply of sliced roasted sirloin cap, thick asparagus spears, caramelized bananas, and cheese rolls.

No, my question is *which* food is so enthralling that she can't stop staring.

I've had this meal many times myself, but tonight, it's oddly more delicious.

Probably because I'm paying attention to the food instead of taking it for granted. I can honestly understand her fascination, and I don't believe I could pick a favorite.

She doesn't leave me to wonder long, as she finally plucks a roll from the spread and holds it up to examine the soft puff of cheesy bread in the glow from the fireplace.

"That is *not* a simple cheese roll. Did the chef put magic in it? Pixie dust? Sprinkles of awesome? How does it taste so good?"

"Essence of magic mushrooms," I deadpan.

"*No*! Oh my gosh, you really do get to try things that normal people—wait. You're joking. *Hayes Rutherford*. Warn me before you make a joke. It actually made you attractive this time."

I jerk my head toward her, but she's already moved past the compliment, and she's sealing her lips around the cheese roll, moaning softly, and thinking is suddenly difficult.

As is sitting still.

And being in fucking *jeans*.

"I'll have sex with you," I announce.

She inhales sharply, makes a noise that has both me and Marshmallow leaping to our feet, and then she's coughing.

I hover while she coughs.

And coughs.

And coughs more, holding up a finger as if to say *I'm okay, this happens all the time, don't worry about it*, which is exactly what Begonia would say if she could talk.

I hand her my glass of wine, and she gulps it, then coughs again.

"I'm okay," she rasps out.

Naturally.

Marshmallow has crawled into her lap and is head-butting her in the chest like the damn dog knows CPR.

"I'm okay," she repeats.

Her hoarse voice hits me right in the testicles and makes me ache.

It shouldn't—she could've choked for real—but I'm rapidly discovering there's little Begonia can do that I don't find attractive.

Hence my incredibly awkward proposition.

Billions of dollars in the bank, growing up in the most elite of societies, nannies and manners lessons and all but going to a damn *finishing school*, and here I am, being rendered awkward as a middle-schooler by a high school art teacher.

"Thank god I didn't choke in front of Angie," she says, a twinkle coming back to her bright eyes as she completely dodges the subject. "She's not the real Angie and probably would've let me die."

I ease back into my chair, afraid if I touch her, I won't stop, and that was *not* the reaction of a woman wanting to take me up on my offer.

Of course it isn't.

She hasn't said another damn word about having sex with me since she first brought it up, and I'm nothing if not effective at shutting down passes.

I've had regrets before, but rejecting her might take top honors as the stupidest thing I've ever done.

And why *would* she want to have sex with me as anything other than a last resort of convenience?

Even at my best, I'm a terrible option for her. And she's seen me not at my worst, but not anywhere near my best either.

"Marshmallow would've saved you," I offer, trying for a joke again.

She doesn't laugh, but instead, nods thoughtfully. "Or Nikolay, I'm sure. He's very nice for being such a terrifying-looking man. Are you ever alone? Honestly? Do you use other people's houses when you're in the area and want a comfortable place to crash but don't have your own nearby? Is that a thing in your crowd? Is that why this is *your* house but everyone else just seems to make themselves at home regardless of what you want? Hyacinth and I would totally share vacation houses all over the world if we didn't have to worry about paying the bills, but then, we share half a brain and we get along better than most families. I think. And really, we'd share summer camps all over the world before we'd share houses, because summer camp is way better than a house."

"Real estate is complicated, and I didn't realize Uncle Antonio would be throwing a party." I was counting on Uncle Antonio doing what he does best and telling everyone that he was headed to my house to take care of what the family says needs taking care of.

Namely, getting me an appropriate wife.

Otherwise, Begonia would've taken one look at this house, realized seven families could live here without seeing one another for at least half a year, and ignored my request for her to stay in my bedroom.

Having an ambush upon arrival?

She didn't even question the size of the house.

Merely the number of inhabitants and their likelihood to be nosy.

As suspected.

I am a bad, bad man, taking advantage of a woman who might not actually have a devious bone in her body, which, again, is highly suspicious. "Why did you abandon your other plans to come interview fifty women for the position of my executive assistant?" I ask her.

It's suddenly imperative to know.

And Begonia doesn't disappoint. "Because the idea of you calling your mother instead was horrifying. She would've had you hitched to one of them by this time tonight."

I grimace.

She does too. "Sorry. That was rude."

"No, it was accurate. And I'm not convinced it was an accidental glitch in the human resources system. Which is neither here nor there. It happened, and I still don't know why you took that on."

She's rubbing her chest as she leans back into the easy chair and stares at the fire, and I want to be her hand

I want to be her hand, rubbing her chest.

What has this woman done to me, and why don't I care?

"I like to help people," she says with a shrug. "You needed help."

Ah.

That's what she's done to me.

She's been nice.

My standards are awful. *I* should probably see the family physician about that. "A chief financial officer should also be able to handle interviews and sorting applicants by himself."

"No, Hayes—the world doesn't work like that. I mean, it does, but it shouldn't. You're not the CFO of Razzle Dazzle because you have good people skills. Your people skills aren't all that great."

"Thank you."

She gives me the *don't sarcasm me when you know I have more to say* look. "And that's totally fine. Not everyone is a people person, nor should they be. You're the CFO because you have other strengths. And you can't shine at what you're best at if you're spending all of your time and putting all of your energy into the things that drain you. Like interviewing fifty applicants when you should've been choosing among four already pre-screened for you. Chad had to interview new assistants all the time. Believe me, I know the process."

I hate Chad, and I want to punch him on principle. "Did you help him narrow his options?"

She snorts. "Mr. Big-Shot Financial Planner asking his art teacher wife for help? Um, no."

I don't even know what Chad looks like, but I'm picturing him bloody and missing a few teeth, with his arm in a sling and both legs in casts, and it's the only thing keeping my blood pressure in check. "While your ex-husband is clearly a twatwaffle, that's exactly the issue. Any other CFO would not have called in a woman he blackmailed into pretending to be his girlfriend to handle that mess either."

"You should say *twatwaffle* more often. It sounds so distinguished when you do it. Also, you're not any other CFO. You're you, and I'm honored that you trusted me to help." She sighs in utter bliss as she bites into another cheese roll. "It says a lot about your good judgment that you know when to ask for help, and a lot about your luck that I just happened to be there."

"I don't want to not be good at the things I'm supposed to be good at."

She shifts in her chair, frowning at me. "I've been teaching high schoolers for about ten years. Every semester, out of all of my students, there are always a handful who walk in with the most amazing talent for painting, or drawing, or sculpting, or studying, but rarely do I see all of those skills together. No one has them all. They're not supposed to. I don't have all of those skills, either, and I don't expect myself to." She tilts her head. "Anymore. I used to think I could do it all, but I've learned to be kind to myself and celebrate my gifts and the things in my control and accept the rest for what they are."

"I rather doubt I have enough of any of the right skills to

do the job." I need to shut up. I need to shut up, but she makes it so damn easy to admit to my fears.

"Your family believes in you."

"They believe in what they want to believe in."

"You know, every semester, I also have a handful of students walk in and tell me they suck at art, and they're only there because they need an easy A. And every year, every last one of those kids walks out of my classroom at the end of the semester still believing they suck at art, but I have yet to find one who didn't have a piece they'd made that they were extraordinarily proud of, and several more that are amazing but that they judge too harshly because we're our own worst critics."

"They make good art because you're a good teacher."

"I'm a terrible teacher. I'm always late turning in grades, I make lesson plans last-minute, and I spend parent-teacher conferences gossiping about old *Golden Girls* episodes instead of talking about how Kelsey or Aiden got a C in drawing for lack of trying."

"You don't give C's."

"Guilty. I'm an easy A. All I ask for is effort. But I *have* given six B's, and it was all about attitude, and I made sure there was nothing going on at home or in their personal lives first, and I finally realized some people are just shits, which makes me sad, so I don't like to dwell on it. But you, Hayes, are not a shit. You're a good man who loves his family but wants them to not badger you to death about getting married. They should trust your instincts."

I snort. They should *not* trust my instincts. On investments and math? Yes. On people issues and relationships? No. Been there, done that, have the ex-girlfriend married to my mortal enemy to prove it.

Begonia glares at me again as only Begonia can—in that special way that makes me feel like it's a glare-hug. There's no heat in it, no matter how much she tries, and I have every last ounce of her focus aimed at me, which should be uncomfortable but isn't, because it's Begonia. "There's nothing wrong with you, and whatever it is you think you've failed at in the past, you didn't fail. You experienced life. You'll do a great job as CFO, with great people supporting you, and if this is truly *not* what you're meant to do, or if it's not what you *want* to do, you'll figure that out and move on to what makes you happy."

"You believe that."

"I do. I believe in everyone."

"But *why*? And why do you drop everything to help people even when they don't deserve it?" I can't let it go. Maybe I want her to tell me I'm awful so that I'll quit being unexpectedly attracted to her. Maybe I want to find the chink in her armor so that I can prove to myself that she's not the goddess I'm beginning to suspect she is. Or maybe I don't understand how one person can believe in so much goodness even *after* being married to a twatwaffle who clearly tried to destroy her spark. Whatever it is, I can't let it go.

"What do you get out of it?" I ask. "I know what I got out of today. I know what your students get out of an easy class, and even out of learning to enjoy some form of art. What do *you*, Begonia Fairchild, get out of doing so much for everyone else?"

"Joy," she says quietly. "I get joy out of knowing I've brightened the world by brightening *someone's* world."

I've spent my life serving my family in one way or another. And I know Razzle Dazzle's entire mission is to entertain people, and thus to also spread their own kind of joy. But *I don't get it*. I don't understand how so much *giving* can be anything but a drain. "Who makes your world better?"

She peers at me, squints one eyelid, then takes my wine and drains the last of my glass.

I lift a brow.

She tries to scowl. "I really don't like when you throw my weaknesses in my face."

I'm so startled that it takes me a moment to find a retort. "Heaven forbid you have a taste of your own medicine."

No one makes her world better.

Jesus.

I need to make her world better. *Someone* needs to make her world better.

She points at me with the wine glass. "I can take my medicine *just fine*. But I'm still working on the right dosage, and I might need to try a different kind of medicine."

"Are you tipsy?"

"No. I'm just a little sleepy, and I can't remember what my medicine is supposed to be, besides leaving Chad, which I did, and I'm happier now, but I'm still...missing something."

If this is Begonia *missing something* in life, I've been missing many, many somethings since I was born. "At least you're looking for yourself."

"It's hard to balance getting enough for yourself when your default is to give to everyone else. Which you have so brutally reminded me."

"That was brutal?"

"It seared my soul, Hayes. Seared. My. Soul."

I can't decide if she's being serious or joking, but I want to smile, and it's difficult to keep my expression straight.

She sighs. "I hate disappointing people, and I disappointed my therapist every time I told her that I'd put someone else's needs above my own since they needed *whatever* more than I did. That's the real reason why I'm not in therapy anymore. I failed. I mean, I didn't. I was projecting. My therapist wasn't *really* disappointed in me. She was pretty good. But I *felt* like I failed. And I *hate* failing at making myself happy when I'm an expert at making people happy except when it comes to me. *I'm a person.* I should be able to make me happy too so that my friends don't have to do it for me. Is there more wine?"

I reach behind the tray to the wine bucket and top her off. "You should be more discerning in picking your friends. Only associate with the ones who appreciate what you do."

"Is that how you pick friends?"

"Yes."

"And how's that working out for you?"

"Unexpectedly well at the moment. I've finally found one who doesn't seem to want me for anything more than my charming company, even if she should have higher standards for herself."

Those big eyes blink at me, surprise flashing across her face as she starts to point to herself, as if she's asking if I mean *her*.

And the fact that I've left her with any doubt makes me want to punch *myself* in the face. "Dog. Down," I order.

Marshmallow leaps off Begonia's lap, sits at attention, and pants happily at me.

"What—" she starts, but she cuts herself off when I drop to my knees in front of her chair, grip her chin, and hold her face close to mine.

"I appreciate you."

"Um, thank you, Hayes. I appreciate you too."

"No, Begonia. *I appreciate you*." Fuck. I'm doing this wrong. "You don't make me feel like the rich, powerful catch of the century."

Her eyebrows do a weird little jig over her eyes, and *fuck* again.

I growl. "I'm not saying this right. I'm trying to say *thank you*, but thank you isn't sufficient, because—*fuck*."

Fuck the words. Fuck talking.

I need to kiss her.

I need to kiss her, and touch her, and taste her, and *show* her.

Our relationship?

Outside these doors, it's pretend. It's fake.

But when I'm with her?

When I'm with her, it feels so very, very real. And I *want* it to be real.

I *want* to trust this.

I want to trust *her*. I want to believe people like Begonia truly exist in the world, and that this isn't a cruel hoax, that she won't move on to shagging my neighbor or the next executive or artist or snake oil salesman who makes her feel wanted more than I do whenever she's gotten what she wants out of this.

But even if my trust is misplaced, she's still done enough for me that I want to give her something in return.

She doesn't resist when I touch my lips to hers.

No, not Begonia.

She leans into me, welcoming my touch, my kiss, *me*.

I know she makes everyone feel this glow, this peace, this sense of happiness just by being near her—it's not something she's doing just for me—but *god*, it's a high I can't get enough of.

She fists my shirt in her hands and holds on as though she's afraid I'll stop. I don't know if she wants *me* or if she'd take anyone, but I know I want to be the one to give her what she wants.

And I won't ask myself if she's thinking of someone else while she's kissing me.

If she'd respond like this for anyone who kissed her when she wanted a kiss.

What the *fuck* was her ex-husband thinking, letting go of a woman who can kiss like this, who can make a man feel *alive* like this, who puts all of herself into everything she does?

Of all the women I could've found in my private sanctuary last week, thank god it was Begonia.

She breaks free of the kiss with a soft whimper, her gaze

falling to her lap, hands still clenching my shirt. "Hayes, you don't have to—"

"Do you want me?"

The towel has fallen off her hair and her robe is gaping open, giving me a glimpse of the curve of her full breasts, rising and falling with her rapid breath. "Of course I do," she whispers.

"Do *not* tell me what you think I want to hear. Tell me what *you* want. Do. You. Want. Me?"

Those gorgeous eyes connect with mine, and it kills me that I can't read people the way she can.

Does that nod mean *yes, I want you*, or does that nod mean *yes, I want you because you're convenient and I want people who want me?*

Do I fucking care?

"This is not a revolving hotel that I keep for my family," I murmur. "I had my staff insist Uncle Antonio come and stay here so you'd have to stay in my bedroom with me under the guise of appearances."

Her gaze doesn't waver, though her lips tip up at the corners. "You *want* me."

"I want you."

"I like being wanted."

"But what do *you* want, Begonia? What do you *want*?"

She studies me, her eyes flickering over my face as her fingers thread into my hair. "This," she whispers.

And then she's kissing me, slow and cautious turning into desperate and reckless, and I'm wearing too many damn clothes.

She nips at my lower lip. I untie her robe and let my hands explore the smooth skin around her ribs. She fists my hair and holds me tighter while she devours my mouth, her eager little tongue hot and slick and perfect, those whimpery moans in the back of her throat making me hard as steel.

It's been a long time since I've kissed a woman I was this

attracted to, and there's a whisper in the back of my brain that I can't shut off.

You don't know her. Can you truly trust her?

I tell it to fuck off as her legs wrap around my middle, tugging me closer.

This wasn't in the contract.

I growl and cup her breasts, finding the tight nubs of her nipples with my thumbs, and she breaks the kiss with a gasp. "Oh my god, that feels so—so good."

"You like me touching your breasts?"

"So—sensitive."

I bend and suck one sweet nipple into my mouth.

"*Yes*," she moans. Her head drops back, and she tightens her legs around me while she holds me to her chest. "More, *please*."

The dog tries to nose in, and I shove him away with my elbow. The scent of her arousal hits me and makes my mouth water.

If she's faking—*no*.

Not Begonia.

And even if she is, I'll make certain she's not for long.

I lick the underside of her breast, and when she squirms and writhes with that panting, breathy *yes yes yes*, I repeat it for the other breast. I suckle and lick and tease, worshipping her breasts and telling all of my internal doubts to go to hell, her gasps and moans the soundtrack that I want playing on repeat every night for the rest of my life.

My family name, my heritage, my bank account, my job— they make me powerful by default, and they're nothing I've earned on my own.

Begonia's reaction to my touch makes me feel like a fucking *god*.

And *that* is all me.

The dog nudges me again.

I nudge him right back. Not hard, but firm.

"*Please*, Hayes," she gasps, and that's all it takes for me to sink back into the moment.

I don't know what the *please* is for, but I know her robe has fallen off her shoulders, leaving her bare from neck to toes, her skin bathed in candlelight, lips parted, eyes dark and hungry, hair loose and wild, and I want this woman.

I want her in my bed. I want her in my shower. I want her in my office.

I want her in my limo. In my helicopter. On my boat.

And I want to deserve her.

My lips slide down her sternum, kissing and licking lower, over her belly, until I reach her exposed pussy.

"*Yes*," she moans when I lick at the wetness between her legs. "Please, *yes*."

"You're exquisite," I murmur against her exposed flesh.

Her body trembles, and she tilts her hips into my mouth.

"And eager." I lick her.

"Oh, god, *so good*."

"How about here?" I twirl my tongue around her clit, and she doesn't reply.

Not with words, that is.

But her high-pitched moan of approval tells me everything I need to know.

For all that I got wrong today, *this*, I'm doing right, and so I lick and tease her again, inhaling her scent, tasting her, pleasing her.

She's not quiet as I devour her pussy, nor is she still, and I love it.

Mind your manners, Hayes. A Rutherford is circumspect.

Fuck that too.

I want her screaming my name.

I want the whole damn household to know she's satisfied.

No, not *satisfied*.

Mindlessly, bonelessly, wholly sated.

My cock aches. My balls ache. She's delicious, and she's

writhing in her chair, head back, arms flinging about until she settles with one hand gripping my hair, the other pinching her own nipple as she rides my face and I eat her like I've never eaten another woman in my life.

I want her to come.

I want her to come all over my face, and then all over my dick. I want to watch her fall dead asleep in that coma that comes after a good, hard fuck, then feel her reach for me in the middle of the night, hungry for more.

"Oh, god, Hayes, I'm—"

Her words are cut off by the splintering shriek of the smoke alarm.

I register the bitter taste of smoke, sense heat, and then—

And then my sprinkler system explodes all over my bedroom.

2 2

Begonia

"GOOD BOY," I SAY TO MARSHMALLOW ONCE AGAIN.

He harumphs and sits at my feet, looking away from me like he's pissed.

Understandable.

He tried to tell us a couple times that I'd knocked the candle over, and we ignored him, because *oh my god*, Hayes Rutherford is a vagina-worshipping king, which I should not be thinking about while he's inside the house with the fire marshal and I'm out here on the fanciest patio I've ever seen in my life—no, it's a *courtyard*, not a patio—chilling in the rapidly cooling evening with sex-hair and a singed silk robe and a pouting dog and, you know, *the rest of his entire family*, who are all dressed and who all know *exactly* what we were doing.

"Are penises really worth it?" Keisha asks me. "I've never understood the thrill. Plus, you have to put up with the man to get the penis, and I've never understood putting up with men either."

"One or two," I tell her. "It makes dating hard."

We stare at each other for half a beat, and then Keisha cracks up.

I was interrupted in the beginning of what promised to be the best orgasm of my life, and I ruined what was left of the cheese rolls in the fire and subsequent dousing from sprinkler water that had *clearly* been in those pipes for *years*, based on the smell of me, Marshmallow, and my robe, and so even though jokes about hard penises would be funny in other circumstances, I barely manage a smile.

Liliane Sussex-Williams makes a delicate huff of disapproval.

Marshmallow gives me the stink eye.

Giovanna Rutherford sighs heavily.

And two gentlemen I haven't met yet cross the courtyard toward the large brick fireplace that Millie's lighting for us. One is unmistakably Hayes's father—they have the same gait, the same eyes, and the same twist of their mouths when they're irritated, plus, he's *Gregory Freaking Rutherford*, president and CEO of Razzle Dazzle, so *of course* I know who he is, even if I don't read the gossip pages—and the other man must be the legendary Uncle Antonio.

I don't know if he's legendary to anyone else, but he's Keisha's father, and I know he's the instigator of today's house party, so he's legendary to me.

"Begonia." Uncle Antonio wins the race to reach me first. "So good to meet you. Never seen Hayes disappear to his bedroom with a woman so fast before. I mean, when he knew people were looking. There was that time in high school he thought he could sneak his girlfriend upstairs, and he was moving pretty quick then too, but he got caught. Pretty sure that boy enjoys the privileges that have come with age. Nice robe."

"Have some decorum, Antonio," Gregory Rutherford murmurs. He glances at me, then at his wife, then back to me, before addressing Millie. "Lovely fire. Do you have some clothes Begonia could borrow?"

"Nope," Millie replies. "I'm naked all the time in the bedroom too, so this is all I brought."

Marshmallow harumphs.

"I'm okay," I tell them. "I like the chilly air. It makes sleeping cozier when you finally get to bed."

Everyone on the patio looks at me sideways.

And thank god, Hayes steps out of the house just then.

His hair still has all the evidence of me gripping it like my life depended on that orgasm he was working on giving me, and I don't know if he's walking stiffly because he's uncomfortable in the jeans or because this entire situation is uncomfortable, or maybe it's both, or neither.

Everyone's attention swings back to him.

"Is the house ruined?"

"Did the rug survive?"

"Was it an electrical problem?"

"Is it totally gutted? Can I do a TikTok in there before you have it demolished?"

Keisha's question comes with a grin that I take to mean she's looking for a reaction.

"Don't be uncouth," Liliane says to her.

"Uncouth is my brand."

"The house is fine, the bedroom salvageable, the rug ruined, the table questionable, and I never liked the latter two anyway." Hayes takes my hand. "Say good night, Begonia."

I lift my hand to wave and parrot a *Good night, Begonia* to Hayes's family, because I'm *that* level of weird and awkward, when Marshmallow growls low in his throat.

A split second later, the "Imperial Death March" rings from Hayes's butt.

He squeezes his eyes shut and sighs. "Your mother?" he guesses.

"That's *my* phone?" I squeak. "Why is my phone in your —oh. You saved it from the fire. Thank you."

Marshmallow growls harder and stalks Hayes's ass.

"Marshmallow! Back. No."

Hayes pulls out my phone, with its sparkly purple case, glances at me, and once again, Marshmallow does what he does best.

He steals the phone and darts off into the night.

"*Marshmallow!*"

"Dear god, what is wrong with that dog?" Giovanna says.

"He's a well-trained support dog who saved our lives by pulling the fire alarm outside our bedroom," Hayes answers. He whistles, and the "Imperial Death March" gets louder, like Marshmallow is actually returning to us.

"If it's not your mother…" he says to me.

"Ex-husband," I whisper.

He stares at me for a beat, the piece still humming along on my phone, before his lips quirk up in an unexpected smile that takes my breath away. "How appropriate."

"I thought so. I'm still looking for the right ring tone for my mom."

Marshmallow trots back onto the lit patio, phone clenched in his jaw, murder written in his eyes.

He and Chad met once or twice.

It didn't go well for either of them.

"Give me the phone, Marshmallow," I order.

He ignores me and approaches Hayes instead, growling low.

Hayes snaps his fingers and holds his hand out.

Marshmallow growls again.

The phone stops ringing, and I breathe a sigh of relief.

"Marshmallow, hand me the phone," Hayes orders.

Marshmallow drops it at his feet.

"That is *the coolest* dog ever," Keisha whispers.

"Broken therapy dog for a broken woman," Liliane murmurs.

"Liliane, kindly see yourself out," Hayes adds as the "Imperial Death March" starts playing again on my phone. "And tell your parents that our engagement is over, much as it has been since the sixth grade."

Marshmallow growls.

I lunge for the phone.

And Hayes holds it out of my reach as he swipes to answer it.

"*Oh my god,*" I gasp.

"Begonia, don't say a word," my ex-husband's nasal, annoying voice says over the speaker. "I made a mistake. I shouldn't have bitched about your credit card bills, and I shouldn't have told you that your clay art shit was ugly, and I shouldn't have used you to warm my hands up late at night when you were sleeping. I can't offer you a billion dollars, but you know he's just playing with you. If you come back now, I can—"

"You can leave her the fuck alone is what you can do," Hayes interrupts. "Lose this number. If Begonia wants to talk to you, she'll be in touch."

Chad sucks in an audible breath that carries across the patio. "You can't talk to me—"

Hayes points to my dog, who's baring his teeth at the phone. "Your turn, Marshmallow. Tell him what happens to anyone who hurts your mama."

The bared teeth turn into a hair-raising growl.

"Good boy." Hayes hangs up the phone. "Now sit."

Marshmallow plops back on his haunches, happy as my stepfather in a pool of bacon.

"Why don't you ever do that for me?" Keisha whispers to Millie.

"You don't have any dick ex-wives because I haven't divorced you yet."

Hayes grabs my hand again. "Once again, say good night, Begonia."

This time, we make it into the house without interruption, with Marshmallow trotting along.

"Are you all right?" Hayes asks me.

"A little mortified, a little grateful, and a little turned on, if I'm being honest."

He steers me through the kitchen to a stairwell leading downstairs. "We're in the last of the guest quarters for tonight. And we're going to have to get engaged."

I almost trip on the stairs. *"Engaged? Are you crazy?"*

"We'll update the agreement. Do you have plans after this weekend? We should extend our arrangement too. We might even have to get married. Amelia in Maine. Liliane here. The fifty women in my office. An engagement or marriage is the only thing that will stop this."

I stare at him.

Does he want to get engaged because he *likes* me, or is this all part of the ruse?

I don't want to get married again. Not for real. I'm still finding *me*. This is an adventure on that path, not the end goal.

And the sex—yes, please, but also, did he do it for me because I asked him to, or because he *likes* me?

I know he likes me. We're friends. With hopefully more benefits.

"Begonia?"

"Is there more wine in the guest quarters?"

"Yes."

"Good. I think I need it."

23

Begonia

HEADACHE? CHECK.

Mouth that tastes like my grandmother's wedding dress freshly out of storage with the mothballs? Check.

Stomach angrier than an arena full of Copper Valley Thrusters fans when that ref made that terribly wrong slashing call against Ares Berger and nearly cost the team the championship? Check.

Missing fake boyfriend who wants to do paperwork to extend our agreement to include a fake engagement after I interrupted him eating me out by setting a tablecloth on fire? Check.

His distrustful mother sitting across from me at the formal dining room table first thing on a Tuesday morning after he also left me a note that we're committed to a charity gala in New York City later this week and I have to go shopping for a dress that will involve Slimzies, borrowed jewels that I will hopefully not lose, and plastering my face with more makeup than The Blue Man Group require in a week? Check, check, and check.

"You don't look well, dear," Giovanna says, as if I didn't attempt to burn the house down last night while her son was going down on me. "Perhaps the country air isn't to your liking?"

"I'm the world's lightest lightweight, and I had three glasses of wine last night."

"Poor dear. Would you like me to ask the chef to make you an omelet? Perhaps some yogurt and granola?"

I will never again believe any interviews that paint Giovanna Rutherford as a saint of a mother.

Yogurt on a hangover stomach?

Gross.

"No, thank you. I'm sure visiting Hayes at work today will make me feel better." *Oof*. I'm catty. Not a good sign. I force a smile and continue. "Or maybe a pickle juice smoothie. Wasn't the moon gorgeous last night? I know you're supposed to wish on a star, but sometimes I wish on the moon when she's that pretty."

"You're quite unique, aren't you, Begonia?"

"Oh, I'm just me. You must meet a *ton* of unique people who make me look normal."

She doesn't take the bait. Out loud, anyway. Her smile behind her coffee cup says the *no, I don't, because there aren't many people odder than you* that she's stifling.

Or possibly I'm reading too much into this because I'm tired and my head hurts and I could really, *really* use a spill-my-guts visit with Hyacinth.

Or a Big Mac.

Definitely a Big Mac.

I do my best to smile at Hayes's mother like I mean it, and not like I'm hoping Liliane Sussex-Williams is gone and Uncle

Antonio and his family are gone and that Giovanna is heading somewhere else today so Marshmallow and I can run around the grounds—or so he can while I flop in the grass and bake in the sunshine—and contemplate where I should go next week when my contract with Hayes is up if he comes to his senses and doesn't continue asking me to extend it.

And maybe also contemplate how I'll try to not be sad when I have to go, and how maybe we'll stay friends and I can text him now and again, even though I know he'll be too busy for me.

I can't stay here.

That much is clear.

And not because Giovanna Rutherford doesn't like me, but because I like Hayes.

I like him entirely too much.

"I'm so sorry to abandon you," I say to her, knowing full well she won't be sorry to see me go, "but I think I need to go lie down."

"Of course, dear. I hope you feel better."

I look down to tell Marshmallow to come along, but he's not there.

Giovanna makes a strangled noise.

And there he is, walking into the formal dining room with a colander on his head and a tall salt shaker clenched in his jaw, tipping it so that he leaves a trail of salt behind him.

I cringe. "My house is Marshmallow-proofed," I say apologetically. "I'll clean that up."

"The housekeeper will take care of it."

I give my dog the stink-eye.

He gives it right back. I think he'll miss Hayes too.

"C'mon, Marshmallow. Time to return your booty."

We head to the kitchen, which is easy to find—you just follow the trail of salt—and when I get there, I'm hesitant to walk in.

It's massive. And fancy. The *kitchen* has an arched ceiling. At least two ovens. Three sinks. A backsplash that was probably hand-painted by one of the Italian greats who was re-animated with some of the Rutherford fortune. Money can buy anything, right?

It takes me a minute to spot the refrigerator because the facing blends in with the cabinets. The island is the size of a continent. The kitchen itself is larger than my entire apartment. And the chef is slicing and dicing things on a cutting board and doesn't look happy at the interruption.

You only live once though, right?

"Hi." I smile and wave like we're not standing ten feet apart. Actually, it might be twenty. This is a *massive* kitchen. "I'm Begonia. Hayes's, um, girlfriend. Did you make that amazing picanha last night? And oh my god, the cheese rolls?"

She snorts. "Child's play," she says in a thick French accent.

"They were my first, and they were amazing." I smile again, which makes my temple throb.

She doesn't.

Maybe her temple's throbbing too.

"I accidentally knocked a candle over and set off the smoke alarms and the in-room sprinklers last night, stood outside in my robe with the entire Rutherford clan while the fire department came, and then my ex-husband called and was on speakerphone when he said Hayes is playing with me and I only get one more chance to take him back. I drowned the complications in a bottle of wine, and I feel basically like ass this morning, and I need to clean up this salt that my dog spilled all over the first floor here. Do you have a favorite hangover cure before I go find the vacuum and make my head split in two with the noise? Because otherwise I'm going to find someone to take me to the nearest McDonald's, and that seems like one more thing that I might do wrong, and I'm trying very hard to not do things wrong today, and I miss my sister, and I wish my ex-husband had this headache instead of me, but he doesn't, at least as far as I'm aware, so I'm just doing the best I can here."

She finishes with six carrots, sets her knife down, and gives me a look that would probably put Giovanna Rutherford herself in her place. "Why did you divorce him?"

"His mother said some not-nice things about me and he didn't defend me."

"Men have no honor. Too afraid of their mothers." She snorts, and I swear she's snorting in a French accent too. Then she points to the other side of her work island, where six stools are lined beneath the countertop. "Sit. I will make you cassoulet, if you don't expire first."

"Hayes defended me to his mother," I whisper.

"Wise man. I will not put too much chili powder in his croissants."

"He likes chili powder in his croissants?"

"No. No one likes chili powder in croissants." She smiles. Not gonna lie—I'm fairly certain it's a smile meant to terrify.

"Do you like your job here?"

"Best job. Mr. Rutherford—he's a good boss." She winks. "And absent so much. I watch home improvement shows on the TV in his office when he is gone. You like coffee?"

"Oh, yes, I *adore* coffee."

She points to a large stainless steel machine on a counter along one stone wall. "You do your coffee. I will do your cassoulet."

I almost tear up. "Thank you."

"No coffee for the dog."

I laugh, thoroughly enjoying the sound of her voice. It's like taking a trip without having to go anywhere. "Agreed."

"I will clean the salt. I gave it to him, I clean it. Good dog. Very funny. And his noise annoys Ms. Sussex-Williams."

"You cheeky devil," I whisper. "Can we be friends? What's your name?"

"This is Françoise, Begonia," Keisha says. Her hair is wild, like she had a very good night. She's in a bright pink kimono, which is gaping open to her belly button and matches the silk pants that are threatening to fall off her tiny frame. She pauses halfway to the coffee maker and dusts off her bare feet with a frown. "Stay on her good side or she'll put olives in your Frosted Flakes."

"Or salt on your feet," Françoise murmurs.

Keisha grins. "I'm gonna call Liliane and tell her Hayes thinks it's sexy when women race barefoot through the front hall. And then I'm going to tell her it's the latest craze—exfoliating your feet just by walking around your own house. What happened? The dog get into the salt?"

I nod.

"Wicked. He's the coolest dog. Can I take him on tour?"

"*No!*"

She laughs. "Ah, man, you didn't sleep well, did you? C'mon. I'll fix your coffee. Françoise has your hangover cure coming, I see. Let's go hide in the gazebo and you can tell me all of your secrets before Millie wakes up and realizes I'm wreaking havoc on the world."

"But the salt—"

"B, the housekeeper vacuums here every day, whether Hayes is in residence or not, so don't sweat it."

"Truth," Françoise agrees. "Annoying as the fuck."

"I'm going to start using that," Keisha says. She affects a French accent herself. "*Liliane is annoying as the fuck too.*"

Françoise's nose twitches, and I don't know if she's amused or if she's plotting Keisha's demise. "Go, she orders. "Have coffee. Spill the kidneys."

"She means beans," Keisha stage-whispers.

"I prefer the kidneys."

I don't know if she's making a joke about wanting to take

people's kidneys, and I don't stick around to find out. Instead, I follow Keisha through making coffee and then out to the gazebo at the edge of the courtyard, overlooking the rolling green hills of the Hudson Valley. I can just glimpse the river tucked in down below too.

"So are you real, or are you the shield?" Keisha asks as soon as we're comfortable.

I frown and don't answer.

And then I sip my coffee and my entire world gets a little brighter. "*Oh my god*. What *is* this?"

"Properly fresh-roasted and fresh-ground Guatemalan beans, though you might've ruined it with all that sugar and cream and cinnamon."

"That machine literally fresh-roasts and fresh-grinds the beans?"

"That's what all the noise was, B."

I sip again. *Savor*, I tell myself.

Screw that, there's more where this came from, at least for today, I tell myself back, though it sounds like Hyacinth instead of like me.

But she's not wrong.

"You didn't answer the question. Real or a shield?"

I hate lying. So I don't. "Do any of us ever know what's going on in a man's mind?"

She laughs. "Excellent avoidance tactic."

"I like him." Also the truth, and more than I wanted to admit to anyone. "But he's so...guarded."

"You would be too if the love of your life married your nemesis."

I pause before gulping more coffee. "Hayes has a nemesis?"

"Brock Sturgis."

I wait.

She waits.

Marshmallow strolls between us, looking back and forth, tongue hanging out, like he's watching a tennis match.

"You don't know who Brock Sturgis is," Keisha finally says. A statement. Not a question, though she's clearly having trouble believing it.

"I don't read the tabloids, and Hayes and I met online." My tongue trips, and I swear she sees through the lie, no matter how much I try to convince myself that *I rented his house online without knowing it wasn't mine to rent* isn't a lie, and is technically the reason we met. So I push ahead. "I didn't know anything about his real life until we met in Maine."

Her nose wrinkles like she's calling me out, but she doesn't say anything out loud. About my lie, anyway. "Brock isn't tabloid bait. Not outside the city. He's old Wall Street money. The Fifth Avenue equivalent of an ambulance chaser now. I was too young when it all went down to really know the nuances, but I know he and Hayes were besties in grade school, then had a major falling out in high school when Hayes realized Brock was copying his homework and spreading rumors about him behind his back. And once Hayes put his foot down, the bullying started. Kids are shits. That's as much of *that* part of the story as you're getting from me. And then after college, Hayes started dating Trixie Melhoff, and he fell in *luuuuuuuurrve*. Not just normal love. Like, even I remember how he could basically talk about nothing but *Trixie this* and *Trixie that* and he was shopping for rings and had already basically proposed when he found out she was sleeping with Brock behind his back."

I gasp.

"Yeah. The guy who almost got Hayes kicked out of fancy high school prep school by claiming Hayes was copying *him*, then saying Hayes had mental health issues and he needed to be institutionalized, like mental health issues are something to be ashamed of, and then sliding the tabloids lies about

Hayes doing drugs to cope with his weird sexual fetishes all through college, and I am *not* saying any more. I'm really not."

"Your family's reputation," I whisper.

She nods emphatically. "Right? Uncle Greg and Aunt Gio were *beside* themselves. I mean, they believed Hayes when he said it was all lies, but the lengths they had to go to for damage control? They were lucky *Hayes is the weird one* is the worst that ever took hold in public. And you know what? I don't like to call women bitches. I think we should support each other, and I think we all have more to give than just chasing billionaires for their money, but that bitch Trixie? She can rot in hell. Most normal women who want to use Hayes would've cozied up to him to get close to Jonas instead, and believe me, plenty did, but *no*. She accepted his proposal while sleeping with his mortal enemy. His former best friend who bullied him all through school. That's like—that's *the worst* kind of betrayal. And that's all I'm saying."

My heart hurts. "Why are people cruel?"

"I don't know. But he hasn't had another serious girlfriend since. I think he tried once or twice, but you know how it is when you're rich and famous. Everyone has an angle. And all of them had angles. So everyone in the family's trying to find someone he could marry without loving so that he doesn't have to go through all of this ridiculous press and publicity with being the last eligible billionaire on the planet. And he's not, for the record. There are like, three single *women* billionaires who are in their thirties and forties, and is anyone talking about them? *No*. Fucking two-faced twats. So. What's your angle? What do I have to murder you for?"

A tear slips down my cheek. I try to swipe it away fast, so she won't see, but another follows.

"Okay, I won't really murder you," Keisha says. "Stop crying. I hate crying. Crying makes me bleeeaaaaaa, you know?" She sticks her tongue out and shudders.

"I wish he'd been born to a normal, middle-class family outside of the spotlight," I whisper.

Her face freezes mid-shudder, and when it moves again, she stares at me in horror. "Fuck, B. That's like, the worst thing you could've ever said."

"Why?"

"Because that's what I wish for him too."

24

From the Text Messages of Hayes and Begonia

BEGONIA: GOOD MORNING, SUNSHINE! SORRY I MISSED YOU leaving. How was breakfast with Merriweather and Winnie? Or ignore me. I know you're busy. We can talk later.

Hayes: It's two in the afternoon.

Begonia: It's still morning in Hawaii. P.s. I should not drink wine again tonight.

Hayes: There's a craft brewery with excellent burgers a short helicopter ride from Sagewood House. Be ready at seven. They have root beer if you're off alcohol altogether.

Begonia: Françoise is making roast duck with some kind of fancy sauce I can't spell, and fingerling potatoes, and brussels sprouts that she swears will taste like they're blessed by the gods, and crème brûlée for dessert.

Hayes: Would you rather have duck at home with my family, or a burger with local flavor?

Begonia: She's going to so much work.

Hayes: She goes to that much work every day. It's her job. She likes it.

Begonia: But people like to feel appreciated.

Hayes: The people at the craft brewery like to feel appreciated too.

Begonia: So we have to do both. I didn't pack my Thanksgiving pants. This could get uglier than me on three glasses of wine.

Hayes: You're oddly adorable on three glasses of wine. I've honestly never had a woman in my bedroom confess to wanting to lick the frost off of windows, and it was more charming than I thought it would be. Especially since there wasn't any frost on the windows. Not in late June.

Begonia: I said I wanted to do that WHEN I WAS SIX, and ONLY on Christmas morning, because MAGIC.

Hayes: You're thirty-two and you still believe in magic.

Begonia: I believe in making magic.

Hayes: And you're quite good at it.

Begonia: You didn't tell me how breakfast went with Merriweather and Winnie.

Hayes: Terrible. They told me what to order, didn't listen to a word I said, sent the tabloids a picture of my left shoe, and stiffed the server.

Begonia: *picture of herself making a horrified face*

Hayes: Teasing, Bluebell. They're perfect, both starting later this week, hence a celebratory dinner OUT instead of in with my nosy family, whom I'll be relocating back to their own houses posthaste.

Begonia: HAYES RUTHERFORD, YOU MADE ANOTHER JOKE. And it was a bad joke at that. Also, who says POSTHASTE? Seriously?

Hayes: I'll have to buy you diamonds to make up for the error in my judgment.

Begonia: I demand a poem in recompense. Recompense.

Ha. That's a fancy word. Don't use it in the poem you write me.

Hayes: I saw an article about you in your hometown paper. You didn't mention you love clay pottery.

Begonia: That article is ancient. You were googling me!

Hayes: Yes, and enjoying it so very immensely that we nearly burned the house down.

Begonia: I'm sitting with YOUR MOTHER and she just asked me why I suddenly went red as an overripe beet. Warn a girl before you say things like that.

Hayes: Begonia, I'm about to say something highly improper and scandalous and it would horrify my mother and will probably make you want to board a helicopter to get to me as soon as humanly possible.

Begonia: I'm turning my phone off until I'm alone.

Hayes: There's a delivery truck on the way to the house right now with a pottery wheel, an industrial-size block of clay, and every clay modeling instrument that the internet insisted you needed to spend an afternoon getting filthy. Perhaps you can give me lessons later.

Begonia: *selfie of herself with her eyes bugging out and a little shiny*

Hayes: You're enjoying the weather. Looks lovely.

Begonia: I make AWFUL pottery.

Hayes: But you enjoy the process.

Begonia: OMG, the truck is pulling up. You weren't joking.

Hayes: You didn't want diamonds or pearls. I had to get creative.

Begonia: I don't know what to say. Thank you feels so very inadequate.

Hayes: Say you'll do dinner with me at the brewery.

Begonia: Of course. Yes. Happily. Can I be coated in clay when we go?

Hayes: I would expect nothing less.

25

Begonia

IT'S ALMOST NINE THIRTY BEFORE HAYES GETS HOME, AND I'M about to crawl out of my skin by the time he walks in the door.

I leap off the stairs, where I'm waiting, the minute the door opens, but he hustles in with his head down, phone against his ear. "No, Dexter, if you want approval, you'll need to send it through the proper channels. I'm not interested in acting as your shortcut. No. No. No. Do I need to say no once more? Call my office and make an appointment if you want to discuss this further. We're done for now. Good night."

He hangs up, drops the phone into a potted plant, and loosens his tie, and all of my own frustrations and worries fade away as concern for him takes hold.

I want to be mad. I want to remind myself that I deserve better than this, but I can't.

For one, this is all pretend.

For two, his profile is etched with weariness, his shoulders are drooping, and the sigh that leaks out of him is like an overstretched balloon finally giving up the last that it has to give.

When he turns his head and spots me, guilt flashes across his features. "Begonia. Apologies. This afternoon turned into one crisis after another, and I lost track of time."

It's so damn familiar.

I'm working late, Begonia. Eat without me.

Sorry I forgot to call. I was tied up.

The boss needed me. You know how it goes.

I know better.

I do.

I know better than to pretend everything's fine and I can roll with this and I wasn't worried he'd died in a helicopter accident, but my indignation is warring with knowing that Hayes Rutherford is a million times the man Chad was, and I'm not talking about his bank account.

Chad wouldn't have walked across the foyer to wrap me in a hug and hold me tight as if he were holding on for dear life the way Hayes is right now, like he truly *didn't* want to be in the office and is glad to be home.

He wouldn't have bought me so much as an at-home clay-painting kit, never mind a pottery wheel and clay.

And Chad and I could've afforded a used pottery wheel and clay.

I'd sometimes stalk them on eBay when I was feeling unsettled.

And I'm not letting Hayes off the hook because he bought me a pottery kit to use at his house, kiln and all, *and* had his staff set it up for me in a room with a window overlooking his solarium with all of the pretty plants and hot tub and indoor waterfall.

I'm letting him off the hook because he has zero obligation to apologize to me, to acknowledge that he made me worry, that he should've called, that he broke our date, because *this is all fake*, but he's doing all the things someone he's in a relationship with deserves anyway.

"You must be famished," he says into my shoulder.

"I had some duck with your family. And it was only mildly awkward when Uncle Antonio started talking about a few women he knows that he could invite out here, and then when your mother asked if he was ready to date again to try to cover for him, and then when Keisha pretended she was whispering to me that they're all a-holes, when she wasn't actually whispering at all and everyone heard her. What about you? Have you eaten?"

"We stock Razzle Dazzle treats in all the offices."

"*Hayes.*"

I can feel his smile as he shifts his head on my shoulder. "I'm shocked, bluebell. You seem the type to embrace snacks for dinner."

"On vacation. Not when you're working fourteen-hour days."

He kisses my neck, sending delightful shivers dancing across my skin. "Apologies for your awful dinner."

"That was actually just the soup course. Dinner itself wasn't all bad. Françoise and I made friends today, so she snuck a live cricket onto your mom's plate, and then Marshmallow tried to save her from the scary cricket and ended up running across the table and almost catching his fur and *another* tablecloth on fire. I think you should have a no-candles rule as long as Marshmallow and I are in residence."

Hayes's whole body is shaking.

"Are you laughing or having serious regrets about bringing me here?"

Marshmallow stalks into the room with an umbrella clenched in his jaw, and he growls low like he's threatening Hayes to not answer that question wrong.

"I'm laughing."

He is. I can hear it, and it makes my stupid back-stabbing heart freaking sing. "At me, or with me?"

"Out of sheer regret that I missed the show. Is my mother packing her bags yet?"

"She says she has to be in Los Angeles for a dinner for some foundation tomorrow."

"Excellent. Did you make lovely art today?"

"Shh. No more talking until you eat something good for you."

He kisses my neck again, and this time, I can't ignore the way his touch electrifies my skin and makes my nipples pebble and sends my vagina into a tailspin of *can we try last night again without the fire and literal sprinklers to put us out, please?*

"F-food," I try to order.

"I believe I'd prefer sleep."

"You need both. And I mean *sleep* in the real sense of the word *sleep*."

"Is the bedroom fixed?"

I sigh. "No. Your housekeeper and Keisha had an argument over whether the table that was under the flaming tablecloth could be saved, and the chairs still smell like smoke and stale water, and apparently having a clay art room assembled in an hour is as far as your money went today."

"Hm." He pulls away from where his breath is tickling my neck, grabs my hand, and drags me deeper into the house, past the formal sitting room in front, the dining room across from it, then the doorway to the east wing, and around the corner and through the arched stone entryway to the massive kitchen.

I smile. "A-*ha*! You *are* hungry."

He hands me a massive picnic basket topped with a blue checkered picnic blanket that's sitting on the island. "Can you hold this?"

"It's a little heavy, but yes, I think I can—*erp*!"

In one swift motion, he hefts me into his arms and heads for the back door, me clutching the picnic basket in my lap, him holding onto me.

"*Hayes.*"

"Robert, close the door behind us, and don't let anyone else leave this house if they want to live," he calls over his shoulder.

"Yes, sir," Robert answers behind us.

"Thank you."

"Don't hurt yourself, sir."

Hayes smiles.

He *smiles*.

"Don't do that," I warn him.

The man isn't sweating or huffing as he carries me out to the courtyard, Marshmallow trotting beside us, which is more than Chad could've done too. "Do what, love?"

"Smile. Do *not* smile."

"I had the most fascinating text messages all day long today." He keeps marching past the edge of the courtyard, me clinging to him like my life depends on it while still wanting to be ready if he drops me and *also* trying not to drop the picnic basket nestled into my lap.

And he's not struggling at all.

Does he work out?

When?

"I wouldn't call our text messages *fascinating.*"

"Jonas is enjoying his honeymoon," he muses, as if he doesn't have a frazzled *me* clinging to his neck and an eager dog leaping around his legs while he strides across the moonlit lawn. "My mother also has opinions about an interior designer for renovating my bedroom suite. Uncle Antonio is sorry he thought Liliane would be a welcome guest. He tells me he helped set up your pottery wheel himself. And Keisha tells me she told you all of my deepest, darkest secrets."

"She only did it because she cares," I say quickly.

"Yes, clearly breaking trust is a sign of caring."

"Would *you* have told me about Brock Sturgis?"

His shoulders bunch. "She truly did tell you everything, didn't she?"

"She didn't go into detail."

"Hm."

"I won't repeat a thing. But I think I understand better why your mom hovers. Everyone worries about you."

"I am not a frail flower, Begonia."

"That's really funny, because technically, a begonia is kind of a frail flower, so it's like you're pointing out that I am when you're not."

"You are *not* a frail flower either. God help the person who mistakes you for one."

"I know I'm not, and I know you're not. You're just…"

"I'm just…?"

"Stuck in a world where you can either let it suck away your soul or be alone. And that's not fair. Or easy, I'd guess. How does everyone else in your family do it?"

"They don't feel it as personally, I suppose. Didn't have the magnitude of betrayal. Or they don't mind. Or they appreciate the luxuries enough that the trade-off is worth it. My father married well. And not in a money sense, but in a trust and true love sense. My parents were high school sweethearts, in fact, from a time before my mother understood what would be expected of her. He's never worried about her stabbing him in the back, nor has he had to. Uncle Antonio didn't fare as well, but he's my mother's brother, so he's shielded from the expectations of being a Rutherford."

"And he's a man," I point out.

Hayes snorts. "That does present another level of protection in the eyes of the world, doesn't it?"

"But you didn't escape it."

"I did for a time, leaving the country to study abroad and

ignoring the tabloids and letting my family handle any issues. Ignorance truly is bliss sometimes."

"Would you tell me what happened?"

"You want details?"

"Yes." I don't want details. I don't want to know the horrific levels of torture that a spoiled high schooler with money and connections could resort to. I see it enough in my own world.

But I want him to know I'd listen if he wants to talk.

"Begonia, this is too lovely of a night to ruin it with old memories that I refuse to let haunt me anymore."

"So, you needed a fake girlfriend because you're perfectly fine and well-adjusted and have no lingering trust issues after your fiancée committed the ultimate betrayal like fifteen years ago?"

"You're so very cruel, yet so very irresistible at the same time. However do you manage?"

"I won't hurt you, you know," I whisper. "If you want to use me to learn to trust someone again, I'm okay with that. And I realize that saying *you can trust me* is basically a red flag that means you probably shouldn't, but—"

"Begonia."

"Yes?"

He doesn't immediately answer, and his steps slow as we approach a line of trees near a hilltop. The lights of the house are distant enough to make this little section of the lawn feel private, and the moon is bright enough that we can see its light reflected in the river in the distance.

He sets me down, then relieves me of the picnic basket and lays out the blanket. "Sit. Have dinner with me and tell me all the good that I missed today."

"You *want* to hear me talk."

He settles onto the blanket, long legs bent, sheds his suit coat, pulls his tie the rest of the way off, then removes his shoes.

It's the shoes that do me in.

I don't know why.

I just know that watching him take his fancy shoes off, here on a picnic blanket under the moonlight, is some kind of catnip to my inner schoolgirl fantasies about saving Prince Charming.

It's like he's removing all of his armor and letting me see him.

All of him. The tender parts and the tired parts and the insecure parts. The simple parts, the basic man under all the billionaire luster who needs nothing more than to know that someone sees him for who he is and loves him for that with no ulterior motives.

Too soon, I tell myself. *Too soon*.

"Is this for you, or is it for me?" I ask as I settle back on my heels beside him, Marshmallow flopping to the ground on top of his shoes. I don't need light to know that my dog is gazing at Hayes as though he invented cheese-filled hotdogs.

Hayes turns to look at me, that lock of unruly hair falling across his broad forehead, his eyes hooded and serious, lips barely parted. "For both of us, I had hoped. You seem to enjoy picnics, and I…I enjoy you."

This man.

He makes me wish we'd met another year from now, when I've fully found myself again, shaken Chad all the way off, learned to stand up to my mother and taught her how to listen to me when I tell her what I want and need, even when she doesn't understand it.

"Is someone listening?" I whisper. "Are there more camera people hiding in the woods?"

He flinches.

And I freeze. "Oh."

"Begonia. No." He grips my hand. "The photographers on Oysterberry Bay—I apologize. I don't—you are correct. I don't trust easily, and I thought it necessary. But here, we're alone. You have my word. This is not for the world. This is for *me*. And, I hope, you."

We're alone. For me.

"I enjoy you too," I whisper.

"You shouldn't. I'm very disagreeable."

I put a finger to his lips.

He captures that hand too, and he pulls it to his mouth, pressing soft kisses to my finger, turning my hand to kiss my knuckles, then turning it again to kiss my palm, my wrist, and up my forearm to the crook of my elbow, holding my gaze in the moonlight and making me feel not like the last woman in the world, but like the only woman in *his* world.

"Hayes," I whisper.

"I would very much like to make love to you under the moonlight, Ms. Fairchild."

My heart tumbles out of my chest and offers itself to him on a clay platter. It's not fancy. Not diamond-encrusted. Not even very pretty sometimes.

But it's what I have, and it's his for the taking.

Even though I know better.

"With my eyes open," he continues, still pressing soft kisses to the bare flesh on my arm, his eyes still holding me captive, "fully aware that I'm with *you*, with you fully aware that you're with *me*."

Butterflies swirl to life in my chest.

This could be a massive mistake. I know better than to get attached right now. And while my brain says this is temporary, my heart says *too late*.

But what's life if not for living? "No fires tonight," I whisper.

His eyes rake over me in the moonlight. "On the contrary, I hope to set you on fire."

Well, then.

My panties won't be in the way. They've self-ignited in a

cloud of *poof*, floating away into the night. My breasts tingle. My vagina aches.

I want him. Naked or in a suit, though this tieless, shoeless, top two buttons of his dress shirt undone thing is exceptionally attractive.

He brushes his thumb over my jawline, shifting on the ground and making my dog grunt between us. "Move, Marshmallow."

The poor pup grunts again.

"I'm going to do unspeakably filthy things to your mother," Hayes informs him, his hand moving to stroke my thigh.

Marshmallow whimpers softly and slinks away, and now I'm laughing.

I'm so turned on I can't think, and I'm laughing.

But only briefly, because the tiger formerly known as Hayes is pouncing, expertly sliding his hands under my shirt and pulling it over my head as he lowers me to the thick, plush blanket.

I part my legs, and he settles between them, the hard ridge of his erection pressing against my center through our clothes, his mouth capturing mine, his hands sliding beneath me while I blindly tackle the buttons on his dress shirt.

My bra suddenly goes loose, the cool air enveloping me a stark contrast to the heat in his gaze and his touch. He tugs one strap down my arm, his fingertips trailing over my skin and stirring my nerve endings like a sandy wind on a warm tropical morning.

I love being touched.

And kissed.

And adored.

I even love that I'm so clumsy right now that I can't get Hayes's shirt buttons undone.

The way he's teasing and licking and nipping at my neck is driving me wild, and I finally give up and yank, sending his buttons flying.

He chuckles into the crook of my neck as his thick, heavy length pulses against me. "Just when I thought you couldn't possibly get any more attractive, bluebell..."

"Want me to do the same to your pants?"

"Yes."

"Are you adding this to my bill?"

"Payable in sexual favors. Where is that sweet nipple I found yesterday? I miss it. Ah. Here it is."

He sucks on the tip of my breast, and the world explodes in song and rainbows around me.

I'm so wet I've soaked through my leggings. The cotton of his undershirt brushes my bare belly, heat radiating off his long, solid body, and I surrender.

There's no history.

No complications.

No questions.

Just *us*.

With him worshipping my breasts while I tug his undershirt over his head and off one arm, then take shaky, overzealous hands to his belt buckle.

He sucks in a short breath, his belly quivering beneath the backs of my hands. "Your fingers are exquisite."

"Your body is extis—etiquette—*oh my god*, I can't talk when I'm this horny."

He chuckles again, his mouth and chest vibrating against me while the moon smiles down on us. "More practice, Begaaaaaa*aaaaaah*..."

I smile and stroke his hard cock again, fisting it in one hand beneath his boxers. "You were saying?"

"D-don't ss-stop."

He has nothing to worry about.

His cock is *exquisite*. Thick and long, hot and silky-smooth, with a wide, blunt tip. "I want to taste you."

He shoves one side of my leggings down. "I want to be inside you."

"I'll rock-paper-scissors you for who's in charge."

God, he has the best laugh. It's like the hills and the river are singing, and it's making me even wetter.

"No negotiations, Ms. *Oh, fuck yes*. Begonia. *Fuck*. No rock p-paper—keep your hands—*yes*."

He buries his head in the crook of my neck, his breath coming short and fast, hips jerking, while I tease his length with my hands, pushing his pants out of the way and cradling his testicles too.

"I love how you feel," I whisper.

He slaps the ground blindly until his hand connects with the picnic basket, and he sends it tumbling, food and all.

I pause. "Hayes?"

"Condom. Inside you. Now."

I can't remember the last time I felt so wanted. So *needed*.

So adored for being me.

Even if it's not real, I intend to treasure tonight for the rest of my life.

I squirm beneath him. "Let me help."

"Got it. You. Strip. For me."

His commanding tone sets my skin on fire and makes my vagina throb. "You like me naked."

"I *need* you naked. I've needed you naked with me all fucking day."

I'm wriggling out of my leggings as fast as I can while he rips open a condom, kneeling back on his heels, his eyes trained on me and my desperate yanking.

"I love when you say *fuck*." I'm breathless and wheezy. Totally not sexy, but his cock is bobbing in the moonlight as he steadies it and rolls the condom down, and the sight of him makes me so wet that my thighs are slick. "It's so improper."

"I intend to fuck you until you can't walk."

"*Yes*." I smell my own arousal as I finally yank my leggings off and reach for him, twisting until we're both on our sides, facing each other on the plush blanket, his erection nudging my clit and making me moan.

Quiet, Begonia, the neighbors will hear.

No.

No.

I shove the old memories out as Hayes kisses me again, his tongue sliding into my mouth with a ragged groan from the back of his throat.

Is he this eager with everyone?

Or is it me?

Shut up, Begonia.

His fingers slip between my thighs, stroking my wet core and teasing my clit, and then I'm on my back, and that's not his fingers anymore. "I want you *now*," he says against my lips.

I tilt my hips, offering all of me to him, my hands gripping his hair. "*Yes.*"

"Slow next time."

"*Yes.*"

He slides inside me, filling and stretching me, and we both groan-sigh together.

"Heaven," he breathes, thrusting into me again while I arch my hips to meet him.

"More," I whimper.

"So tight."

"So hard."

"So fucking *good.*"

He hits that magic spot inside me, and I cry out. "*There,* Hayes. Oh my god, *there.*"

"Louder, Begonia. Scream for me."

"You… feel… so *good.*"

He's a wild animal, completely unleashed, bucking his hips and slamming into me, hitting that sweet spot with every stroke, making my nerve endings tight and deliciously anxious as my release builds inside me, everything tightening and coiling inside me.

"Begonia," Hayes gasps. "Bluebell, I'm so fucking close. Baby, I need you to come. Come all over my cock."

And that's all it takes.

I cry his name as my release washes over me, throbbing and pulsing and squeezing him while he stills, his neck straining, his eyes locked on mine, lips parted while he groans through his own orgasm.

"Begonia," he pants.

I can't speak.

I'm babbling incoherently, my words drifting away into the cool night air while I ride wave after wave of my climax.

It's like my body has been saving up for this for *years*.

And it probably has.

Hayes collapses on top of me, his breath tickling my neck, before the last tremors of my orgasm have finished sending shivers through my body. I stretch my toes, let my legs fall more open, and my arms collapse to the ground too.

And then I giggle.

"Dear god, you're going to murder me with sex, aren't you?" Hayes murmurs.

"Can we do that again?"

"Correction: You would murder me with denying me sex. I would die of blue balls."

I snort-laugh.

He sucks in a breath, his body going still, and I realize my vagina is squeezing his spent cock.

I love this moment.

I'm so very vulnerable. Physically. Mentally. Emotionally.

But also safe.

I know to the deepest parts of me that while this may only be a side benefit of our arrangement, Hayes won't hurt me.

Not on purpose.

I trust him.

He lets me be *me*.

"Are you hungry?" I murmur into his hair as I find the strength to run my fingers through it once more.

He settles his head deeper onto my shoulder. "No," he murmurs. "I'm too content to be hungry." He kisses my collarbone. "Begonia?"

"Hmm?"

"Thank you for being you."

My eyes go hot, and I blink the sensation away as quickly as I can.

This might not be permanent, but it's good, if only to show me what I truly want in a relationship.

To show me what relationships *can* be.

And I will *never* settle for anything less again.

26

Hayes

FOR THE SECOND NIGHT IN A ROW, MY DINNER TASTES AS THOUGH it's been sprinkled with fairy dust and dipped in flavors newly fallen from the heavens.

It's a simple charcuterie picnic, with cheeses and prosciutto and capicola, grapes and figs, honeycomb and cornichons, crackers and dipping sauces.

But it tastes better for watching Begonia enjoy it.

Correction.

It tastes better for helping a very naked Begonia enjoy it.

"What kind of cheese is this?" she asks, leaning over to hold a cube to my mouth.

I eat it off her fingers and chew slowly while she watches me. "No idea. I need another."

I'd swear her smile blossoms from the depths of her soul. It's so wide, uninhibited, and joyful—so very *Begonia*. "Mr. Rutherford, are you trying to get me to feed you again?"

I offer her a fig, which she eats off *my* fingers. "What good is it to have a Greek painting brought to life if she doesn't let me lie with my head in her lap and feed me grapes off the vine?"

"I am *not* a Greek painting."

"Correct. You're much lovelier."

She scoots closer, her bare chest brushing mine as we recline on the blanket in the comfortable summer evening, and she dangles another cube of cheese over my lips. "You may have another sample, but not until you tell me if you've ever camped."

"Like this?"

"No, like in a tent in the woods, roasting hot dogs and marshmallows over the fire and telling ghost stories until you can't sleep because every raccoon or squirrel sounds like *the claw* coming to get you."

"Not recently."

She laughs, free and easy, and I tug her closer to kiss that sweet mouth.

I can't remember the last time I felt free to laugh about the little things.

Or the last time I wanted to.

But she makes me want to smile. And laugh. And sleep outdoors in the light of the moon, wrapped in a blanket with a woman who's asked for so very little and given so very much.

"You've slept outdoors often?" I ask her.

"When I was little, Hyacinth and I used to sleep wherever we got tired when we were running around our Dad's camp all summer long. We woke up once in a canoe."

"On the water?"

"I swore a blood oath to Hy that I'd never, ever, ever reveal more details than that."

I chuckle. "And did you weave your secrets into friend-ship bracelets?"

"We did! And we made candles and tie-dyed T-shirts and that's the first place I ever used a pottery wheel."

"At your father's camp?"

She feeds me a bite of prosciutto as she nods. "He had the most adorable art hut. Every summer after Mom and Dad divorced, we'd spend it out at Camp Funshine. And the minute Mom let us out of the car, Hy would race for the archery range or the ropes course, and I'd dash off in the other direction for the art hut."

Camp Funshine. Of course. It couldn't have been named anything else. "You miss it?"

"Dad gave *so* many kids the best memories of their summers, and we met so many kids from all over the world. There was this girl I met from—oh my gosh, you know what? I can't start, because if I start telling you about all of the people I met there, I would literally never stop."

I smile. That's pure Begonia. "Have you been back as an adult?"

"No. The people who bought it when Dad declared bankruptcy *just* wanted the land. And the lake. And the stables. It's—it's not what it used to be."

There's a sadness in her voice that makes me want to slay dragons. Begonia Fairchild was not born to be *sad*. She was born to make instant best friends at summer sleepaway camp, to leap head-first into any adventure that comes her way, and to lie here with me, naked beneath the summer moon, eating a charcuterie picnic while I wonder what on earth I could ever offer this magical creature to entice her to stay as long as possible.

Somehow in the past two weeks, she's gone from the world's largest inconvenience to my reminder that the world is a place of joy.

"Your father declared bankruptcy." The words leave my mouth, and I cringe.

But Begonia laughs, as if she understands where I was

going. "Yes. It wasn't pleasant, but he survived. I mean, not long, but it wasn't… It wasn't bankruptcy that killed him. That was an accident."

"You weren't terrified at all when I threatened to sue you."

Her cheeky grin flashes in the moonlight. "I would've been sad if you'd followed through and I had to raise funds by putting my great-grandma Eileen's old dildo collection on eBay to afford my own legal fees, but yes, I know I would've survived."

"I'm quite the asshole."

"Hayes. You found *a total stranger* making a disaster of your house."

I grunt and reach for a grape to feed her. "That turned out far better than I expected."

"And look at us now," she agrees.

Look at us now, indeed. "Do you still enjoy camping?"

"I used to, but then—well, then I grew up and did what I thought grown-ups should do, which is dumb, isn't it? Why can't grown-ups have fun too?"

"Are you not having fun tonight, Begonia?"

She wriggles against me, making my cock go harder than it has any right to be given how thoroughly I climaxed not fifteen minutes ago.

And because I've been spending so much time around Begonia, I have an irrational desire to high-five myself for it.

She's not rich. Newly divorced. With her entire plans for her time off thrown into disarray through no fault of her own.

Yet she's the most joyful woman I've ever met, as if she believes the world is made of rainbows and that each experience, from waking up in the morning to having a picnic on the beach, is to be savored.

She's the sun, and I've become a single blade of grass basking in her presence.

She tips the cheese into my mouth, and then she's talking again, her voice washing over me. "I'm having the *best* time.

Do you know what? Summer camp should be a thing for grown-ups too. We should get to play and have fun and let someone else make us cafeteria food after we spend the morning canoeing and swimming and horseback riding, and then get to have grown-up time afterwards."

"You've just described Rutherford family reunions, but without the horrors of cafeteria food, and I honestly don't want to know which of my relatives are engaging in *grown-up* time."

"Did you go to summer camp as a kid? The traditional kind where you sleep away from your parents for a week or more at a time?"

I offer her a bite of brie brushed with honey. "Every summer from six to sixteen, but it was crew—rowing—camp, or lacrosse camp, or math camp, or college application prep camp."

"Did you shoot bows and arrows?"

"No."

"Paddleboard on the lake?"

"No."

"Eat s'mores around the campfire?"

"We had crème brûlée and chocolate lava cakes catered by Michelin-level chefs while we sat around getting lectures about how to apply for college."

She gasps. "Had you *never* had a s'more before our campfire picnic in Maine?"

I crack a grin. Can't help it. "How many Razzle Dazzle films have you seen, bluebell?"

"At least four hundred thirty-seven. I was watching them before Jonas started getting starring roles. I miss the days when Hank Houseman was your main lead. He was too old for me to be attracted to, but I couldn't help myself. Just *shew*."

I roll and pin her beneath me. "How many of those four

hundred thirty-seven Razzle Dazzle films had campfire scenes?"

She purses her lips, and it's nearly impossible to not kiss them.

But I want the reward.

I want to watch the light dawn.

It is *never* disappointing.

And when her eyes go round and her lips part, and then she throws her head back and laughs—*that* is everything.

"Are you telling me lies?" she asks. "*College application prep camp?* You are! You're making that up, and you've had s'mores, and you *did* go to traditional summer sleepaway camp."

"I believe it's called *teasing* when done in the midst of flirting."

"You are the most adorable flirter ever."

"*Adorable?*"

She nods solemnly. "*So* adorable."

I grunt.

Her eyes twinkle and that smile flashes over her face, and she's done it again.

One more point to Begonia for bringing a ray of sunshine into the darkness.

Many more, and I will *not* recover when she leaves.

"Maybe I should show you *adorable*." I tilt my lips to her neck, and her squeal turns into a soft sigh.

"More," she whispers.

More.

I've always wanted *more* too, but my *more* was always solitude, a good biography, an afternoon to work on calculus problems for fun, sometimes cheesecake, sometimes a game of chess with Uncle Antonio or my father.

Now, I want more Begonia.

And I intend to have her as often as I can until this summer is over.

235

27

Begonia

THERE'S NOTHING QUITE LIKE WAKING UP BUCK NAKED IN THE morning light with your fake boyfriend-slash-lover's cousin standing over you. "Did you save some charcuterie for the squirrels and the birds, or did you do something super kinky with it?" Keisha asks.

Hayes grunts, rolls, and throws the picnic blanket over both of our bare bodies. "Go away."

"Your mother's looking for you. Something about the dog and a movie script she was supposed to be evaluating."

I freeze.

"Ignore her," Hayes tells me. "My mother doesn't evaluate movie scripts. Not to say your dog didn't attempt to help her with her perfume, but Marshmallow would not be stealing important paperwork."

Keisha grins. "Nice tattoo, B."

I freeze harder.

Hayes twists a look at me and frowns, and it doesn't take a genius to read his expression. *You have a tattoo?*

"Go away, Keisha, or I'll tell Millie what you do with your drummer when you're on tour," he says, still looking at me like he's silently demanding to know where I have a tattoo and why he hasn't seen it yet.

She gasps. "You *wouldn't*."

"Oh my god, are you cheating?" I cringe and close my eyes. "I don't want to know. No. I don't. Don't ruin this."

"Yes, she's cheating. And her version of *cheating* is three am runs to Baskin-Robbins," Hayes murmurs to me. "She's diabetic, and Millie worries."

"*Shut up*," Keisha squeals.

"It's nothing to be embarrassed about, dear cousin," Hayes says.

"I'm not embarrassed. I don't want to have a fight with Millie if she hears you talking smack and spilling my secrets. And I can have ice cream. *I can*. She overreacts to everything because she loves me so much."

My dog.

My dog.

I jerk my head up, looking around, and I groan.

"Relax, B," Keisha says. "Marshmallow's inside. Françoise has him. She's almost as good with him as Hayes."

Hayes glances at me, the furrowed brow turning into resigned realization. "He took our clothing, didn't he?" he murmurs.

Keisha cackles. "It's *aaaaall* over the downstairs. He took Begonia's bra in to your father, and your mom has your boxers. My dad got the strip of condoms. It's too bad Liliane left, or maybe she could've gotten your tie and Begonia's panties. This is like, the best morning ever."

"How is it I still like her even when she's evil?" I ask Hayes.

He's giving her the growly eye. "I have no idea. I'm not suffering from the same affliction."

She rocks back on her heels, and I realize she's in plain black leggings, which feels almost too bland for Keisha, though her cropped pink sweater is so fluffy, it seems to be made out of cotton candy. "Robert's coming with clothes for both of you," she tells us. "But it was just too fun to catch you sleeping outside naked like randy teenagers."

"Good. I'll have him throw you out." Hayes's hand shifts under the blanket, gripping my hip while his thumb brushes my hip bone, and I wonder how long Robert will take.

Do I have time to sneak under the covers and enjoy an early breakfast?

"But where would I go?" Keisha asks. "You know Millie's allergic to South Carolina this time of year, so that house is out. There's a chance of wildfires out west, so those two houses are out. If I head into the city, I'll eat cheesecake all day, so that's out…"

"Antarctica," Hayes replies.

I shift under the covers, rubbing my pelvis against Hayes's bare body, and his cock immediately stiffens against me.

"Begonia, have you ever seen a K-drama?" Keisha asks. "We should totes have a girls morning and you can explain to me why penises are worth it."

"Don't you have work to do?" Hayes grumbles.

"No one works on a forced sabbatical." She wrinkles her nose, and Hayes cringes, like he's sorry he brought it up.

"Why are you on sabbatical?" I ask.

"Do you know the *best* thing about being a distant Rutherford relative? They seriously cover up some shit. And I like you, B, but I'm not telling."

"Understandable. If you want to talk, though, I'm around."

Hayes scowls at her. "You have three seconds to leave

before I treat you to a full frontal and chase you back to the house *and* tell Begonia all of your secrets. You told her mine. I'll happily spill yours."

She hesitates, but barely. "Fine. I'm going. Come find me for breakfast, Begonia. I want to know how you got that awesome hair color."

And when she actually traipses away, I frown at Hayes. "Have you chased her naked before?"

"No, but she believes I'd do it. That's enough."

"Such a terrible threat, Mr. Rutherford."

Keisha doesn't matter. Marshmallow doesn't matter. Being naked at the edge of a forest without my clothes doesn't matter.

Hayes matters.

And a ruffled but smiling Hayes Rutherford with his cheeks and chin painted with scruff, his hair a tousled, bedheaded mess, and sleepy eyes slowly waking up, might be my favorite version of him.

"It was you or me, and she already has the advantage of seeing some mystery tattoo that I have yet to discover on your body. I have no intention of letting her see it more before I do."

I smile back at him. "You didn't look closely enough in Maine."

"I was quite unaware of who I'd found in Maine."

"And you were tired and cranky and expecting an empty house."

He tilts his head into the crook of my neck again and sighs. "I'm tired of being tired and cranky," he murmurs.

"Are you tired and cranky right now?"

"I'm far more content than I trust."

I run my fingers through his hair and wiggle my hips, enjoying the feel of his rapidly hardening erection against my belly. I can't imagine how vulnerable he must feel to confess that out loud. "Don't question it. Just let yourself have it."

"Begonia, I—"

"Your clothes, Mr. Rutherford," Robert says from nearby. "Merriweather called and reported you've been requested for interviews with several news networks this morning."

I sigh. It's involuntary, and I wish I could stop it, but I can't.

I've been here too many times. *Sorry, Begonia, but if I don't go to my job, I don't get paid. We'll have a glass of wine together tonight.*

Hayes sighs too, and his sigh feels more weary to me than any of my own could ever be. "Why did Merriweather call you?"

"I located your phone in the freezer, sir," Robert replies, which I guess is as solid an answer as anything else would be.

Hayes makes a noise.

I cringe. *Marshmallow.*

"Is that the weirdest place you've ever found a phone?" I ask Robert.

Hayes makes another noise, but it's not like the noises he made when I first met him.

This sounds *far* more amused.

"Today, ma'am," he replies.

"Nikolay would've told me."

Robert doesn't answer. He's somehow staring at me as if I'm breaking some kind of unspoken rule about speaking to billionaires' bodyguards while not actually looking at me, as if he doesn't want to get caught gawking at his boss and his boss's lady friend hiding their naked bits under a picnic blanket.

"We'll be back at the house in fifteen minutes, Robert," Hayes says.

"Certainly, sir. But as a matter of note, your father's requested a video conference over breakfast."

I frown. "Aren't your parents here? I thought Marshmallow took them our clothes."

"We're an early-rising, early-working, early-traveling family," Hayes replies. "Also, never trust Keisha."

"Unless you're broke and lost in Amsterdam," Robert murmurs.

"Or facing down a gang of kangaroos outside Sydney," Hayes agrees. "Fifteen minutes, Robert."

"Yes, sir."

"Thank you for the clothes," I call after him as he heads back toward the house.

Hayes tilts his pelvis, pressing his hard length more firmly against my belly. "I'm quite irritated that your dog stole my condoms. And I would very much like to have been the first person in my family to have studied this tattoo of yours."

I reach between us, wrapping my fingers around his cock. "Guess I'll have to make that up to you."

His eyes slide shut as I find the space and the angle to stroke him.

"Begonia?"

"Yes, Hayes?"

"I will never forget this moment."

My heart warms even as fear dances at the edges of the glow.

I won't either.

And I'm afraid it will be over too soon, but not soon enough to keep me from completely falling.

28

Hayes

I'M DEEP IN DISCUSSION IN MY OFFICE WITH MY BROTHER'S favorite jeweler Thursday afternoon, a couple days after the night in the meadow, when Merriweather knocks on my door. "Mrs. Werenski, Mr. Rutherford."

A brown-haired, round-cheeked, very pregnant Begonia strolls through the door.

And I nearly fall out of my seat.

I know this isn't Begonia. I know this woman is her twin. I've *seen* this woman before, talked with her over video even.

But I had no idea the woman was about to pop, and the sight of a woman who looks so very similar to Begonia carrying a child makes something primal and instinctive and possessive spring to life deep inside me.

I know better. I do.

"Don't make that face," Hyacinth says, though she's not nearly as cheeky as she was on the phone. Her eyes are a bit too wide as she looks around my office and soaks it all in.

"Third pregnancies always make you look like you could deliver any minute from the fifth month on. So. Are you making an honest woman of my sister, or what?"

Merriweather's lips twitch. "Good luck, Mr. Rutherford." She pulls the door shut behind her, leaving me alone with Begonia's twin, Evan the jeweler, and a velvet box of rare diamonds.

I rise and cross the room to kiss her cheek. "Hyacinth. Thank you for coming."

"Oh, you *are* fancy. Are you sure you're in love with my sister? She's as anti-fancy as they get."

"All the more reason to adore her."

Evan clears his throat.

"Hyacinth, meet Mr. Sirotkin. We're hoping you could help us narrow down choices for a surprise for your sister."

"Are those diamonds?"

"Yes, Mrs. Werenski."

"Like, that *whole thing* is a diamond? All of those whole things are diamonds?"

She gestures to the velvet display box lined with two dozen of the best diamonds in North America.

Evan's face doesn't move.

I nod to Hyacinth. "Yes."

She eyes Evan, then me, then Evan, then me again. "I'm trying to decide if I should ask how well you know my sister, or how badly you fucked up."

Not that I had any doubts that this woman is Begonia's twin, but every word out of her mouth is further confirmation that I'm doing the right—and the wrong—things.

She knows her sister better than I do, yet I know Begonia well enough at this point to not be offended by her statement.

"Evan, could you give us a moment?" I ask.

"Shall I leave the jewels?"

"Only if he's buying them for someone else," Hyacinth quips.

I nod, indicating he should take the diamonds with him.

"Your mother's birthday is coming up," he muses as he closes the box.

"Jonas drew the short end of the stick this year. He'll be in touch."

Hyacinth's jaw goes slack. "I keep forgetting you're Jonas Rutherford's brother. Can I touch you again? Maybe have a lick in absentia?"

"No."

"*Phew*. Thank you. If you can be a little more dickish like that, it'll help."

The door clicks shut behind Evan, who's paid too well by my family to breathe a word of anything he just heard, and Hyacinth peers around the room again. "Is this place bugged?"

"No."

"Will Begonia get in trouble with you if I ask rude questions?"

"Your sister could talk her way out of a murder conviction if she were caught holding a bloody knife over the victim. If the police don't stand a chance, I fail to see how I do."

"Because she wouldn't have done it. There would be a logical explanation. Probably that her dog did it, but he was justified."

My lips twitch.

"*Oh my god*, you almost smiled." Her voice drops to a whisper. "Are you seriously dating my sister, or are you blackmailing her with something, or is she doing you a favor? What's going on here? This has *all* the makings of a Razzle Dazzle movie, and Begonia is totally lying to me about *something*, probably a lot of things, and I'm pretty sure you're banging her, but that doesn't mean anything beyond that she's getting some nookie post-divorce so she can get back on that horse for real again soon. I mean, if you're not for real."

I settle onto the edge of my desk and lift my brows at her. "Are you finished?"

"No. Not even close. Is Jonas's marriage real, or was that staged for someone's reputation rehab, because Peyton Baker? *Really?* And if you two were the *two* last eligible male billionaires left on the planet, that would almost be too much, you know? And totally unfair to you, because he'd get all the attention, but then, he always does, doesn't he? It's like I always thought Begonia would resent me for getting all the attention, but she's just so *nice*, and she didn't care that I got to play Annie in the school play and she was stuck in the chorus, because she's always—*oof.*"

Hyacinth bends at the waist and grabs her stomach.

I leap to my feet. "Are you in labor?"

"No, the little bastard just kicked me in the ribs. He doesn't like it when I talk too much." She lifts a finger. "*Do not* say a word. I've heard it all already."

I pinch my lips together, incredibly grateful it was Begonia and not Hyacinth that I found in my hideaway in Maine.

She waves a hand at me. "Your turn. Spill your guts. Why are you dating my sister?"

"She's disarmingly attractive, inside and out, and I can't seem to help myself."

"Did you really make her sign a non-disclosure agreement?"

"I made *you* sign a non-disclosure agreement."

"Yeah, but you're not dating me. You're just tormenting me by not answering my questions after flying me up here on a fancy jet because you thought it would be a nice surprise for my sister."

She has a valid point.

But I still don't answer her question.

She narrows her green eyes at me. "Are you going to hurt Begonia?"

"I will do all in my power to save her any grief, which is

unfortunately easier said than done in my world. But I still promise to go above and beyond to protect her."

That part is undeniably true.

The last time I was with a woman who made me want to crawl across the bed in the middle of the night, wake her with kisses, and make love to her until dawn, she crushed my heart so thoroughly that I haven't honestly let myself be real with anyone since.

She wasn't the first.

She was simply the last. I dated after her, but I never fully let my guard down with anyone.

For years, I've told myself my lack of interest was because my standards were too high, the media attention was too much of a bother, and that I prefer my solitude to the complications that go with relationships.

But it's not entirely true.

Partially true, yes.

But fear—fear has been a major factor for most of my adult life.

Fear and denial.

And now Begonia has brought back to life a part of myself that I'd sworn to bury forever while pretending love and companionship were overrated.

The worst part?

I've missed that part of me, that part that connected with people, that enjoyed people.

I didn't truly understand how lonely I was until Thomas died, and even then, it took Begonia charging through my walls for me to realize I *want* to trust someone again. I don't want to go through the rest of my life regretting not spending time with the people I'll miss when they're gone, and I don't want to go through the rest of my life avoiding pain to the point of sheer loneliness.

Begonia signed our contract extension this morning, but

all the while, I couldn't help but wonder how I might manage to keep her past the summer.

I know the easy answer.

Ask her.

But the easy answer requires a leap of faith I'm not ready to take.

It would require me to let her all the way in.

To fully trust her.

To be worthy of having her trust in return.

And that means not hurting her.

If I can avoid it.

"Do I really get to see her as part of this trip?" Hyacinth asks.

"Naturally. She needs a new dress for a charity gala in the city tomorrow. I assumed you'd be her preferred shopping companion."

"Can I go to the gala?"

"The Rutherfords are known for *not* making scenes."

She cackles, and I know I'm toast.

Begonia will ask, I'll say *of course, my love*, because that's what a doting boyfriend would say, and tomorrow night, my fake girlfriend's twin sister will stuff her bra with cocktail shrimp, drink too many virgin mojitos, pretend to be drunk, and tell the wrong reporter that she thinks we're faking this relationship.

Or so I presume, having met both twins now.

And then I'll have every reason I need to take Begonia on a romantic getaway, where I'll be caught on camera slipping a ring onto her finger, as we contractually agreed to this morning.

I have *zero* desire to hurt her.

I just want to keep her.

For as long as possible.

29

Begonia

I'M CURSING AT A LUMPY, WET CLAY CUP THAT'S FLOPPING ABOUT on the pottery wheel like a flaccid penis on a naked old man riding the tilt-a-whirl wrong, considering if I can blame the lump in my stomach after signing that agreement with Hayes this morning for my poor art skills, when the door to my art studio opens.

"*Don't let Marshmallow in!*" I shriek.

"*Oh my god, you still make penis art!*" Hyacinth shrieks back.

I gasp, blink, gasp again, and then I leap to my feet, all thoughts of my pending fake engagement fleeing my brain. I hurdle the spinning pottery wheel, and dive toward my sister.

My sister.

What is *my sister* doing here? "Look at your belly! I have to hug him!"

"Your hands!"

"Washing machine! Showers! You should see the showers here!" I kiss her belly. I smother her in a hug. I pet her hair. All with hands coated in goopy water. "You're *here*!"

"Oh, B." She's laughing as she hugs me back, the two of us swaying back and forth and hugging and swaying and possibly crying. "I think you just got clay in my mouth."

"There's toothpaste! And spare toothbrushes! That's fixable! What are you doing here?"

"Hayes said you missed me so he sent a fucking private jet to get me and a private nanny to stay behind with my kids and we're going to the spa and taking you shopping for a new fucking dress and *what did you do and how did you meet this man and does he have a secret twin? I don't want another* husband, but I could totally do with a rich lover who buys me fancy dresses and takes me to fancy balls. *Oh my god*, Begonia. Just *oh my god*."

"You can't go to the ball! Rutherfords don't make scenes."

She cracks up.

I crack up.

And I can't stop hugging her.

Not until she *oof*s and shoves me away, squatting and rubbing her belly.

"Aww, did he kick?"

"He does *not* like it when I talk too much." She blows out a breath. "I'm not having a baby this time. I'm having a demon spawn. I know I called Dani a demon spawn when I was pregnant with her too, but I think I mean it this time."

"Oh my god, there are *two* of you?" Keisha's in the doorway, in a feathered jumpsuit today—bright neon blue feathers, for the record—and she's clinging to Marshmallow's leash as he tries to get to Hyacinth.

Or me.

Or the clay.

"The clay!" I shriek.

I let Hyacinth go to leap back across the room and kill the power to the pottery wheel.

"Oh my god, you're Keisha Kourtney," Hyacinth whispers.

"Is that some kind of weird smeared penis art?" Keisha says. "Dude. I do *not* understand straight women."

"It's a cup," I reply.

Though, as I stare down at the stopped wheel, it does not, in fact, look like a cup.

It looks like a semi-flattened crooked penis that needs to see a doctor.

"I'm not the greatest with pottery, but I love how it feels in my hands," I confess.

"That's cool, but if that's also how you treat Hayes's penis, I don't want to know, okay? Oh, hello. Didn't know we were doing the touching thing, but it's cool."

"You're real." Hyacinth pokes Keisha in the feathered arm again. "You're not some kind of mirage or hologram."

"Keisha, this is Hyacinth. She's my twin sister."

"And here I thought she was your illegitimate love child with yourself."

I tilt my head. "Are you and Millie fighting?"

She glares. "No. Yes. Maybe. Do you know your dog weighs more than I do and he's trying very hard to get in there to eat your clay penis and a little *thank you, Keisha, goddess of the sky and feathers and felines* would totally be in order here right about now."

"Marshmallow. Go catch a butterfly," Hyacinth orders.

Marshmallow plops back on his haunches and grins a doggie grin at her.

"Why didn't that work?" Hy whispers.

"He only takes orders from Hayes now. Or sometimes from the chef. Watch this. Marshmallow! Who wants a steak? Who's a good boy who wants a steak?"

My dog tilts his head at me like I'm speaking bear to a

penguin, then lifts a paw to flick at the door handle on the art room like he wants to look behind it and see if Hayes is hiding there to play.

"Why's he on a leash?" I ask Keisha.

"I offered to take him for a walk, but the only place he wants to go is upstairs to check on the progress in the bedroom. And god knows if Hayes wants that room finished, he should probably let the dog pick the decorations. Damn man won't make a decision, and I've had it *up to here* with Aunt Gio telling me I'm wrong about what he'd like. Hayes would *love* a disco ball in his bedroom, and *I paid for it*, so what's the big deal?"

I wipe my hands and give her a sympathetic smile while I ignore her comments on the disco ball. "What's up with you and Millie?"

"She says I'm overdramatic. Can you believe that? I literally get paid to be dramatic. Sometimes I have to overdo it to stay current. And we're touching the feathers again. Honey, I can afford a new jumpsuit, but you're filthy, and it takes about six months to have every one of these sewn on by hand, so can you maybe wait for the touching until I'm back in silk or glitter polyester?"

"Sorry." Hyacinth snatches her hand back from Keisha's outfit again, but she still keeps staring. "You're just so…real."

"Hy, where's Hayes?" I ask.

"At the office. *He put me in a helicopter*. And this big scary guy stared at me the whole time."

"Probably thought you were gonna pull a Marshmallow and try to open the door mid-flight," Keisha says. "Are you both ready to hit the spa? Millie hates the spa, and I have to let her stew while she thinks I'm stewing too. I'll send her a new Porsche and it'll all blow over—she can't resist a good Porsche—but right now, I need someone wrapping my body in seaweed and telling me my pores are gorgeous."

"If Françoise has any seaweed in the kitchen, I could do it

for you," I offer. "I have good clay for masks, and your pores *are* gorgeous."

Keisha's face goes three shades past horrified. "Begonia, I like you a lot, but suggesting DIY spa days in these parts of the social ecosphere is like asking me if I know who Elvis Presley is. You don't ask, because *you just know* the answer."

I grin.

Hyacinth makes a noise that might be a laugh or it might be *don't anger the scary short celebrity by smiling at her when she's having a shit fit.*

And after a long beat, Keisha breaks into laughter. "Oh my god, I'm so glad Hayes finally found someone with a sense of humor. C'mon, ladies. Don't even bother getting changed. The spa will have robes for all of us. You. Begonia's twin. You're gonna have to leave your phone at home because I don't trust you yet. No pictures. Maybe later if you quit gaping at me like that. Nikolay! Nikolay, we need the chopper, please. And Marshmallow needs a babysitter."

Hyacinth makes a face.

"Down the hall, first door on your right," I tell her.

"Stupid pregnancy. I don't know if I can get a spa treatment without having to pee."

Keisha pats her arm. "Sweetie, we only go places where you could literally shit on the table and no one would blink. Don't shit on the table if you can help it, but for real—they can handle it if you need to pause mid-body wrap to take a piss."

Hyacinth waddles down the hallway to the bathroom. Keisha disappears with an order for me to wash my hands and meet her at the helipad in twenty minutes, or she's going without us.

And I take a chance and dial Hayes. I'm planning on leaving him a voicemail, but instead, I get the man himself.

"Good afternoon, Begonia. Having fun today?"

Goosebumps break out on my arms at the sound of his

warm voice. He woke me early this morning after keeping me up late last night, and I can honestly say my body has never been more satisfied. "You brought me Hyacinth."

"You seemed to be missing her."

"I—I was. Thank you."

"My pleasure."

Dammit. My eyes are getting hot again. Chad used to complain about how much time I spent with my sister, even though I never felt like it was enough. And here the man who wants me to agree to fake being engaged to him just *does* it, despite how little time we've known each other. "I don't think I can explain how much this means to me."

"No need, bluebell. Just enjoy your time."

How is it possible that the sweetest man on the entire planet is hiding under that grumpy exterior?

It's a good thing we're having sex now.

I don't know if I could thank him properly with anything less.

"B, you wash up yet?" Keisha calls.

An hour later, we're touching down in New York City.

I text a selfie with Hyacinth and the skyline to Hayes. *OMG! I can see the Empire State Building! Is there anything I should know about spa days and shopping with Keisha?*

He's working, so I don't expect an immediate answer, but I get one anyway. *Tell her to use my credit card and have fun. Follow her lead and don't talk to anyone she says to not talk to. But mostly, have fun.*

We do.

It's limousines and hours of spa treatments at what Keisha tells us is a *secret spa*. But I recognize the name. *Silver Crocus* was the brand of lotion Hayes had at his house in Maine, and the Silver Crocus logo on the spa's front door matches.

This spa is so classy that I'm pretty sure I'm lowering its reputation just by setting foot inside the door. Everything smells like eucalyptus and lavender, the floor is marble, the walls a deep burgundy damask—*to absorb light and sound*, Keisha says—and the light fixtures flicker like candles, even though they're modern bulbs. The orchids, lilies, and crocuses are real, displayed in real crystal vases, and the sheets are smooth as silk, and the towels are fluffy and perfect.

I get my hair touched up so that it glows even brighter, and Hyacinth and I have a couples massage where she only has to get up and pee once. Then there's a body scrub. All three of us have facials in the same room while we're getting pedicures and manicures.

"Usually they'd be separate treatments, but we're on a timeline," Keisha tells us as we recline in heated chairs with organic, fresh-picked cucumbers on our eyes and our feet soaking in bath salts and our hands being massaged with fancy oils before our nails are painted.

We leave carrying the spa robes and our old clothes, along with more sample products that look like full-size products than I could use in three years. *Anything for Hayes Rutherford's girlfriend*, the woman at the counter whispered to me while she slipped two more full bottles of that amazing hand lotion into my bag. *Be sure to tell people you love these, and we'll send you more. Here's a card with our public website. And another with our private website for exclusive clients.*

I have no idea who went shopping for us while we were being buffed and polished to within an inch of our lives, but I'm now in new jeans, an emerald green halter top that matches my eyes, and the most comfortable ankle boots I've ever worn. I'm even in a new bra and panties.

Hyacinth is glowing in a soft pink maternity dress, and Keisha's bodysuit is now black. She's topped her ensemble with a beret and blue-lensed sunglasses.

"You okay to walk two blocks?" she asks Hyacinth.

"I chase two toddlers all day. I can handle walking two blocks by myself."

She nods to someone on her security team, and it's not

until we leave the building and step onto the busy Manhattan street that I understand the question.

And possibly why Keisha's on sabbatical.

"Keisha! Keisha, look here! Keisha, when's your next album? What do you say to the rumors that your ex-girlfriend is dating a man? Were you involved in Thomas Rutherford's death? Is that your cousin's new girlfriend? Begonia! Begonia! Look this way!"

"Keep walking," Keisha murmurs to us as her security team surrounds us. "Don't speak. Either of you. Just keep walking."

Hyacinth grabs my hand.

I squeeze.

And as much as I like people, I'm exhausted by the time we push into a shop two blocks away. "Is it always like that?" I ask Keisha.

"Yep." She waves to someone in the back of the empty shop, and a curvy Black woman glides out with a broad smile.

"Keisha, my darling. So good to see you."

They share air kisses, then Keisha introduces us. "Begonia, Hyacinth, this is Cecily. She's a goddess, and she's going to find us the perfect dresses for the Windsor Gala tomorrow night."

"Lovely to meet you, my angels." Cecily air-kisses my cheeks, then Hyacinth's, and doesn't blink when we both get it wrong in return. "Come, come. I have the *perfect* gowns."

"Oh, I don't think I'm going," Hyacinth says. She points at her baby bump. "I mean, not that you thought I was."

Cecily smiles. "I dressed Emma Roberts during her pregnancy."

"And I have Hayes's credit card, and it would make Begonia's day to know that you're doing dishes in Versace," Keisha adds. "You could go TikTok famous."

Hy gapes at all of us.

I want to tell her no, that she can't have a dress, that this isn't what Hayes meant, that I don't want to waste his money, or use him for his money, but I can't.

The amount of joy this would bring her?

And knowing it's pennies to Hayes?

The man bought me a temporary art studio in his home, sent a private jet for Hyacinth, and Winnie texted me that she's booking Hy's whole family for a two-week all-expenses-paid, no-limits, exclusive-access-pass trip to Razzle Dazzle Village and wanted to check allergies, Hy's due date, and if they prefer cotton, linen, silk, or flannel sheets.

Hayes won't object to a dress.

And if he does, I'll pay him back, no matter how long it takes.

I nod to her. "Hayes would want you to. *I* want you to. Keisha's right. You'd rock the dishes in Versace." I couldn't pick a Versace out of a dress line-up if my pottery wheel depended on it.

"I have died and gone to heaven," Hyacinth whispers.

I want to agree with her.

But I think I'm hitting overwhelm for the day.

The crowd, and the pampering, and Hyacinth being here —it's all amazing.

More than I could've hoped for.

But it's also *not real*.

I mean, yes, my sister is real. The spa was real. The clothing, the dresses, hanging out with Keisha, the reporters—they're all real.

But this dating-a-billionaire lifestyle?

That isn't real.

And I don't want a billionaire.

I don't want a fake relationship. I don't want a fake fiancé.

Right now, I want the man who slept with me under the stars, who went diving under the covers to kiss the hummingbird tattoo on my hip, who smiles just for me, who makes me feel like I'm perfect the way I am and that I deserve to be loved for all of me, not just the convenient parts or the *socially acceptable* parts or the non-annoying parts.

I want the man who makes me believe that two people really can love each other the way love is supposed to be.

But he's not mine.

It's all fake.

And despite making more promises this morning that I would, I don't want to do it anymore.

"Begonia?" Hyacinth asks.

I beam at her. "You're going to be the most gorgeous diaper-changer in the world."

"We're totes getting you the seamstress package so you can have the dress refitted after..." Keisha waves at Hyacinth's belly. "Well, *after*."

I make myself crack up at the look on Keisha's face.

Hyacinth squints at me.

She knows I'm faking it.

But she doesn't press.

She will later. But for now, I point to the anemic display of dresses, which I assume is merely a front for the good stuff somewhere else.

That's how it seems to work in this world. "Let's go have some fun."

30

Hayes

THE OFFICE IS SO HECTIC, I MISS DINNER WITH BEGONIA AND Hyacinth in Manhattan, and even with their late night, I'm home after they are. Friday morning, I'm up before the sun, headed back to Albany, before Begonia's awake.

I miss her.

Despite sleeping next to her all night, I feel as though I haven't seen her in weeks.

It's only been three days since we slept under the moon and stars, but it seems like an eternity. The text message updates she sent while shopping with Keisha and Hyacinth weren't enough. I want to see the light in her eyes and watch her glow as she tells me the story of her day, in bed or over coffee, or in bed with coffee, or while sitting under the stars on a picnic blanket in the hills, and then I want to kiss her and strip her and seduce her until she's screaming my name for all the world to hear.

It's a sure sign this is more than the fake relationship she's signed up for, and it's a sure sign I should cut my losses, tear up our contract, and get out now.

But when I arrive home at six Friday evening, early enough to get ready for the Windsor Charity Gala tonight, there's no *cut your losses* at the top of my mind.

Only *dear god, she's beautiful.*

She and Hyacinth are both in the sitting room in my quarters—easily fixed this morning from the accident early this week once I gave orders to the designer and contractors to only accept Begonia's opinion—each in robes that I suspect they picked up at the spa yesterday, both of them having their hair done.

Begonia's entire face shines like a full moon on a clear night when she spots me. "Hayes! You're home! Guess what? I made a bowl *that looks like a bowl* this morning."

I do not deserve this woman and her sunshine. I know for a fact that packages have begun arriving for her, gifts from companies hoping the world's last eligible billionaire's girlfriend will get caught wearing or using their products in public—and yes, I do mean diamonds, pearls, high-end fashion, and more electronics than you can find at a computer show—yet the first thing she squeals about is making a clay bowl.

How anyone could not adore her is utterly beyond me.

I cross the room, and her stylist retreats as I lean down to kiss her.

I miss kissing her.

Those plump lips and that sweet tongue and her soft noises—she's exquisitely, uniquely perfect.

"Wow," Hyacinth says. "You should keep this one, B. I'm getting turned on just watching."

I pull out of our kiss, and Begonia smiles at me while she wipes at my lips, where I presume I'm now wearing her lipstick. "It's like having two Keishas in the house," she whispers.

"I have another house in the Hamptons. We can be there alone by eight if we leave now."

Begonia laughs. "Of course you do."

"Hello, Mr. Billionaire. You *invited* me." Hyacinth sounds so very similar to my Begonia, but there's no mistaking the difference between them.

"No arguing," Begonia declares as she loosens my tie for me. She glances at her sister. "Not when you're abandoning me right before this ball."

I lift a brow at Hyacinth.

She sighs. "I miss my babies and my husband and my bed and I kinda can't wait to walk through my front door looking like a fucking queen. Plus, this dress is totes amazeballs, but I'd spend half the night tugging it up and down to pee, and I've needed to tell Jerry he's getting snipped for a while, and what better time than now, when I can walk through my front door and start issuing orders like I'm the love child of Martha Stewart and Cleopatra? Begonia swore you wouldn't mind if I took the dress and ran."

I have no idea what my face is doing right now, but I manage to push aside thoughts of Jerry and his impending doom as I nod. "Correct. Enjoy the dress and run."

And I get Begonia to myself tonight.

I hardly mind.

She's already tossing her head back and laughing. "It's not as bad as she makes it sound," she assures me.

Hyacinth snorts. "B, you can't tell a man that. It's *always* as bad as we make it sound."

"Speaking of bad," I interrupt, "Begonia, have you been to a gala before?"

"In Richmond with Chad. Kind of. Not in New York with the *Gossip Girl* crowds."

"If you've seen *Gossip Girl*, you're prepared."

"She hasn't seen it," Hyacinth offers. "She quit reading the gossip magazines because she was upset when some celebrity went into rehab and it was all the headlines were about for *months*, and *Gossip Girl* was like an extension of that."

I remember. And the reminder of Begonia's sensitivity for others makes knowing that my time with her is limited even harder to bear.

"Mr. Rutherford, we need to finish," Begonia's stylist murmurs.

I acquiesce and retreat to my own dressing room, despite the fact that a leisurely shower will have me ready well before Begonia.

And by *leisurely*, yes, I do mean I lock the door and double-check it so that the dog can't get in, close my eyes while the hot water pounds my neck and shoulders, grip my cock, and jerk off to images of Begonia's glorious body and the memories of her panting my name in the meadow.

And nearly two hours later, I'm waiting in the sitting room off the foyer, reading a biography of Catherine the Great and not comprehending a damn word, when I hear voices.

The ladies are ready.

Hyacinth for her private flight home—she's reiterated the request through my staff, and all is prepared for her—and Begonia to accompany me.

I step out of the sitting room, casually stroll to the door for the best vantage point despite wanting to jog, and when I glance up, all I can do is stare.

I've seen Begonia in a gown before. She was lovely for our evening picnic in Maine.

But tonight, she's *more*.

Her bright hair has been trimmed and styled and frames her face, which seems to glow even brighter.

Whatever she's done with her lashes and her eyes—they utterly pop. Her lips are ripe cupid's bow cherries, her cheeks soft and round and perfect. She's selected a few pieces from the family jewels, with emeralds around her neck and dangling from her ears, all complementing her hair.

And the dress—

I'd thought her mermaid dress, as she called it, made her shine.

Tonight's ensemble puts every other dress in existence to shame. It's silver, sparkling in the light of the chandelier, with a strap over one shoulder but bare on the other, the fabric clinging to her from her breasts to her hips and flowing down to the floor, with a slit just high enough to let her thigh play peek-a-boo as she descends the stairs. She looks like an elegant holiday package topped with a bright bow, and I would very much like to unwrap her.

Begonia in her leggings and an oversize T-shirt, coated in clay and muddied water, is beautiful.

Begonia in jeans and a crop top pushing a bike along a dirt path on an island in Maine is perfect.

Begonia dressed to the nines for a gala takes my breath away.

And it's not the dress.

It's *Begonia* in the dress.

I do believe she'll fit in better tonight than I will.

Somehow, she's managed to dress to fit in with the highest of the high-class in Manhattan, but still maintain everything that makes her *her*.

"Aww, B, he's speechless," Hyacinth whispers, and yes, it's every bit as loud as you'd expect of Hyacinth whispering.

Begonia touches her cheek as if she's testing its temperature. "Makeup does this every time," she whispers back in a much more whispery voice.

"Right? Remember freshman homecoming? You were batting them off like maggots on poop."

"*Hyacinth.*"

The brown-haired twin laughs with glee.

She's in a lovely ivory gown, flowing around her belly, crisscrossed with crepe across her breasts and accented with thin, gold-trimmed straps holding it aloft.

And despite their identicalness, she can't hold a candle to Begonia, whose eyes are dancing, smile beaming so bright the sun itself would shield its eyes, her shoulders held back, chin high, as if she were royalty in a previous life and will carry this essence of confidence with her until the end of all time.

"Hayes?" she says softly, though that twinkle leaves no doubt she knows why I'm speechless.

"We're not going," I hear myself say.

One of her newly-sculpted brows arches as she reaches the bottom step. "No?"

"You'll outshine the host, though you'll have her eating out of the palm of your hand within minutes, and then the vultures will descend and they won't stop with what's *in* your hand, but rather they'll attempt to eat *you* alive. You don't belong to this crowd, Begonia. They're too cutthroat, and you're too perfect."

I need to stop talking.

There are witnesses, and I've just nearly confessed to adoring her beyond reason.

She smooths a hand over my lapel. "Hayes. We're going, and I'm going to try caviar and hate it and dribble it down my dress and horrify your crowd, which is *perfect*, since you hate hanging out with them, and then they won't invite you back."

Hyacinth laughs, the sound echoing throughout the foyer. "You two are seriously a match made in heaven. Also, call me when the caviar thing happens so I can talk you down. It will *not* be as bad as you think it is."

Begonia squeezes her sister's hand. "What if I spill red wine on someone wearing a dress like yours?"

"Then Hayes will come to your rescue," Hyacinth replies. "And he gets out of ever going to these things again. Why *don't* you like these things, Hayes? Are they terrible? Or is this just not your crowd?"

The stylist is long gone.

My housekeeper is quietly retreating back upstairs.

Keisha, Millie, and Uncle Antonio have departed.

It's just us.

"Hyacinth, would *you* like to spend your days doing nothing more than operating the preschool's parent club?" Begonia asks.

She shudders. "Hush your mouth."

"High society is to Hayes what preschool parent club is to you. Great for some, but not for all."

"Oh, jeez. At least my kids will eventually outgrow preschool."

I choke on an unexpected laugh, which earns me another of those magnificent Begonia smiles.

"Will Liliane or Amelia be there?" she asks with an innocent bat of her lashes.

I can't stop smiling back at her. "My world is not ready for you, Begonia."

"Keisha operates in your world. They are *more* than ready for me."

The front door opens, and Robert steps inside. "The helicopter is ready, sir."

"Oh my god, *take all the pictures!*" Hyacinth tackles Begonia in a hug. "And can I pee before we get on the helicopter? I can't hug you after I pee or I might have to pee again."

Begonia laughs, then bends to kiss her sister's belly before hugging her tight. "Go on. We'll wait."

Hyacinth waddles deeper into the house to reach the bathroom.

Robert ducks out the front door.

And I turn to settle a hand on Begonia's waist and brush a kiss to her jaw. "You are breathtakingly gorgeous this evening."

"We don't have to go if you don't want to, but I thought…"

"Whatever you thought, you thought correctly. We do, unfortunately, have to go. What's this scent? It's intoxicating."

"You like it?"

"I'm enraptured. You wear it well."

"Keisha gave it to me. She's working on a secret project to take over the world with beauty products on the side."

"Hm."

"Hm?"

"She'll overcharge me exorbitantly to buy the scent so only you can wear it."

Begonia laughs as she arches into my body, but stops suddenly. "Oh my god, you're serious."

"If I have to endure society and people because of my family's success, I may as well reap the benefits of a private perfume for my girlfriend."

My cock is rock-hard, *again*. Touching Begonia's smooth skin, inhaling that delectable fragrance complementing her unique sweet scent, pressing my body against her curves— she's a land Siren, and I am hopelessly devoted to her.

There are so few ways this can end well.

And right now, I don't care.

Right now, all that matters is that she's here, and under whatever guise, right now, she's mine.

31

Begonia

ABOUT A YEAR AGO, CHAD TOOK ME TO A PARTY HOSTED BY HIS financial firm celebrating some kind of big milestone. It was at the fanciest hotel in Richmond, and he shilled out nearly five hundred dollars for us to get a room for the night, and we dined on appetizers of mini quiches and shrimp cocktail and got not quite tipsy enough at the cash bar for me to overcome all of those feelings of being in the absolute wrong place.

Tonight is so similar it hurts, but so different at the same time that I couldn't imagine being anywhere else.

We're not in a hotel. We're at the sea lion pool at Central Park Zoo, with the garden area roped off and guarded by security. Twinkling fairy lights have been added to the trees and bushes at the edges of the walk. The guests at this gala, which benefits an endangered animal foundation, are in attire so fancy that I feel like I'm walking the red carpet at a movie premiere.

Instead of mini quiches and shrimp cocktail, the black-tie

servers are carrying trays of fresh-made sushi, but not just any sushi.

Each piece is a piece of art.

There's also foie gras and caviar and oysters, all in bite-size tarts and puffs and pieces assembled so fancily that I don't think I could eat it without feeling guilty at destroying the beauty of them. And there's a glass something that Hayes tells me is a *verrine*, though I have no idea if the glass or what's in it is the *verrine*.

Free-flowing Dom Perignon instead of Costco wine marked up at the cash bar.

A promise of individual chocolate fountains for dessert.

Individual chocolate fountains.

Let's be real.

That's what I'm most impressed with.

And dessert is even more fascinating because tonight, Hayes himself is basically the human equivalent of a chocolate fountain.

He's surrounded by people who seem eager to dip their fingers in him and lick him and use him to finish off their main course of eating the rest of the world alive.

And it's mostly women.

And that makes me sad.

Not a single one of them *knows* him. And I'd bet a lot of them wouldn't even like him. He's not easy. He's not agreeable. He doesn't let people in.

And he wouldn't like them either.

They *all* deserve better.

And I might not deserve it, but I want to explore the rest of the park instead of standing next to him, faking elegant, sophisticated small talk when I really want to gush about someone's earrings or someone else's hair.

His tight grip on my hand is the only thing keeping me from, well, being totally *me*.

And also sneaking off to explore the rest of the zoo.

Every time I try to interject something into a conversation, I'm steamrolled by someone else speaking not louder, but somehow more commandingly. I laugh too loud. I get funny looks. I hear the whispers.

He'll get tired of her soon. You know how Hayes is. Thinks he's making a point when he's really just making a scene. Don't worry. His mom won't let him actually marry a middle-class suburbanite nobody from—where was it? Does it matter? We know how this ends.

Thank god for the individual chocolate fountains coming.

This is like being back at a party with Chad, but worse.

There, I had a few friends I could sneak away with who also didn't fit. Even when Chad was sending me the *not so loud, Begonia* looks, I knew I could find a corner and a shrimp cocktail and a sympathetic ear.

Here, it's just me and Hayes against the Genteel Army. Keisha's not here. Uncle Antonio's not here. All those sweet people on Oysterberry Bay Island who would've had the time of their lives playing their violins for this event tonight aren't here.

I mean, naturally on that last one, but a girl can dream, right?

The point is—no wonder Hayes hates these things.

I'm smiling through it, laughing as loudly as I want without any dirty looks coming from Hayes himself over it—three points to him—complimenting people on their dresses and jewelry and hairstyles anytime I get an opening—seriously, there's a lot to compliment, but I'm working overtime to find those openings—and sometimes just enjoying watching the sea lions having their late-night swims, when Hayes goes stiff as my former mother-in-law in the presence of a fart joke.

"Hayes Rutherford. Living up to your potential, I see."

I don't know who's talking, but I dislike him on first syllable, and when we both turn to the sound of the voice, the sneer on this man's face tells me everything I need to know.

True evil does exist in the world, and I will fight to my death to defend Hayes's honor.

He squeezes my waist in warning and leaps in to speak before I can, which is impressive. "Sturgis. Mrs. Sturgis."

Oh, *fuck*.

It's his nemesis and former fiancée. Would this be like Hayes meeting Chad?

Am I supposed to punch one of them?

I'm pretty sure Hayes would punch Chad. I've seen that Neanderthal glower a time or two when I've said Chad's name.

But I'm hardly the punching type.

"I see they're letting anyone into these things these days," Sturgis says. I know I could call him Brock, but I don't want to. I like calling him Sturgis. It makes him sound like he's related to a fish.

Hayes goes impossibly stiffer, and I realize it doesn't matter how much formal training he has in social situations or how much time it's been or how immature I'm being in my head.

He doesn't want to be here and is struggling to not make a scene to get away.

"Hi!" I stick a hand out to the platinum blond woman and smile brightly at the couple. I might not have training, but I'm pretty sure I can do this. "I'm Begonia. Lovely to meet you. I mean, as lovely as it can be, given who you are. Your hair is gorgeous. That must've taken forever."

The last woman on earth that Hayes ever loved looks me up and down slowly, not taking my offered hand. I have no idea if I'm doing the subtle insult thing right or wrong, but Hayes is breathing again, so there's that. This woman might not be though, and I don't think it's my attempt at cattiness.

Her dress is pushing her boobs up to her chin and squeezing her waist so tight that her hips jut out oddly beneath the shimmery white fabric. It's like Elvis's jumpsuit had a dress baby with a toga and shrunk.

"I see you're borrowing the Rutherford jewels," Trixie Melhoff-Sturgis says.

Oh, yes.

I remember her name.

How could I not, when she snuck into Hayes's heart and planted explosives there and it's never been the same since? I know she's miserable—you can just tell sometimes. And I know we're not going to stand here one more minute. "The jewels are a dime a dozen in this crowd, aren't they? But the man—Hayes is the real treasure."

Sturgis snorts. "He's not worth the bitcoin I mine."

Oh, for goodness sake. "Are you—are you for real? Do people like you actually say things like that? Oh, sweetie. Good luck with your virtual seven dwarves operation. Excuse us. There's—" I scan the crowd and almost choke on my own spit. "Someone we need to go see," I finish faintly.

Jonas Rutherford is waving at us.

Jonas. Freaking. Rutherford.

I grab Hayes by the hand, yank, and wave back at his brother with my other hand like we've done this a million times.

Excuse me, but *how is this my life right now?*

Hayes blows out a slow breath that I feel all the way in my own toes as he trots along next to me.

Am I running?

I might be running.

I hate insulting people. I hate it more when they make it necessary.

"Do not *ever* change, Begonia," he murmurs.

"Was I mean enough? I'm so bad at mean. But I hated them on sight. Why are they here?"

"Gossip."

"For the record, Hayes Rutherford, I am *very* pissed at you right now."

"What? Why?"

"Because I don't want you to be related to a movie star that I had a massive crush on for half of my life. I want you to be *normal* so that I don't look like I'm only dating you to get close to your brother, because I don't care who you're related to, except for the part where I wish it wasn't him. You really are the jewel here. But *oh my god*, do you have any idea how much Hyacinth would be wetting herself right now even if she weren't pregnant?"

I'm pretty sure I'm whispering softly enough that we're in no danger of being overheard by the fancy clusters of people we're passing, but I'm also pretty sure the slow grin spreading over Hayes's face means he doesn't care if I'm in danger of blowing our story. "I'll give you five million dollars if you'll hug Jonas like you're long-lost siblings."

"I don't want your money, you goober."

"Forgive me, love. It's been a rough three minutes. But please, sell it well, bluebell."

It's the last warning I get before we reach the high table where Jonas freaking Rutherford is sipping champagne, clearly tracking our arrival as he nods to Amelia Shawcross, whom I'm weirdly happy to see, because at least she's familiar.

The movie star's full attention shifts, and his grin widens, eyes crinkling at the corners as he sets his drink down. "Hayes! And Begonia. Nice of you to stop by to say hi."

Oh. My. God.

Hyacinth should've come. She would be in utter heaven.

Hayes nudges me. "Go on," he murmurs.

So I do.

Oh my god, I do.

"Jonas! What are you doing back here already?" I hear

myself say, and then I'm flinging myself at my childhood idol, who laughs as he catches me in a hug that feels so awkward I want to retreat back into the sea lion pool—yes, into the *actual pool*, under the water, and I don't even care if I have a snorkel or scuba gear—and I want to stay there gripping Hayes's hand for the rest of the night.

Confronting a boyfriend's ex-girlfriend and bully of a former best friend?

I'm your woman.

Being normal around his movie star brother?

Why am I such a freaking freak?

"So good to see you again," Jonas says, much more convincingly than I am.

He's lanky and reasonably solid, and he smells pleasantly enough, and looking at him is like looking at a god, though I'd expect a god to be like seventeen feet tall, and he's merely a little under six feet, as you'd expect of a Hollywood hunk, and he is truly a *Hollywood hunk*, but as a man —*blech*.

No offense, Jonas.

But there's still the Hollywood hunk factor short-circuiting my brain.

"Kindly remove your hands from my girlfriend," Hayes says mildly behind us.

"But she gives the best hugs," Jonas replies.

"You're decent, but you're no Hayes," I tell him, which, yes, is a variation on another of the most popular lines ever used in Razzle Dazzle films, and yes, it's the first thing that comes to mind, and yes, I am cringing so hard to myself right now. My chin is hanging on his shoulder, and my voice is a little croaky with the strain.

I am the biggest goober known to gooberdom.

This is where I will actually die of mortification, and I do not embarrass easily.

I'm attacking my fake boyfriend's movie star brother, and

he's letting me, because it makes it look like we're besties, even though we've never met, which means *he knows*.

He pats me on the back and releases me, giving nothing away, because *he's a freaking actor*. Of course he's giving nothing away.

Maybe he doesn't know.

Maybe he's playing along with Hayes dating a *middle-class, suburban nobody* because it amuses him and he likes to irritate his mother.

Maybe he's a good brother.

Hayes slips his hand to the small of my back, his body close enough to make up for all the heat that's left my body as my blood cells flow to my brain to make sense of all of this. "You're back early," he says to Jonas.

"Peyton loves the sea lions."

"Who wouldn't? They're such cute bundles of flub." *They're such cute bundles of flub?* Shut up, Begonia. Shut up, shut up, shut up.

Hayes rubs my back. "Not nearly so much as you, blue-bell. Minus the flub, though you'd be absolutely perfect with or without it."

His eyes are twinkling.

Hayes.

Hayes Rutherford.

Grump supreme. Hater of people. Bigger hater of peopling with people.

And his eyes are *twinkling* as if he knows he's genuinely *funny*.

"Are you enjoying this?" I whisper to him while Jonas turns to take another glass of champagne from a passing server.

"I enjoy everything about you, Begonia," he murmurs back. "Everything."

I glance behind me, where *Sturgis and Mrs. Sturgis* are eyeballing us, and a wave of utter gratitude washes over me.

Hayes is safe here.

Even with the freaking sharks circling.

Jonas is here and has his back.

I have his back.

"Begonia."

Amelia's saying my name.

Shit. Shit, shit, shit. I forgot she was there, and it's making me cuss in my head now.

Also? Amelia would have Hayes's back, I'm pretty sure.

"Amelia!" I leap for her and hug her too, trying for a dainty socialite hug, and instead, our jeweled necklaces get caught up together and our faces are stuck mere inches apart like we're debating kissing each other.

"Um, good to see you," I say.

She smirks. It might actually be a warm smirk. I can't tell, because *I'm a little out of my league* has just changed to *Hayes will never take me out in public again, which means I'm useless as his fake girlfriend, and this is all over. He has to dump me now, because I got his family's jewels tangled with Amelia's.*

"You're quite the breath of fresh air," she murmurs while she reaches behind herself, bringing her face closer to mine while she fiddles with the clasp on her necklace. "These events are rarely so entertaining."

Filed under *the world is so unfair*: my deodorant is failing, while Amelia's lifting her arms and all I can smell are fresh flowers and baby powder and maybe warm chocolate chip cookies?

How do people get to be rich *and* have their armpits smell like warm chocolate chip cookies? And I really want to know what kind of toothpaste she uses, because her breath is remarkably pleasant too.

"I thought that's what the sea lions were for," I say. "For entertainment."

"You get tired of them after the first seven galas of the year with them present."

"Oh my gosh, I could never—"

"I'm aware, Begonia," Amelia says, but there's no snark in her voice. It's all warmth. "I only wish I could've counted on you to slice and dice Brock and Trixie Sturgis's livers."

"I tried, but I don't know if they were smart enough to get the insults."

She makes the same kind of noise in her throat that Hayes has made several times tonight. The kind that made me wonder if I was amusing or annoying him.

Warm hands settle at my neck, igniting goosebumps all over my skin, and I'm suddenly free.

Amelia pulls back too, dangling our intermixed necklaces in hand. "Shall I send yours back once my assistant has solved this little issue?" she says to Hayes.

Not to me.

To Hayes.

We can be friendly, but I get it. We're not friends. And I'm clearly borrowing jewels, because I don't belong here.

"Begonia would love to have her necklace back," he replies. "Thank you."

"Begonia!" Peyton joins us. Yes, Peyton Baker, Jonas's movie star wife who won a Golden Globe and an Emmy this year, which I know because awards shows sometime get exceptions for my no-gossip rule. To my utter astonishment, she grabs my hands and pulls me in to kiss my cheeks in turn, executing the move so flawlessly she manages to make me look like I know what I'm doing with air kisses too. "We were so sorry to miss you at the wedding, but *completely* understood. I'm so glad you're here. How's Hyacinth?"

"She's like a Thanksgiving turkey with her popper thingie stuck in the wing instead of the thigh. Ready to pop, but not fully baked."

Peyton Baker knows who I am.

Peyton Baker. Hollywood's biggest badass leading lady.

She knows who I am, and she knows my sister's name,

and that my sister is pregnant, and I just made the *very worst comparison* ever to turkeys and pregnant woman and I am making no sense, but everyone's still smiling kindly at me.

Good gravy.

Whose life am I living right now?

Why can't Hayes and I dash off to a little cabin in the woods and read and do clay art and talk and get naked and just have fun? *How is he related to these people?*

More importantly, how did I forget that he's related to these people?

Breathe, Begonia. They run out of toilet paper at inopportune times in their bathrooms too. Just regular people. Regular people. Regular people.

"We're so excited for her," Peyton says. "And where's Marshmallow tonight?"

"H-Hayes assigned Nikolay to guard him so he doesn't ruin Françoise's kitchen or redecorate the family portraits."

Jonas laughs. "I love that furry beast."

"He's worth the daily Benadryl." Hayes slips his arm around my waist and squeezes lightly. He's been talking about me. He's been telling his brother about me. And I don't know if this is an act or if they're all merely kind, but I'm getting a warm, squishy feeling in my heart.

They're doing it for Hayes. Not for me.

I know they are.

But I love that he has people who'll look out for him like this.

"Have you gotten to explore the city yet?" Peyton asks me.

I shake my head. "Just a little with Keisha."

And then I remember who *I* am.

Am I world-famous and sophisticated and comfortable here? No. But I'm a people person, and these are *people.* "And what about you?" I ask. "How was the honeymoon?"

Her bright brown eyes light up. "Everything we needed it to be, though unfortunately too short."

"We'll take another one at Christmas," Jonas tells her.

"You should try the Maldives," Amelia says, reminding us all, again, that she's still here. "They're beautiful at Christmas."

"Thank you. We'll add that to the list to consider." Peyton smiles at her, and my heart suddenly aches for Amelia. She's being dismissed. Politely, but still dismissed.

And even *I* can see it.

No wonder Hayes doesn't want to be here.

Even with the kindest of people, there are subtle social hierarchies and digs and rules.

And *are* Jonas and Peyton kind?

I don't know.

I really don't.

"Excuse us," Hayes says to Amelia and his family. "I promised Begonia front-row seats to the feeding."

"You won't really have to fight the crowd," Amelia says.

"Do they do tricks?" Peyton asks. "We'll come with you. Jonas. Where's your phone? Show Begonia the video of the sea lions from our trip to San Francisco when we were filming *Deep in Love*. Amelia, so good to see you again. Have your assistant ping mine. We'll do lunch next time I'm in town."

They do the cheek-kisses, and once more, I get a pang for Amelia.

I shouldn't. She's one more of the women watching Hayes like he's a golden ticket, and even knowing she doesn't want him for him—Hayes told me she's involved with someone her family doesn't like—I can't help feeling sorry for her.

How lonely must it be to not know who your real friends are, and to be hunting for a husband for convenience instead of love?

I want to hug her and tell her to say *fuck the world* and go after what she wants, but it's not my place, and I don't think she wants to hear it from me.

Also, it's not like I don't know how hard that is.

I'm dating a billionaire myself, and my mother is still holding my ex-husband in reserve as her plan for my future when I screw it up with Hayes, which she's convinced I'll do.

And she's not wrong.

I mean, that's actually the plan.

Sigh.

Why can't the world support people doing what it takes to make them happy, instead of what it takes to make other people miserable?

"Do you think they know how lucky they are?" Hayes murmurs to me a few minutes later as we're watching the zookeepers tease the sea lions into doing tricks for fish.

"The zookeeper or the sea lions?"

"Yes."

I slip an arm around his waist and squeeze it too.

He gets it.

He really does.

"I hope so," I whisper.

Once the sea lions are fed, which involves a lot of squealing and pointing on my behalf and a lot of unexpected smiles on his behalf, he tugs my hand. "The interminable self-congratulating about saving a single sea turtle is about to begin," he whispers. "Come with me."

While the crowd around us drifts toward the tables set up on the other side of the sea lion enclosure, Hayes guides me away from the light. It's a gradual departure, when no one's looking, as if he's done this before. He slips behind the catering truck, where there's a break in the security line, and then we're sneaking deeper into a darker part of the zoo.

Nothing is fully dark—not in the city—but the noises of the party are fading behind us, and I can feel the tension leaving him with every step we take away.

"How many times have you disappeared to hide at events like this?" I whisper.

"All of the times."

"Oh."

"Oh?"

"I thought you wanted to sneak away and be alone with me and do something naughty but absolutely irresistible."

He turns me against the back of a building, replies, "Bluebell, for the first time in my life, that's exactly what I want to do," and then he's kissing me.

Everything that's felt messy or awkward or off-kilter tonight fades away into the utter bliss that comes with his mouth on mine.

My own shoulders relax as my clit throbs and my breasts tighten. He grips my ass through my dress, and I curse the material for being so form-fitting.

Even if I wanted to rip the material and wrap my legs around him, I would've needed to be doing some kind of Amelia Shawcross workout to make it happen.

"Fuck, I needed this," he says.

"Your crowd is hard."

He tilts his hips against me, a rueful smile crossing his features in the dim light. "Not as hard as I am."

I arch my belly into the thick ridge of his erection. "You can't *possibly* go through the rest of the night like this. Whatever shall we do?"

"Begonia—"

I tug at his belt. "Shh. Everyone's at the party."

"Just when I think you can't possibly get any more perfect."

"There aren't any reporters stalking in the bushes, are there?"

"Not if they want to live."

"Security?"

"Even if we're caught, they're discreet."

That's all I need to know.

I tackle his pants with more enthusiasm.

He tries to tug my dress up.

"Won't work," I whisper as I plunge my hands down his pants and grip his rigid length.

He groans into my neck, bracing himself with his hands planted against the building on either side of me. "Sweet holy fuck, your hands."

"You have the loveliest penis in the world."

He huffs out a short laugh as his cock pulses harder in my hand. "Your compliments are beyond compare. Dear god, do that again."

He thrusts his hips into my hand as I cradle his balls with the other. He's hard and long, hot and silky smooth. Unintelligible sounds come from his throat as I stroke and tease him, brushing the moisture from the tip of his blunt head, and touching him isn't enough.

I love turning him on.

I love making him feel good.

I love knowing that he'll take care of my needs too, not out of obligation, but because he seems to genuinely enjoy making me feel good.

And I've never gone down on a man in public before, and the thrill of it makes pushing his pants down off his hips and fussing with my skirt so that I can drop to my knees a no-brainer.

"Jesus, Begonia," he pants as I lick the underside of his cock, then suck his broad head into my mouth, twirling my tongue around the silky ridge and tasting his salty flavor.

He grunts like he wants to moan but is trying to be quiet, his hips and thighs quivering. He's still bracing himself against the wall behind me, and my one regret is that he's not gripping my hair.

And that last thought makes me smile around Hayes's cock.

Hello, old Begonia.

I feel so alive right now.

Powerful and desirable and free and open to taking the opportunities the world offers.

No regrets.

Especially with Hayes gasping and groaning softly while I lick and suckle and tease his thick length, sucking him as deep as I can, swirling my tongue around his shaft, and taking him deep again while I play with his testicles and his thighs shake against my arm and hand.

I'm driving him wild, and it's making my clit achy and my panties soaked and my breasts so hot and heavy that there's not enough room in this dress for me to breathe.

It's *exquisite*, to use one of Hayes's favorite words.

I feel like a freaking goddess.

"Begonia," he grunts, and I know he's close.

I can hear it.

I can *feel* it.

I roll his balls in my hand and suck harder, and just as he grunts with his release overtaking him, lights flash.

Then more lights.

He's coming down my throat and the sky is lit up with cameras popping, and *oh my god*.

"Fuck," he grunts, pulling out mid-orgasm.

He twists, but not before I feel a hot, wet stickiness land on my chest.

And then my face is buried in his ass as he barks orders. "Cameras. Hand them over. *Now*."

No, not barks.

Snarls.

"Holy shit, it's really the weird Rutherford brother," a guy says somewhere nearby.

I try to move, but Hayes blocks me. "I said, hand over your cameras."

"Not a fucking chance, bro. Thanks for the shot."

He starts to move, then freezes, like he's torn between chasing away whoever's dashing off with photographic evidence and exposing me to more visibility. "Robert," he barks, and when a tinny voice answers, I realize he's on the phone. "We have a problem."

32

Hayes

IN THE PAST FIFTEEN TO TWENTY YEARS, I'VE MADE AN ART OUT of avoiding anything that will give me regrets.

This evening, I'm living two decades' worth of regrets in the span of under an hour.

"The damage will be minimal," I tell Begonia as we taxi down the runway at JFK. "The paparazzi know my family will pay a pretty penny to squash scandal. My team is on it."

She nods and stares out the window. "Of course. That makes sense."

"We should get married."

The words leave my mouth and I can practically see them traveling the short distance in Jonas's private plane—not mine, since it's still delivering Hyacinth home—from my lips to her ears. I want to snag them back before they register inside her brain, but I can't, and I know it.

I'm also completely, selfishly thrilled with this turn of events.

I marry Begonia so that even if rumors swirl about what we were doing in public and why we disappeared from the gala, the scandal will be outweighed by the news of our wedding.

We were overcome with emotion at my proposal and didn't want to wait another minute to tie the knot.

My family's reputation will take a hit, but not as much as it would if we didn't get married. People tend to forgive you when you *do the right thing*, even if the standards my family are held to are ridiculous.

But tonight, I don't care.

Once I marry Begonia, I'm free.

Free in the sense of not having women swarming every time I'm at an event, even with *my girlfriend*, because *wife* is so much more permanent.

Rutherfords do *not* cheat.

And we can socially ruin anyone who dares to suggest that we should.

I'll no longer be the last eligible billionaire in the world. The damage to my family's name will be minimal.

And I get to keep Begonia.

We're friends.

Friends with benefits.

I'll provide her with a comfortable life and request in return a wife of convenience, at least for a while.

Surely someone else will have joined the ranks of the world's billionaires within a year or two. I'll be written off as *that Rutherford who couldn't hold his marriage together*, convince my family I'm utterly miserable at the idea of having to date, and never have to worry about this again.

With the exception of the horrified gonging in my heart at the thought of letting Begonia go.

She gapes at me from the wide executive chair across from me. "We should *what*?"

"My lawyer will draft a prenup before we land that will

provide a comfortable stipend for you regardless of what happens next. I require at least two full years of marriage in exchange for supporting you in whatever endeavors would make you happiest, from teaching to making your own artwork to exploring anything else that would fill your heart with joy, and at the end of two years, if you've found someone else you would rather be with, I'll grant you a quiet divorce with assistance for transition back to a normal life."

She doesn't answer.

She doesn't have to.

Her agitated green eyes are doing all of the talking for her.

But I wanted my next marriage to be for love, Hayes.

What I wouldn't give to wrap my arms around her and make her all the promises that terrify me to my core.

I'll love you, Begonia. I don't know how not to.

There will never be another woman who affects me the way you do.

You are my one. You are my only one, the one I've waited my whole life for.

But therein is the problem.

Loving her is easy.

Being loved back by her?

She adores everyone.

Who am I to think I could be the man she would love above all others, when a woman like Begonia could have her pick of any man in the world?

Any man in the world. Someone who can love her fully without reservation or fear. Someone who could stand by her side and enjoy *peopling*, as she calls it. Someone who has more to offer her than money.

"I'll do my best to charm your mother, though of course, it's in everyone's best interest if she abhors me. That will make our eventual split easier on you. And I work long hours, as you've clearly realized, so if you wanted to live and work in Richmond as you've been doing, I could commute back to New York during the week, keep my own quarters near you on the weekend, and be as little of an inconvenience in your life as you'd like me to be."

Her chin wobbles, and her eyes go shiny. "That's what you want."

"It's what *must* happen, Begonia. I can't be the cause of scandal to my family, especially given my new position in the company, and I don't know if my influence alone will be enough for you to keep your teaching job if those photos appear anywhere."

It's the best plan.

She becomes mine, for a solid reason, without me having to put my heart on the line.

I can live with knowing I'm not her one greatest love, so long as I get to live with her.

"Take me home," she says quietly.

I blink. "Begonia—"

"Take. Me. Home."

"This is the only clear way to—"

"I love you, Hayes. I. Love. You. And I don't want to. I didn't want to. I just got divorced. I don't fit in your world. I'm still finding myself again. And I could roll with it. I could. You're supposed to love people. That's what makes the world a better place. And you've been nothing but everything I always dreamed I wanted in a partner, except for one thing. You don't love me back. I've spent too many years sacrificing what I deserve for what I thought should've been good enough. I won't do *good enough* with you. I won't do *easy* with you. Or anyone. I will *not* settle for anything less than all-consuming, no-holding-back, nothing-else-matters, we-are-in-this-together, I-love-you-so-much-it-hurts love."

A tear slips down her cheek, and she swipes it away as if it's what's committed the most egregious error of this evening.

It has.

That tear is single-handedly splitting my heart in two. And I have a choice.

I can tell her I love her back, risk that Begonia's love is fickle, that she'll fall in love with someone else as easily as she falls in love with the sunrise each morning, with a funny design on her toast fresh out of the toaster, or with someone's hairstyle at a formal event, and try to do all in my power to keep her, all while never knowing for sure that I'm truly what she wants.

If I'm merely convenient.

The first man to give her a glimpse of better, but not necessarily the man who would be best for her.

Or I can stay safe.

Let her go.

Weather the scandal alone.

And know that I wouldn't have been able to keep her. That this bright, vibrant angel of life couldn't have ever been mine.

Not fully.

She's the sunshine, hurtling about the universe bringing light to all she touches, and I'm the tree.

Solid and dependable. Rooted. With a few broken branches.

But the fact remains—while the tree needs the sunshine, the sunshine will never depend on the tree.

"Do you love me, Hayes?" she whispers. "*Could* you love me?"

For fuck's sake. How could I not? "Begonia, I know very few people in this world who could know you and not love you."

"But do *you* love me?"

Three words.

Three of the most damn impossible words in the English language.

That's what it would take to keep her.

PIPPA GRANT

For tonight.

But what happens tomorrow?

I asked her to pretend to be my girlfriend so that she'd be a shield between me and anyone with an opinion about my love life after I became the world's most eligible billionaire. How ironic, when she's the one who should have men lined up around the block for a chance at her hand.

She's loyal to a fault.

She wouldn't cheat.

But she'll find someone new—possibly someone I know— and she'll be miserable, and then she'll leave me too.

I thought I hurt when Trixie left me.

That grief would be nothing compared to watching Begonia go after convincing myself I could make her happy.

"Hayes?" she whispers.

I rise. "I'll instruct the pilot to change course."

33

Begonia

Hyacinth won't quit knocking on my door.

I know it's her. She has a distinctive knock. It sounds like our mother asking if I took my vitamins.

And just like the last seventeen times she's knocked on my door, I ignore it.

Marshmallow harumphs.

He and I got back to Richmond two nights ago, courtesy of Jonas Rutherford's private jet, since Hyacinth was using Hayes's at the time, and I'm running out of food in my little apartment, and I don't care.

My only plans are to wither away into nothingness, because that will hurt less. Also, if I wither away into nothingness, I don't have to pack my apartment and move back in with my mother, which is probably on the agenda since word got out that I was caught giving a man a blow job in public.

Not really what high school parents want in their kids' art teacher.

My head and a platter are soon to be very intimately related.

I close my eyes and return to snooze-land.

Or try to. Snoozing is hard when you hear your dog unlocking your apartment door.

"Who's a good boy?" Hyacinth says. "Marshmallow is such a good boy. Where's the potty, Marshmallow? Where's the potty before I pee on your mommy's carpet?"

I grunt.

"Oh, B," my sister sighs. "Don't move. I'll be right back."

She's lying.

She's not right back.

But eventually she joins me, which I know not because my eyes are open, but because she's as quiet as a herd of rhinos trying to walk across a field of Legos.

"So it was all fake."

I pry one eye open. "What?"

She waves a tabloid in my face. "You signed a contract to fake being his girlfriend. Why?"

Heat funnels from my chest, up my neck, into my brain, and makes me lightheaded. I'm lying down and I'm lightheaded.

"*What?*"

"That's your signature. I know your signature. How did they get your signature if it was fake? And you were supposed to get *engaged*? What did you *do*? And talk fast, because I guarantee you, this is hitting the morning shows locally any minute, and Mom will be here like she can teleport the minute it does."

I push to sitting, ignore the black dots dancing in my vision, and take the newspaper from her.

That's me.

On my knees.

In the dark.

Giving Hayes a blow job behind a building near the sea lion exhibit.

With a giant blurry spot right in front of my face.

Oh my god.

I fling it away and throw myself back onto the couch. "No," I whisper.

"*Begonia.* Ignore the picture. Also, anyone who comes after you for having sex in public will have to go through me first, because *hello*, that had to be hella fucking hot. But we need to talk about this headline. *The Weird Rutherford Fakes A Girl-friend.* And this contract that they printed. And how I'm going to murder everyone in the Rutherford family for using you like this."

"No."

"Begonia, they have the signed NDA printed in here too. *Talk.* Now. I knew something was up."

"*How?*"

"Hello, twinstinct?"

"No, *how* do they have the contract?"

"So you'd take the fall for the BJ that's threatening to destroy the Rutherford family's reputation. *Duh.* I really hope he did a lot more than setting up the most gorgeous art room I've ever seen for you in that mansion of his, because otherwise, his death will be slow and painful instead of quick and merciful."

"Hy, he wouldn't—"

I cut myself off.

Wouldn't he?

What do I really know about Hayes Rutherford beyond what I wanted to believe?

He stood up to his mother for me, but that was the whole point of the fake relationship. To sell it. To put me between him and her and every other woman in the world.

He treated me like a goddess and told me he liked me for

who I was, but was it all pretend? Is he as good of an actor as his brother?

He couldn't even tell me he loved me.

He preferred letting all of our secrets loose in the tabloids to actually caring about me.

I'd thought I'd cried every last tear I had inside me, but I haven't.

Not by a long shot.

And they're coming hot and hard and fast all over again as I tell Hyacinth everything. The mistake with the vacation rental. Him finding me waxing my bikini line in his bathroom. Marshmallow eating the Maurice Bellitano carving. His mother arriving with a more suitable girlfriend. Skipping the lobster dinner cruise for a picnic on the beach.

Asking him to pop my post-divorce cherry.

His panicked call for me to pick his executive assistants.

Our moonlit picnic when we made love.

Running into the woman who broke him and his former best friend at the gala.

Wanting to hug him and save him and protect him from people who only see him as the world's last eligible billionaire.

But I suppose the joke's on me.

I was never what he actually wanted, no matter how he made me feel.

Hyacinth's cradling my head in her lap and stroking my hair by the time I finish.

"Jerry says he can get you a job at his company," she says. "Just until all of this blows over. To keep you busy, I mean. Until you sue the ever-loving fuck out of that asshole billionaire who's letting you take the fall for all of this."

I squeeze my eyes shut. "Despite it all, Hy, I love him."

"Begonia, you could fall in love with a turd-coated shape-shifting lemur. I realize Mr. Big Bucks was a *little* more handsome than that, and he gave us a good run of thinking he knew you and liked you, but sweetie, *he betrayed you* in the freaking *gossip rags* to save his family's reputation, and *you are going to be okay*. C'mon, Ms. Things Happen For A Reason. You can do private art lessons now. Take advantage of the notoriety and get a page up on Etsy with some of your attempts at spin-art. Sign them, and they'll be worth like, seven times as much."

"I hate math, but even I know seven times zero is zero. And I don't care, Hy. I don't. I don't care about anything."

"You fed your dog today."

"I fed him the whole bag when we got home."

She looks at me, then over near where Marshmallow's dog bowl sits. "Oh. I, ah, see. Does he need to go out?"

"Every freaking hour, but he takes care of it himself."

He's the best dog. Best best best.

"*Begonia.*"

"I've cleaned up seven thousand dog messes in the park from other dogs! If he makes a dozen messes that I don't clean while I'm heartbroken and drowning my sorrows on my couch, then *I don't care*. And if my dog is smart enough to take the elevator down to the parking lot to poop, then find his way back, then why shouldn't he have his freedom to do that?"

"Okay. Okay. I'm texting Jerry. He'll do the whole apartment parking lot. He doesn't mind. He's worried about you."

"You settled."

"What?"

"For Jerry. You settled. I don't want to settle. I want love."

"Oh my god, Begonia. I did not *settle* for Jerry."

"But you complain about him all the time. And the last time he took you on a date was months ago, and it was popcorn and hotdogs in your basement while you hid from the kids."

"Um, hello, that was a *good* date." She rubs her belly, which I can feel behind my head. "Too good, unfortunately.

And I'm sorry I complain about him too much. It's not *him*. Exactly. It's raising two and a half minions and being overwhelmed and settling into—no, not *settling*, not like that—but just having routines and being so busy and forgetting to appreciate all the reasons I fell in love with him in the first place. Like, he gives me foot rubs every night. And he takes the kids to the park every Saturday morning so I can have one morning of bingeing adult TV while I drink my coffee *hot*. And do you remember when the preschool moms all rose up last year to protest Dani saying *fuck*? Jerry was the first one to tell me that our kids will be just fine, because they won't be afraid of profanity and they'll understand how and when to use it and that people are different and see things differently, and he went to the preschool meeting for me and read a list of cuss words and their etymology and talked about how when you stigmatize something, that makes it worse than it is all on its own. *And* he doesn't blink when I drink pickle smoothies or have ice cream dribble down my shirt, *and* he buys me tampons. I know he's not, like, a *billionaire* who can take me to Europe on a moment's notice—which I notice the billionaire who shall not be named didn't do for you, by the way, despite teasing you incessantly about it—or get me tickets to a movie premiere or send me luxury chocolates every day, but he's my prince charming, even when I forget how much he does."

I twist my head to stare up at her for a brief moment, then squeeze my eyes shut.

She loves him.

She doesn't think she settled.

And that's what's important. *Especially* since neither one of us can have a guy like Hayes.

Or who he pretended he was.

"I thought he loved me," I whisper to my sister. "Underneath it all, I thought he was falling in love with me."

Someone else knocks at my door, making Marshmallow growl low in his throat.

I wince. "And now Mom's here."

"If she says the *Chad* word, I'll threaten to never let her see her grandbabies again, and I swear on my loyalty to you above everyone else, I'll mean it."

Marshmallow growls again.

"Begonia?" Mom calls. "Sweetie, open the door. Mommy's here to fix it all."

I whimper.

Hyacinth growls louder than Marshmallow.

The lock clicks, the hinges squeak, and more than one set of footsteps makes my small entryway floor creak. "Honey, don't worry," Mom calls. "I brought Chad, and he forgives you. Let's put this all behind us now, shall we?"

Hyacinth and I lock eyes.

I dive for Marshmallow, and I get lightheaded all over again. Maybe skipping breakfast for the past two days wasn't the greatest idea.

"I'm going to murder them both," Hyacinth says.

I don't dive for her.

The authorities won't put her down if she bites one of them. And I'm pretty sure she won't bite.

Or murder them for real.

And she has that no-fucks-left-to-give third pregnancy glow.

"Begon—*erp.*"

"*Out,*" Hy snarls. "Out, out, *out.* Mother, you're dead to me. Chad, you'll be dead for real if you don't march your loser ass out of this apartment and stay the *fuck* away. You don't get to realize what you lost after it's gone. You get to wallow in misery for the rest of your freaking forever. No, Mother, *dead to me.* Go. *Go.* Before I call Keisha Kourtney and ask her to take Begonia somewhere safe where none of us can ever bother her again, and that means none of us will ever see her again too. *Do you understand?*"

Keisha.

I miss Keisha.

But I don't have the right to call her anymore.

That part of my life? That adventure?

It's over.

And I'm not up for any more right now.

34

Hayes

She fucking betrayed me.

I'm sitting at my desk, staring at the paper hand-delivered by my father this morning, gaping in utter shock.

Begonia exposed our agreement for the world.

My phone won't stop ringing. Not my personal phone, nor my office phone, nor my office cell. Every line, lit up.

Merriweather brought coffee, doctored with sugar and cream and cinnamon, and I nearly threw up just sniffing it, which might've been the point.

Reasonably certain she's on *Team Begonia*, that she's sniffed out that we're no longer together, and that I'm in the doghouse.

Winnie delivered today's calendar and I wanted to crawl under my desk and hide like a five-year-old.

And then my father marched through my door, unannounced, with a tabloid in hand, and set off the biggest bomb of my Monday morning.

"While this has all the makings of a quality Razzle Dazzle film, I didn't expect you'd do it in real life," he says dryly, one ankle crossed over his knee as he sits across from me on my office couch as if this is a casual social visit and not a trip to tell me what a fuck-up I am for getting caught with my dick out in public before being exposed for Begonia being nothing more than a pretend date. "Maybe next time, use a digital document instead of paper. Especially if your fake girlfriend isn't tech-savvy enough to forward it."

She fucking betrayed me.

But what did I deserve?

She told me she loved me, and I told the pilot to turn the plane around.

"I'll issue apologies." My voice is hollow in my own ears. "If you need me to resign—"

"We're held to a ridiculous standard, Hayes. If our family looks merely mortal in the press from time to time, we'll weather the storm."

"This isn't *mortal*. This is *embarrassing*." And it hurts.

It fucking *hurts*.

"It will blow over," my father says.

As if this could possibly just *blow over*.

I glower at him.

I get a mild smile in return.

It makes my ears want to pop off the side of my head to let the pressure out. "For nearly forty damn years, I've bent over backwards to keep from smearing our family's name, and now, with a photo of me getting a goddamn *blow job* on the front page of every tabloid, accompanied by a goddamn *fake relationship* contract, all you have to say is *it'll blow over*?"

He tilts his head as if he's contemplating the question. As if he didn't hear the part where I said *a photo of me getting a goddamn blow job*. As if there's actually any doubt that he's not taking this seriously enough. "You don't enjoy working here, do you?"

"Did you fucking set me up?" I'm on my feet, shouting at my father for the first time in my adult life. My head is pounding even harder, my fingers half-numb, half-twitching, my chest getting hammered so hard by my heart that my lungs are in danger of being collateral damage when it bursts. "Did you set me up so I'd have to step down?"

He doesn't react to that either, but instead waves his hand casually as though he's inviting me to take a seat and have a cigar. "Of course not. But since Thomas passed...you've been different. Some good. Some not so good. I don't know what makes you happy, and your mother and I have been negligent by failing to ask."

Begonia.

Begonia made me happy.

Until she betrayed me.

One good thing to come of this—I can be as unpleasant as I want, reject any potential date as rudely as I wish, and it can't possibly be as bad as the front page of every last gossip magazine and website in the known universe today.

"It's been a difficult time," I bite off. "I'll be fine."

He nods to my desk, where the offensive newspaper glares at both of us. "That's quite the balance sheet collection."

"I like puzzles."

"Especially when you're unhappy."

"I'm not—" I cut myself off with a curse.

While the show my family puts on for the world is fake, and they annoy the ever-loving shit out of me on occasion, my parents' concern for Jonas and me has always been real. I've never doubted that.

They ask for too much—not because they want to, but because of the world we live in—but they worry in equal amounts.

It's why my mother came to Maine—because she worries.

It's why the whole family stayed longer than they should've at the house in Albany.

I'm the one they worry about. Even at almost forty years old. And for as much as I don't like people, I know I need them, and I know I can count on my family.

I sink back into my seat and meet my father's gaze. "I don't know that I'm built to be Razzle Dazzle's CFO."

"Because...?"

Fuck it. What more do I have to hide? "Interviews. Shareholder meetings. Managing a team. *People*. And I hate every goddamn movie this family has ever produced."

He purses his lips thoughtfully. "They're dreadfully repetitive, aren't they?"

And now I'm gawking. "*You* don't like them either?"

"Oh, no, I enjoy them, but we haven't taken a risk since we opened Razzle Dazzle Village when you were a baby. And you're getting old."

Jesus.

Who is this man, and what has he done with my father?

"What would make you happy, Hayes?"

Begonia.

A private island with no one but Begonia.

Food.

Her damn dog.

My father sighs. "Son, life's too short to spend it doing nothing but making other people happy. And god knows we parents get it wrong on occasion when it comes to guessing what that might be. If you're under the impression we expect you to pay us back for anything we've ever given you in life, let me assure you, all we want is for you to do what makes you happy. Not what makes *us* happy. And it's time I put my money where my mouth is, so consider that this offer is as much for me as it is for you. If you're not happy, if you want out...now's the time to take a leap."

He *looks* like my father. He truly does. "Are you ill?"

"No, merely disgusted with myself for taking the easy path for far too long."

I lift my brows and wait.

"Our first film featuring a queer couple is nearly finished." He points to my desk again. "We've done the same thing for so long that we've convinced ourselves the audience wouldn't follow us if we added additional paths, and it's time we move away from the fear and embrace the possibilities of truly living up to what our reputation *should* be. Not a surface-level happy family, but a family of love and support and acceptance. The account sheets will be corrected when we announce it next week. Thomas was aware and had signed off on the various accounting tricks we needed to use for developing the project in complete secret. The rest of the board is ready to handle the media requests we would've had him do, as we've wanted to give you time to settle in before fully feeding you to the sharks. But Hayes, if this isn't where your heart is—and I don't mean the company's growth and expansion into new markets that we should've ventured into before this, but I mean you, in this chair—no one will think any less of you. I'd hoped this job would be an opportunity, but I fear I've actually put you into an obligation instead."

Begonia would be thrilled at this news.

I don't *want* that to be my first thought, but I can't stop it any more than I could stop her from smiling at the sun rising over the sea, or at a small private violin concert, or at her ridiculous dog pretending he could fish for crabs and take them home and cook them himself.

"Think it over," my father says. "If you're not happy, Hayes...let us help you find what would help you get there. And in the meantime, don't let anyone else walk through your door with tabloids in hand."

"*You* just walked through my door with that infernal tabloid in your hand."

"I'm your father. It comes with privileges." He smiles as

he unfolds himself and rises. "But the biggest is worry. The biggest is always the worry."

"I'm fine."

"Are you?"

"As can be."

He looks at my desk one more time. I snag the offending paper and hold it out to him. "Toss this, would you?"

"Never thought she'd be the type to take that to the press," he muses. "Her dog, though…"

I'd point out he barely met her at Sagewood House, but I know my father, and I know he pays attention to more than we think he does. "We're not discussing this."

He shrugs. "Happiness isn't something you can plan, son."

"We're *not* discussing this."

He nods once.

And when he walks out my door, I get the most infuriating sense that he's disappointed in me.

Not because I'm failing at what I'm supposed to do for my family.

But because I'm letting fear stand in the way of the one thing that might finally make me truly happy.

35

Begonia

IT TURNS OUT PAWNING A TWENTY THOUSAND-DOLLAR DRESS doesn't make me happy, but it does give me enough breathing room in my bank account to afford gas, food, and dog supplies for Marshmallow and me to do what we should've done in the first place for my finding-myself post-divorce retreat—borrow Jerry's parents' Outer Banks condo.

And the condo gives me a small degree of privacy too.

I'm a little famous in Richmond right now.

And not for good things.

More for things that have put me on administrative leave from the high school.

I've told Hyacinth that I'll come work for Jerry's company if my new Etsy shop with grief art doesn't pay off.

And considering I haven't been able to bring myself to do any art while I've been grieving here on the beach, there's a high likelihood I'll be donning conservative professional clothes and fetching someone's coffee by the end of July.

No way am I ready to sell Great Grandma Eileen's dildo collection.

Not that I can.

People would figure out that I was the listing person on eBay, associate me with Hayes, and they'd twist the truth to say I sculpted the dildos myself after his penis even though the dildos are like eighty years old.

People are dicks.

And I don't like to think of people as dicks.

But I can't help myself.

Not even when I'm sitting on the beach under a giant umbrella that I paid seventeen dollars to rent for the day, hiding my eyes behind the least-gaudy, big, over-priced plastic sunglasses that I could find in the tourist shop while Marshmallow dances in the surf.

It's only six in the morning and the sun's barely up, so I'm pretty sure we can stay anonymous this way for at least another half-hour.

Possibly forty-five minutes.

Except just as I'm getting comfortable, all of the hairs go up on the back of my neck.

And two seconds later, Giovanna Rutherford plops herself down next to me, right on the sand, in this shimmery pink-ivory pantsuit. "You're a difficult woman to track down when your hair isn't glowing brighter than the sun. The black is striking, but I oddly think I prefer the neon burgundy. It fits you."

I have not had enough coffee or heartbreak healing time for this, and I can't do much more than gawk.

Until reality kicks in.

"You're here to deliver a massive lawsuit, aren't you?" I whimper.

Yes, whimper.

A lawsuit is *not* an adventure.

It's a cold splash of ice water straight off a glacier, and not a pretty glacier either. A big, mean, dirty, ice-spewing, demonic-laughing glacier.

I try to picture it.

And I fail.

Glaciers are really pretty. Even the pictures I've seen of the glaciers in Iceland coated with volcanic ash are pretty.

But lawsuits are *not* pretty.

"Begonia." Giovanna sighs, and it sounds so much like Hayes sighing when he doesn't think I know that the weight of the world is sitting on his shoulders that my eyes get hot and my throat clogs and my sinuses burn. "No, my sweet. I'm here because I owe you an apology."

"This is not helping," I whisper.

"You know about Trixie, I presume."

I nod and try to swipe my eyes without making it obvious that I'm swiping my eyes. I know it's okay to cry.

But I don't want to do it in front of Giovanna.

"You probably don't know about Melinda, Cricket, Elizabeth, Victoria, Emma, Sophia, Emma, Emma, Sophie, Emma, Ella, Odette, and Leah."

I shake my head, something green and ugly growing deep inside me as the list of names gets longer.

"I thought by the fourth Emma, he would've learned," Giovanna says dryly, "but he put his heart out there for every last girl in high school to see, and for so long, he kept insisting that not every woman only wanted to be near him for his family connections, to get closer to Jonas, to ask about a job or an internship with the company, to get a ride to school in our family car every morning, to get flowers delivered weekly, or sometimes diamonds and pearls and exotic chocolates, or whatever in the world her little heart would tell him she secretly yearned for from a store. He even sent a girlfriend a hand-crafted German grandfather clock once. That young man put every ounce of his heart into every relationship he had, *especially* once that awful Sturgis boy decided to

PIPPA GRANT

make his life a living hell in high school. He just wanted to believe that there was good in the world and that he could find it in relationships."

"*Hayes*?"

She nods. "Hayes."

A massive gaping hole opens in my heart for the teenage boy looking for love.

For the boy who *believed* in love.

"He'll tell you now that he saw that three of the Emmas and Cricket and Leah flirted more with Jonas than they did with him, and that he kept dating them to give them something no one else could. That Ella and Odette were only in it for the gifts, and that the rest of them got off on dating *the weird Rutherford with the big trust fund and Razzle Dazzle Village season tickets*. But he didn't at the time. He took a long time to grow into his looks, he didn't have the societal advantage of Jonas's natural charm—and I say that as his mother who thinks he's utterly perfect exactly the way he is—but he'd cut his teeth watching Razzle Dazzle films, and that child believed in the power of love. He believed so hard in the power of love."

"You remember all of their names."

"You will too one day, Begonia. If not for your own children, for Hyacinth's."

I pull my knees to my chest. "A little kid named Aiden shoved my niece Dani on the playground two months ago," I mutter.

She smiles at me. "You'll remember."

"Why are you here? Not to be rude, but—Hayes dumped me, and then he told the whole world we were fake, and—"

"No, he didn't."

"Then who—"

She tilts a brow at me, then shifts her focus to the ocean, where Marshmallow is still dancing about, trying to catch waves in his mouth.

306

"*No*," I whisper.

"Begonia, that dog brought me your signed contract the first night that I was in Maine. I put it back in your luggage for you."

"You knew," I whisper.

"I *suspected* from the minute I laid eyes on you. I *knew* a few hours after that. What I didn't know was what you were hoping to get out of the proximity to my son and my family."

I shake my head, but that doesn't stop my eyes from burning again. "Something new. Anything but my old life. I didn't *want* to fall in love. I just got out of a relationship that was—well, it was lacking. I wanted an adventure. I wanted to live without being told I couldn't do the simplest things that sounded fun. I wanted to find myself. Not lose myself again."

"Are you lost?"

I shake my head. "No. I'm not lost. I'm sad."

"Hayes was never the same after Trixie and Brock," Giovanna says quietly. "I thought he'd come back out of his shell. That I'd see my boy again, the one who believed in the goodness of the world, who had hope, who had so much love to give, but he closed himself off so hard. It was three years before he dated anyone again, and the minute he so much as suspected someone wanted him for anything other than himself, she was out the door. He'd bring the occasional date to an event, but I always assumed it was more to give meddling family members or the press something to talk about than it was because he truly enjoyed his date's company. He was keenly aware that if he was spotted in public with a woman, he'd be labeled a playboy if he was spotted with a different woman anytime in a six-month window after that. He used it to his advantage."

"Why are you telling me this?"

"Because you gave me back my little boy. You made him believe in love again. I have never—*ever*—seen him laugh with another woman the way I've seen him laugh with you.

Or stick up for another woman the way he sticks up for you. And I don't want what happened to him to happen to you merely because he's terrified to love you back."

"*Stop*."

"Thomas's death shook him. It shook all of us. But then Mathias and Jonas both got married too, leaving Hayes as the world's most prominent single man in possession of such a large fortune, if you'll forgive the reference—I was worried he'd do something drastic. I followed him to Maine with Amelia because I didn't want him to do something he'd regret."

"Or something you'd regret."

"Antonio showed up at his house with an eligible bachelorette in tow two years ago, and Hayes retreated to Maine and started dating the mayor there *without* a fake relationship contract." She purses her lips. "Kristine is a lovely woman, but Hayes wouldn't have been happy with her, and he wouldn't have been fair to her either."

"Fair how?"

"She deserves to be loved. We all do."

I twist and bury my head in my knees. She said it herself.

Hayes is terrified to love anyone.

And I can't fix that for him.

God knows I tried to do whatever it took to make Chad love me for me for years. I can't spend another eternity trying to make Hayes not afraid to love me too.

Am I truly that hard to love? "You've made your point. You can go."

"Oh, Begonia, he could so easily love you." She squeezes my shoulder, and I want to tense, but I can't, because she feels safe and kind and she's giving me hope in a way I never would've expected of Giovanna Rutherford. "And he wants to. He does. But big feelings—he hasn't let himself feel them in so long, he just needs time."

"Please don't give me false hope," I whisper.

"You love him."

"What difference does it make? I deserve love. I do. I deserve to be loved back, to not be the one doing all the loving. I don't want to be the woman that a man only appreciates once she's gone."

"Why do you love my son?"

"Because he pays attention and he believes in me." It's such an easy answer. "We were fake. He didn't have to join me for breakfast when we were the only two people in the house. He didn't have to skip that dinner cruise with you to join me for an awkward picnic on the beach. He didn't have to make me tea. He didn't have to tolerate my dog. *With his allergies.* He didn't have to set my phone up on wifi so that I could talk to my sister. He didn't have to fly her in to see me. He didn't have to set up an art studio in his house so that I could make terrible pottery. But he listened. He paid attention. He didn't mock me. He looked at me like I was beautiful, flaws and all. And it wasn't about the money. It was about the *thought.* He's the first man I've known in my adult life who *thought.* And who cared enough to *act* on the thought. And I want—I want him to feel as much love as he made me feel with the simplest little things that no one else has ever done for me before. I want him to know how very much he deserves to be loved and adored."

I swipe at my nose with my shirtsleeve, but I don't try to stop the tears.

I'm not stoic. I'm not upper-crust. I'm not fancy.

I'm me, and I'm a mess, and I'm okay with this.

Giovanna pulls me in for a hug. "No matter what happens between you and Hayes, I hope you know you can call me for anything, anytime. And that's not an offer I've made to any of his other former girlfriends. Ever."

"We were pretend."

"No, Begonia. My sweet child. You most definitely were not pretend."

36

Hayes

IF TIME HEALS ALL WOUNDS, I WOULD VERY MUCH LIKE TIME TO speed the hell up and do its job.

"You have two choices, Romeo," Keisha says to me as she lounges on the couch in my office. "You can remove your foot from your mouth, go apologize, and beg her to take you back, or you can finish the job and retire with all of your investments and go live as a hermit on top of a mountain in the Andes."

"Satellite phones still work in the Andes," Jonas says. He's lounging on my floor. *On my floor.* Just lying there on his back like it's a damn bed, scrolling his phone. I hope it lands on his perfect nose and he has to have stitches. "But here's some good news—some dude named Andreas who's been trading artwork with non-fungible tokens just became the world's newest billionaire. Congrats, Hayes. You're off the hook."

"He's engaged," Keisha says. "To a dude."

"Oh. Ah. Yeah, I see that now. Correction. Sorry, Hayes,

you're still the world's most eligible male billionaire."

"But Hayes can't date anyone for like another six days without getting called a playboy, and god knows your family won't tolerate that. So he has almost another week before he's *truly* in danger."

"They're your family too."

"Only on good days. Hey, what do you think of this statue? I'm thinking Millie needs it for her birthday." She flips her phone around and flashes us.

"Are those breasts?" Jonas asks.

"It's like what would happen if you mashed breasts with ass and added three vaginas."

"Why's it mint green?"

"Would you two *shut up and go away*?" I snap. "*Some* of us have *actual work* to do."

"I'm on the clock," Jonas says. "Next role is a broken-hearted miser hiding from the world in a cabin in the woods. This is character study. I'm absorbing your aura."

"I'm on the clock too," Keisha says. "Your dad's afraid you'll bury your grief in one of your executive assistants, and yes, that's a euphemism, and apparently everyone likes them too much for us to have another situation like the one with Thomas."

I hit the buzzer to call Winnie.

"Yes, Mr. Rutherford?" her tinny voice answers.

"Throw these yahoos out of my office and change the locks."

"They're worried about you, Mr. Rutherford. Although their concerns that either of us would cross professional lines with you are unfounded. Also, tell Keisha that Millie would hate that statue."

"Are you trying to convince me to quit?"

"My brother is a professor of computational physics at this little college in Vermont, and he says he could use a mathematician on his team."

"Once again, are you trying to convince me to quit?"

"No, merely making random conversation since there's not much that makes you happy these days. Excuse me, Mr. Rutherford, but if there's nothing else I can do for you immediately, I have another stack of work from you that needs attention."

Jonas is smothering a grin.

Keisha's flipped herself upside down so that she's dangling off my couch with her feet on my wall. "I could be a CFO. This seems so easy."

I shove up from my seat. "I'm going for a walk."

Jonas also leaps to his feet. "Need a bodyguard? I need to prep for one of those roles too. But hold two seconds. Head rush. Got up too fast."

"Don't you have something else to do?" I mutter.

Keisha wiggles her eyebrows. "Like your wife?"

"Not until her plane touches down from LA tonight."

"I do *not* need you to play bodyguard. I need—"

"Begonia," the two of them answer for me.

Fuck.

I woke up this morning to the realization that it's been ten days since I couldn't tell her I love her back.

Ten.

Days.

Double-digits.

I fell for Begonia in four days. Spent another eight days with her feeling like the very center of her world, and now, we've been apart almost as long, and it's ridiculous to think that I could've found the love of my life in under two weeks, yet the acceptance that it's over won't come.

The conviction that she wanted me for my money, for my family, for my connections, for my friends—it hasn't come.

Even *with* the details of our arrangement leaking to the press, I cannot stay angry with the woman.

I merely have this overwhelming fear that if I go find her, if I tell her how I feel, she will have moved on.

And I'll have let the fear that's ruled my private life for fifteen years destroy the best thing to have ever happened to me.

I glower at my brother and my cousin. "She told the tabloids that we were fake."

Keisha's still lounging upside down like a four-year-old. "I bet Millie six million dollars that Marshmallow had more to do with that than Begonia did."

"Did she seriously take that bet?" Jonas asks.

"No, because she's not a sucker. Also, she called up someone she used to know—don't ask—and they went out riding last night—again, don't ask—and apparently found the 'reporter' who broke the story, and he swore up and down that he was lurking at the edges of Sagewood House's property when a miracle dog appeared and handed him the contract."

"Stop making shit up."

"*I'm not making it up*. That's what Millie told me."

Jonas makes his *I'm thinking* face. "Do you think Begonia would let us borrow Marshmallow on-set? That would be horrific for filming, but can you imagine the end result?"

I leave them in my office, shutting the door behind me and telling my assistants to lock them inside. When I hit the ground floor of the City Hall office building, three women look at me wrong, I realize the odds of the dog being the source for the tabloids is unnaturally high, given who the dog is, and I turn around and get right back in the elevator.

I cannot go on like this.

I don't want to work for Razzle Dazzle.

I don't want to be miserable.

I don't want to be alone.

I want—

I want to fucking *live*.

Exactly like Begonia said she was trying to do in Maine.

I stroll back into my office foyer and look between my assistants.

The two of them exchange their own knowing glances, and then everything turns into a flurry of motion.

Winnie leaps up and shoves a chair under the door handle to block the door of my private office from opening, where I can still hear Jonas and Keisha's muted, unintelligible voices coming through.

Merriweather moves to the small coffee station.

"I don't need coffee," I tell her.

"This is for me."

"What on earth do you—" I start.

Winnie makes an impatient noise. "Mr. Rutherford, you're walking around like a kicked puppy, and it doesn't take geniuses to figure out why. We're having an intervention, or we're both quitting. I probably need a coffee for this too. And I don't drink coffee."

"An intervention?" I repeat.

Merriweather nods. "An intervention. You need your head removed from your nether regions, and we have nothing else left to lose."

"Excuse you—" I start, but once again, Winnie steamrolls me.

"You miss Begonia, because *she's Begonia*, but you won't do anything about it, because *you're you*, which is literally the *only* thing standing between you and Begonia being happy together."

I bristle. "You have not known me *nearly* long enough to—"

"Do you honestly think Begonia would reject you?" Merriweather follows the question by downing a shot of espresso like a champ, then peers at me as if she has nothing better to do than badger me about my personal life.

And I have nothing better to do than answer her, because *I fucking miss Begonia.* "No, but she wouldn't reject *anyone.*"

Winnie snorts. "She divorced her husband. I'd say the woman knows what she *doesn't* want."

"And what she does," Merriweather agrees.

The door to my office jiggles. "Hey! Are you having an intervention without us?" Keisha calls.

Winnie leans back in her chair and props her feet on her desk. She's not wearing shoes, and I should say something, but instead, I'm hanging on her every word. "Did it ever occur to you, Mr. Rutherford, that Begonia is just as afraid of not being loved as you are of not being loved *enough* by her? Do you realize, to even the smallest degree, how unfair that is to her? And how much she's probably hurting right now?"

"Love's a leap." Merriweather pulls a second espresso shot off the coffee maker and lifts it, offering it to me.

I shake my head.

I don't need *coffee.*

"Begonia is Begonia, and she probably has more men vying for her attention now than I have women," I say.

"Probably not, because men are dumb," Merriweather says.

They both peer at me, silently calling me dumb.

I growl.

"Also," Merriweather continues over the hum of the coffee machine, "any man who wants her because of the tabloid coverage will be the kind of man she can see through, and if he's smoother than that, she *needs* you."

"Which would you rather have," Winnie continues as Merriweather takes her second shot, "a safe life without love, or a risky life *with* it?"

"We're basically pulling our hair out over how dense you're being," Merriweather tells me. "*It's Begonia.* One, she clearly adores you. Two, all she really asks in return is that you adore her back. Three, she didn't want to fall in love at all, yet here you both are."

"*She flew across the country to rescue the world's worst dog*. If she can love Marshmallow, *surely*, she can stay loyal to you too."

"Excuse you—" I start again.

Winnie snaps and makes a *zip it* noise. "No, no, you don't get to talk yet. Do you know *anyone* in this world more loyal than Begonia?"

"No."

"Do you know *anyone* in this world who's a bigger dick than her ex-husband?"

"Yes."

"Are *you* a bigger dick than her ex-husband?"

"Only to people who are not Begonia. Probably to people sitting here in my office who should be biting their tongues right now, and who are only still employed because you've *clearly* been talking to her behind my back, and I want to know what you know, and I want to know *now*."

Neither of them is fazed by my glare.

"We haven't talked to her," Winnie says.

"We've talked to other people who know her better."

"They're making suppositions."

"But based on what we know about her—"

"And the way she looked at you—"

"We're assuming we're right."

"So what the *h-e-double-hockey-sticks* are you doing here instead of chasing her down and getting her back?"

"I—"

"She got fired from her teaching job," Keisha yells through my door. "That blow job was a bad look for her."

"Mom said she looked like crap when she tracked her down somewhere in North Carolina too," Jonas adds.

I cross the room in three strides, wrench the chair away, and almost take the door off its hinges. "Our mother went to see Begonia."

It's not a question.

It's an order for him to fill in more information.

My brother shrugs. "She was worried."

I stare at him.

Then stare more.

"She hated Begonia."

"She knew it was fake," Keisha says. "Marshmallow traded her vibrator for Begonia's copy of your signed contract."

Jonas makes a noise I've never heard him make in his life, on- or off-set. "Don't ever say that again."

"What? The part where your mother has a—*mmph*!"

"When?" I ask.

"You want details, talk to her. Pretty sure she was trying to clean up the mess and do what we do best, but it wasn't enough to keep Begonia from getting fired from her job. Sucks too. I heard she's a great art teacher. World needs more of those."

The world needs more *Begonia*.

Period.

And Begonia needs more of knowing that she's loved for exactly who she is.

Not from my mother.

Not from her ex-husband.

Not from any random dickwad who won't appreciate her for exactly what she is.

But from someone like me.

Someone who won't take her for granted. Who knows how wrong relationships can go.

Who's still terrified.

But who might finally be ready to look that old fear in the eye and decide that love is a risk worth taking.

And if I'm wrong—if she's already moved on—if she doesn't want me after all of my fuck-ups—then that's a consequence I'll have to deal with.

Even if I don't have the first clue *how*.

37

Begonia

I'M BACK IN RICHMOND, ONCE AGAIN EYEBALLING A GROUPON for a boat ride out of Virginia Beach after failing to take that leap in the Outer Banks, *again*, when Hyacinth calls.

"Baby?" I ask her, as if she doesn't still have almost three months to go.

"Begonia," she whispers.

A full-body chill washes over me at her tone. "What? *What*?" I whisper-shriek back.

"Camp Funshine sold again."

"*What*? No. *No*. Why didn't we know it was for sale? What are they going to ruin now? We've done this, Hy. I'm not doing it again. *I'm not watching this again*. Not right now. *Not right now*."

"B. Stop. Slow down. Listen. The new owner wants to make it into a camp again."

"*What*?"

"Stop saying *what*?! Just—just stay there. I'm coming to

get you. Get Marshmallow ready for the car."

My stomach is in knots while Marshmallow and I wait for Hyacinth.

When Camp Funshine was sold the first time, we were devastated. It's one of those memories I push down, and I try to remember the good times, not the heartache of knowing it wasn't just Dad losing his camp, but that it was all of the kids losing their summer escape.

It was Hyacinth and me losing *our* place.

Not that I could've afforded it if I'd known it was for sale again, but—

But I love to dream.

And I would've dreamed.

She has both kids in the back of her minivan, and they're flinging Cheerios and Goldfish at Marshmallow, who's strapped in six ways to Sunday so he doesn't try to get out while the van's moving, as we head out of the suburbs and into the hilly countryside.

"Why are we going?" I ask. "What can we do now?"

"They want our advice."

"Now? *Now*? Hello, *warning*."

"Begonia. If this is the only time my kids ever get to see Camp Funshine, *we're fucking going*, okay? If I'd been on the vacation of a lifetime in Australia and my kids were at camp in Europe and I got the call that I had *one chance* to influence what happens to Camp Funshine coming back, *I would've fucking flown around the world six times over to get here*."

I blink back more unwelcome heat in my eyes and nod.

Hy fell in love for the first time at Camp Funshine.

The second time too. And the third. All in one summer.

She lost her virginity out here. Not that we ever would've told Dad or Mom that.

And the pool. The campfire skits. The horseback riding.

The art hut.

My art hut.

"We had the best childhood," I say softly.

She cuts a wet-eyed glance in the rearview mirror, undoubtedly looking at her kids. "The best," she agrees.

I still don't understand why we get *one chance* to go see the property and offer suggestions, but I know Hy's right.

We can't turn down this chance.

If we do it right, maybe we'll get more chances.

We're quiet most of the ride, talking with her kids and Marshmallow when we need to, and after about an hour, we turn off onto a gravel road that used to have a giant sign for Camp Funshine sitting prominently at the corner, but now has a cow.

Just a cow.

Staring at us while we pass.

"Fucking cow," Hy mutters.

"Fucking cow!" Dani parrots from the back seat.

Another quarter mile down the road, my heart squeezes at the sight of the farmhouse that used to be Dad's, the farmhouse where we all lived before the divorce, where Hyacinth and I would sneak out from to go do the ropes courses by flashlight because we thought we were invincible.

It's dilapidated, with peeling paint and a dip in the roof and a saggy porch, which is no surprise.

When it was sold, the new owners made it pretty clear they'd be building a custom mansion deeper into the property.

"Fucking bankruptcy," Hy mutters.

I swipe my eyes. "I miss this place."

"I brought handcuffs. We can strap ourselves to the fence post and refuse to leave. And my purse has enough food to feed all five of us plus the baby for at least four days. Jerry will bring refills. I apologize for not having good potty facilities in my bag too though."

"I love you, Hy."

"I love you too, B."

The gravel road turns into pavement, and soon a massive house with a stone front and arched doorways and a portico and a turret comes into view, right where the dining hall used to be.

Hy flips it off and keeps driving.

"Bad house!" Dani cries in the backseat.

Little Leo, who's barely two, tries to echo her. "Baa how!"

"Show it your fingers, Wee-o!"

"Feeg-aahs!"

"I love those kids," Hy whispers.

The road turns to gravel, then dirt. "Where are we going?" I ask.

She pulls off onto the overgrown former wide pathway to the section of camp that had the pool and the campfire ring-slash-amphitheater and the art hut. She points to a pin on her car's GPS. "There. That's all I got."

My stomach drops as the weeds get thicker around her car and the pin gets closer.

We're going to the art hut.

God, I miss that art hut.

And now I'm wiping tears again, half-furious, half-grateful.

I can't think of the art hut without thinking of Hayes building me an art hut in his house.

I've been doing *so well* at squashing memories of him, but there it is. Welling up and mixing with my favorite childhood memories.

"Fucking art hut," I mutter.

"Aunt B, don't say fuck," Dani says. "It not nice."

"It really doesn't sound right on Aunt Begonia, does it?" Hyacinth says to her daughter.

Dani shakes her head.

"Let me out," I tell her. "I don't want to go."

She ignores me.

"Marshmallow, jailbreak!" I cry.

I turn and watch my dog delicately eat a Goldfish out of my nephew's hand and make no effort to free himself from his straps and harness to rescue me.

"Stop being dramatic," Hy says. "That's my job."

"*I don't want to go.*" *Dammit.* Now I'm crying. "Hy, it's too much. It's—"

She pulls the van to a stop, and I can't avoid it anymore.

There's the art hut.

And just like my relationship with Hayes, it's over.

The door is falling off the hinges. All of the bright designs that campers painted all over the outside of it over the years have washed off with time, so all that's left is a broken gray building missing a few shingles sitting amidst an overgrown field of weeds and baby trees.

The forest wants its art house back.

"B, go on," Hyacinth says. "I have to spray these rugrats down with bug and tick spray before I let them out."

"I'll get them," I offer.

"*Begonia.* Get your ass into that art hut and make sure the toilets still work, because that's the next thing I'm gonna need, and if I'm gonna be peeing in the woods instead, I have to spray my cooch with bug and tick spray too."

"Do *not* spray your cooch with bug and tick spray."

"*Go find me a bathroom.*"

"I'm sure the new owners will—"

"*Go!*"

She's being such a pill, and I get it.

This is hard for her too.

But my stomach is in knots and I want Hayes.

There.

I said it.

I want Hayes.

I don't want to walk into my dad's old art hut, the place I discovered my entire mission in life, all by myself when the last person that I thought could love me tried to recreate it for me and then couldn't tell me he loved me.

I want him here with me.

I want him holding my hand and telling me that I can do this. That I can walk into this building that meant so much to me so long ago and tell *someone else* how to rebuild the dream I let go of forever ago.

God, I miss him. He'd squeeze me in a hug and tell me I can do this, and then he'd tell me he'd buy the whole damn place for me, which I'd tell him was ridiculous and unnecessary because I'm finding another job, a *real* teaching job that's not just summers working for peanuts at a camp, and I can't just pretend I'm a kid at summer camp for the rest of my life.

I don't want him to buy me a camp.

I just want him to love me.

And here I am, thinking I was finally getting over this, and instead sobbing to myself as I walk through the doorway of my dad's art hut to meet some random stranger who's expecting a mature woman who'll have ideas on what to do with a summer camp.

"H-hello?" I call as I push through the creaky door. My voice sounds like two frogs are fighting over a bug in my throat, and I can't stop sniffling, and everything's blurry.

And that's *before* someone inside answers my call.

"Begonia? What's wrong? *Who hurt you?* I'll kill them. I'll fucking—"

I trip at the achingly familiar voice, but I don't fall, because two massive arms and a solid chest are suddenly holding me against the softest fabric in the world, and I smell the Maine seashore, and my heart can't decide if it wants to be in my throat or if it wants to burst out of my chest, because *Hayes is here*.

He's *here*.

"Don't cry." He sounds on the verge of tears himself,

desperate and aching and alone, and it only makes me sob harder. "Begonia. My sweet angel. Please—"

"Don't call me that." I try to push him away, but my arms don't get the message, and instead, they circle his waist and hold on for dear life. *Two more minutes. Just two more minutes of pretending this is real.* "Don't call me that."

His arms tighten around me, and he presses his face into my hair. "I've fucked this up again, haven't I?"

"W-what—you—here?"

"I missed you."

My brain tries to process the words, but all I manage is absorbing the pain in his voice.

The pain, and the fear, and the desperation.

Everything his mom told me comes flooding back, and I squeeze him harder.

I can't be the person who does all the loving. *I can't.* But he's here.

He's here when I need him to be, like he materialized out of thin air, and—*oh my Georgia O'Keefe.*

"You bought my camp."

"It's too much. I know. But I can't go small, Begonia. Not for you. Not when I—when you—it's yours. It's all yours."

"You can't buy my love!"

"I know. *I know!* But I—Begonia. I—"

He stops, cutting himself off abruptly with a curse, the words he won't say hanging in the air between us, and my heart flips inside out.

He bought my dad's camp. He's here. He wants me.

But he can't say the words.

Is he here because he loves me? Or because I'm the easiest path to whatever it is he thinks he needs?

Can I do this?

Can I risk continuing a relationship with a man who might not be able to love me?

"I'm so sorry, Begonia." His voice is hoarse, and I can *feel* his pain. "I should've told you. I—*god*, I haven't said this to anyone in fifteen years. I can't do *words*. Words don't matter. Not when they're tossed about so carelessly, when they're twisted and manipulated and used for anything but what the word is supposed to mean—but I can show you. Begonia, let me show you. *Please*. Please let me show you. Don't leave me before I can learn to believe in the goodness of the words you need to hear."

Oh, my heart.

My battered, bruised, hopeful heart. "You *turned the plane around*."

"I'm sorry. I didn't—I shouldn't have—god, Begonia, I'm so fucking tired of being afraid to live, and you just *breathe* and you live. Even when you're terrified of something, you're *alive* in it. I'm a toad basking in the glory of your rainbow, knowing you don't need me, that you could have your pick of princes and gods and unicorns, but hoping you want me anyway, because you light up my life. You make me smile. You make me hope. You make me want to dance under the stars. And I—I don't know what I have to offer you in return, but whatever it is you want, it's yours. You want my time, it's yours. You want my ears, they're yours. My heart—Begonia. I swear, you stole it the minute you confused me with a dead president, and I don't know *how* that's even possible, but it's the simple truth. I want to be where you are. I want to bask in your sunshine. And I want to show you every single day how perfect and precious and adored you are."

"Hayes." I can barely whisper his name.

"Please tell me I'm not too late. Tell me some lucky fool hasn't swooped in while I was being an idiot."

I shake my head. My legs are quivering. My eyes are leaking. I can feel him trembling too. And I know I'm safe.

"I want to tell you what you want to hear, but the words feel so hollow and insignificant compared to how I feel about you. I can't—I can't minimize what you mean to me by using a phrase that's been ruined in my head."

Hayes-speak for *I love you too much to trivialize it with a Razzle Dazzle line*.

This man.

"Can I say it to you?" I whisper.

"You can say anything to me. You turn every word into magic."

"We're a complicated mess, aren't we?"

"*I'm* a complicated mess, while *you* are utterly perfect. I'm fucking this up again."

"I didn't want this now," I say into his shoulder.

"I'll wait. I'll wait as long as you need. I'll be here."

I'll be here.

It's not *I love you*.

It's better.

Hayes Rutherford doesn't go out of his way to buy summer camps for people he doesn't care about, and he hates peopling with people he doesn't like.

He wouldn't be here if he didn't love me, and he loves me too much to tell me with words that have lost all meaning to him.

"Promise?" I whisper.

"I would promise you anything."

"Just promise you won't leave. Please promise me you won't leave again."

His breath whooshes out like he's been holding it for weeks, and then he's kissing my neck, sending delicious shivers dancing across my skin. "You are my universe, Begonia. My entire world."

I breathe him in and stroke his back, slowly realizing he's in a casual T-shirt. Not a suit or a button-down to be found here. "I missed you," I whisper.

"You'll never have to again. *Never*. You have my word."

I wince.

I don't mean to, but I can't help it. "I know you'll work late—"

"I requested a transfer to a new division. No more long hours, unless they're with you."

I wince again.

I don't want to.

But I can't help myself.

He pulls back, just enough to peer down at me, and once again, I lose my breath.

Okay.

Okay.

I'm pretty sure when a man looks at you that way, you can trust him when he says he'll stop working late. "Family first, and you, Begonia, are my favorite family. And I'm not merely saying that because I'm hoping to entice you to join me as the fourth employee of Razzle Dazzle's new summer camp division."

"Shut. Up." The words fly before I can think, and my vision blurs once again.

He kisses my forehead, my temple, my cheek. "You're welcome to decline, though I'm fairly certain Winnie and Merriweather would be devastated. I'd become unemployed as well, if you do, and would have to spend my days as a mostly useless freeloader happily fetching all the chewed-up wooden works of art your dog can get his jaws on. And that idea does have its own merit. I would be quite content fetching your coffee and tea and art supplies and keeping you from defiling kitchens all day long."

I laugh at the idea of Hayes keeping me from making horrific food. But it feels *right*, too. He cooked so much in Maine, and he seemed to enjoy it, whereas he *clearly* didn't enjoy his job. Or the social life in New York.

"Kids or adults?" I ask.

"I was thinking beef, or chicken, or even tofu. Eating kids is frowned upon, and adults can get rather chewy."

"No, you goofball, *the summer camp*. Is it for kids or adults?"

He smiles at me, warm and amused and bursting with affection, and I lose my breath. "Ah. Of course. The summer camp. Yes."

"*Yes*?"

"Kids or adults. Yes."

"Do you have a plan at all?"

"Yes. Buy a camp, fly to ask Begonia to be my life partner in bringing all of her long-buried dreams to life, and then do whatever she tells me to make that happen."

His smile has grown so broad that his eyes are twinkling, the creases in the corners making him impossibly handsome and irresistible, and I fall in love all over again.

How could I not? "This is you," I whisper, touching the crinkles at the edge of his eye.

"This is me with you," he whispers back. "Only with you."

"It's *you*?" Hyacinth says behind us as Marshmallow barks and lunges for Hayes. "Oh, for fuck's sake. Watch my kids. I'm gonna go find a tick-infested bush to piss in."

Hayes *oof*s and goes down, with Marshmallow licking his face all over while the man himself laughs. Dani stares at Hayes in awe, Leo bursts into tears and tries to follow Hyacinth, but I snag him and swing him around.

My eyeballs are still leaking, but I'm pretty sure this is joy. "There's no crying in art, little Leo," I tell my nephew. "Wanna see where your mama got in trouble for painting an elephant with two trunks?"

"Sit, you furry beast," Hayes says, his voice rich and warm, his eyes shiny as he smiles at my dog.

Marshmallow flips over on his back and grins a happy, tongue-lolling grin at both of us.

"What kind of trouble will he get into at summer camp?" Hayes asks me.

I plop to the floor next to him, Leo in my lap, and press a kiss to his cheek. "There's only one way to find out."

He wraps one arm around me, the other ruffling Marshmallow's fur as the dog climbs into his lap, and he presses a kiss back to my temple. "Thank you for showing me how to live again," he whispers.

"Thank you for knowing what's important," I whisper back.

"I will cherish you until the end of time, my perfect Begonia."

This wasn't what I thought I wanted right now.

But being adored by this man, who knows even more than I do how much love can hurt when it's done wrong? And knowing that he loves me for all of the things that make me *me*?

This is better than any Prince Charming fairytale.

Or maybe, it's my own perfectly imperfect fairytale.

EPILOGUE

Hayes

"Just a few more feet," I tell Begonia.

She clings to my hands, her eyes blindfolded, her steps slow but steady as we reach the end of the gangplank. "Why does it smell like the ocean is right under my feet?"

I hold her by the waist and guide her the last few steps, then tug at her blindfold. "Because it is."

She blinks in the bright sunshine, and then her eyes go round and she shrieks.

"I've got you," I murmur, pulling her tight against me. "And we're not going anywhere. We're docked. Won't leave the pier unless you beg. Cross my heart."

Marshmallow's plastered to my leg, as if he gets just as seasick as Begonia does.

"Whose boat is this?" she asks.

"Mine. And it's a *yacht*, if you don't mind."

"Oh, is that so, Mr. Fancy?" She grins at me as we stand on

my ostentatious vessel, and I find it impossible not to grin back.

"So very so," I reply, parroting a phrase I heard her use with Hyacinth not four hours ago. "You feel okay?"

She leans into me and sucks in a breath so big, I can feel it in my own toes. "Fresh sea air, gorgeous fall trees, sunny skies, and the sweetest, most thoughtful boyfriend in existence holding me and ready to pull me off this boat if I start to feel woozy? I feel so amazing, I might have to dance."

Marshmallow *harumphs*.

"I can too dance," she tells him. "And even if I couldn't, I *should*. Anyone can do anything they enjoy."

"I enjoy doing you," I offer.

And there's that gorgeous Begonia beam. "You knew I'd chicken out if you let me see where we were going."

"I suspected as much."

"You took the leap for me and pulled me along for the ride."

"Bluebell, you've led me to the cliff of so many leaps I never thought I'd take. It's only fair to return the favor."

She laughs. "We are so weird."

"We are so *us*. Would you like a tour?"

When she nods, I loosen my hold on her so that I can turn her to look out to sea. "We are standing on this boat."

"*Yacht*," she corrects.

I smile and point over the covered cockpit. "*That* is the ocean."

Marshmallow sighs.

Begonia cracks up. She twists and points to the Maine shoreline. "What's that?"

"*That* is the most beautiful fall display you'll see anywhere in the world. And it's even more gorgeous when you sail up and down the shoreline, which we'll only do when you're ready."

Violins strike up on shore, and she gasps, then pulls away

and claps her hands. "You hired the Oysterberry Bay Island Orchestra."

"And if you don't feel too ill after your adventure on a boat, I do believe there's a feast waiting for us."

"Hayes."

"Yes, my bluebell?"

She reaches her hands up to hold me by the cheeks. "*This is love*," she whispers.

Ah, this woman. She has my eyeballs suddenly going hot. "And it's my favorite kind of love," I whisper back.

She rises on her tiptoes and presses her lips to mine. "You are my favorite kind of everything."

And this is why it's so easy to love Begonia.

Oh, yes. *Love.*

It hasn't been four full months since she startled the hell out of me at the house she now insists we call Driftwood Manor—*all your houses need names if one has a name, and I was driftwood in your house when you found me*—and in those four months, we've spent most of our time in Virginia, with Begonia making list after list of things that need to be done to the summer camp to bring it back to its original glory, and me making list after list of improvements on her ideas.

Razzle Dazzle does nothing small, even if the end result might *look* like a normal summer camp. I'm not destroying her vision. Merely putting additional support beams beneath it so that it runs as smoothly as if it were the next Razzle Dazzle Village.

But I was talking about love.

And about living with Begonia, who gives it so very freely, to everyone, with no expectation of anything in return and no fear of rejection—*if they don't want love, I can't fix that for them*—that I've rediscovered the meaning of the word.

The way it's meant to be used.

She makes love her own.

She claims it.

She doesn't hide from it or let other people tell her what it is.

And so I'm following her lead, and in our house, there's only real love.

Unselfish, whole-hearted, freely-given love.

This woman is helping me heal my very soul.

And she insists that my easy acceptance of her joy for the little things in the world is something she could never find in another man, nor would she want to.

It's so foreign to me to think that anyone *wouldn't* love her for exactly who she is, and perhaps that, more than anything, means I truly am the right man for her.

It's mind-boggling that simply accepting a person can mean so much, and yet here I stand, contemplating how easily I love this woman who's accepted me and all of my broken and ugly parts too.

She kisses me once more, then goes flat-footed again, drops her hands from my face, and grabs me by the arm. "Show me the dance floor."

I give her the grand tour while the violins play, and as we reach the private quarters below deck, where I intend to give Begonia the *best* part of the tour, Marshmallow appears.

He's soaking wet and carrying a fire extinguisher.

Begonia's eyes go wide.

One wrong squeeze of his jaw, and we'll be covered in the contents of that thing.

"Put it down," I tell him. "And then go dry yourself off."

We have a fifty-fifty shot that the dog will obey.

He's quite a nuisance.

And we can't help but love that about him.

Especially now that the houses we spend the most time in have all been Marshmallow-proofed.

Mostly.

The dog drops the fire extinguisher, shakes his whole body, coating us and the sleeping quarters in wet dog-scented droplets, and Begonia makes a noise that I've learned very well these past few months.

"Let it out, bluebell," I tell her.

She does, and before long, I can't help laughing with her.

She's joy, and she gives *me* joy.

"When we get back to Driftwood Manor, we're locking him in his room, and then I'm going to recreate the day we met," she informs me.

My cock stirs. "Are you?"

"I am." She slips her arms around my neck and smiles at me. "Except without the hot wax and hair dye."

"And the singing?"

She laughs all over again, and I couldn't hold myself back from kissing her if the world depended on it.

There's nothing in the world like my happy Begonia.

"I love you," I murmur against her lips, my heart kicking up as it always does when those three words leave my lips. "I love you and adore you and want to spend the rest of my days cherishing and worshipping you."

She sighs, a contented sound that eases the lingering anxiety I still sometimes feel when I utter that four-letter word, her breath warm and delicious against my skin. "*I love you* isn't enough for how I feel about you."

I kiss her softly, slowly, until she's slipping her hands under my shirt to push it up and over my head, and then her shirt is gone—bra too—and slow and soft won't cut it anymore.

I need her.

I need her more than I need air.

And thanks to a little twist of fate, I'll never be without her again.

BONUS EPILOGUE

Hayes

THERE'S A VAST DIFFERENCE BETWEEN LIVING A LIFE OF obligation and living a life of joy.

I've found I prefer the latter.

Even when it comes with two hundred screaming adolescents hyped-up on sugar sitting in an outdoor amphitheater for campfire skits and the end of the summer marshmallow roast.

Yes, yes, I've spent most of the summer hiding in the main house or the offices, or utilizing the private areas that Begonia insisted be roped off from the campers—and by *roped off*, she means *triple-gated with fences and hedges and trees and monitored with cameras and motion detectors like a prison*, because she *did* grow up as a camper and knows what they're capable of.

And we do enjoy *all* manners of adult activities inside and out of the old farmhouse that we've renovated.

But it's been a remarkably good first summer of camp, especially considering this is the last place that would've ever crossed my mind as a place I'd be happily settled with a woman I found naked in my bathroom just over a year ago.

I insisted we add a few touches as only Razzle Dazzle can, and so the camp food is edible, the beds are comfortable, and the entertainment has been top-notch. It's been a lot of hard work, but at my entire family's insistence, we've intentionally taken a loss on this division in order to fully staff the project and keep Begonia and myself from overworking ourselves.

I barely make forty hours most weeks.

Begonia, meanwhile, squeezes seventy-four thousand hours into every single day, and still has time to sit and eat dinner with me each night, walk our private trails on the land surrounding the campsite that I've acquired for additional privacy, and dance beneath the stars while the woodland creatures watch.

Plus, I insist she takes at least a week off every month. Call it privilege if you must.

I call it making sure Begonia takes time to experience the world instead of making her world solely exist inside the camp boundaries. We often head to Maine, but we've also been to Portugal, Argentina, Hawaii, Iceland, Japan, New Zealand, and a number of European countries, some merely for dinner and the plane ride.

But not Paris.

Despite my regular contributions of a dollar here or five dollars there, and her comfortable camp art director salary that she insists is too much, Begonia is still somehow three years from saving enough for Paris.

It seems she can't help donating to good causes when she has a few dollars in the bank, which suits me just fine.

And I utterly adore watching her occasionally count her piggy bank, and then yell at me when she realizes I've helped.

We've also seen the world's largest ball of string, spent a

week at Razzle Dazzle Village with Hyacinth and her family, took a train ride through the Rocky Mountains, attempted to learn fly fishing, got lost in Tennessee and accidentally crashed a wedding, and got lost in Iowa and accidentally crashed a funeral.

I've never known so much joy in my life, nor had beverages so regularly come out my nose at the dinner table, as I have since finding Begonia singing in my bathroom.

Full disclosure: the nose beverages are generally a result of Hyacinth's visits, and not because Begonia enjoys torturing me.

I'm beverage-free as I stand at the edge of the campfire circle, which is a phrase that does not do the amphitheater justice. Three teenage girls have just re-enacted a pivotal scene from the latest Razzle Dazzle film on the stage, and Hyacinth has shoved her youngest at me so that she can clap the loudest. "That was way better than any acting Jonas Rutherford has ever done!" she calls.

"I can hear you, Hy," Jonas says from my other side.

"She's aware," my mother tells him dryly.

Begonia, who couldn't possibly let the final campfire of the season go without insisting her job as art director also made her final campfire director tonight, squints past the campfire, trying to see us. "Would you look at that?" she says to the campers. "I think my twin sister's here. I can't *see* her, but that sounded like her. Who wants to see me get doubled?"

All forty-two million pre-teens and teenagers erupt in screams of joy.

To meet Begonia is to love her, and I'm reasonably confident she knows every last camper by name.

"This suits Begonia," my mother says as Hyacinth leaves two of her children with us and bounds down the stairs. It's odd how natural it feels to hold her baby, who's a slobbery little boy with mischief written in every ounce of his being.

Unless he's cuddling, which he's perfectly content to do right now, and I'm perfectly content to let him.

"She'd try anything, but you're right," I say to my mother. "This definitely suits her."

"It's fucking late," Dani says, earning a *shh* from her honorary third grandma, aka my mother.

Jerry huffs up to join us, Leo dragging behind him. "Did I miss it? We had a potty problem."

He's a decent guy. Not my first choice for poker night, but then, I'm not the poker night type, so we get along pretty well.

Hyacinth hits the stage with Begonia, and the adolescents go wild.

"She loves this camp," Jerry says. "It's a really good thing you make it pretty clear you can only handle one woman, because Hy would dump me for this camp."

"Don't be ridiculous, Jerry," my mother says. "Hyacinth would never leave you for this camp *or* for Hayes. He gives terrible foot rubs. And she's too busy to fully appreciate camp. Now, once your little ones are old enough to *be* campers…"

"Crap. I've gotta up my game."

Begonia introduces Hyacinth, and the two of them fall into an old routine that I've seen dozens of times, but never the same show twice. It's stories about their time at camp when they were younger, their favorite skits, their most embarrassing moments, and hints of the trouble they got into that they won't tell the campers about, in case the campers come back next year.

"Don't get in trouble," Begonia says to the four hundred million teens and pre-teens.

Hyacinth winks at them.

The crowd roars with laughter.

"This calls for an interruption if you want this place still

338

standing before the corporate retreats start," my father murmurs to me.

I rub my thumb over the velvet box in my pocket. "It does, doesn't it?"

"You sure you want to do this?" Jonas asks.

While I've had a fantastic year, he has not.

Turns out, we Rutherfords are better at navigating public scandals than we thought.

Or possibly we're getting better at letting people see that we're not perfect, and that's exactly as it should be.

"I've never been more sure about anything in my life," I tell him. "Here. Hold the little guy."

He smiles and takes the sleepy bundle. "Good sign."

I head down the closest stairway, following in Hyacinth's footsteps to the stage, where Begonia gasps softly. "Well, this is unusual," she says, meeting me at the edge and holding out a hand to help me up. "Look at this. We get the man responsible for Camp Funshine's reincarnation himself. Now, go easy on Mr. Rutherford, okay? He doesn't like big crowds."

She beams at me, her nose wrinkling a little as if she's asking what I'm up to, and I give her a peck on the cheek that makes the kids around us erupt in cheers.

"Always wondered if that would happen," I murmur to her.

"What brings you to the stage?" she whispers back.

"I missed you."

That smile melts me every time.

"Begonia didn't introduce Mr. Rutherford here properly," Hyacinth announces. "He's actually her *b-o-y-f-r-i-e-n-d*."

The kids squeal even louder.

"We know! We saw them *k-i-s-s-i-n-g*," one of the teenagers yells.

Hyacinth fake-gasps. "Scandalous!"

"Truly," I agree.

It's odd being on a stage, and I still don't know how Jonas

does this—or Begonia, for that matter, as she's out here for campfire skits at least every other week—but her hand is slipped in mine, and she squeezes lightly while she makes a face at the audience.

"Okay, okay, calm down. Grown-ups are allowed to date. And kiss."

"And grown-ups also—" someone starts in the audience, but Begonia's on it.

"Ernie Brown, if you finish that sentence, you don't get to meet any other special guests tonight."

Half the kids snicker.

"Now," she continues, "since our dear Mr. Rutherford has come all the way up to the stage—for the first time *all summer*, I might add—let's see what he has to say." She smiles at me. "And the floor is yours."

I look out over the mass of bodies in the dark, some illuminated by the fire, some farther back and merely shapes and shadows.

And then I look back at Begonia.

"Actually, I'd prefer to just talk to you."

My voice carries, and I hear whispers around us.

Begonia's nose twitches again, and so do her eyebrows. "Right here?"

"It does seem to be one of your favorite places."

And there's that smile again. "I have *many* favorite places."

"That's true," Hyacinth chimes in.

"She's notorious," Jerry calls from the top of the amphitheater.

"Would you two please let him talk?" my mother says.

"Do you realize you're surrounded by people who adore you?" I ask my beautiful bluebell.

She blinks once, and her smile grows wider. "And surrounded by people that I adore in return. This isn't where either of us thought we'd be when we met, is it?"

"Not at all."

I'm smiling too as I glance around at the kids again. Some are bouncing. Grins and smirks abound in this little amphitheater tonight.

"Is he gonna kiss her again?" someone whispers loudly.

"I hope not," Hyacinth whispers back, just as loudly. "Ew."

"What I hope," I say, turning to the audience again, "is that each of you has learned a fraction of what I learn every day about the world and how to live life to the fullest, for having had the privilege of spending it with this lovely woman here."

I squeeze her hand while more squeals and *aww*s rise around us.

"Hayes," she whispers.

I turn back to her. "You, my dear bluebell, have done the impossible. You've taken a cold, battered, hidden heart and taught it the true meaning of love. You've restored my faith in humanity, pulled me back into the world, and brought as much peace to my life as you have joy."

She swipes at her eyes, still smiling. "You make it easy."

"The day we met, the only thing I wanted was peace, quiet, and solitude. And I know I was the last thing you wanted that day too. The universe had other plans for both of us, and I find I want something I never thought could exist for me."

"What's that?"

I drop to one knee, and gasps and squeals explode around me.

But I care simply about one person, and one person only, whose eyes have suddenly gone the size of the fire, and whose lips have rounded into a circle.

"Hayes," she whispers again.

"What I want, Begonia, is to marry my best friend, the woman I adore and cherish beyond reason, the only person on this earth who could make me believe in the honesty of love again. I want to marry you and spend the rest of my life making you as happy as you make me every single day. If you'll have me."

Her eyes are wide and shiny, her smile so bright it could be a star all on its own, and she's squeezing my hand.

"Hayes Rutherford, you know you don't have to marry me to keep me."

"And yet I have an inexplicable urge to stand on a mountaintop and vow to love you for all eternity anyway. I want it all, bluebell. Babies and awkward holiday parties with our families and gray hair and adventure and *life*. I want to tie my life with yours forever."

"Say yes, Ms. Begonia!" someone yells.

"Men are gross! Say no!" a very familiar voice yells back. It seems someone invited Keisha as well.

Begonia laughs, but the merry sound turns into a gasp as I pull the velvet box from my pocket and open it. "I don't mind earning that yes," I tell her softly. "And I don't mind being told no, so long as you'll still keep me."

"I could never tell you no." She swipes at her eyes again, laughing, as she drops to her knees too, then flings herself at me. "I love you, Hayes. I love you and adore you and cherish you and want to spend the rest of my life doing all the things I know to do to make you smile and laugh and also—" she drops her voice "—all those things we shouldn't talk about in front of an audience of horny teenagers."

"Is that a yes?" I ask as I cling to this woman who's given me back everything I've been missing in my life.

"It's a double-triple-quadruple with whipped cream and a cherry on top *yes*," she replies.

And I suddenly realize the error in my plans to propose to her in her very favorite spot on earth.

We have an audience.

Easily solved, though.

I pluck the modest ruby ring out of the box and lift it to her finger. Could I have gotten her a larger ring?

Yes.

Would she have turned me down on principle if I had?

Entirely possible.

"It's the color of my hair," she whispers.

"Exactly right, my love." I start to slide it over her knuckle while the campers cheer around us, when suddenly, a massive pile of fur woofs, leaps between us, knocking us both to our asses.

"*Marshmallow!*" Begonia shrieks.

I look down.

Then at her.

Then at her dog, who's carrying something that looks very much like the first piece of wood I ever saw in his jaws.

But this—this is *not* a Maurice Bellitano original.

Oh, no.

"Is that from Great Grandma Eileen's collection?" I inquire softly.

Begonia's gaze connects with mine, and it's so very identical to the first time Marshmallow stole something from me that I start laughing.

"*Hayes.* The *children*," she hisses. "Tell the dog to take it home."

I would.

And I should. He still only takes orders from me.

But I can't seem to get myself under control.

"Marshmallow, *go home*," Begonia orders.

He ignores her, naturally.

"Go give it to Grandma Giovanna," I manage to push out.

"*Hayes.*"

Her voice is outraged, but her eyes—her eyes are shining in amusement.

And when Marshmallow takes off up the stairs to my mother, the dildo dangling from his jaws, I rise as well, lifting my love with me as I go. "Thank you for spending part of your summer at Camp Funshine," I tell the campers. "Excuse us. I believe this lady is now mine. Jonas, come apologize for us properly, please."

With my famous brother suddenly announced, no one notices as I carry Begonia off the stage.

No one except her, that is. And probably our families.

"Hayes. We *have* to make sure that's the only piece of Great Grandma Eileen's collection that he brought out here," she whispers.

"I'm sure Hyacinth would be delighted to do it for us."

She stares at me a beat longer before she, too, starts laughing. "Do you know how much I love you? *Truly* love you? Simply because you're you?"

I settle her on the ground behind a copse of pine trees, link my arms around her waist. "I have an inkling. And now I'd very much like to show you how much I love you."

And I do.

Just as I intend to show her how much I love her every day for the rest of our lives.

The End

PIPPA GRANT BOOK LIST

The Girl Band Series
Mister McHottie

Stud in the Stacks

Rockaway Bride

The Hero and the Hacktivist

The Thrusters Hockey Series
The Pilot and the Puck-Up

Royally Pucked

Beauty and the Beefcake

Charming as Puck

I Pucking Love You

The Bro Code Series
Flirting with the Frenemy

America's Geekheart

Liar, Liar, Hearts on Fire

The Hot Mess and the Heartthrob

Copper Valley Fireballs Series
Jock Blocked

Real Fake Love

The Grumpy Player Next Door

Standalones
Master Baker *(Bro Code Spin-Off)*

Hot Heir *(Royally Pucked Spin-Off)*

Exes and Ho Ho Hos

Crazy for Loving You

The Last Eligible Billionaire

For a complete, up-to-date book list, visit www.pippagrant.com

---

Pippa Grant writing as Jamie Farrell:

The Misfit Brides Series

Blissed

Matched

Smittened

Sugared

Married

Spiced

Unhitched

The Officers' Ex-Wives Club Series

Her Rebel Heart

Southern Fried Blues

ABOUT THE AUTHOR

Pippa Grant is a USA Today Bestselling author who writes romantic comedies that will make tears run down your leg. When she's not reading, writing or sleeping, she's being crowned employee of the month as a stay-at-home mom and housewife trying to prepare her adorable demon spawn to be productive members of society, all the while fantasizing about long walks on the beach with hot chocolate chip cookies.

Find Pippa at…
www.pippagrant.com
pippa@pippagrant.com

9 781955 930086